The Heart of Winter

The
Heart
of
Winter

A Novel

JONATHAN EVISON

DUTTON

DUTTON

An imprint of Penguin Random House LLC
penguinrandomhouse.com

DUTTON and the D colophon are registered trademarks of Penguin Random House LLC.

LIBRARY OF CONGRESS CATALOGING-IN-PUBLICATION DATA

Names: Evison, Jonathan, author.
Title: The heart of winter: a novel / Jonathan Evison.
Description: [New York]: Dutton, 2024.
Identifiers: LCCN 2024007466 (print) | LCCN 2024007467 (ebook) |
ISBN 9780593473542 (hardcover) | ISBN 9780593473566 (ebook)
Subjects: LCGFT: Novels. Classification: LCC PS3605.V57 H43 2024 (print) |
LCC PS3605.V57 (ebook) | DDC 813/.6—dc23/eng/20240223
LC record available at https://lccn.loc.gov/2024007466
LC ebook record available at https://lccn.loc.gov/2024007467

Printed in Canada

1 3 5 7 9 10 8 6 4 2

BOOK DESIGN BY STEPHANIE KOWALSKY

For Mom

The Heart of Winter

I

Reliable Pleasures

2023

Abe Winter awoke less than rested, autumnal sunlight puddling on his wife's empty side of the bed as he eased himself upright and swung his feet into his waiting slippers. Padding to the bathroom, bleary-eyed, his bladder fit to burst, Abe steadied himself with one hand on the vanity, stooping slightly as he emptied himself into the bowl, the ritual being one of the few reliable pleasures left as he braced himself for what was sure to be his final birthday.

To hear Doc Channing tell it, Abe might make it another six to ten years, so long as he managed his blood pressure and didn't fall down any stairs. But life amounted to more than just a beating heart. Vitality could not be measured by instruments or blood panels, and there was no metric for will, which could only be weighed from the inside. On his way out of the bathroom, Abe paused before the mirror to inspect his personage, frail and cadaverous, rheumy eyed, skin brittle as old parchment, hair gone thin and white as spider silk. He had the look of a man who was liable to get lost on his way to the kitchen, a man easily coerced into sending a sizable check to the next telemarketer who happened to solicit him on the county's last remaining landline. A brutal assessment, perhaps, but one look at his shabby condition was all the confirmation Abe needed. This winter would surely be the end of the road.

While there were still a few loose ends to tie off, arrangements financial and logistical, Abe's goal was to resolve these particulars by the holidays. He'd done his damnedest to outlive Ruth, which had been the plan all along, to spare her the headache of his passing and all the attendant details. But he wasn't going to make it.

As Abe emerged from the bathroom, Megs, the blond Lab they'd inherited as a puppy from their youngest daughter, Maddie, lifted herself with no small effort from her place at the foot of the bed and ambled slowly after Abe as he started down the hallway. Megs was pushing thirteen now, morbidly obese from a sedentary lifestyle and years of table scraps and riddled with lipomas the size of mandarin oranges. It was not unlikely that Megs would be one of those loose ends Abe would have to tie up in advance of his own passing.

He found Ruth in the kitchen, already dressed for the day, a red enameled cast-iron pot of water boiling on the stovetop, a mound of neatly halved new potatoes heaped on the cutting board, cider vinegar and Dijon mustard nearby at the ready, along with a perky bundle of parsley, freshly rinsed.

"The old Streamliner potato salad, eh? French style," he said.

"Ahh, the birthday boy," she said, planting a kiss on his temple.

She was still a beauty at eighty-seven, with a toothsome smile that could disarm the dourest of tax auditors and the same piercing blue eyes that had captivated Abe in 1953, only deeper set now, the corners etched by a lifetime of conviviality and grief.

"I ironed your dress shirt," she said.

"I have to dress up now?"

"And wear a bow tie," said Ruth.

Abe's eight ounces of prune juice and 80 mg carvedilol were waiting for him on the tabletop next to the Saturday edition of the *Kitsap Sun,* that venerable publication that Abe had grown up with back when it was still called the *Bremerton Sun,* a paper that grew thinner and less substantive every month, though the price kept going up, and some days it didn't arrive until nearly ten A.M. Abe supposed that was the price of doing business when you were one of eight remaining subscribers. All the news was on Tweeter now, and the other one, Tickety-tock, where teenagers Gorilla-Gluing body parts to various objects passed as newsworthy.

"I hope Anne and Tim don't get delayed in Denver," said Ruth, offloading the potatoes into the cauldron. "They're expecting a foot of snow in Denver."

"They ought to just stay put," said Abe. "You're making a big deal out of nothing, here. You're treating this like my funeral."

"Not everyone lives to be ninety," Ruth said.

"Well, you're making me wish I hadn't," he said. "And for the record, the day's not over yet. I was born at nine thirty P.M. I could still die, you know?"

These little allusions, morbid quips made in jest regarding his impending demise, had become more frequent of late, as Abe hoped they might help Ruth prepare for the eventuality, if only incrementally. But Ruth was buying none of it.

"You'd love the attention, wouldn't you?" she said. "Dropping dead in front of your entire family."

"Ha," he said. "I'd rather go in my sleep."

"Snoring yourself to death hardly sounds peaceful," Ruth observed.

Abe lowered himself into place and promptly washed the carvedilol down with his prune juice. He figured he must be about the only guy drinking the stuff anymore. An American staple in the last century; fibrous, good source of vitamin C, kept a body regular. But like nightshirts, wristwatches, and the traditional boy-meets-girl narrative, prune juice seemed to have fallen out of style.

Abe turned his attention to the newspaper, startled when the toaster sprung. A moment later, Ruth placed a single slice of lightly buttered sourdough bread in front of him and proceeded to top off his prune juice.

"Easy now," said Abe. "You don't want me to spend the whole party in the bathroom, do you?"

"I told Kyle I'd pick them up at the ferry at three forty," said Ruth. "But he and Soojin insisted on taking Uber."

"Who's Uber?" said Abe. "It's not a dog, is it?"

"It's like a taxi," said Ruth. "Maddie's leaving Corvallis before noon, so she ought to be here by three thirty."

"She's not bringing her puppy, is she?"

Ruth's ensuing silence served to answer that question.

"Great, another puppy."

"Ted and Melissa DeWitt can't make it," Ruth said. "Ted just had a second bypass last month and he's not feeling up to it."

"Geez, did you invite my high school gym instructor while you were at it?" said Abe.

"Del Gundy died thirty years ago, or I might have," said Ruth, setting the colander in the sink. "But I did invite the Jacobsons and the Duncans."

"I thought they were dead."

"Oh, stop it," said Ruth. "Al still golfs."

"Those policies I sold them in '62 are going to waste. Heck, they're liable to outlive their kids at this point."

Yet another reason Abe was ready to call it a day: He couldn't bear the thought of outliving another one of his children. Nearly fifty years on, the loss of Karen still haunted him, as it haunted Ruth, as it haunted all of them. Kyle was turning sixty-four in the spring, and he'd already survived one heart attack. What if he didn't survive the next one? It seemed imperative that Abe move on now, while his children still had some life left in them, while they could still look after Ruth.

After breakfast, Abe retired to the living room, where he lowered himself into his chair, an unoffending beige lift recliner that Ruth had insisted upon. He still hadn't gotten used to the thing after four years. His old green chair had been ratty and, yes, matted with dog fur, and the springs had been shot, and never mind that he could hardly get out of the thing; he missed it all the same. Change, it seemed, was relentless, and make no mistake, it wasn't always progress.

Megs promptly plopped down on the braided rag rug at Abe's feet with a long sigh, imploring Abe with her milky eyes to acknowledge her presence. Abe obliged dutifully with a pat on her head.

"You and me, Megs," he said, without further explanation.

*

One by one, the guests arrived, first Maddie, who, at fifty-three, had been their surprise baby, conceived nearly a decade after Abe and Ruth had agreed to stop growing their family. Three kids had been perfect. They'd hit the jackpot with Anne, Karen, and Kyle. A family of five was chaotic enough. Following the debacle of the 1960s, and all the trouble Anne and Karen had given them, Abe, pushing forty, certainly wasn't prepared to bring any more children into the world, and at thirty-five, Ruth was perhaps no longer ready, either, a fact that her emergency hysterectomy three months after Maddie's delivery seemed to corroborate. The thought had occurred to Abe more than once, in the past five decades, that maybe Maddie wasn't ready to be born into a world she seemed to take so personally—every social injustice or inequity, every heartbreak, defeat, or failure, and yes, every stray puppy.

The new one was called Perry, a shrill Pomeranian who couldn't have weighed five pounds. The instant Maddie set Perry down, the little bugger was harassing poor Megs, yipping and snapping, and sniffing at her hind end with impunity.

"Happy birthday, Dad," said Maddie.

Her hair was still cropped short, a dyed patch of blue on one side, a style Abe might have had a hard time reconciling on a twenty-year-old, but at Maddie's age it seemed beyond a stretch.

Abe was ashamed of his stiffness and ill temper as she hugged him. It wasn't Maddie but the damn Pomeranian who was the source of his discomfiture.

"Can you please do something with that puppy?" he said, a tad more stridently than he'd intended.

"Oh, Abe," scolded Ruth.

Maddie scooped up the Pomeranian, who fell silent immediately for the first time, if only momentarily.

Ruth wiped her hands dry on her apron and kissed Maddie on the cheek. "Don't mind your father. He gets overprotective of that old dog," she offered on Abe's behalf. "I love what you've done with your hair. Very punky! You two get comfortable, I've got more prep to do."

"Can I help, Mom?"

"Yes, by babysitting your father."

Abe and Maddie retired to the living room, the little Pomeranian yipping in her arms.

Kyle and Soojin were next to arrive, by cab, a little after four.

"There's not a single Uber on this island," said Kyle as they made their entrance. "Can you believe that? It's like the nineteenth century around here."

Kyle looked unhealthy, his face drawn, his pallor slightly gray, while Soojin, Kyle's elder by a handful of years, had not seemed to age a day since the mid-1990s. Ruth had lectured Abe two Christmases ago that it was improper to suggest that Soojin's graceful aging had anything to do with her being Korean, that it might be construed as racist, thus Abe was careful not to acknowledge the fact.

"Hey, Pops," said Kyle, leaning over to hug him in the recliner. "How goes it? The big ninety! What's that even called? A nano-something-or-other-genarian?"

For ten years, Kyle had been their youngest child, but he took naturally to the role of middle child upon Maddie's appearance: agreeable, diplomatic, flexible, if not a little quick to compromise. More than any of their children, excepting Karen, who had been a model child before thirteen, Kyle had most aimed to please his parents.

"Hey, I brought you something," he said, handing Abe a box.

"We said no gifts," Ruth reminded him.

"It's nothing," said Kyle. "It's not even wrapped. It just made me think of Dad."

Abe struggled to open the cardboard box for about thirty seconds with his uncooperative digits before Kyle saved him the humiliation, producing a pocketknife and neatly slashing the offending ribbon of packing tape. Inside the box was a framed piece of plexiglass, maybe twelve inches by eight, and an electrical cord neatly coiled in a plastic Ziploc.

"What is it?"

"It's a page magnifier," said Kyle. "Since you won't use the dang Kindle I sent you."

"What am I supposed to do with it?"

"You plug this in, it's got an LED light, you hold the newspaper under it to enlarge the print."

"Ah," said Abe, knowing the magnifier was destined for the closet along with the CarCaddie, the GrandPad, and most recently the compression air massager.

"Thanks, son," he said.

Having beat the snow out of Denver, Anne and Tim were next to arrive, around five thirty, in a rented Taurus. Watching them make their way up the steps, Abe was dogged by the fact that after all these years he still wished Anne could've made it work with Rich Tolbert. Tim was fine, a little on the flaky side, politically speaking, and not exactly a man's man. As though Tim were reading his thoughts, he immediately beat a path to the bathroom, clutching his bladder, while Anne seated herself on the same midcentury modern sofa that she'd routinely fallen asleep on from the second Eisenhower to the Nixon administrations.

At sixty-eight years old, the eldest of the four Winter children,

Anne still held Abe and Ruth accountable for their parenting and had in recent decades reversed the roles on them. It didn't take her long to start in with the downsizing lecture.

"Don't you think it's time you two started thinking about downsizing?" she said to them. "This house, the farm, it's so much work. And look at this place, it hasn't been updated since the seventies."

"That's not true," said Ruth. "We replaced the carpet in 2018. And your father's chair."

"Mom, this place is a museum."

"You hush," Ruth interjected. "And where are we supposed to live, a nursing home? We've been in this house for sixty-four years, we raised you kids in it, why should we give it up now?"

"What do you need with all these rooms?"

"At least your sister will be using one of them, tonight," said Ruth. "You didn't need to book a hotel, you know. You still have your old bedroom."

"Mom, my old bedroom has been a sewing room since 1973. Don't get me wrong, I have great memories of the farm, but in most of them I'm a kid. What are you gonna do when Dad's gone?"

"You talk about him like he's not sitting right next to you."

"Sorry, Dad, just thinking out loud, here," said Anne.

It was a relief when the Duncans and the Jacobsons arrived in tandem, the four of them shrunken and overdressed when Abe and Ruth greeted them on the front porch.

There followed hugs and pleasantries to span the years since any of them had gone out of their way to see one another.

"Looks like you need to get a new coat of paint on those old rockers," said Al Duncan of the twin rocking chairs that had remained fixtures on the front porch for over forty years since Al hand-made them.

"I say better to let them age gracefully," said Abe.

"Speak for yourself," said Al.

The Duncans and Jacobsons stepped into the foyer, proceeding to the living room, where they were greeted by the spectacle of Perry the Pomeranian sexually assaulting poor Megs, who was sprawled indifferently at the foot of Abe's recliner. In a rare act of decorum, Maddie scooped Perry up and set the puppy in her lap as a new round of salutations ensued.

For over sixty years, Al and Terri Duncan and Thom and Nancy Jacobson had been part of the Winters' lives. Anne and Karen and Kyle had grown up with the Duncan kids, John and Jen, along with the Jacobson kids, Frank and Cathy. Their family lives were inextricably linked by dozens of obligations, science fairs, Scouts, volleyball practice, and in the case of the Duncans, even church. Family life had all but forced the three families together. Abe had sold both couples auto, home, and life insurance in the early sixties. Al had been Karen and Kyle's orthodontist. Cathy had gone to senior prom with Kyle. Once the kids were all off to college, the Winters and the Duncans and Jacobsons crossed paths less frequently: chance encounters in the supermarket or on the ferry, office visits, the occasional social call. Still, half a century on, the bonds of their friendship held strong. Such kind people, the Duncans and the Jacobsons, so steadfast and reliable. Every year a Christmas card.

Dinner was quite a production. Pork loin glazed in honey mustard, French potato salad, green beans, Hawaiian rolls, and yellow squash. For dessert, Ruth presented a chocolate layer cake emblazoned with "Happy Birthday, Abe," in cobalt-blue frosting.

They talked largely of the grandchildren and their various doings: Martha, Anne's eldest, and her promotion to senior vice president of the cosmetics corporation; Matt's recent bout with skin cancer; Ben's divorce; Karl's recent second marriage; and Kaylee's newborn, a girl named Lucy. Grandchildren, and now greats; there were too many to keep track of, and while their continuance in the lives of Abe and Ruth was only peripheral, and their presence next to nothing, each of them remained a source of pride, for each of their lives could be traced back to Abe and Ruth, and the little acorn they'd planted seven decades ago, which had grown into a mighty oak, casting its seeds from Oregon, to Colorado, to New Jersey. It was a gift to know that Abe's life had accounted for so many blessings.

With a half glass of red wine warming his blood, a wistfulness overcame Abe. What further proof could he possibly need than to look around the dinner table and know that he had lived his life well? Abe could not help but acknowledge his extraordinarily good fortune. The next time these cherished people assembled in one place, Abe would almost certainly be in a casket.

Watching Ruth, glowing with satisfaction, it was clear she was in her element, as it was equally apparent that she still had a good deal of living to do. She'd get along fine without Abe. She'd still have Bess Delory and the rest of her church friends, and the kids, and the grand-kids, and the Jacobsons and the Duncans.

As dinner wound down, Kyle stood up and tapped his wineglass with his spoon to signal a toast.

"Mom," he said. "First of all, beautiful meal, you really outdid yourself. Thanks for bringing us all together. So nice to see the Dun-cans and the Jacobsons after all these years. I'm an old man myself now, and I've learned some stuff along the way. But most of the im-portant stuff, I learned from you, Dad. Mom, too, of course, but I'll save that speech for her ninetieth. You taught me about responsibil-ity, you taught me about priorities, about integrity and reliability. You taught me how to be a man. But you didn't just tell me these things, Dad, you showed me. You showed us. So, on behalf of everyone at this table, I want to thank you, Dad. Happy ninetieth birthday."

"Hear hear," everybody said in unison.

A few minutes later, in the living room, Abe stationed himself beside his son and draped his arm around him.

"Nice toast, kiddo," he said. "A few tweaks and you can use it again as my eulogy."

"I'm not holding my breath, Pops. You're a perennial."

The comment, though delivered playfully, begged the question:

How long did Kyle really expect Abe to live? Was he on Doc Channing's six-to-ten-year plan? Abe doubted it. Kyle had to know that the end was coming sooner than later.

The Jacobsons were the first to bow out for the evening, and the Duncans took it as their cue to follow. Abe walked the four of them out to the front steps, a slight quaver in his voice as he bid them all farewell with handshakes and hugs, acutely aware that whatever their good intentions might be, it was likely the last time he would ever see any of them, and they him. And it occurred to Abe how fortunate he was to possess such knowledge, so that he could hold it close to his heart, and perhaps, if he clung firmly enough to it, take it with him to the hereafter.

Kyle and Soojin were the next to leave. Having booked a room at the bed-and-breakfast in Eagle Harbor, they phoned for a cab around nine thirty, though it was well after ten by the time it arrived. Again, Abe ushered them out to the porch. Out of all the kids, it seemed the most likely that Abe would live long enough to see Kyle again, as he lived the closest, but you never knew.

Soojin pecked Abe on the cheek and proceeded to the waiting taxi as Abe and Kyle lingered momentarily on the porch. Clutching Kyle by the shoulders, Abe wrapped him in a bear hug, reluctant to let him go. How could it possibly be that Kyle, himself a senior now, long in the tooth, his hair gone thin and gray, his very frame beginning to shrink, was the same little boy who once darted recklessly up and down the stairs and hallways of this very house? Time did not march on methodically, minute by minute, day by day; it sprinted away from us in mad bursts, a thief in flight.

"I love you, Pops," said Kyle, extricating himself from his father's embrace. "Take good care of Mom."

"It's the other way around," said Abe. "She takes care of me."

"Whatever you say, Pops," Kyle said, descending the steps.

Abe lingered on the porch as the cab pulled away up the driveway. Just as it rounded the corner out of sight, he stepped back into the house, where Anne and Tim were in the foyer with Ruth, buttoning up their coats as they readied themselves to leave.

"Daddy, I'm telling you, now is the time to sell this place," said Anne, unable to resist one final overture. "The market is right on the bubble. If you wait any longer, prices will go down. You need to leverage this."

Abe was tempted to ask Anne why she cared so much. What could it possibly matter to her? Was she really concerned about them, or was she simply trying to avoid the eventuality of having to put the house on the market herself when Abe and Ruth were gone?

"If we decide to sell, you'll be the first to know," said Abe, kissing his eldest daughter on the cheek.

Minutes after Anne and Tim left, Maddie started up the rubber-treaded staircase to her old bedroom.

"Good night, sweetie," said Abe.

"Good night, Dad. Sorry Perry was such a spaz."

"It was nothing," he said, waving it off. "Sorry I got grumpy."

"I get it," she said. "Megs is like one of us."

Now the house was quiet at last. But for all the stillness, there lingered a palpable life force, as if the house itself were alive by extension of all that had come to pass under its roof. Megs, free at last of the hectoring Pomeranian, lay still on the floor beside Abe's recliner, her breaths long and labored in slumber. Now and again, a tiny, muffled yip escaped her black jowls from the other side of consciousness.

Abe found Ruth in the kitchen shortly before midnight, handwashing the last of the dinner dishes. Unbeknownst to her, Abe stood for a moment in the doorway, admiring her sturdy figure from behind, her straight back, her hair somehow still not completely gray at eighty-seven.

Ruth left off scrubbing to wipe her hand dry on her apron and proceeded to massage the underside of her jaw just as Abe crept up behind her and wrapped his arms about her waist.

"Tooth still bugging you, huh?"

"I think I'll have to get the darn thing pulled," she said.

Abe spun her around to face him, pressing his lips to her forehead. The weight of his numbered days lay heavily upon him as he gathered her in an embrace. God, how he loved this woman, God, how he'd loved this life.

"It's late," he said. "We can finish cleaning in the morning. Please, come to bed."

Aggressive Measures

2023

It all started with the loose tooth. Number thirty-one, the second molar, back right. Though Ruth dreaded the prospect of another extraction, at eighty-seven, with her gums soft as putty, it wasn't particularly surprising. Things could have been a lot worse at her age. Look at Rose Trembley from church, periodontal disease in her late fifties and dentures by her seventieth birthday. Dr. Jin had already extracted Ruth's second molar on the left side two years ago, once a root canal was no longer an option. The procedure had been quite unpleasant, but not nearly as bad as Ruth had expected. Dr. Jin was a fine oral surgeon whom she trusted implicitly for her meticulous presentation, her consummate professionalism, and her liberal use of anesthesia.

"How long has it been loose?" she asked, peering into Ruth's mouth.

"About two months," she told her.

"Any pain?"

"It's a little achy sometimes. Mostly it's just an annoyance, waggling around back there. I'm afraid I'll swallow it one of these days."

"Let's get an X-ray," she said. "See what we're up against and go from there."

Ruth took this as an encouraging development. It was a long shot, but maybe the tooth could be saved after all. Maybe the wiggling was attributable to a tissue infection, or gum inflammation, or something of the like. Perhaps an antibiotic would cinch up that slacking gum and buttress the molar.

But when had life ever presented Ruth the best-case scenario?

"There's a mass," Dr. Jin explained over the phone the following afternoon. "Could be a cyst, nonodontogenic, possibly an ameloblastoma. I'm going to go ahead and order a biopsy, so we know what we're dealing with."

"A biopsy?"

"Just to be safe," said Dr. Jin.

The following Wednesday morning, Ruth snatched her car keys and her mask off the credenza on her way out the door.

"See you in a little while," she called out to Abe.

"Where you going?" he said, appearing in the foyer.

"I told you yesterday I had to go to town this morning."

"Where, though?"

"T&C," she said.

"Oh, good. Could you pick up some of that homemade sauerkraut from the deli section?"

"Dr. Channing says sauerkraut is loaded with sodium, and that's bad for your blood pressure."

"Yeah," said Abe. "But it's good for my digestion."

"Your digestion isn't the problem," she said with a peck on his cheek.

Though Ruth had always considered herself a terrible liar, she was near certain that she'd avoided Abe's suspicion on this occasion, and so long as she returned with a few items from T&C, she'd be in the clear. Where was the use in worrying anyone when it was probably nothing? Hadn't Dr. Jin said as much herself? Still, as Ruth tried to discount such a possibility, there was a chance that it was something more. It would have been a relief to share the information with somebody, Anne, or Kyle, or Maddie, but Ruth didn't tell a soul about the mass or the biopsy, not even Bess Delory.

Instead, she went about her business as usual the next week, scrupulously adhering to the timeworn rituals and routines that had marked her life with Abe the past twenty or so years. Breakfast at seven A.M., sourdough toast (the twelve-grain was full of lectins), coffee for Ruth, prune juice for Abe along with his medication, after which Ruth rinsed and loaded the breakfast dishes and generally busied herself keeping order in the household, making the bed, feeding Megs and letting her out in the backyard to pee, balancing the checkbook, and taking the recycling out to the bin. All the while, Abe read the newspaper, then dozed for a half hour or so in his chair. Upon awaking, he went to work on the crossword puzzle as he always did, Ruth assisting him when solicited, while she watched HGTV's new *Farmhouse Fixer.*

"Ten-letter word for 'expressionless'?" Abe asked. "Ends with D."

Though Ruth made a brief show of considering the answer, she couldn't begin to get her mind around a crossword in her state of preoccupation. "Ten letters?" she said. "Goodness, I have no idea."

"What about six letters, 'hybrid women's clothing'?"

"I'm not even sure what that means," said Ruth.

Each afternoon that week, according to custom, Ruth prepared their big meal of the day, typically one of the five or six quick and easy dishes she'd adopted since they'd become more health conscious, a menu that included, among other fare, chicken breast with cottage fries, salmon and avocado wrap, shrimp and pasta, and Abe's least favorite of the bunch, quinoa salad. These meals were invariably followed by a nap for Abe, a fifty-minute interval during which he swore he never slept, though his snoring suggested otherwise. That he still refused to wear his CPAP had become a frequent point of dissent in recent months. His unwillingness to endure the minor inconvenience of the device for Ruth's sake was edging toward a legitimate grudge.

"Minor inconvenience?" he said. "You try strapping that contraption on! Every time I open my mouth, I'm like a human leaf blower."

"One of these mornings, you're just not gonna wake up, you know?"

"Good," he said. "Then I won't have to hear about it anymore."

Every evening that week, Abe and Ruth sat together as usual in the living room and watched the five o'clock news, and the six o'clock news, and the seven o'clock news. And for all the normalcy and comfort of the routine, Ruth found it difficult to belie her mounting anxiety regarding the biopsy results. She should have known that after seventy years Abe could see right through her.

"What's eating you?" he asked during a Cialis commercial.

"Eating me?" she said, even as she felt the blood rushing to her face. "What makes you say that?"

"You've been awfully quiet this week," he said.

"Have I?" said Ruth.

"And forgetful, too," he said.

"What did I forget?"

"Well, first you forgot those items at T&C on Wednesday, then, when you went back to get them on Thursday, you forgot your wallet and came back empty-handed. Then there's the fact that you haven't been much help with the crossword this week."

She almost told him then. But given a second chance to come clean, Ruth balked once more.

"I suppose I'm just a little worn out from the party still."

"See? I told you not to make a big production out of it."

"Oh, but it was wonderful, wasn't it?" she said. "Having everybody together like that?"

"It was all well and good," said Abe. "I just worry you push yourself too hard."

"Can't a girl be tired?" she said.

But Abe clearly wasn't convinced, and for good reason, as she would learn in bed that night.

"When were you gonna tell me?" he said.

"Tell you what?"

"About the biopsy," he said. "The referral came in the mail this afternoon."

"Oh, that. Dr. Jin said it's probably nothing," she said.

"So, why didn't you tell me?"

"I didn't want to worry you over nothing."

"Nothing, huh?" he said, turning his back on her.

"Okay, I'm sorry," she said.

But Abe had already settled into an ominous silence. For the next hour, he tossed about under the covers as Ruth lay perfectly still next to him. He had every right to be angry and she knew it. As much as anything, transparency had accounted for the success of their marriage, for it encouraged them to resolve their disputes and overcome their differences, so that they were never left to fester beneath the surface. Frankness and candor begot trust, trust begot connection, connection begot empathy, and ultimately it was empathy that had cemented their partnership by allowing them to absorb their losses and overcome their obstacles collectively.

As small as this evasion on Ruth's part may have seemed on the surface, the omission flew in the face of an accord they'd been honoring since 1954. Thus, it wasn't until Abe's fitful snoring began that Ruth's guilty conscience allowed her to sleep.

When she awoke shortly after dawn the next morning, Abe was not beside her in bed, nor was he occupying the darkened bathroom. Instead, Ruth found him in the kitchen, flat-footed in his ancient slippers, his back turned, too deaf without his hearing aids to sense her watching him from the doorway, his scrawny calves exposed beneath the hem of his old bathrobe, his shoulders stooped, his bald cranium pale and speckled, his bony fingers struggling with a stack of coffee filters even as a pair of blackened eggs wheezed in the skillet and the toaster began smoking.

God, she loved this man. Whatever he may have lacked in utility, he made up in attentiveness and reliability.

Ruth approached him deliberately from the side so as not to

startle him. Still, he was oblivious to her presence as she considered him in profile. Take away the wrinkles, and the age spots, and the chin wattle, and Ruth still recognized the sturdy twenty-year-old Abe Winter she'd first encountered at the University of Washington too many years ago to count.

"I should have told you," she said. "I just thought . . ."

"You're right," said Abe, his eyes evasive. "It's probably nothing."

✶

Winter was almost upon the farm, palpable in the cool, still air of the hallway and the chill of the floorboards penetrating Ruth's slippered feet Thursday morning on her way to the kitchen, where a brisk draft greeted her in the pantry as she gathered the coffee grounds, the filters, and the loaf of sourdough.

Preparing breakfast, she watched Abe out the kitchen window, scraping the ice from the windshield of the old Subaru. Despite his stoop and his diminished work rate, Abe refused to acknowledge the limitations of decrepitude and had managed to remain capable and competent into his ninetieth year, though she hoped he didn't break his neck out there slipping on the ice. Ruth admired Abe's intractable conviction that he could do anything a healthy forty-year-old could do. For all the strength imbued in the young, who thoughtlessly tempted their fates as though it were an act of heroism, it was a fact that they took their vitality and recuperative capacities for granted. Nobody under eighty truly understood what it was to resist—nay, to fight back against—that greatest outside force of all, that thief of minutes and days, death. Everything was a high-risk proposition after eighty. To rage against the dying of the light sometimes meant shoveling the walkway or driving after dark.

Once again, the crisp bite of the coming winter greeted Ruth as she navigated the steps cautiously and proceeded toward the idling car, where Abe hunched behind the wheel like a scarecrow in an overcoat.

"Feels like snow," she said as she fastened her seat belt.

"I hope not," he said. "I'd hate to shovel that damn walkway again this winter. We should have moved to Arizona thirty years ago."

As much as he liked to joke about relocating to sunnier climes and leaving the sodden charms of the island behind, the truth was that Abe, like Ruth, was an islander through and through. They both loved the lush verdancy of the peninsula, the relative lack of traffic or suburban sprawl (though that was changing), and had learned to appreciate the four seasons: fall, fall, fall, and winter.

It was a good thing Ruth had insisted they leave the house early, because traffic was slow with the construction on 305. Not that being late would have mattered, since Dr. Jin kept them waiting for fifteen minutes in the examination room, where the two of them sat in uneasy silence, Abe clutching Ruth's hand in solidarity.

When Dr. Jin finally made her entrance, it was impossible to gauge from her manner whether the news was good or bad.

"Mr. and Mrs. Winter, hello," she said, and wasted no more time on pretense. "Your pathology report came back from the lab, Ruth. Unfortunately, it's not the news we'd hoped for. The mass is . . . not benign."

Dr. Jin gave them the briefest of moments to process the diagnosis.

"The good news," she said, "is that the growth is relatively isolated at this point to the bone, and the margins appear to be clean."

Everything after "not benign" washed right over Ruth as her ears began ringing. For an instant, she thought she might faint from the shock of the news.

"So, you're saying she has cancer?" said Abe.

"Yes," said Dr. Jin.

Again, Dr. Jin granted them a moment to consider the pronouncement.

"What now?" said Ruth, as though from some great distance.

"This calls for aggressive measures," said Dr. Jin. "We need to act quickly. I'm going to refer you to a surgeon, Drew McGonagle at Swedish, one of the very best in the business."

"Just how serious is this?" said Abe.

"We won't really know the full extent of it until Drew gets in there and has a look during the surgery. There's only so much we can glean from the imaging. But it's clear the mass is attacking the bone."

"So, they cut the mass out?" said Abe.

"Yes," said Dr. Jin. "We're talking about considerable bone loss, as well, a large portion of the lower jaw, along with some teeth, and possibly the lymph nodes. We don't know if the tongue has been compromised, or to what extent, nor the surrounding soft tissue."

All the air seemed to vacate the room at once. Ruth could scarcely breathe. Strangely, Dr. Jin's grim assessment of her situation had served to mobilize Ruth's vanity in almost equal measure to her fear of her mortal demise. The prospect of walking around with a stove-in face on the right side, of losing her tongue and mumbling the remainder of her days so no one could understand her, the probability of losing her hair—each of these considerations was hitting her at once, and nearly as terrifying as death itself.

"And then what?" said Ruth. "Are we talking about chemotherapy, here? My hair falls out, I wither away to skin and bones? Honestly, I don't know if I could take it."

"Let's just get you through the surgery first," said Dr. Jin. "I'm not going to lie to you, Ruth. This is going to be a major ordeal, some really rough sledding. But there's a good chance we can eradicate the cancer."

"Is there another option?" she said.

"You could choose not to treat it."

"And?"

"You're probably looking at hospice in four to six months."

"Jesus," said Abe.

"What's the timeline for a surgery?" said Ruth.

"As soon as possible," said Dr. Jin. "Three weeks tops."

On the way home, they drove in silence for a mile or two, Ruth gazing passively out the passenger window at the rash of recent construction spreading before her eyes. How could it be that she was so close to death at that moment, and yet, excepting a loose tooth, she felt perfectly fine? Had she just let the thing rattle around in the back of her mouth or fall out on its own, she might have been dead in four months. And she still might be. Who was to say she'd survive the surgery, or the radiation, at her age? What if the cancer had already migrated elsewhere and Dr. Jin had no way of knowing? It could be anywhere in her body right now, eating away at her, attacking her.

For all the anxiety surrounding her own future, Ruth's thoughts turned to Abe. What would become of him if Ruth went first? Who would take care of him? Anne was half a continent away. Maddie was in Corvallis and could barely take care of herself. It would have to be Kyle, she supposed.

"What about the kids?" said Ruth at last. "Do I even tell them?"

"Of course," said Abe. "You want me to tell them?"

"No," said Ruth. "I'll do it myself."

She couldn't say why she called Kyle first, likely because among her three remaining children, he was her optimist, where Anne was the realist and Maddie the skeptic. Like Kyle, Karen, dead at sixteen, had been an optimist, up until her teen years. How many occasions in the past five decades had Ruth missed Karen's childish optimism, her laughter, her curiosity, her affection? Thank goodness Ruth still had Kyle. She knew she could count on Kyle to remain upbeat upon hearing the news, and he did not disappoint.

"Okay, good, that's good," he said as Ruth walked him through the details. "Swedish is top-notch, and not just regionally, globally. You couldn't be in better hands, Mom. It's not like forty years ago, when a cancer diagnosis was basically a death warrant. They know how to treat it now. The science has come a long way. I know at least ten people who have beat stage four in the past five years. It's good they found the mass when they did."

The call to Kyle managed to buoy her spirits momentarily. Maybe she'd survive this, after all. However, Ruth called Maddie next, who offered an opposing view of the medical prospects.

"You don't have to let them blast you with radiation, you know? It kills everything, good or bad. Have you thought about alternative medicine?"

"I trust Dr. Jin's judgment," said Ruth. "And Swedish has an excellent reputation—and not just regionally, globally."

"Mom, the surgery and the radiation are worse than the cancer. The medical-industrial complex is a sham. Look into holistic oncology options. I went through it with Rupert," she said.

"Rupert was a pug, darling. And he died, as I recall."

"Let me send you some links."

"No, sweetie, it's okay. But I've heard your input, and I promise I'll consider it," Ruth said.

Ruth found herself delaying the call to Anne as long as possible, because she knew Anne would have the most questions and expect the most answers.

"Did you get a second opinion?" she said.

"It's cancer," said Ruth. "What good is a second opinion? I have it or I don't."

"Your insurance will cover the surgery, but what about rehab? Will your Medicare cover that?"

"Honey, I don't know all that at this point," said Ruth.

"Who's gonna take care of you, Mom? Should I fly out there? I can't get away until after Thanksgiving, but—"

"No," said Ruth. "That isn't necessary. We haven't even scheduled the surgery yet. And your father is here to take care of me."

"No offense, Mom, but this is way over Dad's head. You're gonna need actual help. Dad isn't strong enough to help you in and out of bed. He can't take you to the bathroom. He's kind of useless at this point, Mom."

"Don't talk about your father like that," said Ruth.

"All I'm trying to say is that it's too much for you to handle on your own."

Ruth resisted an urge to take her eldest daughter to task. Why couldn't she just be supportive like Kyle? Why, like Maddie, must she always be prescriptive? She knew that they both came from a place of caring, but it didn't make their haranguing any easier to endure. She was exhausted by the time she finally got off the phone. Afterward, she sought out Abe in the living room.

"How'd they take the news?"

"Pretty well, I guess," said Ruth. "Each one differently, as you might imagine."

"You okay?" said Abe.

"Yeah," lied Ruth.

The truth was, she was sick with ambivalence, and dread, and foreboding. And Abe could sense her apprehension. Abe always saw her. Seventy years and counting, and he'd never lost sight of her.

"Sit down," he said. "Let me get you something to drink. What say we watch a DVD? Or one of those home shows?"

"Yes," said Ruth. "I'd like that."

Please, Don't

Winter 1953 marked the beginning of Ruth Warneke's second semester at the University of Washington, where she resided in the women's residence at Leary Hall, a gracefully aging Tudor Gothic on campus, its western façade festooned with ivy, just as Ruth had often dreamed of since freshman year of high school, just as she'd dreamed of one day living in Paris. As the daughter of a mill worker from Shelton, Washington, a rugged outpost of five thousand souls, mired in the muddy backwaters of the Hood Canal, a lumber town with very little to offer a high school valedictorian with bohemian aspirations, Ruth was in love with campus life at UW and doubly enamored with the metropolis of Seattle, its teeming sidewalks and bridges, its architecture, its plunging hills and valleys, its lakes and sounds, and its thousand vistas. Perhaps it wasn't Paris, but it was close to ideal. Ruth was all but living her dream at eighteen.

Content between her studies and her leisurely pursuits of journaling, reading, and secretly writing poetry, along with daily exploring new urban wonders, the museums and shops and cafés, Ruth was not lacking occupation. Surrounded by women her own age, enough of them like-minded to buffer her from homesickness, Ruth did not find herself lacking in companionship, either, and had little interest in courting romance. She'd mostly managed to avoid it through high school, so why start now? Boys and men seemed a distraction with their constant need for validation. While half her housemates at Leary were actively profiling marital candidates, Ruth was unencumbered by any such expectation. There were cheaper ways to find a husband than a college education, anyway. She came to UW to elevate her mind, not her marital prospects.

It was her housemate, the effervescent Mandy Baterman, the daughter of an entertainment attorney from Loma Linda, California, who had already planned her entire life out by seventeen, who coerced Ruth into a blind date with a junior named Abe Winter, as a double with her and her fiancé, Fred Sullivan.

"He's a great guy," Mandy assured Ruth. "Fred played lacrosse with him."

"Lacrosse, huh? What's he studying?"

"Business administration, I think."

"Oh, boy," said Ruth. "He sounds amazing."

"Don't be such a damper, Ruth. You never know, maybe you'll like him."

"If he's so great, why doesn't he have a girl already?"

"Good question," said Mandy. "Maybe he hasn't met the right one."

Convening that Saturday at the bustling student union, the four of them ordered sodas and French-fried potatoes in the commons. As it happened, Abe was quite handsome, something Ruth had not expected; clean-shaven and athletic, lean musculature dressing a long frame, a strong chin, and lively brown eyes. He wore a bow tie, which was a bit of a turnoff; still, she was willing to give him a chance for Mandy's sake more than anything else.

But Ruth immediately found Abe's cockiness off-putting.

"Liberal arts?" he said thirty seconds into their conversation. "What are you gonna do with that when you grow up? Why not something useful like nursing?"

"Or home economics?" said Ruth.

"Sure," said Abe, her sarcasm lost on him.

"And what's so noble about business administration?" said Ruth.

"Well, to begin with, it's applicable to anything," he said.

"So are the liberal arts," she said.

"If you say so," said Abe.

It was apparent at once that they were not made for each other. Their worldviews were hardly compatible. The idea of strolling the hallowed halls of the Henry Art Gallery or sipping café au lait at a coffeehouse with Abe was inconceivable. Worse, within minutes, Ruth had surmised that Abe was a Republican, what with his talk of economic prosperity and limiting big government spending: It couldn't have been clearer if he'd tattooed "I Like Ike" on his big, dumb forehead. Knowing that her father would approve of this only made the distinction worse.

A half hour into their date, Abe already had two strikes against him when you accounted for the bow tie.

"What do you think?" said Mandy in the women's lavatory. "He's a catch, right?"

"I suppose if you like smug," said Ruth.

"He's just confident," said Mandy, powdering her face.

"Yeah, but why?" said Ruth.

"Confidence is good, right? Would you prefer milquetoast?" said Mandy. "And besides, maybe he's just nervous. You never know, Ruthie, give him a break."

"He's wearing a bow tie, Mand."

"Oh, you're such a sorehead. Don't be so quick to judge. Have a good time for once in your life. Or would you rather be in the dorm reading Charles Baudelaire or something?"

"As a matter of fact, yes," said Ruth. "Roethke, even."

"Whoever that is," said Mandy. "Just see how it goes. And play nice, Ruthie."

If only boys were as easy to talk to as Mandy, if only Ruth could let her guard down with men like she could with her girlfriends.

The two couples left the student union and proceeded to the Hub, a hive of activity on a Saturday evening, humming with possibility, with laughter and shouting, the rolling thunder of bowling balls, the sudden clash and clamor of pins, Patti Page's "I Went to Your Wedding" barely perceptible over the public address system, just loud enough to prompt an eye roll from Ruth. The Hub was not entirely what Ruth had imagined in the way of sophistication when she was accepted at UW, not exactly high culture, but it was hard to resist for its pure jubilance and youthful spirit.

Fred went after sodas, while Abe rented the shoes, leaving Ruth and Mandy to wait amidst the throng.

"Don't give up on him because he can't quote Shakespeare, Ruthie," said Mandy.

"He couldn't quote *Howdy Doody*."

"You're insufferable," Mandy said.

"You're right," said Ruth. "I apologize. Maybe I'm the nervous one."

"Fred left me his flask," said Mandy. "Maybe you want a nip in the girls' room; it might loosen you up."

"You mean lower my standards?" said Ruth.

"Ugh, you're impossible," said Mandy. "Don't ruin this for Fred and I."

"You mean 'Fred and me.' *Me* is the object of the verb."

"And stop correcting my grammar."

Mandy was right, of course. Ruth needed to accept people on their own terms and stop projecting her romantic expectations on the world at large. She resolved herself to be open to Abe and whatever he might have to offer.

Perhaps the Hub was an unfortunate place to begin. For, despite his athletic build, Abe quickly proved to be a hopeless bowler, awkward in his approach and reckless in his delivery. Twice within the first three frames, he crossed the foul line. His off-balance recovery after every launch made it look as though he were bowling on ice. He couldn't find the pocket to save his life. When he did manage to hit the headpin, he was left with a nasty split more often than not.

Ruth was a little rusty but not too bad. For all the little town of Shelton may have lacked in high culture, it had not lacked a bowling alley, which was nothing less than the cultural nervous system of the town, outside of the churches. For three years, Ruth had bowled league on Sundays after worship. Friday nights had little else to offer in Shelton that didn't require alcohol or parking on road ends. Thus, it was no surprise that she was out-bowling Abe handily, a fact she may have been relishing a bit too demonstratively for Abe's taste, because the latter was clearly agitated by the seventh frame. When she tried to offer him advice—*measure your approach, follow through on your delivery, quit throwing it so darn hard*—Abe was less than gracious in accepting her input, impatient to restore his pride in the second round, an objective he failed to accomplish, for when it was over, he had bowled a 91 to Ruth's 126.

*

It was bad enough losing to a girl, but the way she kept rubbing it in was downright rude, though she seemed to think she was being cute, a brand of hubris that bespoke what Abe suspected was an indulgent upbringing. Flustered by his dreadful performance, and increasingly annoyed at Ruth's chiding antics, Abe still could not resist a powerful attraction to her beauty, which seemed effortless. How had Fred failed to mention it? The arresting blue eyes. The high cheekbones. The generous figure and graceful carriage. In two-plus years at the U, unable to attract a partner on his own, Abe had conceded to at least a half dozen blind dates at the behest of his fraternity brothers, and all of the dates had either possessed "great personalities" or were "really fun," "super smart," or "very talented," but none of them looked even remotely like Ruth Warneke, whose beauty was worthy of the silver screen.

Abe knew he was blowing his chances with Ruth and was desperate to redeem himself. He was self-aware enough to know that he lacked charm with women, that he suffered from an apparent deficiency of the boyish playfulness and collegiate enthusiasm requisite for a young man of his station. As he emptied his bladder into the urinal, it occurred to Abe that he was born middle-aged, and no doubt Ruth could see it. More than hijinks or adventure, more than the call of youthful appetites, he yearned for routine and order and responsibility. He longed to settle down and root himself like an oak tree. Though barely of legal drinking age, Abe already aspired to be a husband and a father, a stolid presence in the lives of those who depended upon him, reliable, consistent, fair. He possessed all these potentialities, yet in his anxiety to perform, he projected only arrogance and insecurity. It was never like this with men, whom Abe had a facility for persuading.

"Relax," said Fred, stationing himself in front of the adjacent urinal. "Don't try to impress her."

"She's too smart for me," said Abe.

"Nonsense. You just need to lighten up. And don't talk about politics."

"Yeah, I got that," said Abe.

After the Hub, they all piled into Fred's Dodge and drove downtown, where they parked on Mercer and bought tickets at the Uptown for *The Bad and the Beautiful* with Kirk Douglas. Abe didn't dare put his arm around Ruth during the picture, let alone put his hand on her knee. But he couldn't stop himself from sneaking sidelong glances at her, wondering at her thoughts as she watched the screen, her face bathed in the flickering light of the projector, her intelligent eyes penetrating the darkness of the theater, her resting face so considered, so thoughtful, and so unaware of his admiration. God, but he wanted to impress her. How he wished he were Kirk Douglas up on the screen, or even Dick Powell, so he could feel the force of her attentiveness.

The movie wasn't bad, either. Abe had already formulated his remarks on the picture before the final frames played out and was almost as eager to share them as he was to hear Ruth's opinion.

"So, what'd you think?" he asked her on the sidewalk as the four of them strode toward Fred's car.

"I thought it was basically a soap opera, especially the Lana Turner section. One betrayal after the next. I ran out of sympathy about four minutes in."

"That's the point," said Abe. "Shields epitomizes the Hollywood ethos of—"

"Please don't," said Ruth, cutting him off. "I really don't need you to explain it to me. You solicited my opinion, and I provided it."

Horrified by his misstep, Abe felt his face coloring, and he was sure this didn't escape Ruth's notice.

"I'm sorry if that came off as strident," Ruth said. "But honest to goodness, if I had a dollar for every time a man tried to enlighten me."

In the darkened car, the lights of the city blurring past, the young couples proceeded to Belltown for a late dinner at Bob Murray's Dog House. The slogan claimed all roads led to the Dog House, and indeed they must have, for they waited twenty minutes for a table. The entirety of the back wall was adorned with a huge mural testifying to the conceit of the establishment, a road map leading to marital perdition, past redheads, blondes, and brunettes along the way, and terminating at the Dog House, that arguably not-so-unfortunate locale where all roads led for men incapable of monogamy.

"Poor men," said Ruth. "Imagine cheating on your wife with your secretary and ending up in the doghouse. What an indignity. Almost as bad as changing a diaper."

Abe had never known a woman to speak her mind so freely. He was thrilled by Ruth's irreverence, even as it challenged his notions about feminine decorum.

"God, you're right," he said. "And they even make the dog cute, a pup who just can't help himself. Poor little guy."

"He'll be okay. The sign above the doghouse door says welcome," Ruth observed. "And somebody even left our furry philanderer a bone."

When they were finally seated with their menus, everybody ordered boiled ham sandwiches, except for Ruth, who ordered the goose liver.

Conversationally, Abe began to hit his stride as the meal wore on, avoiding politics at all costs and only offering opinions or commentary when solicited. Mostly, he tried to be agreeable. He was in over his head when Ruth turned the subject to poetry or architecture, so he let her carry on, taking the dialogue in whatever direction compelled her. From Abe's perspective, she had some flaky ideas about how the world worked, but she was quite funny, and unexpectedly erudite for a girl raised in the boondocks. This, too, spoke of an indulgent upbringing to Abe.

"How do you know all this stuff?" he asked her.

"Believe me," she said, "there's a lot I don't know about. I'm just faking it most of the time."

Abe was charmed by this display of candor. If only he could wow her with some expertise of his own. But he knew the fundamental principles of accounting and finance were unlikely to impress Ruth Warneke, that she'd have little interest in organizational structure or fiscal design, that she didn't give a whit about lacrosse, and he was no good, anyway. If only she could see his winning qualities: his punctuality, his hygiene, his willingness to be persuaded, to compromise, to show up.

While Abe was loath to share his opinions, Ruth suffered from no such inhibition. During the course of her goose liver sandwich, she espoused her views on everything from civil rights, to forestry, to foreign policy, to social spending, much of it amounting to so much pseudocommunist malarky as far as Abe was concerned. It seemed that poets, or at least those poetically inclined, suffered from such unreasonable optimism that in ceaselessly investigating the world on a cellular level, they completely missed some of the bigger, less convenient realities of human nature and governance. While it was hard to fault them for their noble delusions, there was a certain recklessness to their laissez-faire idealism that was often problematic when faced with, well, real life. Moreover, the idealist rarely footed the bill, practically speaking. But Abe would gladly have picked up the tab for

Ruth's naivety, and listened to her goofy ideas, so long as he could be around her. He didn't want the evening to end, and Fred was one step ahead of him.

"Where should we go next?" he said.

"What about the Blue Moon on Forty-Fifth," said Mandy.

"Isn't that place crawling with subversives?" said Abe, instantly regretting it.

"Oh, for Pete's sake, are you serious?" said Ruth. "You sound like McCarthy."

Having fallen flat on his face again with the remark, Abe had the wherewithal to recover this time. "I was joking," he said. "Geez."

"You and Ruth aren't old enough to get into the Blue Moon without getting lucky," said Fred.

"I'll bet we could get lucky," said Mandy.

"I should probably call it a night," said Ruth. "I'm going to church tomorrow."

"Church?" said Fred.

"Since when?" said Mandy.

"You say it like it's weird," said Ruth.

"I just didn't know you were a church girl," Mandy said.

"I'm not what you would call 'devout,'" said Ruth. "I guess I just miss it, is all. There's something so calming about the routine of it, so peaceful."

Oh, Ruth Warneke! Endlessly surprising, the opposite of Abe in almost every way, and yet, he was helpless to resist her magnetism. He'd never been a churchgoer, never paid much mind to religion, which seemed to present one impractical notion after another.

"I'll go with you," he blurted. "That is, I mean . . . not that you invited me or anything, I just . . ."

"Thanks," said Ruth. "But I like to go alone."

Abe could have easily given up hope at that point. Ruth had basically slammed the door in his face, and yet, he was still compelled to come knocking again and again until she granted him entrance.

"Well, I guess that's a wrap for tonight, then," said Fred.

"Let me get the check," said Abe.

"Is it a national holiday?" said Fred.

"Quit it," said Abe, reaching for his billfold.

Fred drove the girls back to Leary and parked at the curb. Abe and Ruth sat awkwardly in the back of the idling Dodge as Fred and Mandy locked lips in a prolonged farewell. How badly Abe wanted to extend some token of his affection to Ruth. A kiss seemed out of the question, but perhaps he might set his hand atop hers. Before he could summon the nerve to make any such move, however, Ruth, having grown impatient with Fred and Mandy's vulgar display in the front seat, excused herself abruptly.

"Well, it was nice meeting you," she said to Abe. "Night, Fred, night, Mandy."

And then Ruth closed the door, leaving Abe alone with the amorous couple, still fused at the lips, paying Abe no notice at all, as he watched her walk away into the night.

A Few Degrees Colder

2023

It was bitterly cold and spitting rain as Abe hunched over the wheel of the idling Subaru, Ruth beside him in the passenger seat, a cotton knit throw blanket across her lap for warmth, her empty stomach protesting.

"You warm enough?" said Abe.

"Yes, thanks," said Ruth.

"You must be famished," said Abe, as though he could hear her thoughts.

Being famished was only one of the sensations presently rattling around in Ruth's body. And there were far more troubling thoughts vying for position at the front of her mental queue: not surviving the surgery, the nagging and very real possibility of leaving Abe and Megs to fend for themselves. Ruth hoped Abe couldn't intimate those thoughts, as well.

"A few degrees colder and this will turn to snow," Abe observed. "God, I hope not. The hill will be a mess."

"The line is moving, honey," said Ruth.

Indeed, the vehicles in front of them had already begun loading at a crawl, thunk-thunking over the steel ramp onto the car deck, a sensation as familiar as closing the refrigerator, even after all these years since they'd last caught a ferry. Among the first to board, they were ushered clear up front to the open bow of the vessel, from whence Ruth peered out over the choppy surface of the water across the harbor, remembering the old creosote factory, gone for decades. Eagledale, once a smattering of old houses clinging to the shoreline, was built up with bigger houses now, and more of them, crowding out the quaint old seasonal residences. The entire island, even the remotest reaches of the south end, had gone that way the past thirty years, though Bainbridge still managed to maintain some of its woodsy charm, at least from a distance.

Once the ferry had passed Wing Point and cleared the harbor, the Seattle skyline made its appearance to the east under a low, slate-gray cover of clouds. My, how Seattle had grown since Ruth had first laid her hungry eyes on it as a child of ten years old. That was long before the fair, or the needle, or the stadiums, back when Smith Tower was the regional landmark, once the tallest structure west of the Mississippi, its neoclassical elegance now dwarfed, hardly visible in a forest of modular steel and glass.

"You're nervous about driving in the city, aren't you?" said Ruth.

"Why would I be?" said Abe.

"I'd be nervous," she said.

Neither of them had driven in the city in fifteen years. When they made the trip across the sound at all anymore, it was the Kingston run, where they'd park at Kyle's house, five minutes from the terminal in Edmonds. Anne had made them promise they'd take a cab to Swedish, but Abe insisted on driving Ruth himself in the familiarity of her own car. And he was right, it was a comfort, despite the impending anxiety of getting through downtown and up the hill.

Ruth hardly recognized the city anymore. The viaduct was gone, and she found that she missed it somehow. The old ferry terminal had been wholly reimagined, along with the rest of the waterfront. Where the old wharves and brick buildings along Alaskan Way had once offered a soft landing, albeit a grimy, rugged one, maritime travelers were now confronted by a thirty-story wall of urban high-rise development, a steely blockade dedicated to late capitalism that offered little hint of the regional culture that predated it, its lone flourish of frivolity being the great Ferris wheel at Pier 57, a twenty-five-dollar-per-ticket tourist trap that might have been built anywhere. None of the new skyscrapers embodied the dignity or conceit of the Seattle Tower, with its art deco flair, or the King Street Station, with its stately clock tower, or any of the nineteenth-to-mid-twentieth-century structures with their familiar skins of granite, and brick, and terra cotta.

Upon offloading from the boat, Abe's demeanor quickly progressed from visibly anxious to flustered.

"Which damn lane am I supposed to be in here?" he said. "The boat used to empty straight onto Marion. Now I'm two blocks south and there's three lanes. Is that Columbia or Yesler? Can I go straight?"

Ruth knew that to offer any guidance would only agitate him more, especially since she had no idea herself in which lane they ought to be, but if she had to guess she would have stayed in the middle lane. As it happened, Abe ended up doing exactly what Ruth would have done, proceeding straight through the light at Alaskan Way and shooting up Yesler. It should have worked perfectly. But within three blocks, construction diverted them south, and a block after that diverted them back west, then south again, until they were back on Alaskan Way, where, halfway to the stadium, they backtracked north before they finally managed to forge a path east, though not before they almost ended up on I-90 East.

Fifteen minutes later, having circled the block twice, white-knuckled and hunched at the wheel, Abe piloted the Subaru safely into the Swedish parking garage.

"Easy peasy," he said with a feeble smile.

"Looks like the hard part's over, anyway," said Ruth.

Abe gathered Ruth's overnight bag from the back seat, and they struck out in search of the elevator. Checking in on the eighth floor, they were conducted to a pre-op staging area, where a young nurse with brawny forearms and tiny hands presented Ruth with a white, open-backed gown.

"I'm Brooke," she said. "Put this on if you would. And go ahead and lay down in bed."

Ruth let the grammatical blunder pass, a restraint that had taken the better part of fifty years to cultivate, as Brooke pulled the paper curtain closed and stepped out of the room.

"*Lie* down in bed," she whispered to Abe. "*Lay* requires a direct object."

Abe stood by as Ruth disrobed, holding the flimsy garment aloft so that she could easily slip into it. When Brooke returned, she began checking Ruth's vitals with the mechanical efficiency of a seasoned professional.

"Have you had any medications today?"

"No," said Ruth.

"When was the last time you ate?"

"I ate a bowl of cottage cheese around eight thirty last night."

"Excellent," she said. "Everything is in order here. Dr. McGonagle will be in shortly to brief you."

Ten minutes later McGonagle appeared, an impressive figure, maybe six foot two, square-shouldered and deeply tanned, like a man who spent a good deal of time on golf courses. He exuded capability, though it was hard to tell whether it was earned or practiced.

"How are you feeling?" he said, briefly engaging in eye contact before turning his attention to Ruth's chart.

"Good," said Ruth.

"I see you're up six pounds," he said. "That's what we'd hoped to see."

"It was him," she said, indicating Abe. "He all but forced me to eat."

"Well done," said McGonagle. "Have either of you got any questions?"

Again, Ruth let his grammatical gaffe pass.

"How long will the surgery be?" said Abe.

"I can't say until we get in there," he said. "We anticipate some-where in the neighborhood of three hours. As I explained previ-ously, we'll make the incision here, at the jawline, and go in under the flap. You'll likely lose a few teeth and the lymph node along with the bone."

Now that it was about to happen, Ruth found herself impatient to begin, to get the ordeal over with and put it behind her, behind them, to live, or hopefully live, with the results. She was not frightened, not the way she'd expected to be. With three and a half weeks to prepare for the possibilities, she'd resolved herself to put her faith in God, a transfer of agency that allowed Ruth to face the procedure with the same stoicism with which she'd endured childbirth four times, in-cluding fifteen hours of labor with Maddie.

After a twenty-minute wait, two orderlies came for Ruth, station-ing themselves on either side of the bed, and began wheeling her out into the corridor. They paused in their progress long enough for Abe to lean down and gently plant a kiss on Ruth's forehead, even as he clutched her hand in his own.

"I love you," he whispered into her ear. "It'll soon be over, then you can just lay in bed and I''ll take care of you."

"Chickens lay in beds, people lie in them. Didn't they teach you that in business school?"

She could see Abe's eyes were troubled as she gave his hand a final squeeze. Poor, dear Abe looked pale and bewildered standing there in the corridor, slightly stooped, his jaw a little slack, his skin almost transparent under the glare of the fluorescent lights.

Once in the arena, they transferred her onto the operating table beneath the brilliant glow of the surgical lamp. Somebody put the mask in place over her nose and mouth, even as somebody else ad-ministered the IV to her wrist with a dull prick.

The disembodied head of Dr. McGonagle was soon hovering above her, making small talk.

"Tell me about your last vacation," he said. "Where'd you go?"

Before Ruth could answer that seven years prior, she and Abe had flown to his cousin's funeral in Columbus, Ohio, the thought eluded her as her eyelids grew heavy, and darkness fell upon her.

*

Abe waited two hours in reception with nothing but his thoughts to occupy himself before hunger drove him down to the cafeteria, where he ate half a turkey wrap and drank a cup of decaf before returning to his post, alternately inquiring at the desk for updates and dozing off in his chair. Four hours passed, then six, and still no word from the surgeon.

Finally, shortly after dusk, Dr. McGonagle emerged with an update.

"The surgery was more complex than we initially expected," he explained to Abe, who was intent upon the surgeon's every word. "The growth had advanced considerably. Thus, the six-and-a-half-hour surgery."

"Is she okay?" said Abe.

"She did great, she hung in there like a champ," said McGonagle with the pride of a pitching coach. "She's stable now. We're keeping her in the ICU just as a precaution, but she should be in her own room by morning."

"When can I see her?"

"Tomorrow," said McGonagle, setting an encouraging hand upon Abe's stooped shoulder. "You'd best get some rest. Are you at the Silver Cloud?"

"Yes," said Abe.

"Good. Check back in the morning."

McGonagle was in the act of leaving when Abe addressed him once more.

"How did this happen? What caused this?" he said.

McGonagle considered it briefly. "Just bad luck, plain and simple," he said.

The Silver Cloud seemed like a terrible name for a hotel associated with a hospital, where lives hung daily in the balance. Silver clouds seemed to suggest that heaven was the foregone conclusion. The place was reasonably priced, or so Kyle had assured his father, though a hundred fifty-nine plus taxes per night hardly seemed like a bargain when Abe could still remember paying eight bucks a night for the honeymoon suite at the Camlin Hotel. Though the hotel was nicer and the room larger than it needed to be for Abe's purpose, the location couldn't be beat. His sixth-floor window afforded Abe a view directly across the street at Swedish, where Ruth presently lay (or was it *laid*?), apparently stable, and likely insensate.

He ordered a Tuscan chicken sandwich from room service and waited on the bed, still too anxious from the day's events to kick off his shoes. When the food arrived twenty minutes later, he ate half of it without relish, then set the chrome-covered plate out in the hallway.

Anne was the first to call, around six thirty.

"Why haven't you answered my messages?" she said.

"What messages?"

"I left three messages on your cell."

"I don't think my phone works in the hospital," he explained. "Besides, I have no clue how to find my messages, let alone listen to them. You may as well ask me to land on the moon."

"How'd it go?" said Anne.

"It was considerably worse than they thought," he said. "She lost seven teeth, a lymph node, and half her tongue. Not to mention a good portion of her left tibia, now fused to her lower jaw."

"I thought they were just shaving some bone."

"We all thought that," said Abe.

"She's okay, though?"

"She's stable, whatever that means."

"Have you seen her yet?"

"No."

"Where are you now?"

"At a hotel, across the street from the hospital."

"How'd you get there?"

Abe lapsed into silence.

"I told you, it's across the street. I used the crosswalk."

"I mean, how did you get up the hill? Did Kyle pick you up?"

"No," said Abe.

"Then, you took a cab?"

Abe's silence was as good as a confession.

"You drove, didn't you? Dad, when are you going to accept your limitations? There's no shame in being ninety years old, but you can't go about acting like you're thirty-five."

"I got here, didn't I?"

"This time," said Anne. "Do I need to fly out, Dad?"

"No," Abe insisted. "I can take care of her."

"What about Kyle or Maddie?"

"What about them?"

"Can one of them come stay with you for a while, or take shifts, or what about insurance, maybe Medicare will cover some in-home care? Dad, you gotta get some help."

While Abe himself suspected he might be in over his head when it came to caring for Ruth through what promised to be a brutal convalescence, under no circumstances was he prepared to make this concession to his eldest daughter. On the contrary, Anne's skepticism of his ability to care for Ruth only fortified Abe's assertion that he was up to the task.

"She's my wife, I've lived with her for seventy years, I know everything about her, I can damn well take care of her as well as anyone, especially some stranger."

Anne must have convinced Kyle, too, because when he called a half hour later, he broached the subject of his mother's care before he even inquired about the success of the operation.

"So, what happens when she leaves the hospital?"

"We're not there yet," said Abe.

"There's gotta be some kind of aftercare resource in place through Swedish, right? Or what about the Fred Hutch clinic? Let me make some calls."

"No," Abe insisted. "I've got everything covered."

"When can I see her?"

"I'll let you know tomorrow."

"You holding up okay, Dad? You sound tired."

"I am tired," said Abe. "Which is why I need to get some rest. I'll keep you updated."

Even Maddie, their disorganized child, either the most or the least adaptable of their progeny (the jury was still out), was prescriptive regarding her mother's treatment going forward.

"She's not a car, Dad," she observed, the little Pomeranian yipping in the background. "You don't just start removing parts and filling her with chemicals, then run her out on the road again for another fifty thousand miles. She needs some kind of holistic healing, and I don't mean radiation. You cannot do this alone, Daddy. I'm going to drive up on Friday, and we can—"

"No," said Abe. "Thank you, sweetie, but no. Let me handle this."

When Abe finally set his phone down around nine forty-five, he gazed dully at the black sheen of the thirty-six-inch flat-screen in front of the bed, at the burnished, fake-hardwood dresser beneath it, his mind occupying a state beyond exhaustion, mercifully indifferent to the mechanics of the quotidian world. This lasted but the briefest of moments before the pressing reality of his immediate future asserted itself once more.

Finally, Abe kicked off his shoes, then liberated himself from his sweater, then his pants, piling them on the club chair opposite the bed. In only his drawers and T-shirt and socks, he stood at the sixth-floor window and looked across the street at the hospital, still a hive of activity at night—for illness and misfortune never rested.

It had begun to snow lightly. Innumerable windswept flakes, tiny and ephemeral, seeking purchase in the solid world before their time ran out, sticking to anything that would have them, slowly and deliberately beginning to accumulate on the roofs of neighboring buildings, the ledge outside the window, and eventually, on the street below. Somewhere in that great edifice across the way, his wife and best friend, his co-conspirator and confessor, the mother of his three surviving children, lay unconscious in a strange bed, hooked to machines, with tubes up her nose, fighting for her life. It was not even Christmas, and yet already it seemed the heart of winter was upon them.

Where Angels Fear to Tread

1953

A be Winter was a goner for Ruth Warneke, powerless to acquit his imagination of her considerable charms, though both Fred and Mandy had gently made it plain to him that Ruth did not view Abe as companionable. So calling her for a second date was not on the table. Given this singular absence of leverage, Abe had little choice but to lean solely on happenstance to win Ruth's company. Thus, more than ever, when he wasn't daydreaming about Ruth, Abe found himself out and about on campus, neglecting his studies, sometimes crossing and recrossing Red Square in the rain, passing and repassing the student union, loitering in the commons or the Hub, the museum, even walking past Leary to no other purpose than the slim possibility that he might cross paths with Ruth.

In his continued efforts to enhance his eligibility, Abe employed the services of his fraternity brother Brian McCleary—an effortlessly athletic specimen from Huntington Beach, whose blue-eyed, blond-headed visage was lacking in neither confidence nor capability—to instruct Abe in the finer points of bowling, an arrangement comprising a few lessons that Brian consented to at the cost of the bowling and the shoe rental, and a pitcher of beer afterward at the Northlake Tavern. These bowling sessions were largely devoted to Abe's incessant pining for Ruth, a state of affairs that Brian McCleary, to whom everything seemed to come so easily, had little patience for, along with Abe's bowling technique.

"No, no," he said, edging toward exasperation. "You're still coming across your body, Winter! Use the dang arrows on the lane to guide your release, dummy! That's what they're there for! And for Pete's sake, smooth out those mechanics, not so herky-jerky. You look like a marionette up there."

After two weeks and seven sessions, Abe's game had ultimately improved despite the fact that the muscles of his right arm ached at all hours and he seemed to be developing tendinitis in his wrist. With Brian's tutelage, he'd learned to harness his power and control his release enough to consistently score three or four strikes per game, while improving his accuracy enough to mostly avoid splits and pick up the easier spares. His dating game, however, showed no such improvement, as Abe was still clinging to the most tenuous of possibilities, a fool's errand as far as McCleary was concerned.

"Seriously, Winter, why are you so hung up on this girl?" he said over his mug of beer. "She's a looker, I'll give you that, but she sounds kind of stuck-up."

"It's not like that," said Abe.

"So, what is it about her that's got you acting like such a goober?"

"I just like her is all."

"Oh, I see. Very considered, Winter," said McCleary. "I hope you're more prudent in business than dating, or you're never gonna make more than seven grand a year."

The truth of the matter was that Abe had given Ruth plenty of consideration, perhaps an unhealthy amount of consideration seeing as he'd spent a total of only four hours with her. Yes, she was beautiful, confident, poised; those qualities alone might have warranted his burgeoning attraction. Moreover, she was highly intelligent, far more intelligent than Abe considered himself to be, and her sophistication seemed natural to her rather than cultivated, a revelation in light of the fact she grew up in a backwater mill town to a family of modest means, yet another revelation to Abe, who had assumed she'd been pampered. Then there was the simple fact that next to Mandy and most of their housemates at Leary, Ruth seemed like a woman among girls, even as a freshman. But what fascinated Abe most about Ruth may have been their ideological differences, or perhaps not the differences themselves but Ruth's unwavering commitment to her own high-minded ideals, which, despite their naivety and sometimes-fallacious logic, always erred on the side of humanism. In this way, she was the opposite of snobby: Ruth Warneke was very much a woman of the people. Her concern for humanity seemed, like her sophistication, to be native and genuine. Abe was of the mind that what counted more than anything in the end was what he considered to be the incorruptibility of her character.

In addition to bowling, Abe made several visits to the library, where he borrowed volumes of poetry. Not knowing where to begin, he just began working his way alphabetically from Auden to Burns to Coleridge, a practice that did not go unnoticed by some of his fraternity brothers, including Fred Sullivan.

"Winter, you really are goofy," he observed. "I admire the determination and all, but poetry? Just don't start writing it, okay?"

In truth, the poetry did not speak to Abe consistently, and often it was a sheer labor to get through. Some of the poets Abe liked better than others. Baudelaire was interesting, morally complex, plain-spoken enough to agree with Abe's constitution, if a little liberal with his romanticism, and needlessly decadent at times, whereas Eliot's "The Waste Land" was so obscure as to be torturous for Abe. Who was talking? What did any of it mean? Still, that Ruth could comprehend and connect with any of it on such a level as to be genuinely inspired was impressive to Abe and spoke of a character as deep as it was elevated.

It occurred to Abe to compose a poem for Ruth professing his devotion, but he reasoned he would only embarrass himself in doing so; his poetry would be *love* and *dove* and ham-fisted sentiment. She'd probably laugh at the earnestness of it. And heaven knew she'd have a field day with his grammar. If only Abe could make her understand, somehow show Ruth in his own way that he was worthy of her affection. But he hadn't seen her again, and even if he did, what could he ever do to impress someone as erudite as she? It dawned on Abe with aching certainty that his life to this point had been nothing but a series of bad decisions leading to his inability to win the heart of Ruth Warneke, which seemed the great tragedy of his existence. He should have been an English major.

*

Abe Winter would have been the furthest thing from Ruth's mind if it had been left up to her. But both Mandy and Fred continued to lobby on Abe's behalf as winter semester progressed.

"The guy is crazy for you," Mandy told her. "He'd trek the tundra barefoot for you, Ruthie, I swear. Not every guy would do that. I doubt Fred would walk to the market for me. Give him another chance."

That wasn't happening, though, no matter how hard Abe tried to exercise his will and weaken her resistance. The fact was, Ruth had been forced to actively avoid Abe, who had made his presence ubiquitous in recent days. Twice she'd caught him walking to and fro casually in front of Leary and had to sneak out the back door to elude him. She spotted him once at the Henry Art Gallery, standing before a contemporary piece by Roorbach, his head cocked curiously to one side like a springer spaniel confronted with the Fibonacci sequence. According to Fred, Abe Winter had started reading poetry and was now the laughingstock of Sigma Chi.

Frankly, the specter of Abe had become an unwanted distraction in Ruth's life. As it was, the hours of the day were too few to fill her heart and mind with knowledge without having to walk halfway around campus to avoid him. Sooner or later, she knew the situation would have to be resolved in no uncertain terms. And so, when Ruth ran into Abe in front of the student union, where no doubt he'd been running reconnaissance designed to achieve this very end, the unavoidable came to pass.

"Ruth!" he said, as though their meeting were a matter of pure chance.

"Hello, Abe," she said unsmilingly.

"Hey, you owe me a rematch!"

"Oh?"

"Bowling," said Abe.

"No, thanks," Ruth said. "We already did that."

"You got lucky," said Abe.

"Hardly," Ruth said. "You're a dreadful bowler."

"Then what are you afraid of?" said Abe.

What was more embarrassing: that Ruth acknowledged him as any kind of bowler at all, or that owing to her fiercely competitive nature she actually took the bait?

"Okay, fine," she said. "You're on."

The showdown was scheduled for Friday evening at the Hub. There was to be no dinner beforehand. Abe was not to meet Ruth up at Leary, or bring her flowers, or candy, or any such romantic pretense. She was very clear that their meeting wasn't to be a date but a rematch. They would go Dutch on the bowling and the shoes. Ruth would buy her own soda if she drank one at all. They would play but a single game to get it over with as soon as possible. Ruth set the stakes high so she could be rid of him for good.

"When I win," she said, "and I will win, you are never to walk in front of Leary or go out of your way to run into me again, is that clear?"

"What if I win?"

"You won't."

"But if I do?"

"I'll reimburse you for the bowling and the shoes."

"That's not enough," said Abe.

"Fine," she said. "Name it."

"If I win, you let me take you out to dinner," said Abe. "Alone. On a proper date."

Had Ruth entertained any doubt at all as to whether she would ultimately prevail, she never would have agreed to these terms. But Ruth had been rusty the last time out, and her game had improved as the evening progressed, while Abe barely smelled a hundred in three games, topping out at 96.

Ruth dressed frumpily for the occasion in a baggy sweater and rolled-up jeans, exposing her stubbly ankles. She wore no makeup, not even lip balm. She pulled her hair back into a careless bun. For his part, Abe wore a baby-blue oxford shirt with gray pleated slacks, and no bow tie, thank God. He'd nicked himself shaving and neglected to remove the tiny wad of tissue on his neck, which he'd used to staunch the bleeding, an oversight Ruth did not bother bringing to his attention; it would eventually flutter to the hardwood after a few frames.

Whenever possible, Ruth met Abe's attempts at small talk with yeses and nos, careful to maintain a disinterested tone. It was contrary to her nature to behave in such an uncivil manner, and antithetical to everything she had been taught, so why was she rude to him? What was it about Abe Winter she found so distasteful besides his bow ties and his politics? He was well-mannered for the most part, especially for a fraternity boy. He wasn't as much of a know-it-all as most guys Ruth encountered. He was soft-spoken and attentive when he wasn't trying to impress. Was it possible that the very urgency of Abe's affection accounted for Ruth's disinterest? Was it his easy accessibility that made her want to run from him? Could it be that beneath her veneer of assertiveness and worldly conceit, Ruth was still that little girl in Shelton wanting so desperately to escape her beginnings, and that someone like Abe, older and more experienced, someone not willing to agree with her views as a matter of course, someone willing, in fact, to challenge them, threatened to expose that vulnerable girl who had never ventured more than a hundred and ten miles from home? Ruth promptly pushed these troubling thoughts aside as she tied her shoes.

"Ladies first," said Abe, scratching out their names on the score-card. "You'll have to keep tabs; I don't know how. But I trust you."

Ruth hoisted her ball, measured her steps, and let it fly. She hit the pocket perfectly and the pins exploded with a deafening clamor: a no-doubt-about-it strike. She did not, however, gloat on this occasion. Instead, she was all business.

Abe followed with a seven-ten split and didn't pick up either pin with his second ball. It was going to be a long night for Abe even though Ruth was destined to make short work of him. But something happened. He marked in the second and third with spares, then hit a strike in the fourth, and again in the fifth. By the sixth they were neck and neck. Ruth picked up the spare in the seventh, but Abe followed with one of his own.

Now it was Abe's turn to gloat.

"I hope you like French food. I was thinking Maison Blanc downtown."

Abe was a different bowler than he'd been three weeks prior. Clearly, he'd prepared for this match, which seemed a dirty trick to Ruth, like he'd gone out of his way to set her up for failure. And what did he hope to accomplish by this? Did he imagine she wanted him to beat her? Did men really imagine that women yearned to be put in their place? Well, Ruth thought, she would show him where her place was.

But it wasn't to be. Maybe it was the pressure, but Ruth began to fold in the eighth. It started with an embarrassing five-seven-ten split, which she couldn't pick up. She left an open frame again in the ninth. Abe strung together two strikes and a seven in the tenth frame to finish with a 138, to Ruth's 116.

Ruth was not proud of her sulking in the wake of this defeat. It was true, she'd never been a particularly gracious loser, but then, as a lifelong overachiever, she'd had little experience in losing.

"So, this was your plan to win me over, huh? Humiliate me in bowling? Good one."

"I just thought—"

But before Abe could finish, Ruth had already slipped out of her shoes and stormed off to return them at the counter. Abe scrambled after her, and when he pulled even with her, she refused to look at him.

"And by the way," she said, looking straight ahead, "I heard you said something to Fred and Mandy about my native sophistication. Well, let me inform you of something, mister: My sophistication is not native. If it was native, I'd be drinking canned beer in the back of a pickup truck at the end of a dirt road somewhere right now. I'd be pushing paper at the mill, or waiting tables at Jolly Judy's. I worked for my sophistication, I studied, and read, and buckled down, while my friends were out drinking milkshakes and eating burgers. My own parents teased me for my efforts. So, no, Mr. Winter, nothing about me is native. What you see, I invented myself."

If Abe Winter had been a goner for Ruth Warneke before this tirade, he was officially off the rails by the time it was over. The grit of this woman! The spirit, the determination, the independence, were these not the very principles Abe valued above all else? What did it matter if she was a communist sympathizer or a feminist? She embodied all the courage and conviction he could ever desire out of a mate!

Too bad the decision was not his to make.

The evening had been an unmitigated disaster as far as Ruth was concerned. She had no desire to see Abe Winter again, but she was honor bound.

"Well," she said. "Congratulations. This is what you wanted. Pick a date and let's get it over with."

Abe seemed genuinely crestfallen, and Ruth regretted her dismissive tone, if only because she didn't like to hurt people's feelings, even Abe's.

"Look," said Abe. "I get it. You don't like me. You think I'm a bow-tie-wearing square who squeals on communists and thinks the pinnacle of culture is the rule of law. Mandy told me as much. But you don't even know me, really. I just want to be around you. You're smart, you're exciting, you're pretty, and yeah, you're probably out of my league. If you don't want to go to dinner, I understand. I won't hold you to it. Maybe it was a dumb idea. But hey, at least I got to see you again, and now I'm a decent bowler, thanks to you."

"A bet is a bet," she said, sliding her shoes across the counter. "One date. Home by ten o'clock. But that doesn't entitle you to anything more, you understand?"

It was pathetic but almost endearing, his puppy-dog zeal in accepting this lukewarm consolation. It was clear to Ruth she wouldn't be rid of Abe Winter easily.

If nothing else, she had to admire his determination.

*

The only son of Harmon Winter, a general medical practitioner from Shaker Heights, Ohio, a man who never sugarcoated a diagnosis, offered false hope to a patient, or proposed anything but a prudent course of action, young Abe Winter was taught at an early age to value honesty and forthrightness above all else. Without honesty, there was no trust; without trust, every relationship, from doctor-patient to husband-wife, was doomed to failure. Dishonesty was fraudulence, a state that never achieved equilibrium because it was forever forced to seek purchase on some new ground, while honesty abided on the power of its own sure foothold.

Thus, upon the approach of their third date, an occasion certain to make or break his prospects of any future with Ruth Warneke, Abe resolved for the better part of a week, as he daydreamed through *Human Relations in Business and Industry* and *Estate Planning,* to be honest and forthright in presenting himself to Ruth. Rather than try to impress her with hopeless affectations this time around, or apologize for his own preferences, opinions, or proclivities, Abe was determined to be unapologetically his genuine self. And so he wore a bow tie, because he felt his best in a bow tie. And rather than impress Ruth with a fancy French restaurant downtown, they set out from the student union and began walking up the hill past Leeds and the Edmond Meany Hotel, toward the brand-new Dick's Drive-In in Wallingford.

"So, we're walking to a drive-in?" she said as they passed the shoe repair.

"You didn't want me to pick you up," said Abe. "Besides, it's a nice evening for a walk."

"It's thirty-six degrees," she said.

"If you want, we can go back for my car."

"It's fine," said Ruth. "At least it's not raining."

The truth was, despite the cold, Ruth had to admit it was a lovely evening, crisp and clear and throbbing with the sort of urban possibilities that Ruth had always yearned for in Shelton. A steady stream of automobiles filed past, coupes, and wagons, and sedans, black and green and powder blue. Nor were Ruth and Abe the only pedestrians braving the chill evening, as they encountered others out and about on the sidewalks, alone and in tandem, early evening revelers and last-minute shoppers, some striding purposefully, others strolling lazily along their path despite the chill.

"How's the humanities?" said Abe.

"I'm enjoying Lutey's Fine Arts. We're studying architecture right now. It's fascinating, all the factors and considerations that shape the architecture of a place, and how architecture can actually influence our identity, who we are as both individuals and cultures."

"Sounds a little pedantic to me," said Abe, true to himself, but also proud to have used the term *pedantic*.

"Well, you asked," she said. "I suppose you'd rather discuss actuaries."

"I didn't say I didn't want to discuss it," said Abe. "I just said it sounded pedantic."

"What's so pedantic about it?" Ruth said. "Clothing influences our identity, doesn't it, Mr. Bow Tie?"

"Sure, I guess."

"Then, doesn't it follow that the structures we inhabit or experience might also influence who we are as individuals or cultures?"

"For example?" said Abe.

"The Berlin Wall," said Ruth.

"Hmph," said Abe thoughtfully. "You might have something there."

Ruth was pleased by this concession and gratified by her own cleverness. Perhaps Abe wasn't as hardheaded as he seemed on the surface. He was at least willing to consider ideas that ran contrary to his own stuffy reasoning.

"And what about business administration?" she said.

"Well," said Abe, "I can't say that I share your passion when it comes to my own chosen discipline. It's not particularly exciting or thought-provoking in the way that architecture or literature is, but I have found it instructional. It's the sort of knowledge I can apply to nearly any profession."

"So, practical, then," said Ruth.

"I suppose so."

While practical was rather on the vanilla side of character attributes to Ruth's way of thinking, it was hard to fault Abe for it. Somebody had to be practical, or trains would run late and the rules would always be changing. Still, the very condition of practicality seemed like a compromise on some level. Wasn't frivolity the spice of life? It was hard to imagine Abe on a unicycle or hitchhiking on Highway 1. But then, he had proven himself capable of surprising her before. However, the real question was: Why was she thinking about future Abe at all? She had no intention of seeing him after she fulfilled her dreadful obligation, so why speculate?

The parking lot of Dick's was a veritable traffic jam extending two blocks down Forty-Fifth. The evening air was thrumming with cat-calls and car radios, rumbling engines and broken glass, whistles and shouts and hilarity. Among the throng of skirts and sweaters and jeans and letterman jackets, Abe was the only one wearing a bow tie on a Saturday night, so far as Ruth could tell.

The line at every window was stacked ten deep and moved at a crawl. With all the standing around, Ruth soon grew cold. No sooner had she folded her arms than Abe draped his gigantic camel-hair coat over her shoulders, the hem nearly grazing the pavement.

"What about you?" she said.

"I'm from the Midwest," said Abe. "This is like spring. You want my shirt, too?"

God, he was almost cute when he said it, bow tie and all.

When they finally arrived at the front of the queue, they both ordered hamburgers and milkshakes and fries. Ruth seemed a little surprised when Abe suggested they go Dutch.

"Think of it as an investment," said Abe as Ruth dug around in her purse for fifty cents.

With no automobile to accommodate their dining needs, they were forced to sit on the curb, facing the traffic, their greasy bags beside them. Ruth might have been put out by the inconvenience, if not for the novelty. It was something she might have done in high school if she'd ever been cool.

"I hear sidewalk dining is big in the old world," said Abe.

Ruth couldn't suppress her amusement at the observation, the hint of a grin playing at the corners of her mouth. The hot food, along with Abe's jacket, had warmed her considerably. She found that despite herself, she was not at all opposed to Abe's company under the circumstances. Some of his warts were disappearing before her eyes.

"So, Mandy said you've been dabbling in poetry," she said. "Who have you been reading?"

"Just about anything I can get my hands on," said Abe. "Though nobody whose last name begins after F. Working my way toward Wordsworth, I guess you could say. Ought to be there in about ten years."

"And?"

Abe sipped his milkshake thoughtfully.

"I suppose I'm kind of at a loss a lot of the time," he said.

"Much of it is figurative, obviously," said Ruth.

"Exactly," said Abe. "I guess I'm sort of literal. Sometimes the language just seems to get in the way. I like essays and history. I even sort of like instruction manuals."

"That's just masochistic," she said.

"I did like some of Baudelaire," said Abe. *"Flowers of Evil."*

"Les fleurs du mal," said Ruth. "That's one of my favorites. I'm surprised you liked it."

"Me too," said Abe. "That said, I wouldn't want to go into business with the guy."

"Why is that?" said Ruth.

"The man lacks . . . moderation."

"And what about your man in the White House?" said Ruth.

"Ha! Compared to whom, Stevenson?" Abe said. "Anyway, let's not talk about politics."

"Fine by me," said Ruth.

"How's your burger?" said Abe.

"Not bad," she said. "You know, you must be the only person in the world to order a vanilla milkshake."

"They're on the menu, aren't they?" said Abe. "What's wrong with vanilla, anyway?"

"It's so plain," said Ruth.

"Says you," Abe countered. "Vanilla is considerably more flavorful than chocolate. Try it," he said, offering Ruth his shake.

When Ruth sipped from his straw, she knew she'd crossed some line with Abe, some casual yet meaningful boundary of intimacy she'd never intended to broach with him, his lips, her lips, the straw. More troubling still, Abe was right; vanilla, despite its reputation, had more life than the chocolate, more pizzazz, more joie de vivre. Or at least it was sweeter.

"Not bad," she said, chasing it with a sip of her chocolate, its essence now comparatively blunt, lacking the pointed zest of vanilla.

Something was happening. Abe Winter was incrementally wearing down Ruth's defenses with his . . . what, exactly? His Midwesternness? His lack of pretense? His candor? Certainly, it wasn't his wardrobe. But somehow, the same qualities that had initially repelled her about Abe now seemed rather charming in an offbeat way.

Was this what compromise looked like? Was Ruth simply lowering her standards to accommodate Abe? Or was Abe undermining and exceeding her expectations? Either way, Ruth found herself enjoying Abe's company for the first time. His bow-tied visage was suddenly more handsome in the glow of the streetlamp, a bit of gristle clinging to his lower lip as he chewed his burger methodically, gazing clear-eyed and alert out into the traffic. She liked the smell of his jacket, which was the smell of him, earthy and masculine.

"I wonder if it's too late to catch a movie at the Neptune," Ruth said.

"What's playing?"

"Beats me," she said.

"It's worth a try," said Abe, slurping the last of his milkshake. "Let's give it a go."

The Good News

2023

R uth came to in the lackluster light of the recovery room, her consciousness little more than a dull throbbing, her thoughts, all but incomprehensible, running thick as sap. She was not in pain, not in the way she was used to experiencing pain, anyway. From some unseen corner beyond her psychic fog came a relentless electronic bleep, flat and measured in its cadence, as though eight-year-old Maddie were somewhere in the room playing Pong on the old Atari console. Only faintly was Ruth aware of her mummified face or the feeding tube forced rudely up her nose and snaking clear to the back of her throat, a violation that made swallowing exceedingly difficult. If this was anywhere near the new normal, Ruth wanted nothing to do with it. Thus, she opened her eyes only long enough to gather her bearings before she let the fog envelop her once more.

How long she remained in this state, whether thirty seconds or hours, was impossible to tell. But when next she opened her eyes, Dr. McGonagle was standing over her in blue scrubs and a face mask.

"Good morning, welcome back," he said. "How do you feel?"

He couldn't possibly expect her to answer, could he? It was

difficult enough to reason, but communicating with her jaw completely immobilized was obviously out of the question.

McGonagle promptly offered her a pad and pencil to convey her thoughts, but sapped of all her strength, Ruth demurred with a feeble shake of her head.

"You did great, but it's no wonder you're out of sorts," he said. "Once we got in there, things were considerably more complex than we expected. You were in surgery for nearly seven hours. Not a record, but close. The infection had begun to attack the surrounding soft tissue, particularly the tongue and the cheek. Of course, we had to remove the . . ."

At that point, Ruth lost all focus, or rather relinquished it, as the rest of the explanation washed over her like so much indecipherable droning. By the time McGonagle arrived at "but the good news is . . . ," Ruth, half a tongue, a considerable shaving from her left tibia, seven teeth, a lymph node, and the entire bottom right portion of her mandible lighter, had no interest in the good news, or any news at all. Instead, she closed her eyes once more and sought refuge in the slow drip of oblivion.

*

The snow had turned to slush by morning, when Abe left the hotel having skipped both his breakfast and his carvedilol, proceeding directly but carefully over the sloppy sidewalk and across the street to Swedish. When he checked in on the eighth floor, he was informed at the desk that Ruth was still in recovery and likely sleeping, though he was welcome to sit with her.

An orderly soon arrived, escorting Abe through the vestibule and down the corridor. God, but he deplored hospitals for their tidy, antiseptic aspect, their glaring fluorescence, their lifeless air, their vinyl-composite neutrality, and their eerie hum that never failed to set Abe on edge.

Ruth lay motionless on her back in the darkened room, heavily sedated, her sunken eyes closed, her resting countenance a cadaverous veil of imperturbability. The rise and fall of her chest were barely perceptible beneath a thin white blanket. Wrapped in gauze, her face was badly swollen and discolored on the right side, a tube crammed up her left nostril and taped to her upper lip.

Everything about the spectacle was grim and unnatural. To see her that way, wasted and inanimate, shook Abe to the core. She looked comatose lying there. He wondered if it was the machines keeping her alive, for it was difficult to tell where the life support started and Ruth ended. What if she never regained consciousness?

By the time Abe lowered himself into the bedside chair, he was already on the verge of tears. For two and a half hours, Abe slumped in the chair at Ruth's side, hypnotized by the electric blip of the heart monitor, steady as a dripping sink, with no book or magazine to occupy his thoughts as Ruth remained perfectly still, stupefied, and lifeless in the dreary confines of her hospital bed.

At the three-hour point, by which time Abe was lightheaded from hunger, his blood pressure no doubt on the rise, Ruth finally opened her eyes, and Abe lifted himself out of the chair, at once apprehensive and relieved by her emergence.

"There she is," he said, forcing a smile.

The muscles of Ruth's face flexed ever so slightly as she attempted to manufacture her own smile, a feeble attempt yielding only a slight twitch at the left-hand corner of her mouth.

"It's over," said Abe. "You did it."

Abe gathered her bony hand in his own and squeezed it softly.

"You're a tough old broad," he said. "You know that?"

Ruth's eyes projected but a dull glimmer in response.

"You'll be back home in no time," Abe assured her.

A lame consolation, to be sure, and likely an empty promise. Ruth was so underwhelmed by the prospect that she closed her eyes again and slid back into a state of insensibility. Still, Abe stood clutching her hand for five minutes longer, fighting back the lump of grief that had lodged itself in his throat like a briquette.

Lightheaded and a little unsteady, Abe left the recovery room and made his way past the desk to the elevator. On the second floor, he bought a bran muffin and an apple juice in the cafeteria, taking this repast in the solitude of a corner table. It was then he remembered his carvedilol and briefly debated returning to the hotel to fetch it.

Instead, he resumed his post at Ruth's bedside, where he spent the next four hours sitting vigil with nothing to occupy his worries, as nurses came and went; levels were checked, and general appraisals were made, Ruth enduring these ministrations with all the awareness of a human pot roast. Meanwhile, her condition remained unchanged. If she opened her eyes at all, such an occurrence had escaped Abe's notice as he marked the hours to the metronomic beat of the pulmonary monitor.

Around four thirty P.M., McGonagle made an appearance.

"I heard you were here," he said, extending a hand. "Has she been responsive?"

"Barely," said Abe, shaking his hand.

"She'll come around," he said. "Her vitals are on track. She's a strong woman."

"Don't I know it," said Abe.

"We were very aggressive once we got in there," he said. "I'm confident we got it all."

And what if they didn't? Surely, Ruth wouldn't survive a second surgery. What if this whole torturous affair was just prolonging the inevitable? What if the cancer was running rampant somewhere else in her body? What if things got so bad that Abe was forced to make a decision? For as much as both of them had prepared for the inevitability of death, and the mutinous possibilities of failing health, it still seemed impossible that any of this was happening. One day a loose tooth, then, bingo bango, you're looking mortality square in the face.

"How did this happen, Doc?" Abe said. "*Why* did it happen?"

McGonagle set a sympathetic hand on Abe's shoulder. "Just bad luck," he said. "Simple as that. One thing we know about cancer is that it's not very discerning."

Slumped in his chair, Abe ran his hands over his face. So, there it was, the definitive medical explanation: bad luck. It didn't matter what you did to ward off disaster, what precautions you took to avoid it, never mind all the life choices, the kale, and prune juice, and avocados, the lean white meat, the sunscreen, the fish oil, the natural toothpaste, the vitamins, supplements, and medications aimed at protecting the body from grim possibilities; in the end you still had to account for bad luck.

"You look like you could use some rest," said McGonagle. "Give her another night, let's see how things look in the morning. She's only twenty-four hours removed from the surgery, and it was a doozy. Things are liable to look rosier tomorrow."

Tomorrow. The day we all took for granted as we plotted and planned our futures.

"Okay, Doc," said Abe. "You know best."

Abe felt a million years old as he inched his way down the hallway with a full bladder toward the elevator. By the time he reached the bathroom in the first-floor lobby, his teeth were swimming. Abe wasn't sure he'd make it, and it was a close call, to be sure, but when he finally answered it, elbow propped against the tile wall above the urinal, a shiver of pleasure scurried up his spine. It was the first time in weeks that anything had seemed right in the world.

II

All Shook Up

For the second time that Tuesday, all three of them were crying, and it wasn't even noon. The current fiasco had begun with two-year-old Anne marching up and down the hallway, her red-wheeled corn popper thudding relentlessly over the wood floor until the contraption woke baby Karen, who promptly began wailing in her crib. The situation disintegrated from there.

It had taken Ruth forty-five minutes to get Karen down, nursing her all the while as she read aloud to Anne on the sofa: *Teddy the Terrier* (twice), *Winky Dink, Whistle for the Train,* and *Harry the Dirty Dog,* among others, hoping that by some miracle she might be able to get the girls to nap simultaneously. That rare occasion, if achieved, might allow Ruth time to wash the breakfast dishes, start a load of laundry, get out of her bathrobe, check the mailbox, and, heaven permitting, decompress for five, or seven, or ten minutes.

Anne was not having it, however, and remained acutely awake after Ruth eased Karen into her crib and closed the bedroom door but for a one-inch crack. Shepherding Anne to the living room, Ruth stationed her like a mushroom in front of the black-and-white Zenith in hopes that *The Price Is Right* could hold the toddler's attention long enough for Ruth to get dressed. Alas, neither the corny repartee of Bill Cullen nor the relative charms of the contestants, a plumber from Parma, Ohio, a housewife from Sacramento, a schoolteacher from Boise, and an optometrist from Baltimore, offered any incentive for the child to stay put.

That's when the corn popping began. Ruth was still buttoning her dress when the baby awoke and began screeching like a teakettle. Nerve-worn and exhausted, Ruth lost her head, charging out into the hallway, where she let loose a verbal lashing that instantly reduced Anne to a puddle of tears.

Overcome by remorse at once, Ruth tried to right the ship.

"Oh, honey, I'm sorry," pleaded Ruth, squatting down to Anne's level and pulling the child close. "Mommy shouldn't have yelled at you. Mommy was being a bad mommy."

But aggrieved and bewildered, Anne could no more be consoled than the baby, now purple in the face as she choked and sputtered on her own frantic wails, rebuffing Ruth's calming strokes, even refusing the nipple. It was at that point that Ruth, overwhelmed by a hopelessness now familiar, began to sob, too.

What had become of the possibilities of the wide world? Where was the poetry or the song? Where was the leisure time to explore or the impetus to create? With Abe working long hours and her hormones in a frequent uproar, with no time for herself or her interests, nobody to talk to beyond the grocery clerk or the bank teller, hardly time to go to the bathroom, it was hard for Ruth to see past her immediate obligations to that wondrous place she had once aspired to. After two years of convincing herself that she was merely on hiatus from UW, Ruth had finally given up on ever resuming classes once Karen was born, consigning herself to a life of shopping, and nursing, and cleaning, and yes, crying, almost daily, on this occasion so much that Ruth was unable to assuage her grief and frustration until after the baby had ceased howling of her own volition, and little Anne, bless her heart, began to comfort Ruth.

"It's okay, Mommy," she said. "Don't be sad."

Another wave of guilt washed over Ruth as she looked down into Anne's face, registering the child's genuine concern.

"After Mommy feeds Karen, let's go to the playground, how does that sound?" said Ruth.

Once Karen was sated, Ruth dressed the children and conducted them out the front door, where the stroller awaited them on the landing. The fresh air was a welcome diversion from the cloistered house. Ruth was ready to greet the day with renewed optimism. With Anne clinging to the hem of Ruth's coat, they set out on foot, Ruth pushing the stroller south down the rutty sidewalk toward the playground, hoping the six-block stroll would lull Karen back to sleep and an hour at the park might wear out Anne. Much to Ruth's relief, the former objective was achieved within three blocks.

The playground was uncharacteristically quiet at midday, owing perhaps to the promise of rain. Ruth had a bench to herself, Karen asleep in the carriage beside her, as Anne tentatively approached another toddler, a towheaded boy of perhaps three, his mother stationed on the opposite side of the jungle gym. Starving for companionship, Ruth might have engaged the young woman and struck up a conversation but opted instead for the solace of verse. Though she always packed a volume of poetry in her handbag, Blake, or Wordsworth, or Frost, the books served mostly as reminders to Ruth that she still existed somewhere beneath the burden of domestic toil. On this occasion, she'd brought a thin volume of Browning—Elizabeth, not Robert—which she spread open in her lap. But ever watchful of Anne on the merry-go-round, or the Buck-a-Bout, Ruth managed but a single stanza before she was called into service, assisting Anne on the monkey bars.

Barely three years had passed, and already it seemed like another lifetime since that afternoon in July of 1954 at Magnuson Park beach, Abe, the recent graduate, lying beside her in sunglasses, his nose daubed white with zinc oxide, his bare, curly-haired chest already beginning to pinken from the sun, Lake Washington lapping at the shoreline, two dozen kids shouting and splashing in the near distance, when Ruth set aside her dog-eared volume of Keats and spoke in the most matter-of-fact tone she could summon.

"I'm late," she said.

"For what?" said Abe.

Ruth offered only silence in response. After a short interval, Abe shot upright on his beach towel. Turning to Ruth, he lowered his sunglasses and looked her in the eye.

"You mean . . . ?"

"Yes," she said.

Two days later, as they strolled through Volunteer Park, Abe stopped midpath and got down on one knee, fishing a black felt coffer from his pants pocket.

"I know it's not much," said Abe of the half-carat diamond. "But I promise, once we—"

"You're only doing this because of the—"

"No," said Abe. "That's not true. I would have asked you to marry me the first night I met you if I thought I'd had a prayer."

"Oh, Abe," said Ruth. "What will become of us?"

The reply was a soft yes, but it served its purpose. Two weeks later, they were married by the justice of the peace at the courthouse downtown, Fred and Mandy their only witnesses. They deferred a honeymoon until such time as they could afford one. Oh, how quickly the trajectory of Ruth's future had been altered. Down the tubes went the adventuresome path she'd planned for herself, gone the glamour of college life. Indeed, Ruth did not resume her studies in the fall. Instead, she counted the days until motherhood with equal parts dread and hopefulness, the hope being that her new vocation might offer her joy and satisfaction hitherto unknown.

Abe, meanwhile, took a job with the Safeco insurance company. The salary was far from extravagant, but it would do for a family of three. They rented a little green two-bedroom on Roanoke, where nesting helped ease a difficult transition for Ruth as the baby's arrival drew nearer. Despite her frequent physical discomfort, the swelling feet and the constipation, pregnancy allowed Ruth whole days of rest and contemplation. Ruth had been free in those days to wander and wonder, to sate her appetite for newness. But all that changed the minute Anne was born.

Make no mistake, Ruth loved baby Anne every minute of the day, loved her achingly, every inch of her, from her swirl of wispy hair to her placid gray eyes, from her drooly little heart-shaped mouth to her chubby wrists; Ruth adored every tiny finger and toe of her. But all the love in the world could not change the fact that the child all but meant the death of her lifelong ambitions.

The arrival of Karen two years later sealed Ruth's fate as a full-time homemaker. Though Karen was preternaturally composed and mellow for an infant, her appearance doubled Ruth's workload. Now a mother of two, overburdened, listless most of the day, any hint of intellectual stimulation beyond the horizon, Ruth passed her days wavering between anxiety and despair. While she understood that Abe did not account for her malaise, Ruth could not help but resent him, if only because Abe enjoyed a thousand tiny freedoms beyond her purview as a housewife. He lunched at Clark's Top Notch, engaged in substantive conversations with fellow adults, walked down city streets at his own pace, unencumbered by children. Perhaps her biggest misgiving was that in starting a family, Abe had sacrificed so little. In pursuing the career he'd planned for himself all along, he had compromised nothing. In siring his brood without having to contend with the messy consequences of daily life, the dirty diapers, the aching nipples, the constant orchestration required to execute the simplest of household tasks, Abe was unburdened by the perpetual neediness of others, free of the domestic bondage that marked her every waking moment.

It was true that Abe provided for the household without fail, just as he verbally and emotionally supported Ruth and the children in his way, all according to the presumptions, expectations, and customs delineated by the course of human history and biology, as agreed upon by roughly half of the population, the male half. It was plain to see that Abe adored his girls. But bouncing children upon one's knee was not the same as nourishing them at the cost of one's own vitality, just as subsidizing them was not equal to bearing and tending to them.

These thoughts occupied Ruth's mind for twenty minutes at the playground before Anne tripped on a sprinkler head and skinned her palm on the concrete, effectively ending the outing. After much coddling and many assurances, Ruth finally managed to console the child, and they began the journey home, the baby still sleeping, while Anne complained incessantly of hunger all the way to the doorstep.

But before Ruth could finish warming a can of pea soup for the child, Anne fell asleep on the sofa to the theme of *Tic Tac Dough*. And no sooner had Anne succumbed to slumber than baby Karen woke up again and began to fuss.

*

This was not exactly what Abe had had in mind when he chose insurance as his calling. As one of two dozen junior underwriters at the Safeco insurance company, all of them men, all dressed uniformly in white shirts and black pencil ties (Abe having abandoned the bow tie in the name of conformity), hair short and well-kept, heads down as they annotated an endless stream of incoming applications under the vigilant eyes of multiple supervisors, it was difficult to feel as if a body was distinguishing itself in the insurance field.

In they came on the left, and out they went on the right, one file after another, Abe fastidiously processing every application, scouring them for any viable reason not to insure a soul: medical history, obesity, criminal record, pilot's license, any propensity for risk-taking.

Abe made notes in the margins, circling hazards and flagging uncertainties, before sending the memo files off to the typing pool, where two dozen women, dressed uniformly in gray skirts, modest blouses, and black pumps, their hair short and curly, updated files like automatons, promptly dispatching them to the agents.

The Safeco insurance company was a well-oiled machine, and it was not Abe's ambition to be a cog in a machine, but an individual, a man in control of his own concerns and regulations, without having to answer or adhere to the governance of a larger interest. Abe wanted to be an agent, to make a better living for his family, to be his own boss. The financial benefits were not lost on him. He saw the agents with their chronograph watches, driving luxury cars, Cadillacs and Continentals, while Abe and his brethren did the heavy lifting to the tune of twenty-five bucks a week.

While each new day at the Safeco insurance company was roughly the same as the last, some days were worse than others, as was the case with a particular Tuesday in March, when Abe had been taken to task by his supervisor, a thin-lipped, bloodless personage named Scanlon, tall and straight as a lamppost, narrow of shoulder, and stingy of nature, who might have walked straight off the pages of a Dickens novel.

"Mr. Winter," said Mr. Scanlon, looming above Abe's workstation, "were you unaware that Mr. Schwert was a military reservist?"

"No, sir. I was aware."

"I see, yes," said Scanlon unpleasantly. "Then, might I ask why you saw fit to omit this information from your audit?"

"I forgot to note it, sir."

"You forgot?"

"Yessir."

"It just . . . slipped your mind?" suggested Scanlon.

"Yessir."

"I see," Scanlon said, his mouth curling distastefully at the corners. "If I might pose a question, Mr. Winter?"

"Of course, sir."

"How am I to trust your judgment on matters of . . . let us say, incontestability, when something as significant as a man's military status slips your mind?"

"It was an oversight, sir," said Abe.

"And a glaring one," Scanlon observed.

"Also a rare one, sir," said Abe.

"I hope so, Winter. Because I can assure you there are at least ten fresh graduates who would be more than happy to relieve you of your station here at Safeco."

"I don't doubt it, sir," said Abe. "Rest assured, it won't happen again."

Watching Scanlon retreat, the heat of shame and indignation rushed to Abe's face.

His day only got worse from there. At lunch, a solo affair in the murkiest corner of the College Inn, Abe spilled hot coffee in his lap and lost his favorite pen. In the afternoon, he developed a splitting headache poring over the application of a certain James Robert Molinaro, thirty-seven years old, a roofer by trade with two misdemeanor charges (public drunkenness on both counts), both issued ten years prior, shortly after his honorable discharge from the marines. This Molinaro happened to belong to Alcoholics Anonymous and had recently embarked on several mountaineering expeditions, red flags, both. The man was an underwriter's nightmare. But who was Abe to judge? Everyone ought to be insured, as far as he was concerned. In fact, he'd already run the numbers. He could insure every applicant that crossed his desk and the margins would allow for a small profit. There were pecuniary limits, of course, certain financial and moral probabilities to consider, but if Abe was to believe in the American dream, he had to view the playing field as level. To this end, he omitted Molinaro's mountaineering from his memo, an omission that might well cost him his job tomorrow if Scanlon were to catch it. But after four months on the job, Abe was beginning to wonder if that wasn't exactly what he wanted.

He left the office at 5:40, mentally spent, spirits flagging, climbing into his 1947 Nash, its blue paint faded and oxidized, its front fender stove-in, while watching one of the agents pull out of the lot in an Imperial Crown.

The instant he walked through the door, without so much as a hello, Ruth foisted baby Karen on him before he could even take his coat off. The baby immediately began to fuss as Ruth strode down the hallway to the bedroom.

"Where are you going?"

"I'm taking a shower."

"Well, why didn't you take it while—"

Abe stopped himself.

"Wait, I think her diaper is—"

He cut himself short again.

"What should I do with—"

"You'll figure it out," said Ruth.

"But—"

"You can handle it, Abe," she said. "You're a big boy."

For the next five minutes, Abe endeavored to settle baby Karen down.

"You're supposed to be the easy one," he told her.

Abe stroked her head and patted her back, talking to her in funny voices, all the while vexed by his wife's hostility. He understood what Ruth was up against, caring for the girls all day, cooking and cleaning and shopping while he was at work. He knew it had to be difficult. But was it any more difficult than working at the office for eight, sometimes ten hours at a turn, under the constant scrutiny of Scanlon, who appraised Abe's every gesture, scolding him for honest mistakes? Could Ruth's lot possibly be more taxing or humiliating than a bruised ego, a thin wallet, and an uncertain future? How bad could it be? Surely, the baby must sleep a lot of the day, and Abe knew first-hand that Anne could entertain herself for hours on end with a twenty-piece puzzle or a mason jar full of buttons. It couldn't be that hard for Ruth, could it? She had funds, she had peace of mind, she had all the modern conveniences, she had the adoration of her chosen man, yet none of it seemed to be enough for her. There always seemed to be something missing. What happened to the free spirit Abe first met at the Hub, the one who was game for a challenge, the one who surprised him at every turn? And why did Ruth seem to begrudge Abe for his role as breadwinner, as if his vocation were a luxury, as if his office life were something to covet, as if the whole ordeal gave him some pleasure or satisfaction that she had no access to? It wasn't as if Abe were out playing golf or drinking martinis. The fact was, when his nose wasn't buried in a file, when his mind wasn't occupied in analyzing risk, those rare moments at work when Abe managed to elude the ubiquitous eye of his supervisors were spent wishing he were back at home with Ruth and the kids, or better yet, that they were all together on some much-needed sabbatical to the Oregon coast or Snoqualmie Falls. These were the sort of daydreams that got Abe through a day of underwriting.

But every evening when he arrived home, such daydreams wilted under the glare of domestic reality. Ruth was often cranky and short with him, the kids fussy, the house in disarray, and dinner was never waiting.

"There's some pea soup on the range, if you want me to warm it," Ruth said, emerging from her shower in a bathrobe. "I forgot to thaw the hamburger. But there's canned ham."

"Why don't we just go out for dinner?"

"It's too late," she said. "The girls need to eat soon, or they'll start unraveling. And I'd have to change into something nice, and besides, we can't really afford to go—"

"We could drive up to Dick's and eat in the car," said Abe. "Or Burgermaster. Or I could run out for some Chinese."

"It's nearly seven o'clock," she said. "We need to get the girls down by eight or they'll be impossible in the morning."

Thus, it was pea soup and canned ham for dinner, followed by twenty minutes of Andy Williams on NBC. Hardly the Oregon coast. When baby Karen fell asleep in Ruth's arms, bottle in mouth, Ruth retreated to the bedroom and transferred her to the crib, returning shortly thereafter to retrieve Anne.

"Time for night night," she said.

"I want Daddy to tuck me in," said Anne.

A small triumph, perhaps, but enough that Abe was smiling as he scooped Anne up off the sofa and carried her to the bed.

"Shhh," he said as they entered the darkened room. "Don't wake your sister."

"I won't," she said.

Abe pulled back the covers and laid her down in the bed, planting a kiss on her forehead.

"Good night," he said.

"Night, Daddy."

Abe was satisfied with himself when he took his place in bed beside Ruth. For all the disappointments and small indignities he was forced to endure, all the Scanlons, and dented fenders, and unsure futures, his life was not a complete failure, for Abe had the love and adoration of his girls to sustain him.

But when he reached out to touch Ruth, she rolled over on her shoulder, turning her back on him.

"What is it?" he said.

"I'm just tired," she said.

Bright White Corridor

2023

Only dimly through a fog of disassociation was Ruth aware of the urgent beeping, a piercing breedle to which she could assign no source, an alarm that persisted for an indefinite interval before Ruth was besieged by a scrum of nurses and orderlies, foreheads furrowed above masked faces, their movements harried, tones grave and calculated, though the words tumbled listlessly out of their mouths, as if time had slowed down.

"Blood pressure's pluuummeting."

"Acuuute hypotension."

"Get her to I. . . . C . . . U staaaat."

The last things Ruth perceived were the jarring sensation of movement and the dull distant throbbing in her brain as she was trundled at breakneck speed down the bright white corridor.

*

Startled awake by the bleating of his cell phone, Abe found himself momentarily disoriented in the darkness. Groping for the device atop the unfamiliar nightstand, he managed to retrieve it, but not before the call had gone to voicemail, that elusive realm beyond his access. Hardly had he snapped the lamp on and gathered his bearings in the hotel room than the phone sounded again.

"Hello," he said.

The voice on the other end was inaudible.

"Hold on a moment, let me get my hearing aid."

Abe fished the right earbud out of the plastic case on the bedside table and coaxed it into his ear.

"Hello?" he said, the device feeding back.

"Abe Winter?"

"This is him."

"I'm calling from Swedish hospital."

Despite the calming tenor that delivered the news, Abe was overcome by lightheadedness as the information was delivered matter-of-factly.

Twenty minutes later he was across the street in the ICU, where Ruth lay motionless, eyes closed and totally unresponsive. That her heart monitor bleeped at even intervals was little consolation.

"What happened?" Abe asked the attending physician, a young man, perhaps thirty-five, prematurely balding.

"Her blood pressure took a dive in the middle of the night, so we rushed her in here. She's stable now."

"She's unconscious," said Abe. "Is that stable?"

"She needs rest," the doctor assured him. "She's been through an awful lot."

"Why did this happen? Why the blood pressure?" said Abe.

"We don't know."

"You don't know?"

How, with all this medical expertise, the sum of eons of scholarship, of research and observation, how amidst all this specialized equipment, tubes and needles and electrodes, all this miraculous gadgetry, could the definitive prognosis to a critical plunge in blood pressure possibly be "we don't know"?

But there it was, right beside bad luck, not knowing.

For three hours, Abe remained at Ruth's bedside as she faded in and out of consciousness. On those occasions when she emerged fully from her stasis, Abe got to his feet and stood over her, speaking softly as he rested his hand upon her cool, blanketed shoulder.

"You had us all worried," he said. "Thank God you're okay. Are you in pain? What can I do? Should I call the nurse?"

But for all Abe could tell, these queries fell upon deaf ears, for Ruth offered not so much as a nod or a groan. If it weren't for the occasional lolling of her eyeballs or the gentle, almost imperceptible rise and fall of her chest, she may have been comatose.

Still, Abe waited another half hour by her side, wringing his hands, consulting his wristwatch fitfully, until the attending nurse came by on her rounds, checking levels and changing out the nearly depleted banana bag dangling from the IV pole.

"Is she going to be okay?" said Abe.

"We think so," she said.

There it was again in a slightly different guise, the great consolation of uncertainty.

We think so. We don't know. Why did Abe bother asking questions at all? What if the surgery only served to shorten her time on earth? Maybe she would have lived longer, suffered less, if they'd let the cancer run its course and exact its mortal toll. How could it be any worse than this?

Looking down at the ravaged visage of the one person whom he had no intention, nor even the slightest notion, of living without, intubated, senseless, swathed in bandages, Abe searched in vain for the mother of his four children, his best friend, his confidante, his confessor, his moral compass, and his better half in every way. He knew she was in there somewhere; she had to be.

Plans

1959

Five-plus years into their marriage, with a third child on the way, the Winters were outgrowing their little home on Roanoke. But they couldn't afford anything bigger, not in a decent neighborhood, anyway, and not on an underwriter's salary. Four years shy of his thirtieth birthday, Abe had grown to detest his job at Safeco and yearned more than ever to become an agent. As it was, he did more than his share of the heavy lifting at the firm with none of the financial benefits and little room for advancement. It was time to forge his own path.

Though Ruth managed most days to put on a happy face for Abe's benefit, it was clear that her free spirit—that curiosity and appetite for newness, that soulful impetus that had once animated her and driven her into the arms of poetry and art—was flagging under the strain and rigorous routine of her homemaking responsibilities. Abe understood firsthand what she was up against. For two and a half hours every Saturday, he was treated to a little taste of what Ruth endured daily as he was tasked with watching the kids while Ruth shopped and ran errands. Rarely was it as simple as setting them in front of the television or distracting them with playthings. Somebody was usually hungry, or crying, or in need of attention in some way. Harmony was nearly impossible to achieve.

Anne wanted to go to the park, but Karen needed a nap. Too bad she was too big to nap in the baby carriage anymore. Also, too bad she had a dirty diaper, and not the kind Abe could pretend not to notice for another forty-five minutes; it was a ripe one, beginning to test the cloth. Anne wanted fish sticks for lunch, but not until Daddy washed his hands, and not if they were burnt. Karen refused to eat at all, despite Abe's entreaties, though she desperately needed to, because her mood was headed south. She was starting to rub her eyes and glower. Abe burned the fish sticks, of course, so Anne wouldn't eat them. Hunger finally got the better of Karen, who had a meltdown and couldn't be consoled until, mercifully, she fell asleep on the kitchen floor, the tears on her face not yet dry. Anne still wanted to go to the park.

By the time Ruth made it home Saturday afternoons, Abe was ready for a two-week vacation. How Ruth managed it eighty hours a week, he could not fathom.

The way Abe saw it, the time had come to shake things up; time for newness and adventure, time for the Winter family to reinvent themselves. Abe had a plan, a surefire cure to the domestic doldrums that ailed them.

Bainbridge Island. That wooded little utopia of six thousand adventurous souls across Elliott Bay, nine miles and thirty-five minutes by ferry from downtown Seattle. Bainbridge Island, with its offbeat village charm and its wide-open spaces, its untapped potential and affordable real estate. On Bainbridge Island, Ruth could have a garden, a studio even. Heck, they could have a barn, with goats, or a horse. They wouldn't have to lock their doors. The kids could all have their own rooms and run around outside until sundown.

The more Abe envisioned such a life for himself and his family, the more certain he was that their fortunes awaited them across Elliott Bay. He schemed for months, and even missed work one Friday to ferry across the sound and look at home listings at the Sam Clarke Realty office. Still, he did not talk about these plans to Ruth. He didn't want to get her hopes up until he knew he could make it happen. And he had a plan for that, too.

Ready to give his notice any day, Abe took another Friday off at Safeco, feigning illness, and ferried across the bay once more, this time to seize his destiny. He disembarked at the Winslow terminal, shoes buffed to an onyx sheen, briefcase in hand, and headed directly to the heart of town, brimming with purpose and determination. *Don't take no for an answer*, he told himself. *Hit your talking points. Don't appeal to his sentiment, appeal to his fiscal instincts.* For all his certainty, Abe had to reject with every step the likelihood that he was only an imposter, a young man who was in way over his head.

Thus, when Abe waltzed into Bainbridge Island Insurance as though he'd just bought the place, his heart was beating triplets as he handed his freshly minted business card to the girl behind the counter.

"Abe Winter to see Todd Hall," he said.

Abe straightened his tie and checked his breath against an open hand as the receptionist left her station to consult with Hall. Alone in the foyer, Abe cast a look around. The sofa was contemporary, orange faux leather and a little worse for wear. The potted ferns, though ostensibly healthy, needed grooming, cluttered as they were with withered brown stalks. The agents pictured on the wall, four in all, were all over fifty, gray haired, and bespectacled. Clearly, Bainbridge Island Insurance could benefit from an infusion of youth.

The desk girl returned thirty seconds later, escorting Abe to Hall's office, or cubicle, as it were, in the rear of the building. Abe put Todd Hall somewhere in his late forties, a man nearly as wide as the desk he manned, a spot of mustard on his tie, his forehead filmy with perspiration, his thinning hair coaxed in a dozen furrows to one side in a misguided attempt at volume.

"Mr. Winter, is it?" he said.

"Yessir," said Abe.

"How can I help you?"

Small talk was not on the menu. Hall was a man who took his business seriously. Thus, Abe proceeded directly to phase two.

"Mr. Hall," he said. "If you'll give me a moment, I've got an opportunity for you."

"Oh?" said Hall, glancing at the face of his Omega Speedmaster, a far cry from Abe's Timex. But now was not the time to doubt his own worth, because it was Abe who had the leverage.

"Yessir, Mr. Hall, an opportunity for both of us," he said.

"Mm," said Hall.

"It's a real moneymaker," Abe said.

"Is that so?" said Hall, clearly unconvinced.

"You've got this whole island to yourself, am I right? I mean, it's in the name: Bainbridge Island Insurance. This is your domain."

"That's right," said Hall.

"No competition this side of the city. It's open season out here for comprehensive coverage, right? Problem is," said Abe, "your clientele is unmined, Mr. Hall. You're sitting on a fortune here."

His office chair issued a plaintive groan as Hall straightened up. "Okay, you've got my attention," he said.

"It's as simple as two words," said Abe.

"And what might those be?" said Hall.

"Life insurance."

"Keep talking," Hall said doubtfully.

"Life insurance is a higher-commission, higher-gain proposition than any coverage you're offering here. If you think twenty percent on home and auto is profitable, how about eighty percent on whole life?"

For the first time, Hall looked mildly impressed. "Tell me more," he said.

"Not to mention," said Abe, "it's proven that the more lines you can offer a client, the more likely they are to stick with you over the long haul. Persistence is the key to profitability, right?"

"Okay," said Hall. "So, who sells it?"

"He's standing right in front of you, sir."

"What's your background, Winter?"

"Three years at Safeco," said Abe.

"As an agent?"

"Underwriting," said Abe.

Hall slumped perceptibly at this news.

"Hear me out, Mr. Hall. My experience is a benefit. I know the variables, the risks and rewards. I've got the product knowledge, I know the game, I know the markets, and I know who I'll be selling to—young families like myself, in addition to your existing clientele, of course."

"And what makes you think you can sell anything?"

"If you met my wife, you wouldn't ask that question, sir."

"Okay," said Hall. "Sell me some life insurance, then. Right now. I'm forty-three years old, I'm overweight, I smoke, and I'm afraid to die. Just not bad enough to quit smoking."

"You have a wife?" said Abe.

"Of course," said Hall.

"Kids?"

"Boy and a girl, both out of the house."

"I've got two girls myself," said Abe. "Very much in the house, if you know what I mean. Expecting a third in about four months."

"Congratulations," said Hall. "Back to my life insurance. Why should I buy a policy? I'm up to my neck in expenses as it is."

"For your family," said Abe. "That's the real reason you're afraid to die, leaving your family business unfinished. It's your responsibility to have the bases covered, right?"

"You're not wrong," said Hall.

"This isn't just about peace of mind, here, though. This is about financial resources. We're not just gonna protect your family, we're gonna make your family some money doing it. I can sell you a ten-thousand-dollar whole life policy for eighteen to twenty-five dollars a month."

"At my age?"

"Yes."

"As a smoker?"

"Yep."

"Fat?"

"So long as there's no preexisting conditions, yes."

"Ten thousand?"

"Ten thousand," said Abe.

"Not bad," said Hall, sinking back down into his chair, pinching his uppermost chin between thumb and forefinger as he contemplated the possibilities. "Eighty percent, you say?"

"Eighty percent," said Abe. "Split, of course."

"That is good," Hall conceded. "So, what's the catch?"

"There's no catch," said Abe. "Just say the word. You bring me on board, and I'll call the movers and the Realtor before five o'clock today. I'll be making you money inside the month."

"And your family knows about this?"

"It's a surprise," said Abe.

"Helluva surprise," Hall said.

*

They were in the tiny kitchen, the girls finally down for the night, Ruth drying the last of the dinner dishes, when Abe divulged his master plan.

"Bainbridge Island?" said Ruth. "What on earth would make you think I'd ever want to live on an island?"

"It's beautiful!" said Abe. "There's woods, and beaches, and strawberry fields, and—"

"Abe, did it occur to you that I left Shelton for the very reason that I *didn't* want to live in a small town?"

"Bainbridge Island isn't some backwater mill town."

"Actually, it was a mill that put the place on the map," said Ruth.

"Well, it's different than Shelton. It's more . . . I don't know . . . enlightened."

"What is that supposed to mean?"

"It's a poet's paradise!" he said. "All that nature, and fresh air, and the smell of salt water. We could have chickens!"

"Oh, and what do you know about poetry?" she said. "I came to the city because there was culture, museums and bookstores and architecture . . ."

"They've got architecture on Bainbridge," Abe interjected.

"And universities, and theaters, and cafés?" said Ruth.

"I don't know about theaters, but they've got coffee over there," said Abe. "They even have a French restaurant. At least it sounds French—Martinique."

How could he be so clueless? She dreamed of living in Paris, among poets and cathedrals, not on some remote island covered with trees. Did he really imagine that raising chickens was going to fill the mental and spiritual void that had replaced her sense of self, that strawberries and gravel roads were going to magically make her feel like somebody again, that driving five miles to the nearest grocery store was going to imbue her life with that missing sense of purpose she so desperately yearned for, that purpose she'd lost the day she dropped out of UW, a purpose beyond making peanut butter sandwiches, and brushing hair, and reading children's books aloud?

"I don't want to live on Bainbridge Island or any island. I just want . . . I don't even know what I want anymore, but it's not on an island."

"But, honey, you don't understand, I already got the job!"

"What job?"

"The job I've wanted since I graduated college. I already printed business cards."

Sure enough, he fished one out of his billfold and presented it to Ruth.

Stunned, Ruth read the card—*Abe Winter, Agent, Bainbridge Island Insurance*—and fell silent, a molten anger bubbling up behind her ribs. This was never about her, it was always about Abe, what Abe wanted, what Abe decided. Abe, who'd had the opportunity to finish college, and the benefit of a few precious years to grow into himself, to question and identify what it was he wanted out of life and to go after it, while Ruth was left scrubbing toilets and ironing shirts, her dreams, such as they were, gathering dust along with all the unread books piled on the nightstand.

"When were you going to tell me about this?" she said.

"It was a surprise," he said.

"A surprise? A surprise is a gold-plated locket or a diamond brooch, Abe, not this."

"You're gonna love it, I promise," Abe said.

"Love what? Your new job?"

"The island," he said.

"I'm sorry, Abe, but I'm not moving to an island. I feel isolated enough here."

"But, honey, it's already done, I took the job."

"So, commute," she said. "There's people on the island who commute to the city, you'll just be going the other way."

"Ruthie, I bought the house."

Ruth's ears started burning.

"You what? What house?"

"Four bedrooms! It's twice the size of this place. Oh, it's beautiful, Ruthie, you're gonna love it. And get this: It's on five acres—a farm! Our yard is as big as this whole block! It's got a barn, and a henhouse, and a—"

"You bought a house? On an island? Without even telling me? Are you out of your mind? Abe, this . . . do you not understand that this is . . . it's not okay. These are not the kind of decisions you surprise your—your damn spouse with! What were you thinking?"

Abe looked stunned as he fell silent, his eyes seeking out the linoleum.

"Well?" said Ruth.

"I . . . I guess I was thinking that you were unhappy," he said. "That you were stuck, that both of us were stuck. And that moving somewhere would be a good thing. That you'd be excited by the possibilities, the fresh start. That it would be a whole new way of life for us. That we could thrive there."

"So, then, *you* made a mutual decision?" she said. "Just like that, it was settled. Suddenly we're the Swiss Family Winter? Unbelievable. Isn't this the sort of thing we addressed when we made our wedding vows, Abe? Did you forget the 'together' part?"

"Ruthie, maybe if you just give it a chance . . . ?" said Abe.

"It appears you haven't left me much of a choice," she said.

Ruth put the last plate in the rack and walked out of the kitchen in a huff. She didn't speak to Abe for two days. She ironed his shirts according to custom, poured his coffee, and made his toast, but she didn't utter more than the occasional grunt or sigh by way of communication. Not that Abe didn't try to elicit a response.

"Look, the escrow hasn't closed yet. I don't have to take the job, I can stay at Safeco. I never gave my notice."

"What about the baby, Abe? Where will the baby be delivered? There's no hospital on Bainbridge Island."

"I guess I figured . . . I didn't really think about . . ."

"Of course you didn't. What about the schools?"

Abe perked up immediately. "Now, that, I did ask about," he said. "The schools are great. There's a dentist, there's a salon, a feed store."

"Feed store? Is that supposed to be a selling point?"

"There's a library!" said Abe.

Ruth began to soften despite herself. Abe wasn't totally wrong; the newness and change were indeed enticing, loath as she was to admit it. New routines, new possibilities, new friends. Annie could get that dog she was begging for. On the island, Ruth would be closer to her parents in Shelton. And fresh eggs didn't sound so bad after all. Still, it was hard to forgive Abe for the sheer, unmitigated audacity of the whole endeavor. Imagine the conceit of deciding someone else's future without their consent.

"At least let's go out and look at the place Saturday," said Abe.

"What about the kids?"

"Bring them, of course," he said. "It's gonna be their home, too. I mean, if you—if we decide . . ."

"Fine," she said. "We'll look at the place. But that doesn't mean I'm moving there."

"Fair enough," he said. "The decision is yours."

Thus, an uneasy accord was reached, if only temporarily.

Reclamation

1960

Though pride forbade her from conceding as much to Abe, one look at the property on Bainbridge Island and Ruth was already sold. Five hilltop acres of rolling pasture lined with fruit trees: apple, pear, plum, and cherry. Beyond the orchard, an irrigation pond, maybe seventy feet across, hemmed in by maple and alder; an old clapboard barn, splintered but still sturdy. There was a henhouse, half covered, a hundred and forty feet square, and a large vegetable garden, overgrown but ready to reclaim. The entire property, ringed by mature stands of cedar and fir, was accessed via a gravel drive perhaps a quarter mile long. The house itself had been built around the turn of the century and showed some wear and tear with its sloping floors, and blistered paint, and mossy shingles, but it lacked nothing in the way of charm, with its double-hung windows and its wide front porch. That the house and the property required reclamation and upkeep, that the place begged for love and attention, was not a deterrent to Ruth, rather an incentive, an invitation to shape her surroundings. Though he'd gone about it all wrong, and she was still loath to forgive him for it, Abe had been right: The newness and possibility won Ruth over.

They got a dog, what would be the first of many, a little wire-haired Jack Russell terrier they called Rowdy, who lived up to every bit of his name; forever darting, and leaping, and yipping, ferreting out moles and chasing parcel trucks up the driveway.

In her third trimester, she was pulling up carpet and cultivating flower beds when she wasn't tending to their newly adopted hens, an even dozen, Hy-Lines and Orpingtons, acquired for mere dollars from an island farmer named Suimatsu. Daily, with Karen on her hip and Anne beside her, they scattered feed and delighted in watching the hens peck away at the pellets, or the bread heels, or the unfinished oatmeal. Ruth and Anne cleaned the nesting boxes and collected eggs, brown all, of various sizes, far more eggs than they could ever eat, despite all the omelets and egg dips and failed quiche experiments. Twice a week, they walked the surplus eggs to the end of the driveway and set a big basket beside the mailbox with a "Free Eggs" sign, and always somebody helped themselves, if not the neighbors, then the coyotes or the raccoons. The hens were a revelation not for their utilitarian benefits but for their mere presence on the farm. It never failed to delight Ruth, the way they charged the gate when they saw Ruth and the girls coming, the flock of them bounding like some farcical cavalry, useless wings tucked fast against their overplump bodies, bobbing side to side atop their skinny legs as though they were spring-loaded. Anne named every hen—Comet, and Sprite, and Brownie, and Sparkle—though Ruth could scarcely tell them apart from one day to the next.

Abe, for his part, worked long days at the office, building his clientele, while devoting the better part of his weekends to cultivating avocations that spoke to his status as a pillar of the community: Kiwanis and the Sons of Norway, Scouts, attending matches, Little League games, sponsoring parade floats—whatever opportunity presented itself, Abe attended virtually any gathering that might help him pave inroads to the next whole life policy. Thus, Ruth saw Abe less than ever those early days on the island, and yet her life was fuller than ever. Every day Ruth found herself less dependent upon Abe as she grew into herself, gaining confidence with each new task she undertook. It was less the stuff of art and poetry, and more the stuff of utility and purpose, the satisfaction of completing tasks that made a tangible impact on the life of her family and herself, the feeding and watering that accounted for the eggs and vegetables that fed them, the fence that was mended to keep the coyotes out, the gutter that she'd rerouted to save their foundation.

Then there was town, five miles south of the farm. Not exactly what you'd call metropolitan, the little hamlet of Winslow, the entirety of it strung down a single two-lane boulevard hemmed on either side by diagonal parking, a menagerie of brick-and-mortar storefronts, a hardware store, a bank, a Rexall, an appliance store, a barber, a salon, a Christian Science reading room, a white-steepled church at the western end its tallest and most stately structure. Winslow boasted none of the bustle of the city, none of the glorious urban racket, the traffic or construction, nor did Winslow offer the youthful vitality of campus life, a realm that now seemed a part of some distant past. What Winslow did offer was the promise of community, and of fast-growing familiarity, a grocer, and a banker, and a postal clerk who called her by name. In Ruth's enthusiasm for the urbane and the high-minded, she'd all but forgotten those niceties of small-town living that she'd grown up with in Shelton. And yet, unlikely as it seemed for such a small town, Bainbridge Island seemed to be more diverse than Seattle, with its large Japanese and Filipino populations. The influence of these cultures was felt everywhere on the island, woven deep into its fabric, just as sure as the Scandinavian influence; the names—Nakata, Hayashida, Koura, Corpuz, Rapada, Bello—were as ubiquitous as Hansen, and Gunderson, and Olsen, on road signs, park names, businesses, and farms.

Ruth had first encountered the Seabold Church her second week on the island. She was driving the back roads aimlessly in the Buick, attempting to lull Karen to sleep, when she caught a fleeting glimpse

of its white bell tower tucked between the trees. She circled back to
get a better look and was taken by the simple elegance of the structure, its plain façade, its tiny chapel, its cupola dwarfed by the firs and
cedars all around, like a sanctuary tucked within the larger expanse
of an evergreen cathedral.

The very next Sunday, Ruth coaxed the girls into dresses, Ruth
cramming her very pregnant self into a shapeless maternity skirt and
a colorful print smock with an all-around yoke from the Sears catalog. Though Abe had encouraged her to attend, he bowed out at the
last minute.

"You know me, Ruthie," he said. "I'm just not a church guy."

"You believe in God," she observed.

"Sure," he said. "Something like that. I just . . . the Sunday thing,
all that hand-holding and singing, I don't know, it never appealed to
me. Sundays are about football, walking the dog, futzing around the
house."

"You don't watch football."

"Look, honey, I've got nothing against it, really. The God stuff is
more personal for me. I don't need all the theatrics."

Ruth couldn't help but think of that first night at the Dog House
with Fred and Mandy, how Abe had all but begged to accompany Ruth
to church the next day, just to be near her. Now that he'd secured a
future with Ruth, such eager devotion was a thing of the past.

"Besides, I've got that Kiwanis thing," he said.

"Think of the insurance you could sell," said Ruth.

Though intended as sarcasm, the comment was nearly enough to
persuade Abe, before he apparently realized he could just as easily
deploy Ruth to this end.

"That's where you come in," he said.

"I am not shilling insurance policies to the congregation, Abe.
Forget it."

"I'm not asking you to sell policies. Just . . . you know, let it be
known here and there that I sell insurance, mention it when you get

a chance, afterward at coffee and such. I can give you a stack of business cards."

"No!" she said. "Absolutely not."

Despite his lack of shame, it pleased Ruth that Abe was so motivated to succeed financially. It was a comfort to know her children were well provided for. As much as Ruth loved her parents, she'd never known such assurances as a child. Security seemed to breed the kind of confidence you couldn't fake. For was it not easier to take leaps when you had a safety net beneath you, easier to gamble when you had the resources to cover your losses? In Ruth's mind, this was an entitlement everyone should enjoy.

Rather than the curiosity Ruth had expected would meet their appearance for the first time, she and the girls were greeted at Seabold Methodist with smiles and friendly nods as they filed into a pew near the rear of the chapel, a room longer than it was wide, with four gothic windows at even intervals along each wall and eight or ten pews on either side of the aisle. Attendance was robust, perhaps seventy-five or eighty faithful: young families, along with middle-aged and elderly couples. Beyond those initial acknowledgments, the eyes of the congregation were not upon her in those moments before the pastor took his place at the pulpit.

He was a rather young man, not much older than Ruth, square chinned, bright-eyed, and prematurely balding, his figure lean beneath a baggy stole. His sermon comprised a bit about community with a nod to Ecclesiastes that was rather poignant, and a short reading from Galatians. The proceedings shifted to thank-yous and prayers offered on behalf of friends and relatives of the congregation, blessings for a deceased aunt, a sick nephew, a good thought for a daughter gone off to college, all of it punctuated by song. For, more than anything, the service leaned heavily on the hymnal: "I Sing the Almighty Power of God," "Maker, in Whom We Live," and "Joyful, Joyful, We Adore Thee."

It was song that most genuinely embodied fellowship in Ruth's mind, the pulse of the collective, the communing of voices, the comfort of shedding the self, of capitulating to the larger body. It mattered not whether one could hold a tune, for the man or woman or child beside you or across the aisle could elevate you by extension, simply by singing along. That was the beauty of a choral hymn, that in concurrence it was greater than the sum of its parts.

Karen was perfectly well-behaved through it all. Anne stood dutifully when prompted, but unsure of herself, she moved her mouth silently through the hymns.

In closing, the pastor quoted from 1 Peter 3:8:

"'Finally, all of you,'" he said, "'have unity of mind, sympathy, brotherly love, a tender heart, and a humble mind.'"

Afterward, the congregation filed into the fellowship hall, where coffee and snacks were on hand. Anne shyly partook of cookies and cider along with the other children, Karen, on chubby legs, all but attached to Anne's side.

Ruth was standing at the coffee station when she was approached by the organist, a formidable woman nearly six feet tall with a shock of red, curly hair.

"You have a lovely voice," she said.

"Me, are you kidding?" said Ruth.

"I'm not," said the organist. "It was such a . . . well, a relief to hear a new voice."

She reached out a hand, digits long and sturdy, fingertips calloused. Ruth's own hand felt tiny and insufficient in comparison.

"I'm Bess Delory," she announced.

"Ruth Winter," said Ruth. "Those are my daughters, Anne and Karen, over there."

"And this one?" said Bess Delory, indicating Ruth's pregnant belly.

"A boy, we hope," said Ruth.

"And your husband, he's not with us today?"

"Not this time," said Ruth. "He had a Kiwanis event."

Though it behooved her to drop a hint about life insurance at this juncture, Ruth resisted the impulse.

"So," Ruth said. "You mean to say you can actually hear me with all those other voices? Way in the back?"

"Yes," Bess said. "Like an angel amidst a choir of ogres. You have excellent pitch and a genuine vibrato, both rarities around here, though few are lacking in spirit. Between you and me," she said, leaning in to assume a conspiratorial tone, "most everybody else is as flat as the Everglades."

In her months on the island, Ruth had made many acquaintances, some fleeting, some habitual, most all of them pleasant, but she'd yet to meet anybody she could call a friend, someone with whom she could share with absolute candor and no fear of judgment, someone with whom she could laugh, and complain, and gossip. Bess Delory was all that and more. Though their interactions in those formative weeks were limited to the fellowship hall, by the time Kyle was born that winter, they were dear friends.

Kyle was delivered on the farm by a neighbor named Mitsu Nakata, a youthful fifty-year-old midwife who had delivered nearly two dozen island babies in twenty years, some by design and others by necessity. For all Ruth's initial anxiety about a home birth on the island, far from the medical resources of the city, her labor with Kyle proved to be her shortest by a mile. Abe, for the first time, was present for the delivery, pacing about so incessantly that amidst her fierce pushing and gasping and teeth gritting, Ruth's eyes followed his progress around the room until it drove her to distraction.

"Stand still, for heaven's sake!" she shouted.

Abe didn't move another muscle until it was time to squat beside Mitsu and receive the baby.

In possession of good color, clear lungs, and a healthy appetite for nursing (unlike Karen, who had gone mercifully light on Ruth, and even weaned herself at fourteen months), Kyle, like Karen before him, proved to be a mellow baby from the start. Though Ruth never admitted it to anyone, this temperament made Kyle and Karen her favorites in most respects, and she always viewed them as her most self-sufficient children, though there was plenty of evidence to suggest that the distinction rightfully belonged to Anne, who, aside from a colicky condition beyond her control, emerged from infancy into toddlerhood speaking in full sentences, dressing herself, and squirreling away loose change in a jar.

As a newborn, Kyle slept for hours beside Ruth in a bassinet as she sanded shutters and cleared the garden, coaxing the girls to put their busy hands to work weeding the flower beds, turning the soil, and mounding potato plots. Karen especially loved the work. More than the others, she was naturally drawn to the outside world, always picking flowers and collecting pine cones and colored rocks, or conducting funerals for ants and potato bugs. She was such a beauty, Karen, combining the best physical attributes of both Abe and Ruth, and such a sweet, gentle soul.

Late that spring, as the garden was coming into its own, Ruth invited Fred and Mandy out to the farm, an invitation that was long overdue. Fred and Mandy had married the year after Ruth and Abe, and five years later, they remained childless. Mandy was working as a paralegal, and Fred was managing his father's mail advertising business in Renton.

Ruth prepared for their visit all day that Saturday, cooking and cleaning and arranging flowers, while Abe was out shaking hands at the pancake breakfast and Little League jamboree. The impulse to impress Fred and Mandy with her new life was not one she was proud of, but it was one she was powerless to resist, as though she needed it. They both thought Ruth and Abe were crazy to move out of the city, and Ruth wanted to not only redeem the decision but make it look like a stroke of genius: the freshly mowed pasture, the blossoming orchard, the bountiful garden, the polite, well-behaved kids, the charming extra room for guests that they never could've afforded in Seattle, the rustic farm dinner of roast chicken and vegetables, fresh deviled eggs from the hens.

"You guys actually did it," said Fred, wiping the chicken grease from his mouth with a cloth napkin. "Congratulations. I gotta say, it took some intestinal fortitude leaving a good job, a good neighborhood, your friends."

"What do you do about your hair?" said Mandy. "Have they got anyone over here?"

"I hear there's a gal downtown who's pretty good," said Ruth. "But to be honest, I haven't given it much thought—as you can probably tell."

"Stop it!" said Mandy. "You look great. It's hard to believe you've had three kids."

"I concur," chimed in Fred. "You both look great."

Mandy had barely aged since UW. If anything, she seemed more comfortable with her natural beauty. Ruth felt frumpy next to her, with her mousy hair and her baggy jeans.

Once during dinner, Mandy caught Ruth admiring her for a little too long and gave her an inquisitive look.

"Do I have something on my face?" she said.

"It's just so good to see you," said Ruth.

Indeed, it was nice to see Mandy, to have company, validating to have their new lives seen by people who'd known them previously, as if their life weren't 100 percent real until it was witnessed.

"So, what are the possibilities with this place?" Fred inquired. "Could you subdivide the five acres, say four big lots, and put in a couple houses, sell them for a healthy profit?"

"Why on earth would we want to do that?" said Ruth. "We came out here for the space."

"Couldn't do it if we wanted," said Abe. "Minimum lot size is five acres."

"That's too bad," said Fred. "Seems like a guy ought to be able to do whatever he wants with his land if he owns it, don't you think? Free country. Seems like a goofy law to me."

"The thought had crossed my mind," said Abe.

"All it takes is one neighbor with a dollar sign for a heart and you're looking out your window at tract housing instead of fields and forests," said Ruth. "The limits are put in place for everybody."

"I'd say it's owing more to a lack of infrastructure," said Abe.

"Or maybe too much infrastructure," said Fred.

"That could be, too," Abe conceded.

"It's for the common good," said Ruth.

"You're starting to sound like Jack Kennedy," said Abe.

As a man who had essentially bluffed his way into a lucrative career in life insurance, a man who, within a calendar year on the island, had already sponsored a Little League team and a Scout troop, and weekly took out ads in the *Bainbridge Island Review,* Abe had proven himself nothing if not enterprising, a quality that informed his political views as much as anything else. He saw Nixon and the Republican Party as champions of free enterprise and the sort of unfettered American opportunity that allowed the cream to rise to the top, whereas he viewed Kennedy as a meddling interventionist and a blue-blooded phony. If Ruth had to guess, Fred and Mandy's sympathies lay with Nixon's camp. But Ruth had never been reluctant to express an unpopular opinion.

"If that's intended as a slight," she said, "I certainly don't take it as one. I wouldn't trust Nixon with my best serving platter. He's so greasy, he'd probably drop it."

"That's not grease," said Abe. "It's called sweat. It comes from hard work. Besides, Kennedy's too young."

"You know, Nixon is young, too," said Ruth. "He just looks old."

"That's from hard work, too!" said Abe. "At least Nixon's a guy who made his own way up the ladder, unlike your wealthy Harvard boy, who just walked into opportunity like it was his birthright."

"Take it easy, you two," Fred said. "It's only politics."

Irritated as Ruth was by what she considered to be Abe's ideological shortcomings, Fred was right, it was only politics. At the end of the day, Ruth and Abe wanted essentially the same things. But she couldn't help but feel that every year the ideological divide was widening, that Abe saw the world as a set of prescribed principles that were sacrosanct to preserving a certain status quo, while Ruth was always looking to expand her purview.

After dinner, the girls were dispatched up the stairs to their rooms. Abe and Fred retired to the garage with their cans of Rainier as Mandy joined Ruth in the kitchen, helping set Kyle in the playpen, then dealing with the dishes.

"Funny how they disappear at cleanup time," Mandy said, rolling up the sleeves of her blouse.

But before Mandy could pick up a dish towel, Kyle began to fuss.

"You want to hold him?" said Ruth.

"Do I?" said Mandy. "I've been dyin' to get my hands on him. Those cheeks!"

"He just cut a tooth," said Ruth. "That's why he's slobbering so much."

"A tooth! Sheesh. I can't believe it's taken Fred and I almost a year to get out here," Mandy said as Ruth hoisted Kyle out of the playpen and into Mandy's arms.

"It's really not that far, though, is it?" said Ruth.

"No," she said. "It just seems like it with the ferry. And yet, it's like a world away," said Mandy, bouncing Kyle gently as he continued to squirm in her arms.

"I should have invited you six months ago," said Ruth. "But with the baby, and the house, and the whole transition . . ."

"Believe me, sister, I understand. I don't know how you do it. I can barely manage having a job. But look at this, look at you."

Mandy seemed a natural with Kyle on her hip, unperturbed by the boy's fussing and writhing.

"The ferry ride was so romantic," Mandy said. "That is, well, uh, it might have been, if Fred hadn't brought a bunch of paperwork with him. Honestly, he hardly even looks at me anymore."

"Wait'll you have kids," said Ruth.

"If we have kids," said Mandy. "I'm beginning to doubt it."

"Is that what you want?" said Ruth.

Mandy looked at once hopeful and sad, close and faraway. "Ha! You think I know what I want?" she said.

Ruth set her stack of dishes aside. It was good to see Mandy.

"Why don't I pour you a glass of wine?" Ruth said.

"Got anything stronger?" said Mandy.

They retired to the living room, dishes be damned, as Mandy sipped her wine and Kyle fell asleep in her arms.

"Here," said Ruth, reaching out. "I'll take him."

"No way," said Mandy. "C'mon, have one glass with me, Ruthie. Just one."

"If I wasn't nursing, I would," said Ruth.

"My sister swears one glass puts them to sleep."

Ruth finally conceded to four or five ounces in a coffee mug. It was nice to have Mandy pushing her again. Mandy had always believed in her, always tried to press Ruth into situations she thought would be good for Ruth, Abe being the prime example.

"You need a break, Ruthie," she said. "What are you gonna do about day care? Is that even an option out here? Or are you just stuck with the kids all the time?"

"I wouldn't say stuck with them," said Ruth, although the truth was that pretty much every day at some point, she felt exactly that way. It was nearly impossible to shower most days. Not to mention she had zero privacy. And while she enjoyed a good deal of success occupying the girls outdoors, where she could breathe deeply and sink into her surroundings, and she loved that time with them, the idea of sitting down with a book, or pen and paper, was nearly inconceivable.

"Be honest, are you happy, Ruthie?"

"I am," said Ruth. "Really, truly, I mean it. It's a lot, the kids, the farm, but . . . more than half the time I'm happy, like at least sixty-forty."

"God, at this point, I'd take forty-sixty," said Mandy.

Ashamed as Ruth might have been to admit it, that Mandy, childless, professionally advancing Mandy, her figure still taut and perky at twenty-five, was anything less than happy was almost a comfort to Ruth, a roundabout confirmation that abandoning her independence and starting a family had been a good move, after all, even if Ruth hadn't planned it that way. Compromise and sacrifice may have been the rule, but having a family had not been a compromise, had not been a sacrifice in the larger view. Or that is what Ruth was telling herself as she sipped her wine, her arms and bosom and lap mercifully free of children for the moment, her girls likely sleeping, though they hadn't brushed their teeth, her husband in the garage, her old friend sitting across from her, wineglass still half-full.

*

Fred was leaning against the workbench, elbow on the vise, clutching his second can of Rainier as he cast his eyes about the organized clutter of the garage, most of it involving Ruth's projects; half-built rabbit hutches, and painted cupboard doors left to dry.

"I don't know how you do it, pal," said Fred. "I mean, three kids? Living out here in the boondocks. What do you do for excitement?"

"Between the job and the family, believe me, I've got plenty of excitement. It's not glamorous, but it keeps me on my toes."

"What about Ruth? What about living in Paris and finishing college? All that's gone by the wayside?"

"I don't want to say she outgrew it, that wouldn't be fair," said Abe. "I guess in a way she sort of . . . sacrificed it."

"For the common good, you mean?" said Fred.

"Well, when you put it that way," said Abe.

"Maybe she's onto something," Fred said. "Maybe I'm just too tied up in myself. When I think about it, really, what sacrifices have I ever made?"

"You gave me the bed by the window freshman year," said Abe.

"You've got me there," said Fred. "But I didn't want the glare of the sun in the morning, anyway, and my side was quieter because there was no traffic on the other side of the wall."

"Come to think of it, me taking the window was your idea," said Abe. "You're pretty good, Fred, I guess I never realized how good."

"I try," said Fred.

"How's the mail advertising racket, anyway?"

"Growing," he said. "But I'm still hustling. And look at you, Mr. Successful. Ruthie says you're like a pillar of the community, selling life insurance in the cereal aisle."

"You really ought to think about a whole life policy yourself, Fred."

"Yeah, Ruth already gave me the company line," he said. "You two are ruthless."

"Wait'll you have kids," said Abe. "You'll change your tune."

Abruptly, Fred's manner took a sober turn as he set his can of Rainier on the workbench.

"Some days, I don't think we're gonna make it, Abe. For a while, I thought, okay, we'll have a kid, that'll take the pressure off. But the more it doesn't happen, the more I think that's not what I want, not yet. Or maybe not what she wants. I don't know anything anymore, Abe. God, how I long for those days at UW, when the future didn't seem to matter. It was just something to conquer later."

"Have you guys seen a doctor?" said Abe.

"Doctor? Ha. We've seen four doctors. I've . . . you know . . . into plastic cups."

"And?"

"And they gave me a women's catalog to look at, you know, lingerie, bras, that kind of thing."

"And?"

"It's pretty tame stuff. The bra section is okay."

"And?"

Fred heaved a sigh, then took a pull of his beer.

"It's me," said Fred. "Okay? People always assume it's the woman, you know? She's barren or whatever. But it's me, buddy. I'm firing blanks. And you know what, you know what I say?" Fred finished his beer in one gulp and crumpled the can. "Big deal, that's what I say. No offense, but what's so great about kids? I'm busy enough as it is. Mandy swears she wants one, but I really don't think she has any idea how hard it's gonna be, stuck at home. She lives to shop with her girlfriends, she likes her job. I was hoping this would scare her off the idea, like she'd get a little taste of domestic life, watching Ruthie run around after the kids with a baby stuck to her hip? But dang it, your kids are perfect, it's all so perfect here. I don't stand a chance, Abe."

Abe clapped Fred on the shoulder. "Aw, c'mon, Fred, it'll all work out. You two have got a great life."

But even as he said it, the words sounded hollow to Abe. Poor Fred. Abe could no longer even imagine a life without kids. Not that he did much of the heavy lifting, and it wasn't that he couldn't imagine the freedom, because he largely still had that. Half the time, he wasn't even home for dinner, and one or two nights a week, he arrived just in time for a victory lap before the kids went down, sitting Anne and Karen on his knee, regaling them with his exploits in town, slipping them nickels and dimes, before tucking them into bed.

Actually, Abe was acutely aware, not for the first time, of how easy Ruth made it to be a father and a man, and he was so grateful for her, and so grateful for the opportunity to support a family, to be depended upon. He couldn't imagine life without kids. And that was all because of Ruth. He was a lucky son of a gun, Abe Winter.

A Merciful Conclusion

2023

When Ruth finally emerged from her medicated stupor that third day at Swedish, Abe was seated at her bedside in the ICU, nearly five hours after he'd assumed his post there that morning. When she opened her eyes with a groan, Abe set his outdated issue of *Forbes* aside and rose to his feet to greet her awakening. She smiled weakly up at him, moaning in lieu of a salutation.

"Thank God," said Abe. "I was beginning to think you'd never come out of it."

Ruth uttered two syllables, unintelligible, which seemed to originate deep in her throat. Her body refused to cooperate, but her eyes were alert, though Abe could only guess at the thoughts and sensations animating them. Once again, Ruth tried to articulate something, but the result was a string of vowels running together into gibberish. Rolling her eyes slowly back in her head, she lifted her wrist, IV tube and all, and repeated the utterance, motioning toward the side table.

"What is it?" said Abe. "You want me to call someone?"

She shook her head and pantomimed a writing motion.

"Ah, right," said Abe.

Locating the little pad of paper and pen on the side table, he presented them to Ruth, who piloted her bed upright thirty degrees before she began scratching out a note. Her handwriting was that of a six-year-old, oversized and unsteady, but legible.

They're not coming to see me, are they?

"Who?" he said.

The kids, she scrawled.

"I'm not sure," said Abe.

Ruth flipped to a fresh page and began writing once more, her handwriting a little more steady.

Tell them no. I don't want to see anyone.

"Why?"

She scribbled her reply impatiently. *Look at me!*

The effort seemed to sap her energy, and she closed her eyes once more.

Abe set his hand upon hers and gently stroked it.

When she opened her eyes, Ruth endeavored to smile again, but it registered only as a twitch at the corners of her mouth.

"Don't be scared," said Abe. "You're in excellent hands here."

Ruth took up the pen once more and began to write.

Thing I'm scared of is looking in the mirror.

Here she was, practically back from the dead, hours removed from a near-fatal drop in blood pressure, hooked to all manner of machines, tubes in her veins and crammed up her orifices, and yet she could still pretend for his sake that vanity was her biggest concern. God, what a magnificent woman. For all these years, Abe had been determined to outlive her, as though his absence would break her. But she was so much stronger than him. He now understood that her absence would be the end of him.

"Nonsense," he said. "You look perfectly normal."

The truth, of course, was that he had no idea what lay below the gauze and the swelling. She might have looked like Quasimodo. But truer still was the fact that Abe didn't care, that nobody who had ever loved Ruth would care, or even bat an eye at whatever cosmetic revisions may have resulted from the surgery, because Ruth was so much more than a strong jaw or an unblemished face; her presence in their lives outweighed any and all physical considerations.

"We lost our dog sitter," said Abe. "The Callahans are off to Sarasota for the holidays. I'm gonna try to lure Maddie to drive up tonight if she's able. Or I could ask Jen Duncan."

Ruth shook her head firmly, and for the first time, Abe could decipher her words more from their intent than from their enunciation.

"No," she said. "Go home."

A pragmatism hard and shiny as quartz gleamed in her eyes, keenly familiar to Abe after seven decades, beseeching him: *Who will get the mail? What about the chickens? The newspapers will start stacking up. The recycling needs to go out on Wednesday. If you pay the electric after the fifteenth, they'll add a surcharge.*

Again, Abe was humbled by his wife's indomitability. Intubated and unable to speak, yet still likely alert to every detail that populated their daily lives, down to the day of the month.

Not that he regretted a moment of it, but Abe had had many occasions to wonder over the past twenty-five years: How had their lives become so small? It seemed like only three weeks ago that their lives were so hectic with kids and jobs and aspirations, so overrun by obligations and unpredictable variables that they could hardly stop to catch their breath. Cancer wasn't even a possibility. Death was some distant horizon, a fate reserved for the elderly and the unfortunate, a realm far removed from their lives on the farm, where life and abundance prevailed.

"I should stay," he said.

Ruth didn't even bother with grunts and syllables this time; the message was clear in her glower.

"But what if . . . ?" Abe offered.

She shook her head decisively.

"Look, Jen Duncan can look after Megs," Abe said. "I'll just keep the room across the street."

This prompted a deeper furrowing of Ruth's brow. She'd already done the math on the hotel costs. How she managed to juggle such considerations in the face of extinction was barely conceivable. But she was resolute, Abe recognized that much, and had learned long ago to trust such resolve on Ruth's part, or at least not fight it.

Please, she scratched out on the pad. *I'm fine.*

Abe pursed his lips, still not convinced.

An aberration, she wrote, as if she could read his mind. *Won't happen again.*

She looked him straight in the eye and nodded solemnly before turning to a fresh page and setting pen to paper.

I promise, she wrote.

Abe left the hospital late that afternoon and checked out of the Silver Cloud, still uneasy about the decision. The parking came to almost seventy dollars, not to mention the hotel at one fifty-nine a night, expenses he wouldn't dare divulge to Ruth, though she'd probably make inquiries at some point. Not that they were hurting financially, but thrift had become habitual for both Ruth and Abe in the later stages of their lives. It was important to both of them that they leave as much as they could to the kids, and especially the grandkids. Imagine supporting a family in this day and age, or buying a house, or sending your kids to college, or paying for weddings. It used to be that a family could own a home and live comfortably on a single middle-class income. Now it seemed young families were up to their eyeballs in debt, and Abe and Ruth wanted to relieve some of that pressure for their grandchildren. Their liquid assets still amounted to over three hundred thousand dollars, and the farm could probably fetch two million, old house and all. But with three remaining children and five grandchildren, there really wasn't that much money to go around, not as much as they'd hoped. For ever-practical Abe, this had been yet another reason not to linger past his ninetieth year, and yet Ruth's condition now seemed to require that he endure.

Downtown was gridlock at rush hour, and once again the traffic revisions were not helping. Abe missed the four forty-five boat, and the five forty-five was already sold out by the time he got in line. He dozed briefly in the driver's seat before finally loading for the six thirty, which was running twenty minutes late. It was nearly eight o'clock by the time he arrived home, where poor Megs had peed in the foyer. He found a note from Deb Callahan on the dining room table, along with a casserole she'd left in the fridge with heating instructions. The Callahans had been model neighbors for over thirty years, though Deb had never been much of a cook, not like Ruthie. Still, Abe might be forced to heat the casserole at some point.

Abe let Megs out the kitchen door and returned to the foyer with a roll of paper towels to clean up the mess. Flashlight in hand, he took the soiled remains straight outside to the garbage can, then proceeded to the henhouse to shut the chickens in. The night was cool but mercifully dry, a few stars splashed between the parting clouds. Forty years of development all but surrounded their little farm now, cookie-cutter McMansions in varying shades of gray, with hulking three-car garages. So much for the "common good." Despite the sprawl, all was peaceful and still within the Winters' little buffer, the distant traffic on 305 the lone sound penetrating the silence, the beam of Abe's flashlight the only thing illuminating the yard as he moved deliberately across the pasture, wary of ruts and holes. One of these nights, he or Ruth was liable to break a hip.

To Abe's annoyance, the old Orpington with the missing eye, the one Ruthie called Ginger, was still roosting atop the coop. Abe conducted the hen off her perch with the business end of a rake, then spent the next five minutes trying to corral her before he finally finagled her through the door with his foot. He was far too old for such shenanigans. Like most of them, she was an aged, spent hen who never laid anymore, and hardly worth the effort. But eggs or no, Ruthie still loved them as pets.

Sure enough, Abe retrieved but a half dozen eggs from the nesting boxes, a meager haul, particularly after a two-day absence. It was clear from the pungent odor emanating from the boxes that he'd need to clean them out tomorrow. They may not have laid much anymore, but that didn't stop them from pooping everywhere. One of the heating lamps was burned out, and Abe knew the temperature was bound to fall below freezing before the night was over. He had half a mind to leave the bulb for morning, but his sense of duty—to Ruthie more than the hens—kicked in just in time, and with a sigh, he plodded across the pasture to the shed in the darkness. There were no heat lamp bulbs to be found among the musty clutter of the shelves, but Abe found a thirty-watt incandescent, which would do the job. As he trudged back to the henhouse, it occurred to him how many of these little tasks fell on Ruth: the care of the animals, the orchard, the garden. Most of Abe's contributions to the farm and the family had come from behind a desk, and such utility as that was decades removed, whereas Ruth had kept up with the same chores she'd been doing for sixty years, while Abe futzed around with crosswords and fell asleep in chairs.

By the time Abe returned to the house for good, he was faint with exhaustion and fell back heavily in his La-Z-Boy without reaching for the TV remote. He could have called it a night right then and there, but he knew he had to update the kids.

And so, one by one, he called them.

"We're coming out for Christmas," insisted Anne.

"I don't think it's a good idea," said Abe.

"Of course it's a good idea," she said. "Don't worry, Dad, we'll stay in a hotel and spend the days with you and Mom and help out. It'll give you a break."

"A break from what? I haven't done anything yet," he said.

"Believe me, that will change once Mom gets home," said Anne. "You'll be helping her in the shower, back and forth to the bathroom, you'll be preparing her meals, you might even be feeding her from what I understand. You're gonna need a hand, Dad. And it will be good for Mom to see everybody."

"So, everybody's coming?"

"Maddie is still looking for somebody to cover for her at work, but that's the plan."

Despite Anne's assurances, Abe could summon no enthusiasm for the holidays. The mere prospect of celebrating Christmas under the circumstances sounded dreary and exhausting. But how could he turn his children away? He thought of all those times when the kids were in their twenties and thirties, when Abe and Ruth had begged them to come out for the holidays and bring the grandchildren, but more often than not, everybody was too busy. Now Abe didn't want all the fuss, and he was sure Ruth wouldn't want it, either, but they'd gone and invited themselves. There'd be a lineup for the bathroom. Who was gonna cook a goose? Abe would have to make a trip to the Christmas tree farm. How would he carry the damn thing in the house by himself? He'd have to stock the refrigerator.

"No presents," said Abe.

"Fine by me," said Anne. "This is about being together."

Abe was tempted to add "one last time," but now his impending exit had been deferred, for who knew how long? He couldn't leave Ruthie in this condition. Four or five weeks ago, she hadn't really needed him, he served no real function in her life beyond predictable company, but now she was depending on him, and Abe wasn't at all sure he was up to the task, let alone hosting a family Christmas.

Abe called Kyle next and gave him the update on his mother.

"I'm gonna go see her after work tomorrow," said Kyle.

"No," said Abe. "She doesn't want to see anybody."

"What do you mean, she doesn't want to see anybody?"

"More accurately: She doesn't want to be seen by anybody."

"That's ridiculous," said Kyle. "How bad could it be?"

"You can call her, though," Abe said. "Once she's in a regular room. She won't be able to talk back, but she'll hear your voice if the nurse holds the phone for her."

"It's that bad, huh?"

"I don't think Christmas is such a good idea," said Abe. "But Annie is really pushing for it."

"We'll take care of everything, Dad, the food, all of it. Don't freak out. All you have to do is watch football."

Where Anne always seemed to work Abe up during the course of their exchanges, Kyle had a way of settling him down. And Maddie, well, she was Maddie.

"Good news," she said. "I've got somebody to fill in on the twenty-sixth."

"You're bringing your dog, aren't you?" said Abe.

"That's okay, isn't it? Megs and Perry get along great," she said.

"He just humps her the whole time," lamented Abe.

"They're dogs, Dad. They do dog stuff."

No, Maddie would never grow up, it was hopeless to think so at this point. After all, she had never married, never had children, never maintained a serious romantic relationship for more than two years, she was already AARP material, so what would compel her toward adulthood now?

"Can we not do gifts this year?" she said. "I'm a little thin financially."

"No gifts," said Abe. "It's already been decided."

Abe never could see the use in gifts once everybody was out of the house; Christmas had always been for the kids. But some people couldn't help themselves, specifically, Anne. Abe preferred Thanksgiving to Christmas, but this year, under the shadow of Ruth's impending surgery, they hadn't cooked a turkey for the first time in over sixty years.

By the time Abe finished his call with Maddie, he'd already decided to gift her a few thousand bucks to help ease her pressure. Of course, Ruth would insist they offer the other kids the same in the name of fairness. That they were still calling them kids and giving them money seemed a little absurd.

Abe settled back into his easy chair, while sad-eyed Megs sprawled on the braided rug at his feet, looking up at him. Even as his eyelids grew heavy, Abe thought of poor Ruthie, all alone in that cold hospital. Life was a relentless war of attrition, to love was torturous, for love ravaged you and brought you to your knees; it broke your will, over and over, until death seemed like a merciful conclusion.

What Was Left of Her

R uth spent three days in the ICU after the sudden drop in blood pressure that nearly ended her life. Three days in a dazed torpor, during which she refused to let Abe or anyone else visit her. As much of a comfort as Abe's presence might have been, the idea of his trekking back and forth from the island to the city at his age was more worrisome than her own recovery. And the cost of a hotel was a ridiculous expense to incur just to see her scratch out a few sentences on a pad of paper. Like clockwork, Abe called twice daily and spoke to her at length, though she could hardly respond. Still, there was solace in hearing his voice, as he mostly imparted to her the mundane details of his days.

"That damn Ginger was on the roof again last night. It's murder getting her in. She should spend less time up there roosting and more time laying eggs. Incidentally, Bess Delory has left three messages on the home phone. I called her this morning and gave her an update. Told her I'd keep her posted. Sooner or later, she's gonna wanna come to visit you, Ruthie. You gotta understand, people want to be there for you."

"Nn nn!" blurted Ruth.

"I figured you'd say that," said Abe. "I told her as much. Pastor Persun has been calling, too, I owe her an update. Of course, folks in the congregation are asking about visiting, too."

"Nn."

"I know, I know," said Abe. "No visitors. Can't say I understand it, but I'll honor it. You're really not gonna like the news I have for you, though."

"Ut ow?" muttered Ruth.

"The kids have invited themselves to Christmas. All of them."

"Nn nn, nn!"

"I told them it was a bad idea, but you know Annie, once she's got an idea in her head, she's like a dog after a bone."

The thought of all of them at Christmas was overwhelming; it was only days away, and Ruth couldn't walk, couldn't even speak, and certainly couldn't orchestrate a holiday gathering. Who would see to all the arrangements? How would she feed them all? But if Anne had made her mind up about it, Ruth knew it was useless to oppose her. Where her first child had come by such obstinacy, Ruth could not say, but she'd learned not to resist Anne's will by the time Anne was fourteen years old. My God, how teenage Anne had tested them. It took all the strength Ruth could muster to resolve herself to the reality of Christmas.

On her fifth day at Swedish, Ruth was transferred to a private room on the eighth floor, where she finally had her own bathroom, though she couldn't get out of bed to utilize it without the aid of a nurse. She remained adamant with regard to permitting Abe or anyone else to visit her, even Bess Delory, who, along with Abe, Kyle, and Anne, called her daily. Bess kept her abreast of church news: Jessie Hayward's son, Ron, had suffered a coronary event. Lynn Mugrage's granddaughter was off to Boise State again after a semester off, they'd offered a blessing for her last Sunday. Attendance in Sunday school was down to three kids the past two weeks.

Kyle's calls consisted mostly of encouragement: *You've got this,*

Mom. At least it's just radiation, not chemo. You dodged a bullet there. They'll have you back home in no time. Anne says you can re-hab in Silverdale, so you won't be so far from Dad. Of course, we'll bring you home for Christmas. I can get you there and back.

Though everybody meant well, even the phone calls, the simple act of listening, of trying to concentrate through the dulling sensation of painkillers and the throbbing of her traumatized face, were enough to exhaust Ruth. She slept sixteen hours at a stretch and spent the remainder of her time trying to attain a state of slumber. Each day, the pain of her jaw grew stronger as the swelling subsided. And the real pain had yet to begin. Dr. McGonagle had warned her at the outset that the recovery period was bound to be worse than the surgery itself, a regimen that included six weeks of radiation on the right side of her face, a scorching, blistering, irradiated assault on her soft tissue that would leave her mouth burned and ravaged, both inside and out. Moreover, for the first time since infancy, she would be totally dependent on others, most notably Abe, for the simplest of tasks, all the feeding and toileting and transportation she'd formerly taken for granted.

Who was to say she'd ever recover fully, or regain even half her vitality? What if she never returned to a normal life? What if being bedridden was the new reality? Clearly, she'd never again appear normal, not with a leg bone for a jaw and an eight-inch scar from ear to chin, not with seven missing teeth and half a tongue. My God, there was hardly anything left of her face. Why did she even want to live, when she might be taking her meals from a straw the rest of her days, when she couldn't taste her food or feel her tongue? These were questions Ruth had spent a great deal of time with in recent weeks, since the moment she received the biopsy results.

What would account for her will to live going forward? A worthwhile life didn't amount to utility alone. Of course, Abe still needed her, of course Bess still needed her, and Megs, and the hens, and her garden, so she was plenty needed, and yes, that provided some motivation to live. To be needed, after all, was a blessing; to be central to the lives of others was an honor and a responsibility. To love and protect those she held dear had been a principal theme in her life. But was it enough to endure the suffering that lay ahead? At what point did survival become a law of diminishing returns?

Ruth could argue that in her late eighties she'd already passed that juncture, already outlived her usefulness. Yes, she was still acting as church assistant treasurer, still on the board of directors for the Bainbridge Historical Society, which, to be fair, beyond an occasional vote of nominal significance, was a symbolic position as much as anything else. She still worked the strawberry shortcake stand in the T&C parking lot every Fourth of July. But were these small measures of utility enough to abide as a mere shadow of her old self? Who wants to buy strawberry shortcake from an old woman with half a face? Surely, someone else at Seabold Methodist could execute her responsibilities as assistant treasurer. It didn't take Alan Greenspan to count the weekly offerings, or write the deposit slips, or drop them off at the bank, nor did being on the parsonage committee require any degree of expertise; the job was as rudimentary as making sure they slapped a coat of paint on the place and laid new carpet every couple years for the incoming pastor. Then there were her grown children, and grandchildren, and now great-grandchildren, two of whom she'd never even met, and to none of whom Ruth served any particular function. While she wasn't without use, the world was hardly dependent on her participation.

The painless alternative to enduring, of course, was to have not survived the surgery at all, to have succumbed to the anesthesia and never regained consciousness. No doubt, that would've been easier. But when had life ever been easy? Sure, Ruth had suffered. She'd grown up on the edge of poverty. She'd outlived a child, every parent's worst nightmare. Like so many women before her and after her, she'd downsized her dreams long ago. What mattered to Ruth more than anything in the end wasn't dreams and aspirations. It wasn't enough to sit back and admire one's accomplishments. What made life truly precious could not be measured by achievement, or even service. To live fully was not an obligation or an act of faith, it wasn't a state of being at all, but a capacity, a willingness to engage the smallest and most unexpected aspects of being alive, to remain curious and open to the unforeseen and hitherto unrecognizable. To live fully was to observe like a poet, and though Ruth had not written nearly enough verse in recent years, nor read nearly enough poetry beyond an occasional psalm or a bit of Ecclesiastes on Sunday morning, she was still—as she had always been—a poet at heart, living in the quality of sunlight as it angled through the kitchen window, abandoning herself to the greater glory, capitulating to the harmonic fabric of the congregation joined in song, feeling the breeze on her face as though it was not just moving air but the touch of infinitude. To live fully was to recognize and acknowledge the tiniest of beauties, those ever-present, immutable though often elusive truths, pure and simple as a raindrop on a daisy.

The question remained whether Ruth could now live such a life. Could she still recognize all that was holy when she could barely recognize herself? Would the wind ever feel right on her disfigured face?

Ruth had plenty of time to consider these questions in the hospital, as her healing progressed more slowly than expected. The swelling came down but was still considerable days after the surgery. Her blood pressure and heart rate were still unstable. She still couldn't get out of bed on her own. To make matters worse, her weight was down, and her stomach had started rejecting the nourishment she received through the feeding tube. She began to vomit frequently, a disconcerting development for the medical staff, who scrambled for solutions, altering the schedule and contents of her diet. But the vomiting continued as Ruth complained of near-constant stomach pain. While Ruth's stay at Swedish had initially been factored at roughly a week, it was becoming increasingly apparent that, whether or not she wanted to, she would not be discharged in time for Christmas.

The Changing View

1969

In the ten years since Abe walked into Bainbridge Island Insurance and talked his way into a job, he'd been the cash cow of the agency. A few of the older agents had dropped out within six months of Abe's arrival, and their replacements were hard-pressed to perform anywhere near Abe's sales threshold. Not only had he virtually cornered the island market in full life, the game was changing, and Abe was ahead of it, offering PUAs and term riders to existing customers while stacking up big commissions not only for the benefit of himself and his family, but for Todd Hall and the agency, as well. Abe had also brought a lot of business lines into the mix at BII—commercial, auto, bank. In the meantime, through his tireless outreach and hustle, he'd made himself the face of the agency and a well-regarded figure in the community at large.

Abe's Bainbridge Island Insurance Seagulls, coached by Dick Wyman, who once pitched in the Detroit Tigers farm system, were nothing less than a Little League dynasty, in their baby-blue pinstripes. They had the sharpest uniforms; and the best equipment, and old Dick even persuaded the twelve-year-olds to wear their hair short. Every Fourth of July and Scotch Broom Parade, Abe was near the front of the procession, usually riding shotgun in Bill Ostenson's 1927 Model T roadster, waving at spectators, familiar faces many, pelting the kids with hard candy and Tootsie Rolls out the open convertible as they inched down Winslow Way, where midway through town Abe never failed to smile as they passed the Bainbridge Island Insurance Office, three doors down from the Winslow Clinic.

The first half of the 1960s had been very good to the Winters financially, as they'd been for much of America. The Winters were on their way to paying off the farm, they were stacking up savings, and Abe's earnings provided an abundant life for his kids, one heavily complemented by Ruth's tireless organization, guidance, and dependability at home. They were a good team, Abe and Ruth. Even as the country seemed to grow more divided, with reason and moderation on the wane, and discord and dissension on the rise, the status quo in doubt, the Winters endured and even thrived despite their differences.

Thanks chiefly to Abe, Bainbridge Island Insurance accumulated profits at a rate that had allowed Todd and Jean Hall to buy a vacation home on Lake Chelan and take a two-week vacation in Acapulco every February. Not to mention the powder-blue Caddy Todd drove to work when he wasn't driving the Olds 98 convertible with its overhead valves and telescopic steering wheel. Abe, by contrast, was at the helm of a wood-paneled Country Squire wagon—in fairness, a choice he owed to his growing family more than his income.

Though Abe was living the good life, it wasn't quite all that he'd yearned for when he'd decided the agent's life was for him, back when he was an underwriter at Safeco, a few years removed from UW. Despite his prosperity, Abe was feeling a little stuck professionally.

Abe's father used to say: "Unless you're the lead dog on the team, the view never changes."

The time had come for Abe to take the lead.

Todd Hall was pushing fifty-five, if he wasn't already there. Todd's own sales numbers had begun a steady decline the day Abe joined the agency, and yet, all these years later, his standard of living was still more extravagant than Abe's. In fact, Todd had given up sales entirely three years prior to manage the agency exclusively, while Abe was still making him money hand over fist. Not that he begrudged Todd this bounty. After all, Todd had given him the opportunity in the first place. Todd had mentored Abe, though the latter had learned everything Todd had to teach him within a couple of years. And without Todd Hall, there would have been no farm, no life on Bainbridge Island, no growing savings account, no investment portfolio.

That said, if Abe bought Todd out (a big if), Abe would no longer have to split those commissions with anybody. Sure, he'd have a little overhead if he owned the agency, but he could make money a whole lot faster with a little more effort. And if Abe brought in younger, more savvy agents, he could make that nut with even less effort. The clincher was that such a transfer of ownership would be beneficial to Todd, as well.

"Think of it, buddy," Abe said over lunch in the murky confines of the Tillicum Room in the rear of the Martinique, where Todd was enjoying a double MacNaughton on the rocks with his prime rib, and Abe a lime and soda with his lemon glazed chicken. "Be honest," said Abe. "Twenty-five years in the game, right?"

"Twenty-seven," said Todd. "But who's counting?"

"You gotta be burnt, pal," Abe said.

"To a crisp," said Todd.

"You're going to get out eventually, right? You gotta."

"Eventually, yeah. That's the plan," said Todd.

"So, why wait?" Abe asked. "Let's say I buy you out today on a ten-year contract at eight and a quarter percent. No more sweating it out with the applications, no more carrying the weight for the incompetent agents, no more phone calls, no sales work, no having to be anywhere or put out any fires. You can just sit by a pool or go hit a round of golf at Wing Point. Think of the time you'll have with Jean. You can travel, go to Scotland, go to the Bahamas, go see the pyramids. And the beauty of it all, the real reason you ought to just jump now, is that you'll be stacking up cash the entire time. Just imagine it: You shoot a dang birdie on the seventh hole, and you make a stack of cash at the same time. You're finally reading *War and Peace,* but you're doing it in sunglasses and swim trunks, and guess what? You just made three hundred bucks. How does that sound, Todd?"

"Keep talking," said Todd.

Abe kept talking until halfway through Todd's second MacNaughton, when Todd, by then mentally bronzed in swim trunks and well-read in the pre-revolutionary Russians, had no recourse but to sell the agency to Abe.

Once again, Abe had managed to talk his way up another rung of the ladder. In twenty years, he could take that final step and sell the agency, just as Todd had sold it to him. But in the meantime, he'd be lead dog, and the view would only get better and better.

While buying the agency may have been a financial coup, the wealth came at a cost, and what it cost Abe was time, and headaches, and never-ending responsibilities, not the least of which was pulling in new agents and training them. His first hire was a young man named Ted DeWitt, straight out of Central Washington University. Good-looking kid, great with the numbers and details, though not nearly as personable or charming as Abe would've liked. It was pretty clear that DeWitt wouldn't last long in sales, but Abe needed bodies, and he was desperate to get some younger blood in the office. The island was getting younger, and Abe needed younger agents.

But not just anyone could sell insurance. It took a certain warmth and a knack for engendering trust; a firm (but not too firm) handshake; an ability to actively listen to the mind-numbingly prosaic concerns of the average consumer; a facility for modulating one's voice—tone, timbre, volume—when the moment called for it. In short, it took a certain charisma. His fellow Kiwanian Jim Mathison, from the chamber of commerce, was a young man with a good deal of charisma and, Abe thought, a lot of promise going to waste.

"C'mon, Jim," said Abe. "I'm telling you you've got the gift. I mean, Bainbridge Auto Freight? What even is that?"

"Well, Abe, maybe it's not as glamorous as insurance sales, but it's stable. I've got a three-year-old kid, and Kelly's pregnant with number two. Now is hardly the time to change careers."

Not only did Abe fail to recruit Jim Mathison, it would take him six years to sell Jim and Kelly a policy.

Owning the agency was a good deal more work than Abe had anticipated. Beyond staffing, Abe found himself overseeing the office in such detail that he was tasked with choosing between wallpaper swatches and office furniture when he wasn't delegating, motivating, or educating the other agents, whose personal problems somehow became his personal problems, all while continuing to sell policies himself across all lines and remaining the face of the agency.

It wasn't long before the added obligations began to take their toll on the home front. Where Abe used to arrive home late several nights a week, he hardly ever made it home for dinner anymore, instead eating takeout from the Lemon Tree at his desk, if he took dinner at all.

Ruth, having no doubt grown weary of his absence and all the responsibility that fell upon her with the kids and the property, seemed to grow distant as 1969 wore on. Abe's attempts—albeit blundering—at intimacy were usually met with aloofness, or a strained enthusiasm when there was any at all. More and more, their dialogues seemed to focus on the kids or the farm, and rarely on their conditions or plans as husband and wife. At times theirs seemed to resemble a business partnership more than a marriage. Ruth lived her daily life, Abe lived his.

While nightly in bed, Abe expressed his curiosity about Ruth's days, this curiosity was not reciprocal, as Ruth seemed to entertain little interest about his daily life. Abe could hardly blame her for being bored by the insurance racket, and maybe she'd heard it all before, but couldn't she see what it meant for her and Annie, and Karen, and Kyle? Yes, it was hard work, but weren't their lives full? For that, couldn't Abe expect a little gratitude, a little indulgence in return, even if it was feigned?

Though Ruth professed to love her life on the farm when pressed, more often she seemed discontent, especially during the summer, when the kids were out of school, when she had less time to herself. She seemed restless during these months, as though she wanted to be somewhere else. It was true that Abe owed them all a vacation, and he was planning a trip to Arizona in the fall, even if it meant taking the kids out of school.

In addition to this gradual growing apart, the kids, particularly Anne, were taking a toll on their union. Quickly approaching her fourteenth birthday, Anne had finished eighth grade in less than commendable fashion, with plummeting grades and a burgeoning antisocial streak. She wanted nothing to do with her parents or her younger siblings. When she was home at all, Anne sequestered herself behind her bedroom door, sometimes with music, sometimes talking on the phone with a friend, the phone cord stretched to its limit from the hallway. But as often as not, Anne dwelled amidst conspicuous silence in her room, her thoughts and actions unknown to Abe or Ruth. The child was annoyed when summoned, irritable when questioned, and less than enthusiastic when forced to comply with anything. No cheerfulness could seem to arouse her spirits or stir her from her state of teenage torpor. Apathy seemed to be the rule with Anne in those days. Given every opportunity to thrive, given a beautiful home, and good schools, and a reliable moral compass, that any child of Abe's should entertain indifference was unacceptable.

How to handle Anne's behavior provided yet another point of contention for Abe and Ruth. Over and over, their ideological differences clashed, whether it was Ruth's flaky politics, or her lax parenting, or her willful naivety regarding certain inconvenient realities of the world.

"It's those kids she's hanging out with," insisted Abe. "The Carlson girl, Gus Fromm's kid, the Dolinger boy. They're bad influences. The loud music, the scraggly hair, the torn jeans, the antiestablishment crap. You know what the Carlson girl and—"

"Kari," said Ruth. "Her name is Kari."

"Well, you know what Kari and Fromm's daughter—"

"Melissa," said Ruth.

"Well, you know what those two have in common? They're older than Annie. Worse, they've both got older siblings. Gus's got an eighteen-year-old son that wants to burn American flags."

"His name is Steven."

"I don't care what his name is, it's all bad news. The Dolinger boy smokes cigarettes, I've seen him out back of the bowling alley. And the older Carlson girl is apparently some kind of feminist agitator in Berkeley now. What are these kids up in arms about, anyway? They've got a great way of life, thanks to the grit of their forebears; they're secure; they've got good futures in front of them. They're insured. The young Blacks, the Latins, now, that I can understand—they've got a legitimate beef. But Gus Fromm's kid? C'mon, Annie, they're just malcontents, spoiled brats playing at being adults."

"This isn't about anybody else's kids, Abe. This is about Anne. You've got to understand, it's hormones," Ruth said. "Anne's got a good head on her shoulders, it's just a hard time for her right now, she's going through a lot."

"Like what? What's so hard about going to school and pulling Cs and living on a farm? We should have grounded her after last semester when she started getting Bs. We should've kept making her go to church on Sunday."

"You don't go," Ruth observed.

"That's different," he said. "The point is, we're not holding her accountable, plain and simple."

"Abe, she needs to learn to account for herself, don't you see?"

"I don't really see it that way, Ruth. I think you're taking a very laissez-faire attitude about all of this. I think Annie needs guidance, structure, some rules. What I don't think she needs is to be running around with kids that are two grades ahead of her."

"She's precocious, Abe. Where are they gonna run around, anyway?

It's Bainbridge Island. It's not like they're going to get tied up in some criminal underworld."

"You watch," warned Abe. "Pretty soon, Anne will start infecting Karen. After all, Karen looks up to Anne. What kind of example is her older sister setting for her by dating troublemakers?"

"She's not dating anyone," insisted Ruth. "If you're talking about Jeff Kleist, he's just a friend. They've been classmates since second grade. They got through algebra together. Abe, you're blowing this all out of proportion. Anne will be fine. Karen will be fine. Kyle will be fine. Just let them get through these awkward years."

What about us? That's what Abe wanted to ask. Would they be fine? What could Abe do to reinvigorate their marriage? What could he do to be a better husband, when he was already doing the best he knew how?

*

Though she invariably defended Anne's recent behavior, Ruth found it almost as vexing as Abe did. After all, what had Ruth ever done but nurture and indulge Anne, guide her, comfort her, support her, even when that meant giving her some space, like the last six months that she'd spent locked away in secrecy? In return, Ruth's efforts were greeted with sullenness and resentment, and a snotty brand of semi-cooperation when she got any at all. As the eldest sibling, Anne had always proved helpful with Karen or Kyle, whether it was occupying them on Ruth's behalf, persuading them, or, as Abe had alluded to, guiding them by example. Well, not anymore. Anne was all about Anne these days. She could no longer be bothered by Karen or Kyle, no matter how much they idolized her and studied her every move.

"Ugh," she would say. "Can you please tell them to leave me alone?" or "Why does Karen have to come?" or "Can't they use the other bathroom? It's so annoying!"

Moreover, Anne refused to go to church anymore.

"You said I could decide for myself when I was old enough," Anne said. "Well, I'm old enough. Tell God not to take it personally. You shouldn't, either."

Anne might have been pregnant or suicidal for all Ruth knew. It didn't matter how Ruth tried to elicit information about the girl's life. She was anything but forthright around the dinner table, fielding Ruth's frequent queries with offhanded *yes*es and *no*s and *I don't know*s, if Ruth was lucky enough to get that much. Mostly, Anne's communications consisted of grunts or sighs or eye rolls.

Then there was Abe, stellar provider but absentee husband and father. For all his child-rearing philosophies and his contempt for Ruth's own, he sure didn't practice parenting much. An occasional game of catch with Kyle on a Saturday, a lame insurance joke for Karen's benefit (*What's the difference between an actuary and an accountant?*), or an occasional admonishment or directive, usually directed in anger at teenage Anne. Never mind that Ruth had the best appliances and ample resources at her disposal. Children weren't something to be bought, they weren't domestic chores to be executed like laundry or errands, children were needy, complicated, hormonal souls who no matter their age existed in a state of perpetual transition, and transitions were always tough. Ruth could have used some help in the parenting department.

As for the state of their marriage, by 1969 it seemed that Ruth and Abe had little in common anymore, so little that Ruth was frequently forced to wonder if they ever really had. She'd always believed that despite their differing worldviews and polarized opinions, they shared the same values at the end of the day. But what were those values, exactly, if not family?

With Abe AWOL and Anne no longer her helper and friend, Ruth dwelled in a state of isolation on the farm, not unlike the Roanoke days, when she was left to dirty diapers and playground picnics, with no adult company all day long. Her dealings outside the farm were largely transactional. After Mandy and Fred had divorced three years prior, loyalties had proven tricky, and Ruth spoke to Mandy less and less until she hadn't spoken to her in over a year. Thank heavens for Bess Delory, her wit, and wisdom, and companionship.

"It's not you, honey, trust me," Bess assured her as the two women kneeled side by side weeding Ruth's flower beds. "There's only two things you can do to get a man's attention after fifteen years of marriage. The first is dent the car. And the second takes about four minutes. What you need is more projects, Ruthie."

"Look around you," said Ruth. "I've got the garden, the orchard, the chickens, a pond that needs dredging."

"What about a greenhouse?"

"For what?"

"Tomatoes, chili peppers, herbs, you name it," said Bess. "Honey, you could grow orchids in a greenhouse."

Bess was right; the busier Ruth kept herself, the healthier her mindset. The more tasks Ruth could devote herself to, particularly tasks that served to gratify her sense of creative purpose or independence, the happier she was likely to be.

The trouble began with a visit to Island Gardens on Winslow Way, where, seeking guidance for her new greenhouse, Ruth was referred to a contractor and master gardener on the north end of the island named Leonard Haruto, a young widower specializing in greenhouses. Ruth contacted Haruto by telephone, and they scheduled a consultation at the farm, where Ruth had already staked out a flat building site for the structure.

Leonard Haruto arrived the following Wednesday in an old red pickup truck, scrupulously maintained, with *Haruto Design* emblazoned on both doors. He hopped out of the driver's seat nimbly, clutching a clipboard in his right hand. Framed by medium-length dark hair, his smiling face was open and perfectly symmetrical, a countenance that engendered trust almost immediately.

After they'd exchanged pleasantries, Ruth led Haruto to the back of the house.

"A beautiful garden," he observed on their way past the neat rows of raised beds, lettuce, spinach, fennel, and mustard greens, then past the brimming flower garden. "Your canna lilies are impressive," said Leonard. "I wish mine looked that good. Not enough sun at my place."

Nor did Ruth's hydrangeas or lilacs escape Leonard Haruto's keen eye.

"You've maintained those hydrangeas well," he said.

Ruth could feel herself blushing at the compliment and found herself simultaneously annoyed when Karen cut them off in front of the building site.

"Is it really gonna be that big?" she said.

"Go back up to the house, honey," said Ruth. "Mr. Haruto and I are talking about business things."

Leonard Haruto was not a large man, nor was he powerfully built, but he carried himself with noble grace. Clearly, he was athletic, and strong despite his slight frame, which could be seen in the sinew of his lean arms. But what attracted Ruth most to Haruto, when she considered him alongside big lumbering Abe, was an almost feminine aspect, not only in the effortless grace of his comportment but in his unapologetic passion for gardening.

For the better part of a decade on the farm, Abe had never even noticed Ruth's hydrangeas or lilacs, let alone noted the way she fussed over them, fighting back the shade-making menace of cedar limbs so that her lilacs could receive proper sun, deadheading her hydrangeas every winter so that next year's blooms could flourish. Haruto noticed all of this, acknowledging the care and expertise that Ruth poured into her garden. Regarding the orchard, however, Leonard was a little less complimentary.

"Good trees, but you're pruning the stone fruit too early in the year. Wait until late summer, you'll get a higher yield."

Expense was not an issue for Ruth where the greenhouse was concerned. Abe was not cheap in that respect. Whatever the greenhouse cost, he would be willing to pay. She suspected this sort of

financial latitude on the part of an otherwise fiscally responsible Abe
was owing to vanity. Abe liked to see his money put to use in ways
that he could easily admire. Despite this lack of budget restraints,
Haruto was conscientious enough to talk Ruth's twelve-by-thirty
footprint down to ten by sixteen.

"It's too big, you won't require that much space for your pur-
poses," he insisted. "Besides, it'll cost you a fortune to heat in winter
if you're planning on exotics."

Ruth found herself more than willing to defer to Leonard Haruto
on this or any other gardening matter. She was awed by his knowledge and equally compelled by his gentle, easy confidence as he imparted it. How thrilling it was to discuss something besides term life
insurance or school calendars.

It took the better part of two weeks to construct the greenhouse
from the concrete slab up, Haruto working five days a week, arriving
at nine A.M. and leaving in the afternoon. The first few days, Ruth left
Leonard to his work as he marked the area, dug the foundation, built
the forms, and finally poured the concrete and raked it smooth and
perfectly flat. Occasionally, she peered out the window to admire
Leonard's progress and the methodical way he went about his work:
sure, precise, but unhurried. There was a certain poetry to it. Rather
than throw himself at the job, he let the work come to him.

By the third afternoon, Ruth began bringing Leonard pitchers of
water and sandwiches, lingering at the construction site as he partook of them. Each day, their familiarity grew. Ruth shooed Kyle
and Karen off when they dared interrupt her conversations with
Leonard. They were the most stimulating conversations Ruth had engaged in since college, lively, and thoughtful, and unpredictable. With
Leonard, she spoke of gardening and island life, and places they'd
seen, though neither of them had strayed beyond the Pacific North-
west. And to Ruth's delight, they even talked about poetry. It was
clear that Leonard could apprehend poetry in a way that Abe was
never able to.

"Real poetry is to live a beautiful life," he told her, taking a measurement.

"That's a beautiful thought," said Ruth.

"It is not mine," said Leonard. "It's Bashō's."

"Bashō!" said Ruth. "How well I remember him from college! 'Come, see the true flowers of this pained world.'"

"Indeed," said Leonard. "The true flowers."

"Where did you learn Bashō?" Ruth said.

Leonard averted his eyes to the measuring tape, as though the question embarrassed him. "From Atsuko's mother."

"Atsuko?"

"Atsuko was my wife."

For three days, every glance at Leonard's ring finger had served as a reminder to Ruth of the underlying sadness in Leonard's placid demeanor, though this was the first time he'd made any reference to his wife. Ruth understood that it was not an invitation to delve further into the subject, but she could not resist her curiosity.

"What was she like?"

"My mother-in-law? She was formidable. She was only four foot ten, but she—"

"No, Atsuko," said Ruth, who felt the blood rushing to her face. Was it rude to make such an inquiry, especially with such keen interest?

Again, Leonard's eyes sought refuge in his tasks. "Atsuko was . . . also formidable," said Leonard. "But in a quieter way."

Here, Leonard offered nothing further, whether because he believed this characterization to be sufficiently informative or, more likely, because he wished to speak no further of Atsuko. But Ruth could not help herself.

"By formidable, you mean . . . ?"

Leonard considered, eyes still on his work.

"Confident," he said. "Determined. Strong. Everything I wasn't."

With this, Leonard fell silent once more as he set to mounting a bracket, which Ruth took as a wordless appeal to jettison the topic. Yet it took considerable restraint to abandon her line of questioning. For Ruth felt she had to know. She was less interested in Atsuko's passing and more in her living embodiment: Was she beautiful? Was she bright? How had they first met? And how was it that Leonard's loss, or, more precisely, his endurance in the face of such privation, rendered him so hopelessly compelling to Ruth? It was as though she was trying to convince herself that her attraction to Leonard was rooted in her pity for him, and that this sympathy allowed her to entertain an otherwise indiscreet impulse.

As the days wore on and Ruth's interest grew keener still, Leonard Haruto seemed largely oblivious of her admiration. When the work was completed, Ruth couldn't bear to see her new companion go. Thus, she extended Leonard's employment, not as a contractor but as a gardening consultant. Leonard would oversee the setup and the stocking of the greenhouse, help her select her exotics, educate her in their care and maintenance. In this capacity, Leonard returned to the farm on a half dozen occasions. Ruth savored every moment. How wonderful it was to be learning things again! Despite his vocation as a builder, Leonard had small, soft hands that fascinated Ruth with their facility as he turned the soil between his fingers or dexterously demonstrated how to prune her hibiscus.

Though it had never been her intention, Ruth became bolder in initiating little intimacies with Leonard, grazing shoulders and hands as they worked side by side in the greenhouse. To feel his body so close was to recall an exhilaration she had not known in ages, had in fact never quite known with Abe, about whom she'd entertained reservations from the moment she met him, moral, ideological, and, yes, physical. His bearish embrace, his big, clumsy fingers, his impatience to consummate the act of intimacy, as if it were a job to be completed. Whereas Leonard was a portrait of physical patience, shy in engaging, a state quite likely owing to his sense of decorum and the fact that Ruth was a married woman, but Ruth didn't care. Daily, she pushed

Leonard closer to the precipice until finally, one afternoon in the greenhouse, Leonard relented, if only reluctantly, acquiescing to Ruth's advances as she all but trapped him in a corner, her heart thumping like a kettle drum.

Ruth and Haruto had been in their embrace less than five seconds when Anne walked through the greenhouse door, interrupting them.

Ruth pulled away instantly from Leonard, who averted his eyes as Anne fled the scene.

Visibly bewildered and presumably racked with guilt, Leonard still could not take his eyes off his shoe tops as he attempted a response.

"I . . ."

"Go," said Ruth. "Please."

Leonard Haruto took leave of the farm immediately, his red truck trailing a cloud of dust as it disappeared up the long driveway.

When Ruth caught up to Anne in the kitchen, she sent Karen and Kyle outside to play.

"But a few minutes ago, you told us to play inside," Karen observed.

"Do as you're told, young lady," said Ruth, ashamed of her scolding tone.

Not until Karen and Kyle were safely outside and out of earshot did Ruth dare to speak.

"What happened out there . . . it was—"

"I saw what it was," said Anne. "I don't want to know any more than that."

"It was only—"

"I don't care, Mom," Anne said, her tone venomous. "Really, I don't even want to know. That's between you and Dad."

And those were the last words Anne ever said on the matter. For the five remaining weeks of summer, Ruth's indiscretion with Leonard Haruto remained Anne and Ruth's secret, a knowledge that passed surreptitiously between them in the most fleeting of glances, always with a nagging knowledge on Ruth's part that whether Anne had any intention, or was even capable, of exercising it, she held massive leverage over Ruth, until that intolerable fact became her oppressor and, coupled with her own guilt, compelled Ruth to come clean with Abe, a confession sure to subject their marriage to the biggest test yet.

She disclosed her trespass as they lay in bed, about the only place they ever spoke at any length anymore. Expecting the worst, Ruth could scarcely believe it when Abe took the news calmly, almost matter-of-factly.

"Who else knows about this?" he said.

"Nobody," lied Ruth.

"Good," he said. "This can't get out, do you understand? And that means not telling Bess, either."

"Of course not," said Ruth. "I understand."

That his biggest concern was running damage control was not only shocking but disappointing.

"This Leonard, how do you know he won't go blabbing all over town?" Abe said.

"I just know," she said. "It's not his nature."

"Hmph, his nature," said Abe. "I'm supposed to trust a man who fools around with a married woman?"

"I initiated it," said Ruth. "He didn't want to. He tried to—"

"Stop!" said Abe. "I don't know want to hear another word. Why tell me at all if you're the only ones who know? Why not just pretend it never happened?"

"Because I owe you the truth. It was in our vows," said Ruth. "I'm telling you because I have to be accountable for my actions before either of us can forgive me."

Abe frowned, brow deeply furrowed, staring holes into the dresser opposite the bed.

"*If* you can forgive me," Ruth said.

Abe lingered in a deep silence, the duration of which was unnerving to Ruth, who was hanging on his next syllable. But it never came. Instead, Abe snapped off the lamp without another word, pulled the covers over him, and rolled away from her in bed.

Was it over? Had she been forgiven?

That Abe could absorb this news and make so little ado, that he would greet it with so little anger, or disillusionment, or even surprise, was almost enough to make Ruth want to jump in the car and drive to Leonard Haruto's house and fall into his arms. Lying there stiffly next to Abe in bed, it occurred to Ruth that he might indeed have taken the news harder if she'd dented the car instead of making a cuckold of him. But later that night, she felt him tossing wakefully beside her for hours, until he finally got out of bed, stepped into his slippers, and retreated to the kitchen.

After a moment, Ruth crept down the hallway after Abe and peered around the corner into the kitchen, unbeknownst to him. He was sitting at the breakfast table, clutching a glass of milk, head bowed, tears streaming down his face.

Ruth knew better than to try to comfort him, which would only exacerbate the wound to his pride, so she left him there with his grief and returned to bed, where she lay awake half the night.

Closed Doors

1969

That Ruth's indiscretion had only been a kiss, that the event had been isolated rather than serialized, and that she had not consummated her amour with Leonard Haruto was of little consolation to Abe. Nor did the fact that he'd never entertained such treachery himself serve as fuel for his hostility. Abe's misgivings were mostly with himself following the affair, if it could be called one. He began to wonder—at his desk, in the car, standing at the register at Winslow Drugs—whether he hadn't permitted or even encouraged Ruth's disloyalty. Perhaps the deficit in their marriage was owing not to Ruth's nature, which had never shown itself to be duplicitous, but to his own failings as a husband and lover? Whatever need had inclined Ruth toward such recklessness, it must have been an imperative that Abe had been unable or unwilling to fulfill.

Self-pity dogged Abe for weeks, a wistful awareness that despite all his efforts, he was not enough. Doubt was his constant companion as he executed a thorough inventory of his failures. Though he'd worked hard to provide for his wife and family; striven relentlessly to serve as a model husband; kept Ruth's photograph on his desktop for all to see at the office; brought flowers and candy when custom prescribed (birthdays, anniversaries, insensitive remarks); indulged her interests, from chickens to gardens to greenhouses, with little regard to expense; endured the naivety and misguided good intentions of her politics—none of it had been enough. Leonard Haruto, this gardener and handyman, had offered Ruth something that Abe could not. But what?

This sense that he was lacking despite his every effort hectored Abe from the time he took his first sip of morning coffee in the kitchen, not six feet from Ruth, whose manner remained one of sheepish acquiescence in the weeks following her confession, until his final waking moments of the day as he lay beside her in bed, close enough to feel her warmth, yet miles away. Abe almost relished his own vulnerability as one might derive gratification from an achy bruise, begging to be touched. Poor, jilted Abe, not good enough despite his noble efforts.

It took weeks for this pitiful melancholy to harden into something resembling outrage. How could she? The ingratitude! He'd busted his tail to provide a life for Ruth. Hell, he'd essentially moved to Bainbridge Island for her. Abe was no farmer, but he'd bought a farm for Ruth, because he knew she would take to the lifestyle. And she did. She loved her gardening and her hens, she loved reaping the fruits of her labors. She never lacked for anything so far as Abe could see. He provided all of it for her, and his thank-you was Leonard Haruto?

But Abe did not act upon his anger. Instead, like it was a candle, he let his indignation burn down gradually of its own accord. Not that he didn't go out of his way to make Ruth suffer. While he may not have visited his anger on Ruth explicitly, he tortured her with his inaccessibility and seeming indifference. It was almost as if he was daring Ruth to seek fulfillment elsewhere, as if in his passivity he was offering her a choice: Keep your bucolic life on the farm with your healthy, good-looking children, your fresh eggs and flowers and pears, your husband willing to foot the bill for your fancies (even if he did not share them), willing to work overtime so that there would always be more than enough for you and your children (unlike your own impoverished childhood), or walk away from all of it, leave it behind and run to Leonard Haruto.

Abe reasoned that Ruth needed him. So, he bet on himself, which meant forcing Ruth to take the lead in their reconciliation, to recognize and acknowledge that what she had so recklessly jeopardized was a life that many would aspire to. It was up to Ruth to win Abe back.

More than anyone, Anne may have inadvertently encouraged their marital accord by presenting them with a common adversary, a challenge that required Abe and Ruth to maintain an uneasy alliance as parents, if nothing else.

"What is she rebelling against? That's what I want to know," said Abe, pacing the living room floor, impelled by Anne's most recent display of audacity, her refusal to man the Bainbridge Island Insurance booth and hand out leaflets during the Rotary auction, a vocation she considered beneath her dignity. *No way, Dad. I'm not a puppet for the establishment!*

"We can't take it personally," Ruth insisted.

"Well, we're the ones that have to live with her, so how else are we supposed to take it?"

"It's not just Anne, Abe. It's all of them, her friends. It might be her whole generation, the way things are looking."

"Baloney!" said Abe. "I see plenty of decent kids out there, and a lot of them are serving their country."

"She's fourteen years old," said Ruth.

"Exactly," said Abe. "So, why does she get to hold us hostage? She's begging me to teach her how to drive; how am I supposed to trust her with the station wagon? She doesn't work, doesn't contribute anything to the household, all she does is defy us. These kids crap on everything we've granted them with our hard work, and yet, look at them: They're lazy, permissive, and for all their complaining about the status quo, they don't offer any solutions—just slogans and hair, grubby jeans and guitars. You know what she said the other day? She said America is soulless, it's all about suppression and commercialism. Where does she even get this stuff?"

"She's not entirely wrong, you know," said Ruth.

"Good heavens," said Abe. "Not you, too? Go ask some kid in China about suppression. Just how the hell has America suppressed our lovely daughter? She lacks for nothing!"

"I think it's about more than her," said Ruth.

But unwilling to listen, Abe waved the idea off. "I just hope to God she outgrows it," he said. "And that it doesn't infect Karen."

"It's not a disease," said Ruth.

"We'll see about that," said Abe.

Despite their philosophical differences, abetted by habit and necessity, Abe and Ruth gradually achieved equilibrium once more. Three months after the fact, Abe made his amends with Ruth in the station wagon. Anne was babysitting Karen and Kyle, and Abe had surprised Ruth with a rare night out, dinner at the Martinique.

"I can see things from your perspective now," he said, his eyes on the road as they drove south in the spitting rain, stands of fir on one side, sodden farmland on the other. "I dragged you out here to this island, away from your coffeehouses and museums and all the things you cherished about the city, then I just left you here by yourself with the kids to hold it all together, thinking I was doing you a favor. I wasn't here for you enough, and I'm sorry. You never asked for any of this."

"Maybe not," she said. "But you were right to think you were doing me a favor. It's a beautiful life here, one I didn't see for myself, and I love it, I truly do. Then you got busy. And I understood. But the longer you stayed busy, the harder it was to understand. We already had everything we needed, but still you were gone all the time. I began to feel invisible."

"I'm sorry," said Abe.

"It's no excuse," said Ruth. "I might have said something, I should have pushed you harder, I could've expressed my needs instead of expecting you to intuit them."

"I should have intuited them," he said. "I'm your husband."

"It's still no excuse," said Ruth.

They deferred to silence for a moment, Ruth gazing out the side window at the fields.

"I think we understand each other better now," she said.

Among the few dining options in town, the Martinique was Ruth's preferred destination, and thus had become Abe's default preference. It wasn't that the Martinique's Parisian fare exceeded Abe's expectation that particular evening, for he knew exactly what to expect from his boeuf bourguignon (too rich, too heavy, undercooked), it was the company that surprised. Ruth was effervescent. It was as though some obstacle, having stood between them, obscuring their view of one another, had been suddenly removed and they could see each other as never before. Ruth was her lively old self, but something more, as if she'd actually grown beyond what she'd once aspired to be. She was engaged, curious, optimistic; she seemed to laugh more freely, even at Abe's lame jokes. Maybe he ought to buy Leonard Haruto a thank-you card for his trouble. Whatever that flirtation amounted to, it seemed to have unlocked something in his wife.

In a rather rare display of intemperance, they finished a bottle of chardonnay between them, and a glass of Pernod, thus Abe and Ruth were both tipsy when they arrived home to find Kyle and Karen in front of the television, and Anne where else but in her room, the strains of some husky-voiced rock 'n' roller audible through the closed door.

"Lights off at ten," said Abe.

"Don't forget to brush your teeth," said Ruth as they walked past them into the bedroom, where they wasted little time removing their clothes and turning off the lamp.

No sooner did they lie side by side in the darkness than Abe felt the warmth of Ruth's hand on his chest, slowly working its way down his torso, and soon his blood was rushing in the same direction.

*

"I'm late," Ruth said as she topped off Abe's coffee at the kitchen table, where Abe's face was buried in the *Post-Intelligencer,* a paper he still read begrudgingly every morning despite having almost canceled his subscription after their endorsement of Jack Kennedy nearly a decade ago.

"Late for what?" he said.

"That's what you said the first time," said Ruth.

Abe lowered the *PI* slowly as the reality dawned on him. Ruth could almost hear his thoughts: Another child? Now? All these years later? He could hardly stand the other three at this point.

"That's great," he said. "Right? I mean, isn't it? We've got the room. We make great kids."

Even less certain than Abe, Ruth leaned into these assurances. "At least we know what to expect by now," said Ruth.

"Oh, boy, do we," said Abe, setting his paper aside to reach for Ruth's hand. When he had hold of it, he pulled her in close, slapping her playfully on the backside with his free hand.

"I suppose I better give Mitsu Nakata a call," she said, pulling away from him.

Ultimately, the pregnancy, unplanned and previously unwanted, served to galvanize their marriage. After years of growing apart, Abe and Ruth were collaborating once more on a mutual project: Theodore, if it was a boy, or Madeline, if it was a girl.

At twelve weeks, they resolved to tell the kids, who had failed to notice the slight change in their mother's abdomen. They gathered them in the living room after dinner one evening, a feat that required no small amount of finagling, and in the case of Anne, a legitimate threat to her precious sovereignty.

"Ugh," said Anne upon hearing the announcement.

"Is this a joke?" said Karen.

"No," said Ruth.

"As if it's not chaotic enough around here," said Anne. "It's impossible to get any privacy as it is."

"I don't want a little brother," said Kyle.

"Well," said Abe, "then you better hope it's a girl."

"I want a little sister even less, I'm already outnumbered."

"I don't know what to tell you, buddy."

In the meantime, it seemed that Ruth's impropriety with Leonard Haruto, or more precisely its resolution, had continued to pay dividends for their marriage. How else could she explain that Abe was more present than ever before with this pregnancy, not just physically but emotionally? For the first time in over fifteen years of marriage, Abe began to express a tenderness hitherto unknown, little flourishes of affection—a peck on the cheek in passing, a brief shoulder rub at the breakfast table, the occasional foot massage in the evening. He was more attentive to Ruth, anticipating her needs and considering her comfort as never before. He brought her tea in the evenings when she was sprawled on the sofa with her legs splayed, her inner thighs sweating, her collapsed arches aching. Though she deemed herself unsightly, already bigger and more cumbersome in her second trimester than she'd ever been in her third, Abe professed to admire her shape. Despite her condition, their couplings became more frequent and more ardent. Had it been possible to impregnate Ruth twice, Abe almost certainly would have succeeded in the endeavor.

The baby was born in August of 1970. Ten years after she'd helped steward Kyle into the world, Mitsu Nakata delivered the baby in the living room of the farmhouse. She was a Madeline, not a Theodore, a designation promptly shortened to Maddie. Eight pounds, nine ounces, ostensibly healthy, with good color and a formidable set of lungs.

Everything was different with Maddie from the start. It wasn't just Abe. Now, with the benefit of an additional decade of experience and maturity, Ruth found herself more composed in the face of the inevitable difficulties presented by child-rearing. Now that she could foresee problems and anticipate the infant's needs more proficiently, momentary setbacks did not devolve so quickly into calamities, and calmness usually prevailed. Where she had always taken the lead with Anne and Karen and Kyle, Ruth allowed Maddie to soothe herself, which she always did eventually. Sometimes that meant letting her cry for a few minutes while she packed Kyle's lunch or scratched out a grocery list.

Abe was more attentive to Maddie than he'd been with the other three infants. He held her more and looked more comfortable doing so. Like Ruth, he no longer panicked at the first sign of trouble and, as often as not, was able to finesse Maddie himself rather than handing her off to Ruth.

Though their lives returned to relative normalcy, it was impossible to avoid the lingering specter of Leonard Haruto on an island as small as Bainbridge. Surely, Abe must have seen Leonard piloting his red truck down Winslow Way past Bainbridge Island Insurance, his name embellishing the door like a taunt. Ruth could not imagine what that must have been like for Abe.

It was only by sheer diligence that Ruth managed to avoid run-ins with Leonard. When in town, she remained ever awake to the possibility that Leonard might be mailing a letter, or popping into T&C for a carton of eggs, or doing business at Bainbridge Gardens. On several such occasions, she'd spotted Leonard before he saw her and, dodging into the canned vegetable aisle or behind a pallet of fertilizer, had managed to escape his notice. But such contingencies were unsustainable. A reunion was unavoidable.

Of all places, it came to pass at the dump on a Saturday afternoon, where Ruth was purging the farm of four Hefty bags bursting with busted and cast-off toys, puzzles with missing pieces, broken mixers, mateless socks, cracked baby bottles, curlers, combs with broken teeth, dried-up jars of wood glue, and all manner of household detritus.

Both Ruth and Leonard pretended not to see each other at the pay station, a charade that proved untenable once Leonard backed his red truck full of scrap wood right next to the station wagon. Their eyes crossed fleetingly before Leonard diverted his attention to the bed of his truck as he slipped into a pair of leather gloves. The thought that Leonard Haruto should feel shame for an unwanted transaction he was all but powerless to stop had troubled Ruth for a year. Bad enough to have injured her husband; she had also wronged Leonard by assaulting him in the greenhouse.

Side by side like strangers at the edge of the landfill, heaving their refuse into the abyss, Ruth could no longer endure the silence. She turned to Leonard Haruto and looked at him until she managed to hold his gaze.

"I owe you an apology," she said.

Sometimes all it took was an acknowledgment, for that simple apology helped Ruth close the door on Leonard Haruto, once and for all. It should have come as a relief. So why, on the drive home, did Ruth find her spirits flagging? Was it because her life began to feel like a series of closing doors, eschewing one possibility after another? Was it because she saw a future where fewer and fewer doors would open for her, a future where her appetites, and yearnings, and aspirations— romance, poetry, Paris—would one by one be left out in the cold? Or was it something else?

When Ruth arrived back at the farm in the afternoon, she hesitated on the front porch. She had yet to open the door, and already she could hear the kettle screeching, the TV blaring, and the baby wailing over the thrum of rock 'n' roll music from behind the closed door of Anne's bedroom. Ruth lingered a moment to gather resolve, a little prayer upon her lips:

Dear God, please give me the strength to get through this day.

III

It's That Time of Year

2023

Maddie was the first to show up for Christmas. She arrived unannounced a little after nine thirty P.M. the night before Christmas Eve and let herself in after a token knock. She found Abe alone in the living room, half-asleep in his recliner, something with Jeremy Irons playing on the old TV, the volume down low, Megs sprawled at the foot of the chair, her chest rising and falling with each breath. The old Lab lifted her head when Perry the Pomeranian charged into the living room and started yipping.

"Perry!" scolded Maddie.

To Abe's surprise, the dog fell silent, though he couldn't help sniffing around Megs's posterior, and Megs just plopped her head back down and paid the Pomeranian little notice beyond the occasional swipe of the tail, presumably aimed at discouraging her assailant.

Maddie dropped her duffel on the floor as Abe eased himself up from his chair to greet her, feeling every one of his ninety years. Her hair was still cropped short in front but was a little longer in back, a different shade of blue than it had been at his birthday party.

"Daddy," she said as they embraced. "How are you holding up?"

"Reasonably well," he lied.

The truth was he didn't know what to do with himself without Ruth around.

After the hug, Abe lowered himself back into his chair and, snatching up the remote, turned the TV off.

"I decided to just leave after work today," she said. "Boy, what a fiasco. There was a big pileup on 5 south of Portland. Then the usual construction through downtown, which I swear has been nonstop for fifteen years. You have anything to sip on around here?"

Before Abe could provide an answer, Maddie was in the kitchen, rummaging around the liquor cabinet. Abe knew without looking that it was slim pickings in there: some ancient vermouth, probably vinegar by now; a pint of Myers's dark rum half crystalized into brown sugar; some port from the first Bush administration; and a half-empty bottle of Pernod. Maddie returned to the living room with two snifters, dusty, no doubt, and the bottle of Pernod.

"How about it?" she said.

"What the hell," said Abe. "It's almost Christmas."

Abe hadn't had a drop of alcohol since his ninetieth, and he felt it almost immediately, that warm suffusion of well-being. The way the licorice-infused vapor expanded in his sinuses was a delicious sensation that offered immediate relief from his recent state of anxiety. It reminded Abe of the Martinique on Winslow Way, the very night Maddie was conceived.

"Geez, Dad," said Maddie. "You need to restock the liquor cabinet. I feel like I'm drinking cough syrup."

"I like it," he said.

"Must be an old-person thing," she said.

"You're not exactly young, you know?" Abe observed.

"Well, compared to you," she said, corkscrewing her face at the taste of the Pernod.

They fell silent for a moment, Maddie looking around the room.

"This place is like a family museum," she said.

"So, what's wrong with that?" said Abe.

"I mean, nothing, I guess," said Maddie. "But they make flat-screen TVs now, you know, for like the past thirty years. I can't believe that old thing even works with your cable."

"I've got an adapter," said Abe.

"It must weigh a hundred pounds," she said of the bulky old set.

"Good thing I don't have to lift it," said Abe.

Maddie continued her inventory of the living room. "Are those the same curtains from when I was a kid?"

"Maybe, how should I know? What's your point?"

"Nothing," said Maddie. "It's just that everything is the same around here."

"And that's a bad thing?"

"I didn't mean that," said Maddie. "It's just kind of . . . eerie, I guess. Like the Land Where Time Stood Still."

Why did their children never stop judging them? Everything had been fine until around age eleven or twelve: Abe and Ruth could do no wrong. Then the kids hit their teens, and it was one slander after another, and it never let up. Here they were in their fifties and sixties still disparaging their ways, telling Abe and Ruth to move on, to let go of those very things that constituted the fabric of their lives.

Maddie could see she'd hit a nerve.

"Dad, really, I didn't mean anything by it," she said. "It was just an observation. I like that the farm is timeless."

Couched in those terms, the idea was a little more palatable to Abe but still not a fair appraisal.

"I wouldn't say that, either," he said. "Plenty has changed around here. You know this house is nearly a hundred and forty years old, right? It was old when your mother and I bought it. That oak out front, in the middle of the roundabout, you planted it as a seedling when you were maybe two years old; you could barely walk. You used to waddle around in overalls, toting a bucket of water, blackberry jam on your face, your big diaper protruding in back. Every damn day, it was all we could do to stop you from pulling the dang seedling out of the ground or drowning it, you were so eager to watch it grow. By the time you turned five, it was taller than you. By the time you graduated high school, it was taller than the house. Look at it now."

They withdrew into silence once more, sustaining the thoughtful note Abe had struck. During this lull in the conversation, he considered his youngest child there on the sofa, her dyed blue hair gone gray at the roots, sipping her Pernod philosophically as she leveled the crosshairs of her recollection inward, the corners of her mouth drooping slightly at whatever she confronted there.

Was Maddie happy? Was she fulfilled, with more than half her life behind her, no children, no real prospects for a better life on the horizon? It was difficult to think so. Now Abe admonished himself for judging her.

"I always think of Karen this time of year," Maddie said at last, her enunciation beginning to soften at the edges, her voice a little huskier. "I hardly remember her. But I remember that first Christmas without her."

Abe remembered it, too, and all too well. Fifty years had done little to diminish the clarity of that dark period. The further it receded into the past, the more he forgot the days, and months, and years surrounding it, and the decades preceding it, like it was the one fixed point in an otherwise fluid sea of memory.

Maddie must have guessed at his state of mind.

"She was your favorite, wasn't she? You and Mom."

"You were my favorite," Abe said without pause. "Don't tell the others."

Of course, he would've said the same thing to Anne or Kyle. In some ways, it was true Maddie was his favorite, even if she hadn't quite lived up to what Abe viewed as her potential. He'd been more involved in the formative years of Maddie's upbringing than he had been with Anne, or Kyle, or Karen, which is to say, he was around more. Maddie was probably their most agreeable child temperamentally, all things considered. She gave them the least grief, the least drama, and the least trouble growing up. But it was also true that in many ways Karen had been Abe's favorite, because she was the most independent, the most steadfast in her pursuits. She earned good grades effortlessly, never complaining about homework, never requiring a parental prodding to address it, or any other responsibility that landed within her purview. Not that Karen wasn't a freethinker; she was very creative and very thoughtful. But she was also the most stable and reliable in her adherence to Abe's principles of hard work and responsibility, a bias Abe subscribed to long before her death turned their lives upside down, and one, in the end, he could never resolve with the final eighteen months of her life, an uncharacteristic period about which he would always harbor doubts and misgivings.

But now, half a lifetime on, it was Maddie who was Abe's biggest ally among the remaining children, Maddie whom he could count on to come to his defense if Anne or Kyle bullied him.

Perry the Pomeranian was by now asleep on Maddie's lap, just as Megs was deep in slumber on her old rug, her breathing pronounced and labored, her pink, nippled belly protruding, the nubs of her sagging black gums trembling with every exhalation.

"I remember when Megs was just a puppy," she said.

"It wasn't that long ago," said Abe.

"Seems like forever," said Maddie. "What's it been, twelve years since I brought her to you?"

"Something like that," said Abe, who found himself wanting to change the subject.

"Have you taken her to the vet lately?"

"Not lately," said Abe.

"She's getting old, Dad. Slowing down."

"I've noticed," he said.

"It won't be long before . . ."

"Yes, I'm well aware of that."

They may as well have been talking about Abe.

"How long has she been breathing like that?" said Maddie.

"Couple years," said Abe, but the truth was he'd noticed a difference in recent months, as her breathing became more labored and her movement more sluggish.

Maddie polished off her Pernod and set the empty snifter on the coffee table in front of her. "Well," she said. "I'm wiped, Dad. I'm gonna hit the sack."

"Good night, sweetie," he said as she retired upstairs to her childhood room.

Abe wasted no time in turning in, himself. It was late, nearly midnight, and the next few days were sure to be exhausting. He set his empty snifter next to Maddie's, retreated to the bedroom, stripped down to his drawers and his socks, and assumed his place under the covers, Ruth's absence resting heavily beside him.

*

Kyle and Soojin arrived around eleven A.M. the following morning, Christmas Eve, Kyle obscured by the five-foot Christmas tree he was carrying, a scraggly fir, none too full.

"There weren't many left," he said before anyone could comment on its scrawniness.

Anne and Tim arrived three hours later, their arms loaded with wrapped presents, though they'd all explicitly agreed against gifts in advance.

"Oh, Dad, where's your holiday spirit? It's fun. We don't expect anything, we just like to buy gifts! Does someone want to help Tim with the groceries? We loaded up at T&C."

Anne had not lied when she'd said she'd take care of everything. Tim and Kyle carted in no less than ten bags of groceries from the trunk of the rented sedan: fruits and vegetables, all manner of snacks, an eight-pound ham, a twelve-pound turkey, two half gallons of egg-nog, flatbread pizzas, deli salads, beer, wine, Irish whiskey. Knowing how pricey T&C was (not like the old days), Abe figured Anne must have spent four hundred bucks, at least.

"Let me pay for this," said Abe as she stocked the cupboards and fridge.

"Absolutely not," said Anne. "Kyle already chipped in."

Willful and inflexible as his eldest daughter could be, Abe could not fault Anne for her generosity, nor for her industry. Soon the whole house smelled of cooking. When she wasn't preparing for dinner, she was in the attic, where she dug out the old boxes of ornaments and the Christmas plates and set to work decorating the tree and setting the table.

Abe couldn't recall the last time the old farmhouse was so steeped in holiday cheer; it had to be twenty-five years. The mantel was soon adorned with a wreath and a poinsettia, flanked by Christmas cards from the Duncans and Jacobsons. But for all the effort, and the brave faces everybody donned for the occasion, the gaiety felt entirely cosmetic. Ruth's absence hung like a dark cloud over the festivities. Anne was an imposter in the kitchen. It should've been Ruth buzzing around the house, Ruth adorning the hearth, Ruth arranging presents under the tree, for this house, this farm, it was nothing if not Ruth's domain. Christmas be damned, Abe should've been at Swedish today, sitting bedside with Ruth. The thought of her alone in that sterile room, contemplating her future, her mortality, her disfigurement, was almost too much to bear. Despite Ruth's assurances, and her insistence that Abe was not to visit her daily, she needed him. She could not get through this alone. Abe should've insisted on being there for her regardless of her entreaties, just as he should have encouraged the kids and Bess Delory to pay her visits, despite her resistance. Because Ruth needed them, too. But instead of dictating the healthier course of action, the one that might have served to comfort and distract Ruth, grant her the assurance that she would not have to face it all alone, Abe had caved in to her wishes, which were the same as always: to cause as little inconvenience as possible for everybody else. Only now could he admit that in doing so, he'd taken the easy way out. And here he was, about to sit down to a family feast, while Ruth languished in solitude.

Though Abe aspired to joviality at the dinner table, he was unable to manufacture any. There was a little talk of grandkids: Ben had met somebody new, Martha was considering early retirement, great-granddaughter Lucy was already talking in sentences. Though he ought to have felt something, Abe ate joylessly and in silence, leaving the kids to talk among themselves. After the meal, they all retreated to the living room, an occurrence that seemed natural enough at first, until Abe suddenly felt like he was the center of attention. Indeed, they all seemed to be gathered around him, sitting forward in their respective seats, as if they were waiting for him to make an announcement.

"What?" he said.

Exchanging a glance with Anne, Kyle took the lead.

"Dad," he said. "The three of us have been talking."

"Okay," said Abe warily.

"We know you think Mom ought to come straight home from the hospital," said Anne.

"Well, of course, I think—"

Anne fashioned a yield gesture with both hands. "Just hear us out, Dad," she said.

"Just what the heck is this all about?" Abe said, appealing to Maddie, who couldn't look him in the eye.

"Dad, we've looked into it," said Kyle. "There's an aftercare facility out past the Poulsbo junction on the way to Silverdale. It's called Twin Pines."

"It sounds like a cemetery," said Abe.

"It's not," said Anne. "It's a facility that exists exactly for situations like this."

"Like what?" Abe said.

"Post-surgery recovery. It's not just old people, either," said Anne. "Mom will get round-the-clock care there, all the post-op medical attention she needs, the feeding and nutrition, the physical therapy."

"She can get physical therapy at the Winslow Clinic," Abe said. "I can feed her right here at home."

"At Twin Pines, they'll monitor Mom's progress in ways that you simply can't," Anne said.

"She's right," said Kyle. "They will."

"You keep saying 'will,'" Abe said, leveling his gaze like a challenge at Anne and Kyle, side by side on the sofa.

When neither of them said anything, Abe appealed silently to Maddie.

"I think they're right," said Maddie. "I don't agree with the radiation, but this isn't that. She needs to be monitored. What if her blood pressure goes haywire again? We just can't take that chance."

Abe felt a heat rise from the pit of his stomach to his tingling scalp, equal parts anger and embarrassment.

"So, that's what this is? Some sort of intervention?" he said.

"Dad, we just need you to understand where we're coming from," pleaded Anne.

Unbelievable. Who did they think they were that they could defy the wishes of their parents? Never mind they were old themselves, they were still, at least in Abe's mind, children. While he knew they had no legal power over him, he also suspected that it was useless to defy them, for he was but a feeble old man in their eyes, and as much as he resented them for it, they were not wrong to intercede. But he wasn't going to roll over.

"And what does your mother have to say about all this?" said Abe. "Does she get any input in the matter, or do you intend to strong-arm her like me?"

"We'll talk to Mom when we see her tomorrow," said Kyle.

"Trust me," said Anne. "She'll see the wisdom in it."

*

Phase two of Operation Twin Pines, consigning Ruth to an aftercare fate she had no say in, would come to a head at Swedish the next morning, Christmas Day, when Abe and all three children piled into Anne's rented sedan and ferried across Elliott Bay to the city, leaving the spouses at the farm to fend for themselves.

"Let me and Kyle do the talking," Anne said in the car. "We need your blessing on this, Dad. It's what's best for Mom. So, keep your opinions to yourself, please."

Abe neither consented to nor resisted this directive, gazing silently out the side window at a deserted downtown Seattle, almost unrecognizable, scarcely a soul or an automobile to be seen amidst the crisscrossing corridors of steel and glass. A mere ten minutes after they disembarked the *Walla Walla,* the four of them were crowded around Ruth in her hospital bed.

The feeding tube had finally been removed from her nose, and the bandages had come off. Nobody was shocked, so far as Abe could tell.

"I can't even tell the difference," said Maddie, God bless her.

"You're just saying that," said Ruth.

In the days since Abe's last in-person visit, Ruth's speech had improved markedly and was only slightly garbled. To Abe's eyes, the results of the facial reconstruction were not nearly as glaring as he'd anticipated. McGonagle had done an admirable job of reconstructing the jaw. From straight on, the difference was negligible. But for some lingering swelling of the soft tissue, the frontal aspect presented only a slight asymmetry. The eight-inch scar running from earlobe to chin along the underside of her new mandible was mostly hidden from view. Only from the side was the disfigurement significant, a prominent though not extreme concavity below her right ear, which amounted to a sunken cheek, owing largely to the loss of so many teeth. While considerable, the renovation was nothing to inspire nightmares in children, as Ruth had feared.

Knowing what was to come, Abe found the small talk excruciating: details about yesterday's ham, vagaries of air travel, news of the spouses.

"Just get on with it already," said Abe.

"What's got into you?" said Ruth.

"Tell her."

"Mom, we've all been talking," said Anne.

As always, Ruth listened patiently through the first half of Anne and Kyle's proposition, until she could no longer hold what was left of her tongue.

"I want to go home," she said, crossing her arms resolutely.

"But, Mom," said Kyle.

"I want to sleep in my own bed, next to my husband. I want to see my hens, and Megs. I want to watch my own TV."

"That's what I told them," said Abe, who was immediately reprimanded with an icy glare from Anne.

"We talked about this, Dad. It's what's best for Mom."

"Says you," Abe said.

"Says all of us," Anne said. "And the doctors will back us up on this."

"Let me worry about the doctors," said Abe. "I can drive her to appointments. I can give her medications; it doesn't take Marcus Welby, MD, to make her a smoothie."

"It's not that simple, Dad."

Ruth's pulse quickened as the debate raged on. The audacity of them to think they could decide her fate. She had birthed them and reared them, guided them not only through childhood and adolescence and adulthood but well into middle age, advising them, talking them down off ledges, sending them money and airline tickets. At what point did they presume the balance of power had shifted? Ruth may have been old, but she was in no way mentally feeble; she could outreason all three of them, if only she could summon the vitality. For, livid though she was, put-upon by the arrogance of her children, by the gravity of the situation, her uncertain future, the grim harbinger of their unwanted Christmas visit in the first place, all of them crammed into that suffocating little room, the painkillers coursing through her veins, the sum of all of it seemed to drain the sap out of her, and Ruth found herself all but powerless to advocate for her own wishes. Perhaps, too, it was that at least part of her knew her children were right, she did require constant care, and despite her insistence, she could barely get around with a walker, and when she managed with the aid of a nurse, the endeavor exhausted her within four steps. It was all too much to ask of Abe, though she knew he would do anything for her.

It was as though Abe could intimate these thoughts and was determined to fight this battle for her.

"That's it," he said. "I'm not hearing another word of any of this."

"Dad, we already—"

"You listen to me, young lady," Abe said to his sixty-eight-year-old daughter. "They can keep her here at the hospital as long as they see fit. And from what I understand, that's a few more days. After that, she comes home. Does everybody understand? I'm caring for her. Me, her husband, nobody else. If any of you would like to stay around and help me, okay, fine. But she's coming back to the farm. Isn't that right, Ruthie?"

Ruth was near the edge of sleep then, but she managed to smile, nodding once in approval.

Gonzo

Senior year, Anne began dating a boy named Royce Holiday, a second-year student at Seattle Central Community College, the older brother of her classmate Tracy Holiday, whom she'd known since seventh-grade choir. Royce Holiday was a cadaverously thin, hirsute youth of twenty, who wore a scraggly attempt at a beard and answered to the self-appointed moniker "Gonzo." So far as Ruth could surmise, Royce Holiday did not own a pair of shoes that were closed at the toe, nor a pair of pants that were not made of denim and riddled with holes. Despite his deficits in the arena of grooming, the boy was thoughtful and opinionated, qualities for which Ruth could hardly fault him.

Abe, however, disliked the boy immediately and comprehensively, a sentiment he shared with Ruth in bed the night of their first meeting, a dinner at the farm during which the boy had neglected to remove his floppy, wide-brimmed leather Minnetonka hat and continuously talked with his mouth full.

"Gonzo? You've got to be kidding me," he said. "It's a good name for a chimpanzee, maybe, but not my daughter's boyfriend."

"Oh, he's not so bad," said Ruth.

"Compared to who, Charles Manson? Did you hear him at dinner tonight? What was all that baloney about repression? His father owns a brokerage! He could be attending an Ivy League college if he had any gumption."

"He was talking about Bangladesh," said Ruth. "I think it's admirable he's advocating for human rights."

"Well, maybe he should concentrate on his own struggles—like trying to liberate that unruly mop of his with a hairbrush. Who knows what might be hiding in there?"

"Anne likes him," said Ruth.

"She also likes mayonnaise on bananas."

"The kids like him, too," said Ruth. "Did you see him with the baby? And the way Karen looks at him? And Kyle?"

"That scares me, too," said Abe. "This Gonzo's not exactly what I consider a great role model, Ruth."

"At least he's not a druggie."

"Not that we know about. He looks enough like one. What's he studying, anyway? Certainly not hygiene."

"Oh, Abe, give the poor kid a break," Ruth pleaded. "It's the style."

"He looks like a hobo," said Abe. "They all look like hobos."

"Look what these kids are up against. At least they're nonviolent, at least they're trying to make a difference."

"I'll tell you what really bothers me about this Gonzo character," said Abe. "For all that hair and the dirty clothes and whatnot, he's slick. Just like his old man the broker. He may not look it, but he is. I don't trust him, Ruthie. Mark my words, he's gonna hurt Annie one of these days."

Whatever Abe thought of him, it was true that the younger kids idolized Gonzo, who gifted Kyle his old baseball card collection and Karen her first stack of LPs, a selection that included Bob Dylan, Mercy, the Box Tops, and Creedence Clearwater Revival, all music Abe could not stand with its squalling guitars and self-important messaging. He liked Dylan least of all. Dylan, "the poet," with his nasal tones and warbling murmurations.

"What's wrong with Elvis Presley?" Abe asked rhetorically.

"As I recall, you didn't like him, either," said Ruth. "Perry Como was more your speed."

"At least the man could sing," said Abe. "Not like this Dylan character, who sounds like a jackass in heat."

Like just about everything else, Ruth and Abe didn't agree on Royce Holiday. Where Abe saw an incorrigible rebel with no cause, Ruth saw a boy from a good family who was just finding himself. Ruth appreciated that Royce allowed Karen and Kyle to tag along with Anne and him to the Lemon Tree, or Crazy Eric's in Poulsbo for hamburgers and milkshakes, or the bookstore, or the library, even when Anne protested the matter.

"Aw, c'mon, Annie," Gonzo would say. "They're cooped up on that farm all afternoon. They're kids, let 'em have a little fun. They won't bug us."

Whatever virtues Gonzo may have possessed, Abe blamed the influence of Royce Holiday more than Anne for the change that came over Karen sophomore year of high school. As far as Abe was concerned, Gonzo was polluting Anne's impressionable little sister with his warmed-over hippie posturing, his lazy opinions, and his half-baked ideologies. In wayfaring around the greater Puget Sound region in rags and that goofy hat, decrying the evils of the establishment, rejecting the customs and institutions that were the glue of this great nation, refusing to honor the timeworn social contracts that had made America the greatest country on Earth, Gonzo, it seemed to Abe, was inviting his daughter, both of his daughters, to drop out, to disengage from the promise of a prosperous future.

Karen's grades dipped, though not quite precipitously enough to draw disciplinary action from Abe, at least not at first. Even Ruth could see a slipping of standards with Karen, not only academically but socially, where she was no longer engaged with friends as frequently as she'd once been. Moreover, she'd become less communicative with Ruth in recent months, certainly not a unique phenomenon among teenagers but still a troubling development because it seemed out of character for Karen. Though hormones could account for some of it, Ruth worried it was more complex than that. Increasingly, her attempts at familiarity with Karen were greeted with monosyllabic responses or evasion. To tease intimacy out of Karen, once so forthcoming, became an exercise in finesse.

"Sweetie, why don't you ever go to Deb Carnes's house anymore?" Ruth inquired innocently, setting Karen's breakfast in front of her. "You haven't called Heather Bohannon in weeks. Did you three have some kind of falling-out?"

"No," said Karen. "Everyone's just busy with stuff."

"Well, that's too bad," observed Ruth. "You kids ought to leave some time for fun in your life."

The irony of the statement was not lost on Ruth, who'd spent the entirety of middle and high school with her face in a book, having never felt a need to surround herself with friends. But Karen had always been a social animal, and this sudden turnabout in her daughter's social life added to Ruth's anxiety that all was not well with Karen. When Ruth broached the subject with Abe, it was clear he didn't share her concern.

"She's fourteen, what do you expect?"

"Maybe she should talk to somebody," said Ruth.

"You want me to talk to her?" said Abe.

"That's not what I had in mind."

"She's fine, Ruthie, she's a teenager," he said. "But whatever you think is right."

As the weeks wore on, Karen continued to withdraw further into herself, and Ruth attempted to pursue the matter, most often at the breakfast table before the bus, the only interval her children seemed to have the time of day for her anymore.

"I heard from Bev Eckert there's a dance tomorrow night. Have you picked out what you're gonna wear?"

"I'm not going," she said.

"Not going? Sweetie, it's not like you to miss a dance. Is something wrong?"

"No," said Karen. "Quit asking me that. Who wants to go to some stupid dance? All they play is terrible music. And all the kids just stand around looking stupid."

"Did nobody ask you?" said Ruth. "Is that it?"

"Who cares if anybody asked me? Either way, it's dumb."

"What about Heather and Deb, are they going?"

"How should I know?" said Karen. "They don't even talk to me."

"What happened? Did you have some sort of rift?"

"Yeah, me," said Karen. "I'm the rift."

"What does that mean?" said Ruth.

"It means they think I'm weird," said Karen. "Everybody thinks I'm weird."

"Weird how?"

"How should I know? Just weird. The things I say, the way I act."

Oh, how Ruth remembered that feeling of not fitting in, of feeling like an outsider, of being considered weird. And how much more complex was the world now than it was when Ruth was a girl?

"Oh, they're just jealous," said Ruth.

"Of what?" said Karen.

"Your maturity," ventured Ruth.

"Yeah, right, Mom."

Determined to get to the bottom of the issue, Ruth made the fatal error of taking matters into her own hands, calling Heather Bohannon's mom, Grace, in an attempt to glean any insight she might have to offer. This conversation soon got back to Heather, Karen, and everybody else at Bainbridge High School.

"Thanks a lot, Mom!" she shouted, arriving home from school the following afternoon. "That really helped! God, what were you thinking?"

"Honey, I was just trying to—"

"Stay out of my life! God, I just wanna get out of here!" she said, storming off to her bedroom and slamming the door behind her.

How had they arrived here? Once their most reliable and least troublesome child, Karen, like Anne before her, began sequestering herself in her room with greater frequency, listening to the records that so offended Abe's sensibilities. In addition, her interest in extra-curricular activities had reached an all-time low; no more math club or drama, and especially no school dances. As she had with Anne, Ruth partially attributed these changes to hormones, although if she was being honest with herself, she secretly suspected that outside cultural forces, those forces that Bainbridge Island, for better or worse, had always seemed impervious to, were also at work on Karen. She had developed a taste for the larger world, an appetite that island life, for all its charms, could not seem to sate, a sentiment Ruth could relate to from her teenage exile in Shelton. This restlessness only got worse once Anne was out of the house and off to Bellingham with Royce Holiday, leaving Karen alone with her hopelessly uncool parents and her annoying little brother.

"It's so boring here without Gonzo and Anne," Karen complained. "There's nothing to do. I can't do anything cool anymore."

"Nonsense," said Ruth.

"Name one thing!"

"Bowling," said Ruth.

"I hate bowling."

"Why don't you join drama again?"

"It's so bogus," she said. "The plays they choose are totally stupid. *Our Town*? Gimme a break, Mom."

"Oh, I don't know, I rather liked *The Snow Queen*. I thought you were wonderful as Gerda."

"What a bore," she said. "Fairy tales."

"What about a job?" said Ruth. "You could always babysit."

"No way," she said. "I'm not changing diapers or playing Chutes and Ladders all night for a lousy three bucks. I want to hang out in town, actually do things."

"Well, what's to stop you?" said Ruth. "You can always walk to Winslow after school."

"I mean Seattle."

"Well, we can certainly go to Seattle one of these weekends,"

Ruth said. "It'd be fun. Maybe we'll go to the zoo. Or the arboretum. Dad and I could show you the UW campus."

"I don't mean with you guys. I mean by myself. I feel like a prisoner on this island."

"You'll have to ask your father about going to Seattle."

"He'll just say no, like he does to everything."

"That's not true."

"Oh, isn't it? The Zeppelin concert, the Laserium, even the dumb skating rink—all big fat nos."

"He's only looking out for your well-being," said Ruth. "It's his responsibility as your father."

But Karen obviously wasn't buying it. Her relationship with Abe grew increasingly contentious as the months wore on. The more Karen railed against his authority, the harder Abe pushed back.

"Absolutely not," he said about Karen going to Seattle. "Senior year, maybe. And only if you get your grades back up."

But Karen did not get her grades up. The second semester of sophomore year, they fell from Bs to Cs. No matter that she was grounded for this offense; she just wanted to stay in her room anyway. When Abe took her record player away, it did not provide the incentive he'd hoped for. Her grades continued to slide.

"This all started with Anne and that damn Royce Holiday," Abe complained to Ruth.

"Careful, Abe, he may just end up being your son-in-law."

"Over my dead body," said Abe. "He's the one that's filled our daughters' noggins with all his warmed-over hippie malarky. Dropping out? That's their answer to everything? That's how they're gonna solve the world's problems? By ignoring them? Just keep on truckin', huh?"

Karen seemed intent on putting Abe in an early grave with her defiance, and her aloofness, and her shoddy academic performance. And no measure of discipline seemed to improve matters. When, after a late evening at the office, Abe happened to catch Karen disembarking the five thirty boat from Seattle with Tracy Holiday and the Dolinger boy, he grounded her for two weeks. When, on the third night of her sentence, she snuck out her bedroom window and didn't return until two A.M., Abe grounded her for an additional month and stripped her of her phone privileges. None of it persuaded Karen to change her ways. Winter semester she received a D in biology, a new academic low. She continued her unauthorized forays into the city, arriving home smelling of cigarettes and retreating straight to her room with hardly a word. Such was her defiance, at barely fifteen years old, that it seemed they could not govern the child at all.

At his wit's end, Abe all but relinquished his parental authority over Karen, opting instead for the path of least resistance. While Anne may have been a handful those last years of high school, Karen proved a burden too heavy to bear. Though Abe was not proud of the fact, it had been a relief to cede his authority. There was no getting through to her. Let her have her damn record player back. Let her hang out with riffraff. Let her learn the hard way.

Twelve-year-old Kyle, meanwhile, short of eating them out of house and home, presented few challenges. He adhered to the rules, pulled As and Bs at Commodore Middle School without much fuss, performed his chores around the farm, turned his bedroom lights out at nine P.M., limited his TV consumption to three hours per day, and rarely defied a parental directive. Still, it seemed they were losing Kyle, too. He no longer entertained his former enthusiasm where family activities were concerned—game nights, movie nights, evening walks, those customs that had made them feel like a family unit. Like his sisters before him, he longed for sovereignty and independence.

It didn't seem fair, being a parent. You worked, you planned, you executed. You provided for them, sacrificed for them, worried for them, guided them, and comforted them, and what did you get in return? Where was the appreciation? What happened to solidarity, to loyalty, to valuing family above all else? After ten years old they wanted very little to do with you, it seemed. You were their taxi driver at best. At fifteen, you were the archenemy. They didn't even want your rides anymore; they accepted your money as though they were doing you a favor, sought your blessings begrudgingly. And once they were out of the nest, you were lucky to get a phone call or any kind of acknowledgment at all for your years of effort.

Had they spoiled their children, was that the problem? Had they not instilled in Anne and Karen and Kyle the proper sense of gratitude or respect? Had Abe and Ruth painted themselves into this corner by inviting their children to take their endless support and service for granted? Abe could only imagine how Ruth must have felt at such a thankless return on her investment. For Ruth had done 85 percent of the parenting. Ruth was the one who had sacrificed her autonomy, her dreams, her mornings and afternoons and evenings. Ruth had given the prime of her life to those children. How many novels and books of poetry had gathered dust on her nightstand because she could never quite find a moment to herself? How much self-care had she deferred to bestow that attention on Anne, or Karen, or Kyle?

Thank goodness for little Maddie, the one child who still appreciated and wanted to be around her parents, the only one who did not judge or defy them. Maddie still wanted to follow her mother around the farm, gathering eggs, harvesting vegetables, still wanted to help unload the dishwasher and fold the laundry, to stroll the aisles of Town & Country or Winslow Hardware with Mommy. And Maddie still adored Abe, though he was usually home late from the office and often absent on the weekend. Maddie did not begrudge these truancies, rather treated Daddy's presence as a novelty, begging him to play Candy Land, or admire her most recent indecipherable Crayola masterpiece—a tree that looked like a mushroom cloud, a flower as tall as a house, a fox shaped like a coffee table with ears.

Despite Abe's fatigue, when called upon, he never failed to oblige these requests, because he now knew from experience that these precious occasions were numbered. The day would come, and all too soon, when he'd no longer be viewed as a coveted playmate, or someone whose approval was to be greedily sought, but an adversary, an obstacle.

A Softer Landing

1973

In the months since Anne began attending Western Washington University, Abe and Ruth had received no more than a half dozen phone calls from Bellingham, vague briefs and assurances regarding her opaque life up north, invariably accompanied by a request for financial relief. Never mind that she and Gonzo had been to Seattle for no less than four concerts in the interim, a mere ferry ride away, and had not bothered to call upon them, or even offer them the opportunity to hop a ferry themselves so that they might treat them to dinner or write them a check.

Abe blamed Gonzo, of course, Gonzo, the freeloader (though his parents were wealthy); Gonzo, who had failed to accrue the necessary credits at SCC to transfer to WWU but followed Anne up to Bellingham anyway, where, despite Anne's lame assertions, he used her as a meal ticket and a benefactor; Gonzo, who protested inequity ceaselessly, preached a new world order, but practiced only sloth. Abe had given up hope that Anne would outgrow Gonzo. He was certain that the useless malingerer would hurt his daughter, and only then would they see the end of him.

When Anne finally did come from Bellingham for break, it was no surprise when Gonzo accompanied her. Rather than gracing his own parents with his ineffectual presence, he stayed on the farm with Anne, all too comfortable lounging on the sofa, kicking his feet up on the coffee table, eating for three days at the Winter table, and never lifting a finger around the farm. Abe hardly engaged the boy, who made little effort to ingratiate himself or even avoid Abe's notice, as if lazing about the house and grazing upon the fruits of Abe's labor were his birthright.

Worse than the boy's imposition on their hospitality, or the impunity with which he helped himself to whatever he pleased, was the way Gonzo managed to methodically vanquish fifteen-year-old Karen's once-good judgment (as he had with Anne before her), right in front of Abe's ears. They all but worshipped him, waiting breathlessly on his every word as though it were gospel. What was all Gonzo's self-important dogma but machismo dressed up in long hair and counterfeit sensitivity? None of it even the least bit creative or original or even timely, merely the warmed-over counterculture gruel of 1967, an ethos rooted in disengagement and political contrarianism, antiauthority, antiestablishment, a total disregard for the social contracts and sensible order that previous generations had constructed on their behalf so that they need not know the poverty and struggle of their forebears. Why did Abe permit the wayward son of a wealthy stockbroker, an unmitigated self-made failure, an ideological clown, to hypnotize his daughters?

Only once during their stay did Abe manage to procure an audience alone with Anne, and it was only by accident. In the kitchen at seven A.M., Abe was sipping his coffee and reading the *Sun*. Ruth, having cleared his plate, was already out planting bulbs. The rest of the household was still sleeping—especially Gonzo, who never arose before eleven—when Anne crept into the kitchen, surprised to find Abe there.

"Oh, Dad, hey."

Abe knew he should have attempted a softer landing, offered at least some morning pleasantry or novel commentary on the weather, anything. But he was brimming with intent. Abe made little effort to modulate his volume.

"He's not worthy of you, damn it."

"Good morning to you, too," she said, pouring herself a cup of black coffee.

"I mean it, Anne. You're wasting your time with this rascal. He has no prospects, he's a walking cliché, he's not even good-looking so far as I can tell under all that hair."

"Says you."

"I don't want him filling Karen's head with all that baloney."

"Karen's no dummy, Dad. She knows the score."

"And what might the score be?" said Abe.

Anne sat down at the table as Abe lowered his newspaper. "Do we have to fight, Daddy?"

"I'm sorry, sweetie, but I don't like to see my daughter wasting her life with a man—no, no, he's not even a man, he's a boy—who is so obviously beneath her in every way."

"You sound so bourgeois, Daddy. Royce is great. He's thoughtful, and he's caring, and he's good to me."

"I don't see it," said Abe.

"Maybe you just don't recognize it," Anne said.

But Abe knew what he saw, and that was a charlatan with a guitar and a dirty leather hat, though he was powerless to convince his daughters as much.

By the fifth day of their stay, Abe was more than ready to bid Anne goodbye in the morning. As much as he loved his eldest daughter, as much as he wanted to save her from her lapse in judgment, he could not endure her bad decisions and was tired of feeding her boyfriend. Upon the final night of Anne's stay, unable to sleep, Abe found himself in the kitchen after midnight, rummaging through the refrigerator, when he heard voices on the back porch. Anne and Royce, he assumed, probably out there smoking reefer, though he could not smell it. If that was the case, if Abe could catch them in the act, he would finally have the definitive reason he so yearned for to throw Royce Holiday out on his ear. He was almost hoping he'd catch them smoking a joint. But when Abe proceeded to the porch for an inspection, he found Anne and Gonzo locked in an embrace, necking arduously on the porch swing.

Abe cleared his throat with aplomb.

When they broke off their embrace suddenly, and Anne spun around to face her father, Abe found that it was not Anne at all. It was Karen. Stunned by this realization, it took him a moment to find his voice, and when he did it was taut with rage and confusion.

"Go to your room this instant," he commanded Karen.

Karen complied, swiftly and without protest.

Royce Holiday was still caught like a deer in the headlights as Karen darted through the screen door and up the stairs. It was the first time Abe had seen Royce Holiday without his dirty leather hat, which had tumbled to the ground by his feet at some point during their canoodling. Only now could Abe see that the boy was prematurely balding.

"You think you're a pretty smooth operator, don't you, Mr. Holiday?"

For once, Royce Holiday had no answer.

"You think you've got everything figured out, eh, Gonzo?"

Here, Abe nearly succumbed to the urge to pull him out of his seat by the shirt collar and commence whaling on him, but somehow, he managed to control his fury, perhaps because he feared he might beat the life out of Royce Holiday. Rarely had such a violent impulse possessed Abe.

"What's your father gonna think when he finds out you violated a fifteen-year-old girl, huh, wise guy?"

"But I didn't—we just—it wasn't—"

"What's your girlfriend going to think when she finds out you made a pass at her kid sister?"

"I didn't make a pass at her. She was the one—"

"Shut your mouth and listen, Royce," said Abe. "One more word and I'll knock your front teeth out."

Indeed, Abe's fist was clenched.

Even in his shock and dismay, Royce Holiday could not belie a hint of smugness, a defiant glint in the eye that seemed to dare Abe to unleash his violence and watch his father sue him for everything he had.

A second wave of violence welled up inside Abe. It took all the restraint he could summon not to slap the hubris right out of Royce Holiday.

"This is what's going to happen," said Abe. "You're going to get up out of your seat and you're going to leave this house immediately. No explanations, no goodbyes. You're going to walk up that driveway, and I don't ever want to see you again, do you understand? You will not speak to Anne or Karen from this moment forward. You will not see them. You will not so much as write them a postcard. If I find out you do, there will be consequences, young man."

"But she's the one who threw herself at me," said Gonzo.

Royce Holiday didn't see the blow coming and neither did Abe, a hard slap across the face that spun Gonzo around in the swing and brought him to one knee on the porch. Before Abe could visit further violence on the boy, Royce covered up with both arms, scurrying down the steps and up the driveway at a sprint, floppy hat in hand.

Abe marched upstairs and woke Anne out of bed, sparing her no details regarding recent events.

"Where is he now?" said Anne. "Is he hurt?"

That she could still express concern for him after what Abe had just told her angered Abe anew. He did not raise a fool.

"Just what the hell is wrong with you?" he demanded.

"I love him," said Anne.

"Not anymore you don't!"

"I'm an adult, Dad! You no longer get to decide who I—"

"What's all the commotion?"

It was Ruth, standing in the doorway now, and behind her, skulking in the shadows, Karen.

"Our Mr. Gonzo was on the porch taking advantage of your daughter," explained Abe. "And I don't mean Anne. The other one."

Ruth turned to Karen in disbelief. "Is this true?"

Karen replied with a telling silence.

"Where is he now?" said Ruth.

"Halfway to Fletcher Bay is my guess," said Abe. "With a very sore face."

"You didn't hurt him?" said Ruth.

"I'm sorry, Anne!" blurted Karen. "It just sort of . . . happened."

"It's not your fault," said Anne.

"Who's to say it's not her fault?" Abe said. "According to Royce, she started it."

"It's Royce," said Anne. "Every time."

"You mean it's not the first time?" said Ruth.

"Unbelievable," said Abe.

"Relax, it's harmless," said Anne. "It doesn't mean anything to him."

"Of course it doesn't!" shouted Abe.

If she really loved him as she claimed, and Abe had every reason to doubt it, how could she forgive him so easily, when it had taken Abe months to forgive Ruth after Leonard Haruto?

Anne left for Bellingham in the morning without saying goodbye. Abe and Ruth awoke just in time to see her pulling away in the '67 Rambler they'd sent her off to college in, a cloud of dust in her wake as she disappeared up the driveway.

When Karen came downstairs for breakfast, long after her sister had taken leave, Abe greeted her with stony silence. He could barely look at her as they ate, Karen mostly pushing food around on her plate.

"How could you?" Abe finally said with a forkful of eggs. "Have you no shame at all? Your sister's boyfriend?"

"You don't understand," said Karen.

"Oh," said Abe, dropping his fork. "Don't I? Just what in the hell is it that I don't understand? Even if the boy threw himself at you— and he claims it was the other way around—is that any excuse to oblige him? You might have pushed him away or offered any kind of resistance. But that's not what you did, is it? Instead, you brought shame on yourself and your sister, on me and your mother. So, what am I failing to comprehend?"

Even as Abe berated Karen, he was admonishing Ruth, too, for the impropriety he'd sworn he'd already forgiven.

"I didn't raise a tramp," said Abe, regretting it immediately.

Karen pushed off from the table, upending her chair, and stormed out of the kitchen and through the back door into a steady drizzle. Ruth pushed her own plate away and removed herself from the kitchen without a word, leaving Abe seated alone at the breakfast table, flummoxed. How was he the bad guy? He couldn't possibly be expected to condone such conduct, could he? Let alone under his own roof! It was a slap in the face for all Abe's hard work and sacrifice, everything he'd tried to impart to his children about personal responsibility, and loyalty, and common decency. But the more he stewed at the breakfast table and rationalized his own vexation, the more the shame crept in. He'd been too hard on her. She was just a teenager, she was impressionable. Obviously, the Holiday boy was the real culprit. He had no business raising his voice at her like that or calling her a tramp.

It was four in the afternoon when Principal Roe called to inform Ruth of Karen's absence from school. She'd been scheduled to deliver a speech fourth period but never returned from lunch. Ruth called Abe at the office, but neither of them felt any reason to panic. Karen had continued to demonstrate a flair for "acting out," whether that meant phone calls from the principal or cigarette butts in the garden beds. She routinely snuck out at night without any real consequences. It was easy to imagine Karen skipping out on a speech or a test. After all, Gonzo had already convinced his daughters that academic achievement was a dead-end street, that conformity to the rules in any guise was an offense against the new world order, that adults were phony, all the Holden Caulfield crap he'd repurposed to his own selfish ends. So her absence on a Wednesday was hardly grounds for panic. She was probably in Seattle, smoking cigarettes.

But when Karen didn't return to the farm by dinner, Ruth began calling her friends' houses to make inquiries; Tara Hewson, Lynn Gary, the Munger girl, Kristen or Kirsten. Nobody had seen Karen after third period.

Once eleven o'clock rolled around, Ruth and Abe were indignant. If she'd missed the late ferry or had decided to sleep at a friend's house (God forbid, not another grown man), the least she could do was call. They'd been so lenient as it was, so forgiving with their ever-moving boundaries, so understanding and accommodating of Karen's irascible and unpredictable behavior of late, for the child to disregard their authority altogether came as a slap in the face.

But by one A.M. that indignation had turned to concern.

"Should we call the sheriff?" said Ruth, beside him in bed.

"Don't you think she's at a friend's house?"

"What if she's not? What if she's stuck in the city?"

"Okay, maybe we should call," said Abe.

Three days. Three agonizing days with the Kitsap County Sheriff's Office on alert; calls to friends' houses made time and again; students pulled from classes and questioned; ferry workers and business owners canvassed; Xeroxed flyers posted on reader boards and telephone poles, as though Karen were a missing pet; endless speculations chased down blind alleys; and no answers, nothing. For all anyone knew, Karen had vanished.

Adrift

It was disingenuous to blame Gonzo for Karen's inexplicable flight. Nor could Ruth fault Karen for the ignorance of youth, any more than she could blame the influence of Karen's older sister. So, who was at fault? How had Karen, her little helper, her effervescent thespian, she of the good grades and the agreeable personality, strayed so far, so fast? Somehow, someone had failed Karen, and Ruth was at a loss as to how to account for this. Sure, Karen had done her share of misanthropic teenage brooding, a rite of passage she and Abe had already endured with Anne, the stuff of Central Casting, really. But where were the signs of something more troubling?

On the fourth day, Karen finally phoned home. Ruth answered the call after the first ring.

"Oh, thank God," she said upon hearing her daughter's voice. "Where on earth are you?"

"Spokane," she said.

"Spokane? Sweetheart, what are you doing in Spokane? Where in Spokane?"

"I'm at a diner," she said.

"Stay where you are, we're coming to get you," said Ruth.

"No," said Karen. "Look, I didn't call to talk, Mom. I only called to let you know I was okay."

"Karen, what's wrong? Why did you run off?"

"It's a long story, Mom."

"Well, I'm ready to hear it," said Ruth, her concern edging toward anger.

"I don't want to talk about it," Karen said.

"Listen here, missy. You owe your mother an explanation, whether you feel like talking or not."

Ruth knew this tack came with a risk, but how else could she demand accountability? Still, she softened her manner immediately for fear of losing her. "Are you in trouble, sweetie? What is it?"

"It's nothing."

"Karen, come back to the island, whatever it is, we'll work through it."

"I'm not coming back to the stupid rock," she said. "I hate it there."

"How could you hate it? It's your home. It's been nothing but good to you. It's not like you've had it hard, Karen. What's gotten into you?"

"I don't want to get into all of this, okay? I'm fine, I'm safe, I just wanted you to know. I'm sorry I didn't call earlier."

"Do you have any idea what you've put your father and me through?"

"I said I was sorry."

"Karen, we've been worried sick, we thought you were dead."

"Well, I'm not. Look, I've gotta go, Mom. Somebody's waiting for the phone. I'll call you in a few days. You can guilt-trip me then."

"Don't you dare hang up that—"

But Karen hung up. Paralyzed, Ruth continued to clutch the humming receiver long afterward.

It was a week before they heard from Karen again. As before, it was Ruth who answered the phone before it had time to ring twice.

"Boise?" she said upon learning of her daughter's whereabouts. "Idaho? What are you doing in Idaho? Who are you with?"

"I'm with a friend," she said. "I'm fine. I'm just letting you know—"

"What friend?" said Ruth. "Whose idea was this?"

"Look, Mom, I'm okay. That's all you need to know."

"As a matter of fact, I'm gonna need to know a lot more than that, young lady. You are not an adult."

"Close enough," she said.

"Is that so?" said Ruth. "Well, you're sure not acting like one."

"I don't wanna fight, Mom. I gotta go."

"No, please, don't hang up," pleaded Ruth, willing to concede. "Do you have a place to stay? Do you need money?"

"No, I'm fine," said Karen.

"How can you be fine?" said Ruth. "What are you doing for money?"

Ruth could hear somebody talking in the background, though the voice was obscured, the words muffled as though Karen had cupped her hand over the mouthpiece. But it was a male voice, Ruth was quite sure.

"Who is that?" said Ruth. "Who's with you? Is that Royce?"

"I gotta go, Mom," said Karen.

"Karen, honey, just let us—"

But before Ruth could persuade her, the line was humming a dial tone.

She was with the Holiday boy; it had to be him. The realization came as a relief. For all his faults, at least Ruth was acquainted with the boy, knew where he came from, and knew where to find his parents. Better that Karen was with Royce Holiday than all alone out there.

Ruth called Anne in Bellingham, pressing her for some word on Gonzo or his whereabouts.

"I told you, Mom. I haven't seen him since Dad chased him off. Not even a phone call. Yeah, thanks, Dad."

"Do you think it's possible he ran off with your sister?"

"I mean, anything is possible with Gonzo, but I seriously doubt it."

192 * Jonathan Evison

"Why?"

"She's just a kid, Mom."

"Well, he wasn't treating her like a kid on the porch that night."

"Whatever Dad saw that night was nothing, trust me, Mom. Geez, he was probably just teaching her how to kiss or something. Or maybe he was just stoned and kissing my kid sister seemed like a good idea at the time. Maybe Karen really did throw herself at him, who knows? He'll try anything once. Gonzo does whatever Gonzo wants. He can pretty much be with whoever he wants, so why would he run off with Karen?"

Ruth offered only silence in lieu of a reply. Once the silence lingered for five or six seconds, Anne caught her meaning.

"Oh, c'mon, Mom, really?" said Anne. "You can't possibly think that Gonzo is actually like . . . ?"

"Well, I . . ."

Anne sounded as though she could hardly suppress her laughter.

"Trust me, Mom. He's not in love with a fifteen-year-old. But it's possible he went on one of his walkabouts. Last fall, he took off to Mendocino, but he likes to do that stuff solo. I mean, I suppose Karen might have tagged along. But I really can't see it."

"What about Idaho?" said Ruth.

"What's in Idaho?" Anne said.

"That's what I'd like to know. Did Royce ever say anything about Boise?"

"Why would he?" said Anne. "Isn't it like the potato capital of the world or something? Look, Mom, believe it or not, Karen is gonna be fine. She can take care of herself."

"You just said yourself she was a kid."

"She's been around enough," said Anne.

But despite Anne's assurances that Karen could take care of herself, there was no getting past Ruth's motherly intuition that all was not well.

Ruth found Dick and Barbara Holiday listed in the phone book.

"We haven't seen or heard from Royce since Christmas," Barbara Holiday explained. "His father wasn't happy when he dropped out of SCC. They had a bit of a row about it, but he left on good terms."

"Has he ever expressed any interest in Idaho? Does he have friends or relatives there?"

"Idaho? Heck no. Why do you ask?"

But a brief silence was enough for Barbara to comprehend the implication.

"Surely you don't think my son has run away with your fifteen-year-old daughter?" said Barbara Holiday, incredulous. "That seems very unlikely to me. Outrageous, in fact."

Ruth resisted the urge to tell Barbara about that night on the porch. Such an imputation was likely to put the Holidays even more on the defensive, when she and Abe needed every ally they could find.

Abe alerted authorities in Boise, a step that did little to inspire optimism and yielded even less in the way of results. For over a week, Ruth waited by the phone, each day less rested, her nerves frayed ragged. The speculation was maddening. Was Karen with Royce, or was she with somebody else? And if so, who? Why Boise? Why not San Francisco or Los Angeles or Portland?

As it turned out, Boise was never a destination. Two weeks later Karen finally called again, this time from Helena, Montana. She sounded more unlike herself than ever, edgy, impatient, as though each mile she trekked east, each new town, each cryptic phone call, signified a further degree of separation, an estrangement beyond physical distance. Still, Ruth was desperate to bridge that distance.

"Honey, there's something you're not telling us, what is it?" said Ruth. "Who are you with? Who is this friend? Is this somebody I know? Is it the Holiday boy?"

"No," she said.

"Are you in trouble?" said Ruth. "You're not . . ."

"No!" said Karen, as though it was an insult to even suggest such a thing.

"Karen, honey, there's no trouble we can't handle together. Please, let us come get you."

"No," she said.

Forced to employ the heavy artillery, Ruth foisted the receiver on Abe.

"Here, your father wants to speak to you," she said.

Abe seemed in no way prepared to confront his daughter.

"Karen, this is your father."

"Yeah, I sort of figured that out."

"You are to come home, and that's an order. This nonsense has gone on long enough, your mother is on the verge of a nervous breakdown," he said.

"And I suppose that's my fault?"

"As a matter of fact, it is," said Abe.

"This is your strategy to get me to come home, blame me?"

Sensing he was about to lose her, Abe eased up on the gas. "Look," he said. "I'm sorry, whatever we did, we apologize. We'll make it right, whatever it takes, we'll make it happen. They've got counselors for this kind of thing. I'm going to wire you money tomorrow morning, I'll find a Western Union. Just give me your word that—"

But Abe's entreaty met with an abrupt dial tone.

Once again, he alerted the local authorities, this time the Helena sheriff's department, to whom he provided yet another description: long, straight brown hair; brown eyes; fair skinned; about five foot four. She was dressed in jeans and a red knit sweater last they saw her. But who really knew what Karen looked like three weeks and two states later? She might have shaved her head for all they knew.

Abe sighed heavily as he replaced the handset.

"Well, so much for that," he said. "She's bound to run out of money soon."

"That's it?" said Ruth. "That's all you're going to do?"

"What am I supposed to do?" said Abe.

"I don't know," said Ruth. "Go after her?"

"What, just drive to Montana, when we don't even know where she is?"

"She's in Helena," said Ruth.

"And I'm supposed to find her? She could be anywhere, it's a city, Ruthie."

"It's a town."

"And it's six hundred miles away! She could be long gone by the time I get there. And to where? Anywhere."

"I'll go myself, then," said Ruth.

"Don't be ridiculous," he said.

"Then do something!"

The following afternoon, Abe met with a private investigator in Seattle named Byrd, who kept an office above a bathhouse in Pioneer Square. Byrd, squat as a cedar stump and neatly bearded, bore a striking resemblance to KIRO 7's sports anchor, Wayne Cody. Whether owing to his tiny, unventilated workplace smelling of bromide and stale cigarettes, or the mustard stain on the front of his linen guayabera, Byrd didn't exactly inspire Abe's confidence.

"So, any problems at home?"

"No," said Abe.

"How's your relationship with the girl?"

"Fine, normal, what are you insinuating? Are you a detective or a family therapist?" said Abe.

"Just trying to get a read on the situation, Mr. Winter."

"Well, the situation is my daughter ran off, possibly with a fellow named Royce Holiday."

Byrd jotted down a note on a sheet of yellow paper already riddled with miscellany, phone numbers scribbled hastily, doodles in the margin. "Family acquaintance, this Holiday?"

"Of a sort, yes."

"What sort?"

"My daughter's boyfriend."

"Okay, so, she may have run off with her boyfriend," said Byrd.

"He was dating my other daughter, actually."

Byrd arched an eyebrow and scribbled a note. "Holiday, he's a minor, too?"

"No. He's twenty, I think. Maybe twenty-one."

"Do you recall your last conversation with Karen?"

Abe grew increasingly uncomfortable as Byrd piled on the questions, as though the man were cross-examining him and believed Abe was somehow culpable. By the time Abe left Byrd's office and began ambling back to Colman Dock in the rain, his irritability had achieved such a pitch that his heart was racing. Byrd had a lot of nerve insinuating that he had anything to do with Karen's disappearance. He had half a mind to wring Karen's neck when they finally got her back. How could she do this to them?

It was eight days before they heard back from Byrd.

"I tracked down the Holiday kid," he told Abe. "He's living in a garage in Alderwood with an uncle. Says he hasn't seen Karen in weeks, since the night you threatened him, says he hasn't left the area. His story checks out with the uncle, who'd just as soon be rid of the kid, as far as I can tell. I poked around in Helena—hospitals, YWCA, the high school; you never know, maybe she's got a friend there. Distributed over a hundred flyers. Now we wait. In the meantime, if you want, I can go ahead and—"

"Never mind," said Abe. "We'll handle it from here."

Ruth didn't take the news well.

"What do you mean, you called him off?" she demanded.

"We've got flyers all over Helena. There's nothing to do but wait, hope somebody recognizes her, or maybe she sees herself on a telephone pole and realizes what the hell she's putting us through."

"What's the matter with you?" said Ruth. "How can you be so callous? This is your daughter we're talking about. Is this about the money, is that why you called this Byrd off?"

"Of course it's not about the money. I'm just being realistic. What else can we do? I'm telling you, whatever is going on with her, she'll get past it, Ruth. I promise, she'll come home eventually."

"And if she doesn't? What if she's been abducted or . . . ?"

"Trust me," said Abe. "She'll be back."

How could he be so sure Karen was in no danger? Where was the evidence? And what could it possibly hurt to have somebody out there searching for their daughter?

Karen finally called again, nine days later. This time it was Abe who fielded the call. Karen was thirty miles outside of Reno.

"You listen here, young lady," said Abe.

But before he could berate her, Ruth wrested the phone from him with a withering glare.

"Sweetie, please, let us come get you," she pleaded. "Whatever is going on, whatever may have happened, we can deal with it. Just tell us where you are and—"

"Stop," said Karen. "You're wasting your energy."

"Why are you doing this to us?" said Ruth.

"I'm not doing anything to you," said Karen. "Quit saying that. What I do with my life is not about you."

It seemed as though Karen were holding them hostage, punishing them for some reason Ruth could not comprehend.

The next morning, Abe hired another private investigator, a fellow from Reno named Campion, a referral from Byrd. Campion spent two weeks beating the streets of Reno, one dead end to the next. Truck stops, motels, hostels, questioning the girls on Virginia Street. It was incomprehensible to Ruth that they'd broached the prospect of their daughter working the streets of Reno at sixteen, and it was a possibility Abe refused to entertain altogether.

"Ridiculous," he said.

"Then where is she getting the money to live?"

"Who knows? Friends. She'll run out of options eventually, and when she does, she'll come home."

Though Abe continued to insist as much for Ruth's peace of

mind, his own confidence had already begun to waver. He called Campion from the office every morning hoping for news, and invariably he'd turned up nothing. By the third week, Campion's investigation was running on fumes.

"We haven't got a single hit on the flyers. If she was ever here, there's a good chance she's gone by now."

That served as Campion's three-thousand-two-hundred-and-eighty-dollar explanation.

"I can keep looking, asking around," he said. "But without any leads . . ."

Once again, the search was suspended. As the weeks of not knowing wore on, running into months, Karen's absence began to tell on Ruth and Abe's marriage. It seemed to Ruth that Abe ought to bear at least some of the responsibility for Karen's running away. After all, it was Abe who'd admonished her so sternly that morning she stormed out of the kitchen into the rain. And wasn't it Abe who had been the one denying Karen all along, prohibiting the rock concerts and the trips to the city with her friends? By forbidding these freedoms, by grounding her on those occasions when she did not comply, by depriving her of telephone privileges, he had as much as imprisoned her, cut her off from her friends, from the outside world she'd so longed to explore. Moreover, Abe had given Karen something to defy, to rebel against. When denying her failed to do the trick, when his authority had been found wanting, it seemed to Ruth that Abe had just given up and stopped parenting Karen altogether. That is, until the night he caught her necking with Royce Holiday and blew his top. God knows, he shouldn't have shamed her at the breakfast table the following morning. If he'd handled the situation with a little finesse, she might have never run off.

As far as Abe was concerned, Ruth's lax parenting was what was at least partially responsible for their wayward daughter. Maybe if Ruth had been more of a mother to Karen, instead of trying to be her friend. Instead, she indulged Karen, acquiesced at every turn, never held her accountable, always leaving it to Abe to be the heavy, so much so that it damaged his relationship with Karen. Ruth should have listened to him. Hadn't he been right about Royce Holiday from the beginning? It was Royce Holiday's influence, his lazy worldview, his defiance of authority in any guise, his denial of timeworn customs, that had started Anne and Karen down the wrong path. And what did Ruth do except stick up for Royce Holiday at every turn?

"Me?" said Ruth, incredulous in the kitchen after dinner, four months after Karen's disappearance. "You're the one who drove her off with your iron fist! All her friends went to see this Led Zeppelin, he's apparently very popular, but not poor Karen, she wasn't allowed, the only one. And what was the harm in the laser show?"

"It wasn't the concerts; it was the city! I was only protecting our daughter."

"From whom exactly, this Pink Floyd character? You treated her like a child."

"She is a child!" said Abe. "Just look at the decisions she makes! Maybe if you might have helped me set some parameters. Maybe I did drive her off, but you might have shared the responsibility a little."

Somehow, their marriage managed to endure these disputes, as it had endured Abe's singular decision to uproot their lives in Seattle fifteen years prior, as it had endured his habitual absenteeism and workaholism, as it had endured Leonard Haruto. Still, the ugliness had to exact a toll.

On numerous occasions, Abe dreamed of Karen, dreams so vivid he could all but reach out and touch her. Karen sitting beside an old woman on a Greyhound bus, gazing out a rain-streaked window. Karen on a street corner, a gray kitten wrapped in her arms, asking a policeman for directions. Karen as a girl of six or seven, a purple halo of grape juice ringing her mouth, bouncing on a trampoline, laughter bubbling up out of her each time she sprung back into the air. As desperately as Abe yearned to address Karen's visage, he was tormented by his inability to speak. Still, it was a comfort to see her.

But as the months wore on, Abe stopped dreaming of Karen and began to accept the possibility that she was not coming back, not any time soon, that she was already beyond their reach.

Though Abe put little stock in it, he accompanied Ruth to church most Sundays, holding her hand as she clung to a diminishing hope, praying with the congregation that her child would regain her senses, that she would come home, or at least let her family come to her. But there arrived no more assurances, no letters or phone calls from Karen. By fall, it seemed she was already a ghost.

Ministrations

2024

Arriving on the hospital's ground floor, Kyle wheeled Ruth out of the elevator, navigating the crowded lobby to the foyer, while Abe was tasked with lugging Ruth's walker. Though it weighed very little, the apparatus was cumbersome. It might have been easier to simply utilize the damn contrivance as it was intended instead of dragging it clumsily through the throng, clipping shins and elbows at every turn, but Abe's pride would not allow it.

"You wait with Mom," said Kyle when they reached the outer entrance. "I'll go back round to the garage and pull up in front of the sliding doors."

Abe was doing his stubborn best to begrudge the fact that Kyle was there upon Anne's insistence to accompany them through the transition. The truth was, though, it was a relief to have Kyle on hand for the discharge, and especially for what promised to be a harrowing drive through downtown to the terminal.

Abe stood behind Ruth like a sentry as they looked out at the steady traffic on Pine.

"You comfortable?" he asked her.

"A lil chilly," she said.

Indeed, every time the sliding doors opened and closed, an arctic wind rushed into the vestibule. Abe stooped to rearrange her lap blanket so that it covered her arms as far as the elbows.

"Ank ou," she said, her speech still muddled by the ravages of the surgery that had taken half her tongue.

A few minutes later, Kyle pulled up, jumped out of the driver's seat, and circled the Bronco, leaving it to idle at the curb. Wheeling Ruth as close as he could to the vehicle, he set the brakes on the wheelchair and opened the rear passenger door. Snow was falling again, wet flakes filtering down from above like bits of tissue, dissolving on contact. The pewter sky crowding down on them promised more flurries to come.

"Okay, Dad, together, now," said Kyle.

One on either side of her, they clutched Ruth under the arms and carefully hoisted her out of the chair, guiding her into the back seat. Awkward though the transfer was, it wasn't hard; Ruth was light as a feather pillow.

"Easy peasy," said Kyle, who opened the rear hatch and stowed the walker. "Hop in, Dad."

But instead of the front passenger seat, Abe followed him around the rear of the car to the driver's side.

"I'll sit in back with your mother," he said.

Though barely noon, it might have been dusk it was so dim, particularly in the back of the Bronco amidst the black leather interior. In silence, they traversed the hill in fits and starts, missing nearly every light. Clutching Ruth's liver-spotted hand, Abe could hardly bear to look at her, still unaccustomed to what now passed as her jaw. It wasn't like it sounded, though. It was less the loss of any physical beauty that unnerved Abe and more the loss of vitality: the deliberateness of her every movement, as though it might break her; the new fear draped like a veil over her eyes; the dissipation of her very presence. Ruthie would always maintain her beauty, no deformity could compromise that, but he was unprepared to see her diminished in such a capacity. To witness her confined to a hospital bed after her surgery was one thing, but how would it be back at the farm, in her own kitchen, her own bed?

"Looks like we're missing the twelve twenty-five," said Kyle, stalled in traffic at Third and Madison. "You okay back there, Ma?"

"Fine, dear."

They remained in the vehicle for the ferry crossing, mostly in silence. It was after two by the time they arrived at the farm, and the snow had turned to rain. The familiar sight of the place was an immediate salve to Ruth's beleaguered spirit, a sight she'd thought she might never see again: the grass field once mowed to stubble now knee-high; the overgrown orchard, now punctuated with dozens of tiny volunteers; the pond, protected from ice beneath its thick blanket of algae; the dilapidated barn somehow still standing, its truss folding in on itself. And the old farmhouse itself, badly in need of a new coat of white paint, the wood of the blue shutters gone punky from the relentless assault of moisture, yet, in its way, the domicile more formidable than ever in its decrepitude, like a squat old prairie woman brandishing a rifle.

The driveway was a muddy morass; thus, Kyle hefted his mother out of the back seat in spite of her protests and conveyed her in the manner of a newlywed up the steps to the landing as Abe fumbled with the keys at the front door.

God, but it was good to be home in that old house. Gripping her walker, Ruth paused in the foyer to breathe in the familiar scent of the place, the slightly camphorous odor of old cedar mixed with dog hair and dust, and from the kitchen, halfway across the house, still the faint remnants of fifty thousand meals prepared.

As ever, the hallway was drafty as Ruth inched her way toward the bedroom, Abe and Kyle trailing nervously behind in case she faltered.

"How's the leg?" said Abe.

"Fine," Ruth lied.

In reality, the limb seared and pulsated deep beneath the muscle, in the spot occupied by what was left of her tibia. Ruth wasn't even sure she could make it to the bedroom.

"You sure?" said Kyle.

"Positive," she snapped, immediately ashamed of her irritability.

When she finally arrived at the foot of the bed, exhausted from the effort, she yearned only to climb under the covers, but her full bladder harassed her.

"I need to use the lavatory," she announced.

Oh, but Ruth abhorred the new normal, this dependency on others to execute the simplest of bodily functions.

Kyle took her by the elbow as though to lead her to the bathroom before Abe intervened.

"I'll handle this," said Abe.

And thus began Ruth's care at the tender if less-than-expert hands of her husband, who'd changed but a handful of diapers in his life, bandaged five or six scraped knees, and could barely survive a common cold himself. For seven decades, Ruth had cared for Abe, ministered to his ailments, from his aching lumbar to his plantar fasciitis, from his tension headaches to his gallstones, from his peptic ulcer to his bruised ego, and now the tables were turned, and Ruth didn't like it one bit.

Over the course of the next forty-eight hours, Abe would assist her to the toilet on at least a dozen occasions without incident, including several times in the middle of the night. Snapping on the bedside lamp, he would circle to her side of the bed, position the walker, then stand by drowsily just outside the bathroom doorway as she endured the runs. Ignoring the malodor as he lifted her off the toilet seat, Abe disposed of her soiled pad, heavy with moisture, then fumbled to extract its replacement from the package and secure it around her waist before finally helping her up with her drawers. He shepherded her to the sink on the strength of his elbow as she washed her hands one at a time. Delivering her to her walker outside the doorway, he followed her back to bed, only to repeat the sequence two hours later.

By day, Abe served her applesauce and probiotic yogurt, pureed yams, pureed beets, pureed lentils, rice and black beans, pureed cheer, and encouragement, and affirmation, as Ruth drank the food down, dabbing her own chin after every bite. Abe assisted her on and off the mattress, where she spent the majority of her hours. Two or three times a day, he persuaded her to leave the darkened confines of the bedroom at the back of the house, coaxing her to the kitchen or the living room to watch TV, even to the front porch in the rain just so she could look out upon the sodden farm. Ruth complied mostly for Abe's sake, for every one of these activities left her exhausted. At once grateful for and humiliated by the constant care and attention, at times Ruth missed the solitude of her hospital room. Somehow it was easier to heal alone, to lick one's wounds in isolation, than beneath the watchful eyes of a worried husband. Add to that Kyle's presence as reluctant arbiter, who owing to proximity was his siblings' consensus pick to oversee the transition. Ruth found his ubiquity suffocating; he was always checking in on Ruth while she was trying to doze off, perpetually monitoring Abe's ministrations when he wasn't taking his father to task for various offenses, from leaving the freezer door open to spattering the kitchen window with pureed carrots. Funny how Ruth had been yearning for the companionship of her children for decades, but now that one of them was a fixture on the farm, she wished he'd go home to his own wife in Edmonds and leave Abe to care for her alone.

Indeed, if Kyle's constant supervision was an annoyance to Ruth, it was a burden to Abe. It was like Abe was auditioning for his own job. The added pressure only seemed to undermine his ability to execute the most basic tasks.

Dad, you left the toilet seat up again!

That's way too hot, Dad! You're gonna burn her mouth!

You forgot to turn off the shower, you're gonna flood this place, Dad!

The cumulative effect of Kyle's micromanagement drove Abe beyond the edge of despair, squarely into the realm of outright indignation. The nerve of him, his own child, belittling his every effort, correcting his every little oversight or omission, mediating his every move, as if Abe, or at least Ruth, had not taught him how to tie his own shoe and wipe his own bottom. Kyle treated Abe as if he were inept, a feeble old man, incapable of caring for himself, let alone anyone else.

That's not the way you do it.

You can't leave her alone like that, Dad.

That's too quick, you're supposed to ease her up.

The constant editing and auditing and redressing finally achieved critical mass on the evening of the fifth day, when Abe snapped.

"How about you just get off my back?" he said. "Believe it or not, I don't need your help."

"I'm not so sure about that, Dad, no offense. Last night, you left the gas on."

"The damn knob sticks," said Abe.

"You could have killed us all," he said.

"Well, I didn't. If you want to be useful, find some 3-in-One oil in the garage and fix it."

That evening, Kyle phoned Anne with a progress report from the living room, Abe eavesdropping as he loaded the dishwasher.

"I mean, there's times when he seems sort of out of it, but I think he can handle it," said Kyle. "He sure seems convinced he can do it. I'm a little worried about him driving her around, honestly. But I guess it's only Poulsbo."

Abe wanted so badly to grab the phone from Kyle and give Anne a piece of his own mind. The audacity. The presumption. The indignity. It seemed a cruel arrangement that one's children, the very nurslings who once drooled on your shirt collar and threw up on your lapel, who wet the bed and crapped on the floor, those helpless lumps of adipose who depended upon you for every little comfort, nay, for their very survival, one day grew into sanctimonious, domineering, irredeemable despots, hell-bent on infantilizing you as though it were the natural order. At what point did they reckon they'd surpassed you in wisdom and experience? When was the torch passed? At sixty, at seventy, at eighty? No, there was nothing natural about this order.

The following evening, to everybody's relief, Kyle finally consented to leave.

"You're sure about this, Dad?" he said in the foyer, duffel in hand.

"Of course I'm sure."

"Mom?"

"Yes."

"Remember, Twin Pines is only seventeen miles," he said. "It's fully covered by Medicare. Great facilities, on-site rehab, twenty-four-hour care. You could visit Mom every—"

"Go," said Abe.

Abe watched from the front step as Kyle climbed into the car, honking once as he pulled away. It wasn't until Abe watched the Bronco disappear up the driveway that he released the breath it seemed he'd been holding for a week.

Following a fitful night's sleep, Abe woke before Ruth and crept to the kitchen, where he concocted a smoothie of yogurt and greens, frozen mixed berries, and fruit juice, amending it with a powdered dietary supplement. He poured it out into a glass and brought it to her in bed, sitting patiently beside her on the edge of the mattress as she ingested it through a straw. After breakfast, Abe retreated to the kitchen, where he rinsed Ruth's glass and placed it in the dishwasher. Returning to the bedroom, he assisted her to the toilet and sat her down before removing himself to the doorway and closing the door three-quarters of the way. It was apparent from her groaning that she was still suffering from diarrhea. When he heard the toilet flush, Abe retrieved her and helped her to her feet, where Ruth held fast to his shoulders as he replaced her soiled pad and pulled up her underwear.

Back in the bedroom, Abe helped Ruth into her jeans, now hopelessly baggy on her balsa-wood frame, the back pockets drooping halfway to the hollows of her knees. Goodness, she couldn't have weighed ninety pounds.

"You're gonna need a belt for these," said Abe.

Around nine thirty, Abe pulled the Subaru up to the front porch and ever-so-deliberately guided Ruth down the steps to her walker, then lowered her into the passenger seat, clipping the cant rail with the top of her head.

"Oh, my God, I'm so sorry," he said.

"It's nothing," said Ruth.

At the doctor's office, Abe waited in the lobby, thumbing through an issue of *Popular Science* for the better part of an hour. How corporations helped fuel the big business of spying. Seismic sensors reveal the true intensity of explosions in Ukraine. Your car could be capturing data on your sex life. Doubtful.

When Ruth finally emerged from physical therapy, ushered down the corridor at a snail's pace by a nurse practitioner, she was noticeably hunched and gray in the face, perhaps discouraged at her lack of progress.

"She did amazing," said the nurse. "She's a trooper."

Abe could see how much Ruth abhorred the implications of such a statement, how exceeding expectations only wounded her pride, as it only served to remind her how low those expectations were.

Once they were settled in the car, Abe took Ruth's silence as an invitation not to converse. Instead, he gripped the wheel with both hands and peered straight ahead, eyes on the road. It was stop-and-go through Poulsbo on 305 with all the signals. Abe remembered when there were no lights at all. No shopping centers or Dairy Queens, no Subways or strip malls, just the Evergreen Motel and the service station, and, later, the short-lived Mark-it Foods where they shopped but once.

Before they reached the new roundabout at Johnson Road, its very presence an offense to Abe, Ruth had already dozed off in the passenger seat. Instead of driving straight to the farm, Abe decided to buy her some clearly needed rest, thus he picked up Miller Road at West Day and drove south past the Grand Forest and Fletcher Bay to

Lynwood Center, where it was shocking to see how developed the area had become: a second shopping center tastefully rendered in matching Tudor across the street from the original, kitty-corner to a trio of three-story apartment buildings. It seemed like only last year when it was just the old theater and Walt's grocery, old Walt with his generous mustache and exorbitant prices.

Abe piloted the Subaru past the old post office, now abandoned and sagging, though the adjacent storefront was under reconstruction. Abe proceeded on Point White Drive as Ruth continued sleeping, her head canted slightly to the side, exposing the entirety of her ravaged jaw, the sunken cheek, and the long incision below the ear, running raised and pink the length of her mandible. Glancing sidelong at his wife, Abe was humbled by her strength and endurance.

All told, Abe drove for thirty-five minutes on the south end of the island, around Point White along Rich Passage, north to Crystal Springs, before turning back south and down Baker Hill to complete the loop. Finally, he began winding his way back north to the farm, where he awoke Ruth gently, leading her into the house on her walker, then straight to the bedroom without a word.

When Abe felt she was sufficiently rested, he coaxed her out of the bedroom and situated her on the sofa as he prepared her a mug of tepid beef broth. She took her nourishment again through a straw, as side by side on the sofa they watched the tail end of the six o'clock news, then half of the seven o'clock news before Ruth was once again sapped of energy.

"I can hardly keep my head up," she said. "I'm gonna call it a night."

Assisting her to the bathroom, Abe stood by as she gargled her disinfectant mouth rinse before he helped lower her onto the toilet seat.

Finally, he followed Ruth to the bed, standing by as she settled in beneath the covers.

"I've got an idea," he said.

"Mm," said Ruth, eyes half-closed.

Abe withdrew briefly to the dresser, where a dozen books were stacked willy-nilly, as they had been for years. Such a pile had existed in some shape or form their entire lives on the farm. Abe selected a tome at random, then joined Ruth under the covers, flipping on the bedside lamp. Lying there beside her, Abe began reading aloud from a dusty volume of John Donne.

> *Thou hast made me, and shall thy work decay?*
> *Repair me now, for now mine end doth haste,*
> *I run to death, and death meets me as fast,*
> *And all my pleasures are like yesterday;*
> *I dare not move my dim eyes any way,*
> *Despair behind, and death before doth cast*
> *Such terror, and my feebled flesh doth waste*
> *By sin in it, which it towards hell doth weigh.*
> *Only thou art above, and when towards thee*
> *By thy leave I can look, I rise again;*
> *But our old subtle foe so tempteth me,*
> *That not one hour I can myself sustain;*
> *Thy grace may wing me to prevent his art,*
> *And thou like adamant draw mine iron heart.*

"Well, that was uplifting," observed Ruth drowsily.

"Was it?" said Abe.

"I was being facetious," she said.

"Ah," he said.

"You know," said Ruth, "Donne was never really my cup of tea when I was younger. His tone always sounded a little stodgy to my ear."

"I just picked it off the pile," said Abe. "I can pick a different one."

"No, no," said Ruth. "Keep reading. I'm finding I like it more now. I like the metaphysical conceit, and I like the vulnerability. I never recognized it before."

Whatever that meant. God, what a woman, though. Nearly nine decades on this earth, and still mentally limber, still willing to be open-minded, still game to reconsider ideas and opinions she once held as truths. How different from Abe, who clung to the ideas he'd always known, the ideas that had served him well as a young man, the principles that fit him like a trusty old pair of slippers.

Abe read on in the steadiest tenor he could muster, his voice dry and brittle at the edges, baffled by the mellifluous language, oblivious to most of its intent or meaning, but determined to do the poems justice for his wife's sake. After a few more stanzas, Ruth began to snore, and Abe set the book aside, snapping off the light. For twenty minutes he lay in the darkness, trying to get his head around the meaning of the death poem and getting nowhere. Was it really as simple as heaven or hell for this Donne fellow? Finally, Abe was too exhausted to pursue the matter further. Never in his life had Abe been so thoroughly played out. Sleep fell upon him heavily, like six feet of dirt.

When Abe awoke, it was morning; dull-witted, he turned to discover Ruth's side of the bed empty. Bolting upright dazedly, he registered Ruth's walker upended in the bathroom doorway. Heaving himself out of bed, he nearly lost his balance as the room pitched sideways and the world spun counterclockwise. He righted himself against the dresser for an instant before he rushed to the bathroom. Arriving there, he discovered his worst fear confirmed: There lay Ruth, sprawled unconscious on the tile at the foot of the toilet, blood pooling beneath her head.

The Void

1973

For eight months, Ruth clung to hope in the face of a despair that might have been debilitating were it not for the support of her community. Every Sunday, without fail, the congregation of Seabold Methodist Church prayed that Karen might return safely to the bosom of her family, that the child would regain her senses and let her family reclaim her, or at the very least call home. But there arrived no letters or postcards, not so much as another phone call from Ruth's wayward daughter. Karen might have been literally anywhere, or worse, nowhere at all.

Her absence was ubiquitous, an aching hollow in Ruth's chest every time she passed Karen's empty bedroom, where Lynyrd Skynyrd soundlessly gathered dust on the turntable. To launder the pair of dirty jeans heaped at the foot of the bed according to protocol, to fold and replace them in the bottom drawer of the dresser, would have been admitting defeat, for as long as they remained there on the floor like unfinished business, Karen's absence was only temporary. Likewise, Ruth resisted the urge to confiscate the half pack of Kool menthols stashed covertly in the back of the desk drawer—first, there would be a lecture on the perils of smoking.

Ruth felt the sting of Karen's absence each time she gazed across
the dinner table at the vacant seat next to Kyle. Whereas a year ago,
Karen's taciturn presence at the dinner table had seemed a largely
futile exercise in civility, now Ruth would have traded anything for
Karen's grudging attendance. Most acutely of all, Ruth felt Karen's
absence in the invisible chasm of culpability that seemed to exist between her and Abe, where all their unresolved arguments finally took
shelter and fortified themselves. Still, somehow the household managed to function, if only by avoidance.

Never had Ruth's faith been so thoroughly tested. It was her dear
friend Bess Delory who rode shotgun through the cruel odyssey of
Karen's dereliction, with phone calls daily, lunches twice a week, and
whenever possible, a helping hand around the farm, weeding, and
feeding, and mowing, her shock of red hair barely contained beneath
an old red bandana, her bawdy laughter a salve against the relentless
grating of the unknowable. But all the support in the world, all the
faith, could only go so far in buffering Ruth from those grim possibilities that comprised the rule of the universe. It was only through the
accumulation of days and the architecture of routine that Ruth could
even begin to accept the unacceptable. And she knew she must.

Eleven months and twelve days after Karen had left Bainbridge
High School following third period, Ruth received the call from the
Bernalillo County sheriff's department shortly before seven P.M. The
instant the reluctant messenger identified himself as Lieutenant
Frank McCombs, Ruth knew that the news was of the worst possible
variety. In an instant, all hope was extinguished.

A demolition contractor had discovered Karen's body in a resi-
dential squat south of the city, lifeless amidst the squalor of a back
room in total disarray. The image Ruth conjured was sure to haunt
her the rest of her days, a scene as vivid as anything out of her own
experience: the stained and mottled mattress in the corner, the cra-
tered plaster walls, the floor riddled with mouse droppings and refuse,
a soiled sheet draped over the window to block out the sunlight and
the glare of curious eyes.

Numb with disbelief, Ruth lowered herself into a chair at the kitchen table, gutted, ears ringing as Lieutenant McCombs, probably a father himself, was forced to explain to Ruth that no foul play was suspected in Karen's loss of life. There was no note to accompany Karen's demise, and thus no explanation, and her death was ruled accidental pending a toxicology report, but the implication was clear without Lieutenant McCombs's having to say it: Karen had more than likely taken her own life.

He was so sorry, Lieutenant McCombs, so very sorry to bring her this news.

Ruth clutched the handset until the line began to blare its re-monstrance, the shrill, staccato alarm barely penetrating her stupe-faction. Neither could Maddie's insistent tug at the sleeve of her blouse elicit any reaction. Ruth was still clutching the receiver when Abe arrived home an hour later, unaware of his daughter's passing. To utter the words was unnecessary, for the conclusion was plastered upon Ruth's stricken face, mouth agape, eyes stunned senseless.

Abe froze in the middle of the kitchen as the blood drained from his own face.

"No," he said. "There must be some mistake."

Only then did a lone whimper escape Ruth as she threw her arms around Abe as though she were drowning.

"No," Abe repeated, this time barely a whisper.

The days that followed were a blur of tortured faces and uneaten tuna casseroles. Were it not for the tasks and endless arrangements set before her, Ruth might have retreated to the bedroom, climbed under the covers, closed her eyes, and never opened them again. But the world demanded her participation.

Worse than the guilt that dogged her every waking moment was the speculation that clung to Ruth like a shadow when she was forced to engage the necessities of the outside world. Though her neighbors and fellow congregants showed her only kindness, Ruth could hear their thoughts, as she would hear them for years to come: *What could possibly have been wrong in the Winter household that the poor girl would run off and take her own life?* What made it all the worse was that Ruth had no answers.

Abe, for his part, receded still further into a shell of emotional impenetrability, as though constitutionally incapable of accepting Karen's death. In Ruth's darkest hour, she found him largely unavailable, unwilling or unable to share her grief. Her own doubt and self-disgust only seemed to alienate him further.

"What's wrong with you?" she demanded, face puffy, voice hoarse from squalling.

His expression remained impassive, blank as a prairie. Behind his glassed-over eyes, Ruth could see nothing, no suffering in any guise. On those occasions when Abe capitulated, mechanically volunteering a shoulder for Ruth to cry on, he was stiff and immovable as ever.

"Where are you?" Ruth cried, pounding his chest with clenched fists. "What's wrong with you?"

Abe neither budged nor defended himself against her assault, merely absorbed the blows silently.

*

Over a hundred people attended Karen's memorial service on a Saturday afternoon near the end of March: neighbors, friends, congregants, bundled in jackets and scarves, huddled on folding chairs. Though KOMO 4's resident meteorologist and wiseacre, Ray Ramsey, had promised a "drizmal" day, nobody had expected snow that late in the season, and yet down it came in slurry streaks, wet and windblown, sopping the mossy grounds of Hillcrest Cemetery, the gathered riddling its flat grass expanse with their soggy footprints. Nobody dared to ask why not an indoor service. Instead, they sat in silence, somber and stoic and shivering, the wet snow stinging their faces.

Abe and Ruth were stationed in the front row, Kyle between them, and Anne on the end, their faces ravaged by the biting wind. Kyle held his mother's hand, while Abe's hands remained in his own lap, balled into fists. For beneath the numbness of the trauma burned a seething anger lacking any focus—anger at the world and at himself; anger at Karen and every friend who couldn't save her, every soul who ever rejected or hurt her; anger at the weather he could not control; anger at Ray goddamn Ramsey and his stupid plaid jacket. But most of all, anger at God for not existing, and anger at every gullible fool of every color or persuasion or affiliation who ever deigned to believe in such fairy tales.

The unraveling cotton cuff of Pastor Nordan's long johns shirt was just visible beneath his wet stole as he cleared his throat and looked kindly upon those gathered before him. In a practiced tone, at once humble and reverent, he addressed the dearly beloved and bereaved, speaking on the brevity of our days on earth and acknowledging the Lord's blueprint—often inexplicable—for each one of us. He spoke of God's mercy, and his divine wisdom, as Abe's fists throbbed restlessly in the frigid air. Where was the mercy? Where was the wisdom in his daughter's suicide? Any cosmic design that allowed for such a thing was born of depravity; any deity so impotent or inhumane as to permit such a thing was no God at all but a fiend. For what shepherd led his lambs to slaughter?

Still, Nordan, the charlatan, the journeyman on a two-year loan to Seabold from the clergy, the same man who immediately upon his appointment had requested a new refrigerator and Radarange for the parsonage, begged his almighty God not to hinder His children, for they belonged to the kingdom of heaven.

Unable to endure the lies, Abe let the useless words wash past him and gave his eye to wandering. There were Al and Terri Duncan in the second row, next to Thom and Nancy Jacobson. Across the aisle from Anne, one row back, Abe recognized Burt Brainard, to whom he'd sold a ten-thousand-dollar term life plan four years back, though Brainard had never been what Abe would consider a family friend.

Dubious, Abe leaned across Kyle's lap and whispered to Ruth: "What the hell is Burt Brainard doing here?"

"Shush," she scolded.

And there were Jim and Kelly Mathison. Jim was a sometime associate at the chamber, sure, a nice enough guy, but what was he doing at his daughter's funeral? Abe was about to ask Ruth as much, but before he could she shut him down with a withering look.

As Pastor Nordan waxed on about the glories awaiting Karen in heaven, Abe's restless eyes continued to appraise the mourners; he now toggled his head unapologetically three and four rows behind him. There were the Bohannon girl and the Dolinger boy. There were Karen's former drama teacher, Mrs. Nielsen, and Karen's old Girl Scout leader, Kate Dearsley, and behind her, Ruth's fellow Methodist congregant and onetime whist partner Jacqueline Hobbs. What were any of them doing here? Were they truly in attendance, suffering this "drizmal" weather to say goodbye to Karen, to support the family, or was their presence at the service more akin to rubbernecking at the scene of a traffic accident? None of them had done a thing to save Karen.

At first, Abe did not recognize the young man standing off to the side, slightly back from the assembly, medium hair, thinning on top but a bit shaggy over the ears, no jacket, no hat, no scarf, just shirt-sleeves and aviator sunglasses despite the dreary winter light. He was a few years too old to be a friend of Karen's and too young to be a teacher. It was only after the service, as the last of the mourners were fanning out, when Abe paused halfway to the car to wait for Ruth, Kyle, and Anne, that Abe recognized the boy.

Before he even knew what he was doing, Abe had the boy around the neck as Anne and Ruth both tried desperately to pull Abe off of him, even as other mourners came hurrying to intervene, their dress shoes squelching across the muddy lawn at a trot.

"You sonofabitch!" Abe screamed, throttling the boy. "You did this!"

The slick ground beneath Abe's feet gave way, and in an instant, he was weightless and plummeting backward, the winter sky pressing down on him as the back of his skull was rocked by a violent impact with the ground, a collision that arrived like a lightning bolt.

Abe was seeing stars when he regained consciousness surrounded by a murmuring throng. Of all people, Jim Mathison was down on one knee, consoling Abe, wife Kelly flanking his right shoulder, and Burt Brainard beside her.

"You're okay, big guy," said Jim. "Just take a minute."

Jim helped Abe to his feet, standing with him as Abe gathered his bearings while the others began to disperse, whispering among themselves. Abe was too far removed from the situation to be embarrassed. Even the anger had left him by the time he shook off his overcoat and wiped the mud from his hair. Canvassing the area, Abe saw no sign of Royce Holiday, who had no doubt taken flight. Neither was there any sign of Ruth or Anne, who had also fled the shameful exhibition.

Now that Burt Brainard had established there was no further assistance to be offered, only Kyle remained, standing there bewildered beside Jim and Kelly Mathison, whose pitying expressions served only to heighten Abe's shame.

"Everything is gonna be okay," Jim told Abe, kneading his shoulder.

"Thanks," said Abe.

"You need a ride?" Jim asked.

"No," said Abe. "Thank you."

"Look, if there's anything Kelly and I can do, anything at all . . ."

"Appreciate that, Jim. I'll keep it in mind."

Ruth did not return home after the service. Only later would Abe learn that she'd accompanied Bess Delory to her house off Manzanita, where she would stay for the next two nights. Nor did Anne return to the farm after the fiasco at the cemetery but retreated to her old friend Lynn Bryndleson's house in Port Madison before driving back to Bellingham the following morning.

Abe drove Kyle home through the sleet, the squeaking of the windshield wipers the only sound penetrating the silence. Clearly, the boy needed to hear something, some assurance or explanation, but Abe had nothing to offer him.

Finally, it was Kyle who interrupted the stillness as they rounded the head of the bay.

"Geez, Dad, are you okay?"

"Yeah," said Abe, even as a pinching in his chest caused him to grimace. "How about you, kiddo?"

"Yeah," he said. "Kinda. I mean, I guess so."

Abe stared into the near distance beyond the windshield, a slurry wash of green coming at him at forty miles per hour.

"You're a good boy," Abe observed flatly.

"Okay," said Kyle.

That was the last they spoke until they pulled up in front of the darkened house at four in the afternoon, where two of the hens were huddling for warmth beneath the front porch, runoff pouring down the rain gutters in sheets not two feet from them. Abe and Kyle sat in the car for a moment, the sleet slapping the windshield like guano, the motor still idling.

God, how Abe wished he felt something, or knew what to say, or what to do next.

Abe finally turned off the ignition, and they both remained seated. After ten seconds of deafening silence, Kyle piled out of the passenger seat, and Abe followed the boy's cue, trailing him up the steps into the house. As Kyle shuffled listlessly up the stairs to his bedroom, Abe knew he ought to do something, cook the boy some dinner, at least call out to him, remind him once again that he was a good boy. But he didn't, because somehow, he couldn't.

Everything Abe had ever thought he knew no longer mattered; everything he had once believed—all the principles he'd adhered to throughout his life, all the tools he'd spent decades devising, all the ways and means that had formed his master plan for life—was meaningless and could do nothing to serve him in this hour of need.

When he heard Kyle's door close upstairs, Abe gravitated to the kitchen and turned on the light before realizing he had no purpose there, no appetite, no desire or motivation to clear the dirty dishes piled in the sink. He turned off the light and stepped back out of the kitchen into the darkened hallway, where he stood for a moment, not knowing which direction to turn, nor how to proceed. Without even knowing how he got there, he found himself standing in Karen's bedroom in the dim light before dusk, bereft, numb to the world, but somewhere deep within him achingly, unrelentingly alive, and wishing it weren't so.

Clauses of Incontestability

1976

Abe spent more time at the office than ever. When there wasn't work to be done, he made work, and if there wasn't work to be made, he made phone calls, friendly check-ins to preferred clients, and when there were no phone calls to be made, he stayed late in the office anyway, balancing his checkbook, organizing his Rolodex, watering the plants, or just kicking his legs up on the desk and reading the *Bainbridge Review,* or the *Sun,* or the *P-I,* sometimes twice in the same day for distraction, anything to avoid going home.

The sum of all the blame and remonstration that attended the unutterable nature of Karen's death had exploded the Winter family, scattering them in every direction. Anne rarely made the drive down from Bellingham anymore, or even called. Kyle, like Abe, managed to keep himself busy, lettering in three sports sophomore year, always attending practices or games, rarely returning home before sundown during the week, eating his warmed-up dinner alone in the kitchen. On weekends, he had more practices, or open gym, or friends to meet at the Kel-Lin Drive-in, or in Scott Nickell's garage, where they tinkered endlessly with car engines, though still a year removed from their driver's licenses. Saturday and Sunday nights, Kyle bused tables at Aida's in the new mall, taking his staff dinner at the restaurant. All told, Abe probably saw the boy forty-five minutes a week.

Even Duke, the once irrepressible six-year-old border collie, was apparently depressed, spending whole afternoons under the front porch, chin on his forepaws, gazing dolefully out at the farm.

For Ruth's part, as far as Abe could ascertain, she mostly languished around the farm, much like Duke, while Maddie and Kyle were at school, letting the flower beds go to seed, neglecting the vegetable garden and the orchard, permitting the hens to range freely and the dishes to stack up in the sink. Some afternoons, she ate lunch with Bess Delory, and on Sundays she had church, but other than that, she didn't appear to get out much. God knows, Abe didn't take her anywhere.

Abe and Ruth had always made an oddly paired couple, ever since that first double date at the Dog House in 1953, and all along they'd had their differences of opinion, and taste, and even principle. The fact was, they hardly agreed on anything. But the distance between Abe and Ruth had never been greater than it was in the wake of Karen's death. Now that Anne was all but estranged, and Karen was gone, and Kyle was never home, it seemed Maddie was the only glue holding the family together. Though Anne was beyond his sphere of influence, and Karen was dead, and Kyle was well on his way to being a man, there was still time to protect Maddie, to guide her, to ensure that she never strayed down the same path as Karen, if it was even possible to influence such outcomes. Abe would not fail again for lack of trying. Even as he was repelled by the possibility of his home life, he yearned for a return to the fullness and clear purpose of the old ways. So, why wasn't he at the farm, putting his life back together?

Instead, most nights, Abe was at the office hours after closing, avoiding the home front, as he was the evening that he ran across Jim Mathison's obituary in the *Review*. Swinging his feet off the desk, Abe hunched over the paper and read the remembrance in disbelief. Jim

Mathison was only thirty-eight years old. Survived by his wife, Kelly, his twelve-year-old son, Michael, and his eight-year-old daughter, Mary Beth. Jim had chartered the Kiwanis financial assistance fund and headed up the scholarship program. He was a seven-year veteran of the chamber of commerce. He coached the BI park district Little League Shamrocks. Jim Mathison was a good man by any measure. The obit failed to elucidate the particulars of Jim's death but to say that his demise was unforeseen, and like Karen's, accidental. As a man who measured lives as an occupation, a man who weighed and considered a life's hazards and limitations, its risks and rewards, who deemed a life insurable or not, Abe found this lack of information maddening.

It couldn't have been eighteen months since Abe had sold Jim Mathison a forty-thousand-dollar life policy, which was a blessing for his family. Despite this terrible turn of events, at least Kelly and the kids would be granted a modicum of financial security to buffer them from the loss. As Abe recalled, his former protégé Ted DeWitt had adjusted Jim's Safeco policy, thus Abe ought to call Ted and make sure the payout was in process. In the meantime, he would call Kelly in the morning and pay his respects, send some flowers, and make a hundred-dollar donation in memoriam to Jim's Kiwanis fund.

The following day, Abe called Kelly according to plan.

"Kelly, I'm just devastated," he said. "I can't begin to tell you how sorry I am for your loss. Jim was a good man. If there's anything I can do, anything at all, really, let me know. I'm going to chase down that claim for you, make sure your check's running on schedule."

"Thank you, Abe, that's very kind," she said, her voice faltering. "We're gonna need every penny we can get."

Unable to continue, Kelly broke down, as Abe indulged her silence.

"Forgive me," she said finally.

"No, no. I'm so sorry, Kelly," Abe said. "Really, I mean it, if there's anything I can do to help. Anything."

Indeed, the offer was more than a sentimental token or a professional courtesy, it was a lifeline extended in earnest, though Abe didn't quite understand the impetus himself. Perhaps it was their small kindness at Karen's funeral after Abe had gone berserk on Royce Holiday. For all his familiarity with Jim and Kelly Mathison, they hadn't really been friends. And yet, Abe was genuinely willing to do anything to help Kelly Mathison and her kids through this ordeal, whatever that looked like: financial, administrative, personal. He would have made the funeral arrangements had she asked, driven out to Rolling Bay and taken the garbage to the curb, whatever it took to help ease the burden of their loss. The irony of this was not lost on Abe. All but useless to his own disintegrating family, persistently absent, yet ready to serve another man's family, perhaps as a nostrum for the guilt and shame of his failures.

"I just don't understand how he could do this to us," Kelly sputtered.

"It was an accident," said Abe.

"Is that what you think?" said Kelly. "Eighteen years and he never left the gas on, not once, nobody's ever left the gas on. Besides, he never sits in the kitchen unless he's eating, and only late at night. Then suddenly, when the kids and I just happen to be at my sister's house for the weekend, he shuts himself in the kitchen and neglects to turn the gas off?"

Kelly needed to stop talking immediately if she didn't want to kiss her settlement goodbye, but she couldn't seem to help herself now that she'd found a trusted confidant in Abe. It had yet to dawn on Abe why she might have chosen him of all people.

"Why do they do it, Abe? I never thought he was capable of this. I really didn't. How could I not see it?"

It was clear Kelly was oblivious to the implications attending such candor, or she wouldn't have been telling Abe any of this. But what did Kelly Mathison know about clauses of incontestability? The truth was, most folks who weren't Abe didn't have a clue as to the

limitations of their coverage; nobody read the small print. What could
the manner of her husband's death possibly matter to Kelly Mathison
in her grief? But because of his familiarity with the policy, Abe
was visited suddenly by the profound discomfort of knowing that
Kelly Mathison was unwittingly playing his hand for him. He was le-
gally, if not morally, obligated to share this information with Safeco,
but how could he? How could he tell a bereaved wife and mother of
two that not only had she lost her husband, but the policy wouldn't
pay out?

"Kelly," said Abe. "There's something here I'm not sure you're understanding regarding the policy."

"I'm sorry," she said. "My God, why am I dumping this on you?
What is it? Do I need to sign something?"

"Kelly, there's something called an incontestability clause in Jim's
policy. Well, in every life insurance policy, actually."

Abe was about to drop the bomb, but considering poor Kelly
Mathison on the other end of the line, ravaged by grief, he couldn't do
it, not yet.

To withhold this knowledge went against every principle Abe had
ever adhered to, not only as an insurance agent but as a man. Transparency had always been the ideal; to obfuscate the truth only complicated the world needlessly. The truth itself was incontestable. If
agreements were not binding, what was to serve as the bedrock of
order or justice, what was to prevent the landslide of moral collapse?
Add to what would be a grave ethical failure on Abe's part the inherent
risk of his participation in perpetrating such a fraud, and the plan
was downright foolish. Abe could lose his license; his reputation
would be destroyed. He could go to jail. But the alternative was to
destroy what remained of the Mathison family, to single-handedly
render their future irredeemable. What chance did they have without
the settlement? Bad enough their lives should be blown to smither-
eens, that those poor children would be forced to live with the knowledge of their father's willful abandonment, his final resounding act of

cowardice; that they should suffer further privation, lose their home, their livelihood, lose their opportunity to go to college, was unthinkable.

Abe couldn't stop picturing Jim, slumped at the kitchen table, pants soiled in front, gray faced, sightless eyes peering at the tabletop into the abyss. Did Kelly find him there like that? One of the children? How could he be so goddamn selfish? How could he leave them to wonder the rest of their days whether they might have saved him? Could he not see that in doing so he was punishing them?

"What am I gonna do, Abe?" Kelly Mathison pleaded. "How am I supposed to go on—no husband, no father for my children? What's left?"

"It's okay, Kelly," Abe assured her. "You're gonna get through this."

Never had doing the right thing been such a fraught decision, never had the world seemed less black-and-white to Abe.

Ted DeWitt came to work for Abe shortly after Abe bought the agency from Todd Hall. Ted was just a kid of twenty-two, a recent CWU grad who looked the part, well-groomed, clean-cut, but it was soon evident that he was a terrible salesman. He had no gift of gab, and his manner tended toward the brisk. Exchanges were best executed efficiently in Ted DeWitt's mind. What Ted did possess was excellent clerical and organizational skills. His files were perfect, his work was tidy, he was scrupulous, detail oriented, a great rule follower.

Abe liked the kid, he really did, but he didn't need Ted at Bainbridge Island Insurance, he needed salesmen. After a year, it fell on Abe to tell him as much. He broke the news to him on a Friday evening after work in the back bar at Aida's.

"Look, son, I'm not gonna lie to you, you're not cut out for the sales side. I don't need your numbers to see that. But here's the thing: You're talented, you're meticulous, you're a perfect fit for the company side. And you said yourself you'd like to move to the city. This island is no place to meet your future wife. Let me make some calls for you."

Indeed, it was Abe who lined Ted up with a job at Safeco, where he'd been thriving for six years, met his wife, and now had a toddler.

Twenty minutes after Abe concluded his conversation with Kelly Mathison, he phoned Ted DeWitt at Safeco.

"Ted, Abe Winter."

"Abe!" said Ted. "Holy moly! It's been a while!"

"Geez, maybe two, three years?" said Abe.

"Longer," said Ted.

"Look, Ted, there's a claim you adjusted, I wrote the policy early last year, a family friend here on the island, tragic situation, an accident. I just want to make sure the payout is on schedule."

"Let me grab the file," said Ted. "What'd you say the name was?"

"Mathison, James."

"You wouldn't have a policy number handy?"

"Sorry," said Abe.

"I'll find it," said Ted. "I'll get back to you by end of day."

As promised, Ted called back two hours later.

"Here's the thing, Abe," he said. "I'm not really satisfied with the accidental death in this case. I should probably flag it. I mean, say this wasn't an accident, we gotta consider the clause of—"

"Don't do it, Ted," said Abe. "This was an accident, you understand? Pure and simple. You're gonna have to trust me on this."

"What about the commission? Or SUI?"

"They don't need to know," said Abe. "Just don't flag it, and everything will just . . . take care of itself."

The line fell silent momentarily.

"Abe, what are you asking me here? Are you asking me to commit insurance fraud?"

And there was Abe, frozen at the moral crossroads, caught in the headlights.

"I'm just asking you not to flag it, Ted. As a personal favor. For old times."

Ted never provided Abe explicitly with an answer one way or another; their call was left open-ended, and Abe assumed hopefully that

Ted would comply to honor their history together. But for weeks, Abe was on pins and needles as he awaited news of the settlement. Was the claim still under review? Had Ted flagged the cause of death after all? Three times during the impasse, Kelly Mathison called to inquire about the settlement.

"These things take a while to process," he assured her. "Just routine stuff, lotta channels, et cetera, no reason to worry."

Twice, Abe phoned Ted DeWitt to inquire about the settlement's approval, a reckless move if ever there was one, for should the commission ever divine Abe's keen interest in the matter, there was sure to be an investigation, and SUI would no doubt crucify him.

"That settlement we talked about," said Abe. "Any word?"

Ted's momentary silence was an unspoken remonstration.

"Routine audit," he said at last. "Shouldn't be any hang-ups."

"Thank you, Ted."

"Just doing my job," said Ted, his tone anything but pleased. "You'll hear from the company."

Despite Ted's assurances, Abe felt worse about the prospects after the call. Would Ted DeWitt actually report him after all Abe had done for him? But why would he string Abe along like that, why act as though he'd help, then do the opposite? Why not decline Abe's ask from the get-go? Even more agonizing was the reality that there was nothing more Abe could do to press Ted for confirmation; he was at the mercy of Ted DeWitt as his livelihood, along with the Mathison family's fate, hung in the balance.

For weeks, Abe was nervous to the point of distraction. On edge, he couldn't concentrate. His monthly sales hit an all-time low. Any moment he might get a call from SUI. He didn't dare risk further correspondence with Ted. After eight weeks without word, Abe was convinced he was part of an ongoing investigation. What would become of all he'd built, the company, the farm? Should he start reorganizing his assets to protect them? He could have strangled Ted DeWitt, the duplicitous little prick. One evening, after two uncharacteristic martinis at the Lemon Tree, Abe even considered ferrying over to the city and showing up on Ted's doorstep just to give him a piece of his mind, right in front of his family. Let his wife and kid see what a heartless bastard he was, letting a bereaved family suffer the ignominy of poverty and destitution, when all he had to do was check a few boxes.

God, what had Abe been thinking by going against the foundational principle of transparency? Why would he risk everything for somebody else's family? And how could he reasonably expect Ted DeWitt to be complicit in such a scheme wherein he had absolutely nothing to gain and everything to lose? When Abe framed the dilemma in those terms, he couldn't blame Ted for reporting him.

Just when Abe was convinced that his hypocrisy would come crashing down upon him, that what was left of the USS *Winter* would soon be sunk, he got the word from Safeco. Nearly three months after Abe had initiated his ill-advised scheme to save the Mathisons, he received a letter from corporate informing him that the claim had been approved, and that the settlement check would be disbursed by courier to Abe's office within five business days.

Such was Abe's relief that he laughed out loud in spite of himself. To think he'd ever doubted Ted DeWitt!

Three days later, upon another "drizmal" island afternoon, Abe set out to hand-deliver the check to Kelly Mathison. When he rang the bell, Kelly met him at the door barefoot in jeans and a sweatshirt.

"I've got something for you," said Abe, presenting the envelope.

Kelly looked momentarily stunned, then threw her arms around Abe, clutching him so fiercely about the trunk that he could feel her fingernails digging into his back as though they were looking for purchase.

"It's all there," he said.

When Kelly finally relinquished her grip and recomposed herself, she invited Abe into the kitchen for a cup of coffee.

"Look, Kelly," said Abe, setting the envelope on the table. "There's something I've got to say about all of this, and it's very important. Strictly between us, I don't know who you've told what in terms of family, friends, and the like. But from now on, what you told me about Jim, how he died, the circumstances, you can't tell anybody that, okay? If the insurance company ever caught wind of it, there would be trouble, big trouble, you understand? It was an accident, and that's the end of it."

Though Abe was making Kelly Mathison complicit in the deception with this briefing, it was a necessary safeguard for everybody involved.

"Of course," she said, wiping her eyes.

"Good," said Abe. "If they were to find out that he . . . that it wasn't an accident, they . . ."

"I understand," said Kelly.

They deferred to silence momentarily, Abe sipping his coffee as Kelly moved nervously about the kitchen looking for purpose. Abe found himself at a loss for what to say to her that hadn't already been said.

"Here, let me top you off," she said.

"No, no," said Abe. "I'm good. It'll keep me up all night."

"Well, how about a sandwich?"

"I had a late lunch at the office," said Abe.

"Oh, Abe, let me get you something," she said.

She moved to the refrigerator and opened the fridge, which, for all its bareness, was in disarray.

"Really, I'm good," said Abe. "Thank you. Sit, sit."

It was a relief when Kelly shut the refrigerator. Something about its bare shelves and untidiness made him sad. All that space probably once occupied by family leftovers and Jim's favorite beer. A fridge that in a former life demanded organization just to accommodate its bounty. Once the center of family life, eating had become an afterthought. How well Abe knew that feeling, even today.

Seated again, Kelly exhaled the breath she'd been holding in, and

Abe watched as the nervous vitality drained from her being. She looked wooden in its absence.

"Don't take this the wrong way, Abe," she said from some great distance. "The money will go a long way, it will. But I still just . . ." She averted her eyes. "I don't understand why he did this, Abe. Like he was punishing us."

"He wasn't trying to hurt you," Abe said.

"Then why?"

"We'll never know," said Abe.

"How can I keep going?" said Kelly. "Why should I keep going?"

"Because you have to," he said.

Abe left Kelly Mathison bereft on the front landing and drove back to Bainbridge Island Insurance in the downpour.

That night, when he should've been home hours ago, Abe sat at his desk in the darkened office and listened to the rain tap ceaselessly on the roof, staring at nothing, trying to disengage from the world. No newspaper, no busy work, no distraction. As he was gazing out across the floor past the empty desks to the foyer, there came a stirring from deep in his chest, almost like the first rumblings of acid indigestion. But when he tried to swallow the sensation as he might swallow a burp, the reservoir of his pent-up grief came rushing up like molten lava to the base of his esophagus. The dam finally broke. Abe cried for twenty minutes without pause, wept until his throat was sore, until his sinuses were ravaged. And when these paroxysms finally subsided, Abe slumped in his chair, strangely hopeful.

Shortly before ten that night, he returned to the farm in the old Ford wagon, where he found Kyle in the kitchen, still clad in his dirty football uniform, eating a giant bowl of macaroni and drinking milk straight from the carton. As Abe stood watching him for a moment without comment, he felt another welling in his chest.

"Um, can I help you?" said Kyle.

"I love you," said Abe.

"Uh, all right," said Kyle. "Everything okay, Dad?"

"Yeah," said Abe. "I think it is."

Abe padded up the stairs a different man than when he'd left the farm that morning, and every other morning for the past two years. He crept into Maddie's darkened room and hovered above the bed looking down on her, watching the gentle rise and fall of her chest as she slept, the slightest hint of a smile playing at the corners of her mouth. He could only marvel at the child's grit, her effervescence in the face of everything going on around her. How was she happy? Abe could not say. But he was determined to do everything in his power to keep her that way.

Leaving Maddie's door cracked open, Abe continued down the hallway to the bedroom, where he began to undress quietly in the darkness.

"I was starting to worry," murmured Ruth drowsily.

"I'm sorry," he said. "I should have called."

"Mm," she said.

Abe piled his slacks on the wicker chair, set his shirt atop them, leaving his socks balled on the floor beside his shoes, before climbing under the covers in briefs and T-shirt.

Though Ruth did not stir, Abe felt her flinch when he set his hand upon her bare shoulder and began to gently knead until her body slackened.

"What I mean," said Abe, "is that I'm sorry. For the past couple years. Christ, for the past twenty. Yesterday. This morning. Karen. Me. I've been lost, Ruthie, and I'm sorry. I guess I couldn't see past myself most days. I should have been doing more."

IV

Slack

2024

When Abe rolled her onto her back and cradled her head in his lap, Ruth was conscious, but only dimly, her eyes glazed and insensible, her expression slack, a string of saliva clinging to her chin.

"Ruthie, talk to me," he said.

She groaned, and when her lips moved, she managed a slur of unintelligible syllables. Her hair was matted with blood in back; Abe could feel it, slippery between his fingers. He placed a folded towel on the floor and lowered her head back down upon it.

"Everything is gonna be okay," Abe assured her, a churning nausea at work in his gut.

Almost as pressing as Ruth's condition was the awful realization of his own negligence. How could he let this happen? If Ruth did not survive this ordeal, he would never forgive himself.

Abe clambered to his feet unsteadily, and the room began to spin once more as he felt his way along the wall to the basin, then into the bedroom, navigating four feet of open ground to the dresser, where he braced himself once more as he reached for the telephone.

It took less than five minutes for the paramedics to arrive. Forty years ago, it would have taken thirty-five; when they moved to the island in 1959 it might have taken two hours. For all that was wrong with the world, some things got better, and more efficient, but clearly Abe was not among them, standing by helplessly, still dizzy, the flashing lights playing havoc with his ninety-year-old synapses, several drops of urine spotting the front of his pajama pants as the EMTs loaded Ruth onto the gurney and into the ambulance.

*

"I hate to say it, Dad, but we warned you this would happen," said Anne, who had managed to wrangle an early flight out of Denver, rented a car at Sea-Tac, and driven clear around the Tacoma narrows to Silverdale, all before Abe could formulate a defense.

Standing beside him in the corridor, Kyle set a hand upon Abe's shoulder in solidarity, though it was still clear he was in agreement with his sister.

"You can't do this alone, Dad," he said.

The gradually accelerating slide into indignity had finally reached avalanche proportions. Abe's inadequacy and incompetence had ultimately rendered him defenseless against the will of his children. What could he possibly say to redeem himself? If only Maddie had been there to defend him, maybe then Abe would've stood a chance. At this point, he'd be lucky if Anne and Kyle didn't consign both of them to a nursing home.

"She was supposed to wake me up, that was the routine," Abe said, a last-ditch effort to save face. "If your mother wouldn't have been so proud, she would have nudged me like usual, and I would have helped her to the bathroom, and we wouldn't be here right now."

"So, like, in an alternative universe?" said Anne.

"Go to hell," said Abe.

Indeed, his daughter's condescension burned. Who anointed Anne judge and jury? Anybody might have slept through the ordeal. Likewise, anybody might have slipped in the night and banged their head on the toilet. It was an accident, not a crime.

"I've already made the arrangements at Twin Pines," said Kyle. "We were lucky to get a bed on this notice. Like I said, Medicare will cover it for a month. We can go back to the drawing board after that."

"What does that mean?" said Abe.

"One day at a time," said Anne.

There it was: the subtle decree that his own future was no longer negotiable, that Ruth's fate lay firmly in the hands of his children.

"What does your mother think about all of this?" said Abe.

"How should I know?" said Anne. "Why don't you go in there and ask her?"

"Look, Dad," Kyle said. "It doesn't matter what Mom says. We gotta do what's best for her. She needs proper care; we've been saying it all along."

Though there was no sign of internal bleeding, Ruth was to remain at St. Mike's through the night, where her progress would be monitored. Anne and Kyle booked rooms at the Quality Inn, rather than stay at the farm, which might have been an affront to Abe had he not begrudged their interference in his life.

"Dad, you should just crash in my room," said Kyle. "I asked for two queens."

But Abe refused.

"What about Megs?" he said. "You didn't think of that, did you?"

"She's just a dog," said Kyle. "Call the Callahans, have them let her out."

"She's gotta eat, too," said Abe. "Remember?"

"So, the Callahans can feed her."

"I've gotta stop at the grocery store, she's out of wet food," Abe lied. There were at least six cans in the pantry.

"It's not like she's gonna starve," said Anne.

"Hell, she could stand to miss a few meals," said Kyle.

"It's gonna be dark soon," said Anne. "You don't need to be driving around in the dark. And what if it snows?"

But Abe was adamant. There was more at stake than Megs's appetite or a good night's sleep. There was the principle.

Abe drove home, clutching the wheel, squinting through the darkness on Highway 3. Halfway to Poulsbo it did indeed begin to snow, big, fat, wet flakes, swirling and diving in the headlights, playing tricks on Abe's eyes. When he arrived back at the farm, he opened the door and called out Megs's name. He turned the porch light on as Megs emerged from the house and descended the front steps.

Abe took a seat on his porch rocker as he waited for Megs to pee. Al Duncan wasn't wrong about the old chairs, he ought to have taken better care of them over the years. They'd served the Winters so well, through countless summer evenings, stretching back over four decades. How many times had he and Ruth rocked gently, side by side, looking out through the spring rain at the sodden farm? How many conversations and reminiscences, how many hours of easy silence, had they shared out there on those chairs to a chorus of heat-dazed crickets? It felt wrong, one of the rockers being empty.

When Megs struggled up the steps, she proceeded directly to her raggedy old bed between the two rockers and laid herself down heavily with a sigh. There, the two of them remained in silence for five or ten minutes, watching as the snow began to gather on the driveway.

*

The following morning, Ruth was discharged with seven stitches in the back of her head. She was relocated to Twin Pines, where Anne, Kyle, and Abe were all waiting to oversee the transition as she was loaded off the ambulance, past reception, down the corridor to Room 4.

Even as Ruth was deposited in her new bed with the help of two orderlies, she could see Abe, Anne, and Kyle in the hallway through the open door, obviously discussing her fate. It was clear from Abe's body language that he was making some sort of stand. He looked ridiculous, stooped and disheveled and half-crazy. His lips were parched and receding, his wispy hair in disarray. He'd buttoned up his shirt wrong, so there was a little pucker at his sternum where the button and the hole were misaligned. It was hard to imagine he was persuading Anne or Kyle in any way, but it wasn't for lack of trying.

God, how Ruth loved him.

Her new room was just as Ruth had anticipated, drab and institutional, a menagerie of chrome and plastic utility, partitioned crosswise by a thick, gray curtain, blocking off the window. From the other side of the curtain, Ruth could hear the steady hiss of a mechanical ventilator, punctuated abruptly by an unnerving cessation every three seconds. Though she had no idea who occupied the other bed, they were apparently in worse shape than Ruth. But that was no consolation. Though some of her vitality was returning, Ruth was still shaken by her setback. If this was to be the new normal, condemned to live the remainder of her days enfeebled and unable to tend to her own basic needs, Ruth would have preferred death.

Her days at Twin Pines were a portrait of routine: At 6:40 A.M., she was given a breakfast of pureed protein and a chocolate-flavored Glucerna, which she took through two straws. Though the nurses pushed liquids on her constantly, Ruth partook of what she reasoned to be the bare minimum, trying to avoid the indignity of assisted toilet trips.

Every couple of hours, an aide popped in to check her vitals and ask a litany of routine questions regarding Ruth's pain, appetite, mobility, vitality, and comfort. Lunches consisted of flavorless mashed potatoes, no doubt of the powdered variety; pureed chicken and vegetables; and a dessert cup of lime Jell-O or chocolate-and-vanilla-swirl pudding. These repasts were invariably accompanied by the ceaseless hiss and pause of the ventilator on the other side of the curtain.

After lunch followed physical and speech therapy on alternating days. Physical therapy saw Ruth wheeled to the "gym," a cloistered, low-ceilinged room, perhaps fifteen feet by thirty feet, with padded floors and three-hundred-sixty-degree handrails, the entirety of its square footage crowded with treadmills, yoga balls, and steps leading nowhere. Here Ruth was subjected to an excruciating sequence of leg stretches and routine practices such as getting in and out of her wheelchair and climbing the steps.

For speech therapy, Ruth remained in her bed, where she was made to recite the alphabet endlessly when she wasn't practicing words with "s" and "j" sounds: *glasses,* and *messy,* and *castle,* and *jaw,* and *joke,* and *pajamas.* Additionally, she was compelled to contort her mouth into all manner of positions and hold it open for twenty seconds at a time, all so she might one day be reasonably intelligible again. Ruth hated the way she sounded, like her mouth was half-full of water and she had a fingerling potato for a tongue.

Over the course of that first week, though their communications through the drawn curtain were infrequent, Ruth learned that her roommate was named Tish, and she'd been there for three weeks, and her Medicaid was about to run out. Tish was only seventy-five years old, a divorcee more than half her life, with one child, a CPA living in Gig Harbor who had not visited in the weeks she'd been at Twin Pines.

Every other day, Ruth was assisted into a plastic chair, where she submitted to a sponge bath and a change of gown while her sheets were replaced. Visiting hours presented Ruth's lone relief from the tedium of patient care, Abe being her sole frequenter by design. Not only did Ruth not wish her friends and fellow congregants to see her in such miserable condition, but she didn't want to inconvenience them with the forty-minute round-trip drive. Every afternoon without fail, Abe arrived at Twin Pines to sit bedside, reading aloud to her, talking about everything and nothing at all, flipping through the five or six available TV channels, or sometimes just sitting quietly beside Ruth as she dozed off. He was always there when she awoke.

But on the seventh day, Ruth was given to understand when her breakfast arrived that the snow had returned and was beginning to stick. It seemed certain that Abe would not make the trek on bad roads, though she might have expected him to call and tell her as much. Maybe the phone lines were down. What would see her through the afternoon? She was out of unread magazines. Though Abe had brought her a few volumes of poetry, somehow the optimism of Browning or the sensual charm of Keats seemed out of place in the dreary confines of her room at Twin Pines. And there was sure to be nothing on TV to relieve the ennui of Abe's absence.

After speech therapy, compelled by tedium and disappointment, Ruth solicited the orderly to help her out of bed and wheel her out to the lobby with a thin cotton blanket on her lap for warmth, setting Ruth before the huge picture window to leave her there, looking out at the snow. There were nearly four inches of accumulation, enough to bow evergreen limbs and likely render the less traveled roads all but impassable.

Ruth gazed out at the parked cars huddled in the lot gathering snow. Even as she was appraising the scene, she saw the Subaru crest the rise into the lot and immediately start going sideways down the incline, skating narrowly past the line of parked cars before straightening out miraculously, not two feet from sideswiping a van. Ruth watched in disbelief as Abe piled out of the driver's side clutching a canvas grocery bag and began the harrowing trip across the lot in his galoshes. Breathlessly from her wheelchair, Ruth tracked her husband's methodical progress, every slip, slide, and potentially disastrous misstep of the way, until he reached the glass doors intact against all odds, yanking his stocking cap off his head as if it were an annoyance and shaking the snow off it as he stepped into Twin Pines.

He squelched in his galoshes right past Ruth toward the front desk before she called him back. His thin hair was more disheveled than ever as he clutched his wool cap in one hand and the canvas bag in the other, the collar of his mackinaw jacket folded under on one side. Several days unshaven, his chin stubble had caught a bit of blue-gray lint. To see his stooped figure framed in the picture window, the snow fluttering down behind him, his jaw slightly agape, his expression blank, it seemed a miracle that her husband wasn't stranded in a ditch somewhere along the way.

"What were you thinking, driving out here in this mess?" Ruth demanded.

"Aw, it's just a little snow," Abe said, waving it off. "The roads were fine."

But Ruth knew how he'd grown to hate driving in the snow.

"You shouldn't have come," she said.

"Well, tough luck," said Abe. "I'm here. I brought you a new stack of magazines, and some books."

He dug the stack of magazines out of the bag and piled them in her lap.

"You wanna go back to the room?" he said.

"Sure," said Ruth.

As Abe pushed her down the corridor, Ruth flipped through the magazines, touched to see the new *Poets & Writers,* which meant Abe must have made a special trip to Eagle Harbor Books. Back in the room, Abe helped her out of the wheelchair and into the bed, which proved a more difficult task than it had been at home, the bed being a good foot higher off the ground.

"Bess keeps calling the house," said Abe. "She wants to visit, and I don't know how much longer I can hold her off."

"Fine," Ruth conceded. "But only Bess. Please nobody else. Not the Duncans or the Jacobsons. And not in this weather."

"Got it," said Abe. "She'll be glad to hear it."

They lapsed into silence, or near silence, as the ventilator chuffed softly behind the curtain. Abe reached for the remote and turned on the TV, though neither of them paid the screen much notice.

"So, the kids," said Abe at last.

"What about them?"

"They keep pushing me, they're relentless," he said.

"About?"

"About after."

"After I die?"

"No, no," said Abe. "After this place. In two or three weeks."

"I come home," she said.

"Exactly," he said. "They keep leaning on me to sell the farm."

"Maddie?"

"Well, no, not Maddie," Abe said. "Mostly Anne, but Kyle is on board."

"And what do you tell them?" said Ruth.

"Hell no, of course," Abe said. "Too bad if they don't want the farm. I do, and you do. Right?"

He sounded a little unsure on the last.

"Of course," Ruth assured him.

There it was in plainspoken certainty, the sum of their adult lives, everything Ruth and Abe had built together in nearly seventy years of marriage, all the work, and sacrifice, and vision, the goal of providing a bounty for their children, a wholesome, stable environment in a beautiful setting, a place where Ruth and Abe had crafted memory upon memory for Anne, and Karen, and Kyle, and Maddie, birthday parties, weddings, countless holidays, the endless reiteration of the seasons and all their attending joys, the kiddie pools and leaf piles to jump in, and her children didn't care enough to preserve it. What a life.

"How's Megs?" she said.

"Eh," said Abe. "Not so good. She peed on the floor again last night."

"Maybe it's time," Ruth said.

"No," said Abe. "We're not there yet."

He might have been talking about himself, or Ruth, for that matter.

"You probably shouldn't leave her alone too long," said Ruth.

"She'll be okay," said Abe. "I put a towel down."

Poor Megs. Poor Abe, poor Ruth. If you were lucky enough to live a full life, they left you a towel to pee on in the end.

Thankfully, temperatures had risen during the three hours of Abe's visit, and the snow was on its way to melting by the time Abe left Silverdale for the farm. Ruth made him promise he'd call when he arrived safely home, but she was already asleep when the call came in, an orderly later informed her.

Late that night, Ruth was awakened by the sudden whoosh of her roommate's ventilator being removed, even as the lights came on and a pair of harried paramedics wheeled in an empty gurney, disappearing behind the curtain, loading Tish on, and moments later reemerging with her, hurrying her out the door and down the corridor.

For forty-five minutes following Tish's urgent evacuation, Ruth's mind raced with speculation and concern for her bunkmate. But despite her inquiries to the orderly who came to check on Ruth an hour later, no information was forthcoming. Eventually, Ruth fell back to sleep.

In the morning, a different orderly pulled back the curtain, and sunlight flooded in from the window. And from that day forward, Ruth had the room to herself.

There You Go Again

1980

Thanksgiving 1980 was relatively quiet. Wrestling season had just kicked off, so Kyle was unable to make the trip home from Indiana Tech, where he'd just begun in his second year on scholarship. It was mostly a family affair at the farm, the lone exception being that Anne had brought her new boyfriend, Rich Tolbert, home to meet the parents. He was the first mate she'd brought home since Royce Holiday had disappeared into the night some seven years earlier. There had been a handful of other relationships, but none of them enduring. Someone named Chet, who only lasted three or four months. Another guy named Dave, whom Anne had met at a friend's barbecue the summer she'd first moved to the city from Bellingham. As recently as the previous year, Anne had been seeing an older gentleman named Seth, a pilot for Continental Airlines, a relationship that was on again, off again for a year. But Ruth never met one of them. Anne must have really liked this Rich Tolbert if she was bringing him home.

"Make a good impression," Ruth said to Abe as she readied the dinner table an hour in advance of their arrival. "Don't start in with the politics."

"Another hippie?" said Abe.

"I don't think so," said Ruth. "He's some kind of investment banker."

"That sounds promising."

Upon first meeting, Rich Tolbert struck Ruth as morbidly awkward, though sufficiently polite. He seemed like a sensible enough fellow, very professional, and owned a house in Redmond. Though Abe eventually took a shine to him as the afternoon progressed, Ruth couldn't quite understand the attraction. Rich Tolbert was nothing if not unremarkable. He was vaguely handsome but not virile. What was Anne thinking? At least Gonzo, for all his defects, had possessed a little pluck, a certain rakish charm, a cow-eyed mystique that lurked beneath the brim of his dirty hat. Rich Tolbert was all pointed eyes and elbows. His observations were pedestrian. His opinions were safe. Even his wardrobe was lackluster: pleated khakis and a white button-up shirt. At least he wasn't wearing a bow tie. But in Abe's mind, Rich Tolbert had one admirable quality that trumped practically all others: He was a Republican.

As dinner progressed, Abe, to his own satisfaction, methodically managed to lure Rich out of his shell and elicit his political sympathies.

"What do you think about all this economic policy talk, Rich?"

"Well, if you want to stimulate the economy," said Rich, "you've got to offer people incentives. They can't spend money if they don't have it."

"Exactly," said Abe.

"It's just common sense," Rich said.

"You're darn right," said Abe. "And common sense is at an all-time low in the Oval Office, if you ask me."

"Nobody's accountable," Rich said. "They just make excuses."

"You've got that right," said Abe. "That's what America's been missing the past twenty years, accountability, and fiscal responsibility, the kind of leadership that inspires confidence as a nation. No more kowtowing to Iranians, or communists, or anyone else. We need real leadership, someone to jump-start this economy, someone who believes in free enterprise and America putting their best foot forward. I'm tired of conceding on every front. Ruth's man, the peanut farmer, he just hasn't got enough backbone."

"Baloney," said Ruth. "You talk about fiscal responsibility and free enterprise, when really you mean cutting social programs."

"There you go again," said Abe.

"Now you're just parroting the old boob," said Ruth.

"C'mon, Ruthie," pleaded Abe. "We're talking about cutting bureaucratic fat here, not social programs. Am I right, Rich?"

Rich nodded his assent matter-of-factly, though also, Ruth noticed, somewhat apologetically. He seemed to know his audience, and he was losing Ruth.

"Oh, let's not talk about politics," Ruth said.

Rich was more than happy to concur and ate the remainder of his dinner in silence.

After the meal, Anne took her mother's cue to join her in clearing the dishes and hauling them to the kitchen.

"He's so quiet," said Ruth, wiping a dish dry.

"He's just shy," said Anne. "Once he opens up, he has a lot to say."

"Mm," said Ruth.

"Dad likes him," said Anne.

"Yes, he does," said Ruth. "And I like him, too."

"Do you?"

"Yes, of course." But really, Ruth had to think hard of something nice to say about Rich. "He's nice."

When the dishes were racked and drying, Ruth and Anne joined Abe and Rich in the living room, where they were watching the news in silent tandem rather than conversing. Anne proceeded straight to the television and turned it off.

"Hey, what's the big idea?" said Abe.

"Dad, Mom, me and Rich have an announcement. Rich, you want to tell them?"

Rich seemed mortified by the prospect. "You go ahead and tell them," he said.

Ruth's first thought was: *Please don't let her be pregnant with this guy.*

"Mom, Dad," said Anne, "Rich and I are engaged! We're getting married in the spring."

Though she was sure her disappointment was palpable, Ruth manufactured a smile. "That's wonderful, honey," she said.

"Congratulations, you two!" said Abe.

For all the worrying Ruth and Abe had done about Anne finding love after the unmitigated disaster of Royce Holiday, her last serious boyfriend, the news should have come as a relief. But it didn't, not for Ruth, anyway. Something felt off, though Ruth was powerless to share these feelings with Anne.

In bed that night, after Anne and Rich had returned to the city, Ruth lay shoulder to shoulder with Abe as he skimmed the obituaries in the murky light of the bedside lamp.

"Well, that was quick, don't you think?" said Ruth.

"When you know, you know," said Abe. "I was half-convinced I wanted to marry you the night you humiliated me at the bowling alley."

"Doesn't he strike you as a little . . . conservative?" said Ruth.

"What's wrong with that?" said Abe.

"I mean, for Anne," Ruth said. "He just doesn't seem like her type. He's so . . . buttoned up."

"Well, he's no Royce Holiday, that's for damn sure. I think we can both be thankful for that."

"I suppose," said Ruth.

"I don't get it," said Abe. "You don't like this guy. What's not to like? He's polite. He's responsible. He doesn't bring a guitar to the dinner table."

"He's just a little . . ."

"A little what . . . ?"

"Reserved, I guess."

"So, what's wrong with exercising a little restraint? Does everybody gotta yammer every time a thought takes shape in their head?"

"Maybe *dull* is the word I was looking for," said Ruth.

"You said the same thing about me—to your friends, anyway."

"Touché," said Ruth.

"Look, Ruthie, maybe he's not a poet. But he seems like good husband material to me, dependable, not full of surprises. He's not the type that's gonna run around on her."

"I suppose you're right about all of that," said Ruth. "I just have a bad intuition about it."

"Let it go," said Abe. "She's a big girl, she knows what she's doing."

By acknowledging her reservations about Rich Tolbert as a suitable mate for her eldest child, wasn't Ruth essentially saying she'd made a mistake herself and didn't want Anne to make the same one? The revelation stung. How could Ruth even entertain such a thought after twenty-six years of marriage? Abe deserved better than that. They'd both had their misgivings over the years, and yes, the long road of their marriage had been largely unpaved and full of potholes, but they'd made it this far, hadn't they? Who was Ruth to want more for her daughter? Anne would be lucky to partner with someone as steadfast as her father. Maybe Rich Tolbert was Abe's equal, and Ruth just couldn't see it.

The wedding planning fell almost entirely on Ruth's shoulders, and despite her reservations, she put her heart and soul into making Anne's big day perfect. The ceremony and the reception were to be held on the farm, this being the one facet of the master plan that Abe approved of wholeheartedly, for even accounting for the Porta Potties, and the tables, and the chairs, and the tents, and the caterer, and the band, it was still considerably cheaper than renting Kiana Lodge.

Ruth held Anne's hand through the entire sometimes overwhelming ordeal, helping Anne select the votives, and the floral arrangements, and the dresses for the bridesmaids, and the caterer, and the cake. Abe, meanwhile, wrote the checks, often begrudgingly.

"Why do we need a dance floor? The reception's outside. What's wrong with the lawn?"

"Sign the check, Abe."

Abe's protestations extended to the invitations, as well.

"The Duncans and the Jacobsons, sure, of course. But the Dolingers?" said Abe. "Why do the Dolingers have to come? I've never even met them."

"Kenny Dolinger is Anne's friend from high school," Ruth explained.

"The smoker from the bowling alley parking lot, yeah, I remember. That was over ten years ago," he said.

"Abe, stop it," she scolded.

"Okay, fine, invite Kenny Dolinger. But why the parents?"

"Abe," said Ruth.

"Fine," he said, waving it off. "But don't complain to me when our nest egg has dwindled to nothing and we're living out of the station wagon."

This exaggeration was, of course, patently absurd. The Winters were more than set for the future, from college, to weddings, to retirement and beyond. Abe had tucked 10 percent of their income aside from the start and invested wisely all along. The farm was nearly paid off and was now valued at four times what they'd paid for it in 1959. Abe was simply getting stingy in middle age. To his credit, though, he was willing in the end to loosen the purse strings, if only reluctantly, and get out of Ruth's way.

Anne's wedding was a late May affair, and the farm had never looked more beautiful or inviting, the cherry trees in blossom, the sprawling lawn still green from the rain, the flower beds brimming purple and pink and yellow. Miraculously, even the weather cooperated. They couldn't have asked for more glorious conditions: sixty-five degrees and sunny, the kind of burgeoning spring magnificence that Californians took for granted, the promise of summer whispering upon its gentle breeze, the kind of rare and unseasonable occasion that never failed to inspire false hope in Western Washingtonians, who would have to wait until August for its actual arrival.

A hundred and fifty people attended the ceremony, the numbers skewing decidedly toward the bride's side of the aisle, with the Tolbert contingent accounting for less than forty friends and family members situated on the groom's side. The Dolingers were in attendance.

The altar stood at the foot of the orchard, where white cherry blossoms rained down like confetti, several collecting upon the shoulders of Pastor Dearsley's stole as he awaited the bride and groom. Above him the sky was blue; beyond him, the pond, sheltered beneath the cedars, glistened with a glassy green sheen of algae.

From Ruth's seat in the front row, Abe looked totally unprepared for the flood of emotions that overwhelmed him as he escorted his eldest daughter down the aisle, through the colonnade of fruit trees toward the altar, his face red, cheeks shiny with tears.

And when Anne and Rich took their vows, almost shyly, their sun-kissed faces radiating optimism, Ruth set aside her reservations in that moment and believed in them. In the light of all that beauty, their differences seemed trivial.

Ah, such a lovely day it had been: blue skies and blossoms, birdsong and boundless green grass! And that elusive grace; Ruth, too, had felt it in the air. Then came the reception, the dining, and dancing, and laughter, all the joyous harbingers of the wonderful days that lay ahead, the magnificent promise of a stable future spread out before them. Love had been indomitable that afternoon. And when the stars fell upon the merriment, the music echoing in the treetops, the children, up way past their bedtimes, hopped up on root beer and wedding cake, darting between revelers on the dance floor, harmony was all but assured.

★

A marriage is not built in a day to last. Rather, it is shaped gradually and methodically to withstand the ruinous effects of time and outside

254 * Jonathan Evison

forces beyond the control of its principal players. Like all institutions, a marriage requires maintaining, and amending, for it is more than a binding commitment, it is a process, one that demands participation, a willingness to absorb, to accept, to reassess. Ruth didn't need a marriage counselor to tell her any of that, she'd learned it in the trenches, and was still learning after twenty-six years. After the vows, and the bouquets, and the trip to Honolulu, marriage was mostly work.

Within nine months of Anne and Rich's wedding, it seemed clear that they were headed for trouble, and barring any seismic shifts in their relationship, likely toward a divorce. While this situation elicited Ruth's sympathy, it also provoked a significant degree of annoyance and antipathy. More than the dissolution of their association, it was the principles at stake that bothered Ruth: unconditional loyalty, devotion, responsibility, all those qualities comprising the covenant of marriage. Surely, Ruth and Abe had provided their daughter a sufficient example, hadn't they? Or was it possible that Anne's thoughts were informed by the enduring dissent that had marked Ruth's marriage to Abe? Had Anne, in essence, having borne witness to this uneasy union her entire life, glimpsed the future in the form of her parents' marriage and decided that wedlock was akin to a padlock? Had Anne resolved that the notion of growing old together wasn't worth all the quibbling and ideological schisms that attended such an abiding obligation? Or was the decision simply a generational default? Had the American age of prosperity overindulged Anne's generation? Had their "laissez-faire" attitude—as Abe liked to put it—toward everything from sexual mores to economics to religion spelled the end of traditionalism?

Anne's disillusionment with Rich marked a turn in her relationship with Ruth, with whom she came to share her misgivings about her husband with increasing candor.

"He's like one of those zombies," Anne complained. "Four months of therapy, and we're still going round and round in circles. What do I do?"

This represented the first time that any of her children had solicited Ruth's input on a romantic matter. Certainly, Anne had never
sought her guidance over the course of a half dozen boyfriends dating
all the way back to the eighth grade. Though Ruth had never cared for
Rich Tolbert in the first place, and the preceding months had done
little to change her opinion, she felt nonetheless morally compelled to
encourage her daughter to save the marriage.

"Revisit your vows," said Ruth.

"We've done that already, Mom," she said. "The contract is void."

"Redraft it, then."

"It's hopeless, I'm telling you. He's an immovable object *and* an
irresistible force," Anne said. "He won't try anything new, not even in
a restaurant. He orders the same thing from the menu every time."

"He knows what he likes," observed Ruth. "Like your father."

"Does he, though?" said Anne. "How can he know what he likes
when he won't try anything? I swear, it's like he was born fifty years
old. He literally drives me insane. The way he chews ice, the way he
sleeps with four pillows, the way he never talks about his job. I can't
take it anymore."

"So, that's it? You're just gonna give up?" Ruth said. "A few bumps
in the road and you're ready to call the whole marriage quits?"

"Well?" said Anne. "What can I do? We're incompatible."

Ruth might have told her so, but she held her tongue. Instead,
she could only offer Anne a different sort of tough love, which was to
hold her responsible for her own part in the collapse of her marriage.

"I guess I thought he would change," pursued Anne.

"You thought you could change him?"

"No," said Anne. "I just thought he'd evolve."

"Have you?"

"What is that supposed to mean?"

"Sometimes marriage is a compromise," said Ruth.

"Spare me the clichés, Mom, will you?"

Cliché or not, as far as Ruth was concerned, that marriage was a compromise cut about as close to the bone of matrimony as you possibly could. After a quarter of a century, Ruth knew this all too well, and she supposed Abe knew it, too. Where exactly was the crime in compromising? Was this who we'd become? A nation of self-serving egocentrics, our only allegiance to our inflexible ideals?

No, Ruth could not accept as much. If there was one thing that she and Abe could agree on, that had helped account for their longevity, it was this: Sometimes it was necessary to acquiesce, to tolerate and accept the beliefs or needs of others to achieve harmony. If everybody refused to concede the gratification of their will at every juncture, where would we find ourselves in twenty, forty, fifty years? Somebody had to build bridges across the divide.

Despite Ruth's encouragement, Anne and Rich filed for divorce at the end of '81, but it was already a foregone conclusion by then. The primary consolation of their bifurcation was that there were no children to muddy the waters, their split was not acrimonious, the property was distributed evenly, and all in all, it might have been much worse. Anne went her way, and Rich went his. Still, Ruth could not shake the feeling that on some larger scale the concession of their vows, like so many things at the dawn of that shiny new decade, was a small step backward for the institution of marriage.

Nothing Could Be Finer

1985

With her fiftieth birthday approaching, Ruth came to discover that change, a concept once conceived as a course of action to be plotted and planned like a European vacation, was in fact less like a journey and more like a malady, one that exhibited new symptoms daily: foggy brain, flagging vitality, persistent irritability, hot flashes. And those were only the physical manifestations. After decades of personal abnegation and domestic administration, Ruth's search for self-coherence was nosing toward a crisis. With Maddie already looking at colleges, with the last of the Lego bins and Lincoln Logs and stuffed animals already stowed in the attic, the fully empty nest once envisioned as respite from servitude was suddenly a prospect Ruth dreaded. My God, the house would be so empty. What would she do with herself?

These pressing questions had flooded in on Ruth, wave after wave of uncertainty battering the hull of her identity until she woke up at forty-nine feeling shipwrecked, marooned with a mutinous body on an island where nobody could reach her. She knew better than to solicit her husband's aid, for he would most likely chalk it up to hormones, and he would only be half-right. Her children would tell her to get over it. And how could she expect childless, unmarried Bess Delory to understand? Ultimately, it would be a stranger who threw Ruth a life preserver.

Ruth was shopping at Town & Country one weekday afternoon, listlessly combing the produce department for the customary provisions (spinach, apples, squash, russet potatoes), when she encountered a striking young woman, perhaps Anne's age or slightly older, slim and athletic with dark cropped hair, hefting in her tattooed arms what appeared to be a giant, psoriatic melon the likes of which Ruth had never seen. In truth, it had been the young woman herself as much as the mystery fruit that had aroused Ruth's curiosity: the vaguely Polynesian tattoos snaking up her arms, the short, lustrous hair that still managed to look feminine, the remarkable ease with which she seemed to carry her beauty. By Bainbridge Island standards, she was exotic.

"Pardon me," said Ruth, approaching her tentatively. "But . . . may I ask, what exactly is that you're holding?"

"It's jackfruit," said the young woman.

"Ah," said Ruth. "It looks tropical."

The woman's smile was contagious, and Ruth found herself smiling.

"It is," said the young woman.

"So, like a pineapple, then?"

"You'd think so," she said. "But it's actually more like a giant fig."

"What do you do with it?" said Ruth. "I mean, if you don't mind my asking. Am I being nosy? It's just that I've never even heard of it."

"Not at all," she said. "The jackfruit is unappreciated in North America. They love it in Thailand."

Ruth felt so ordinary next to this lithe young woman. Here she was in her frumpy jeans, the same hairstyle she'd worn for fifteen years, with her yellow squash and russet potatoes; what could possibly be less exotic?

"When they're unripe like this, I use them as a meat substitute," she said.

"Oh?" said Ruth.

"I'm a vegetarian," she explained.

No wonder she was so skinny.

"I'm Tiana, by the way," she said, extending a firm handshake.

"Ruth," said Ruth.

"You look familiar," she said. "Have I seen you at the Stream-liner?"

"I've never been," said Ruth.

"Never? Well, we need to change that," said Tiana.

And thus, an unlikely friendship began with an invite for coffee at the Streamliner Diner. What exactly Tiana saw in Ruth that she would extend such an invitation, Ruth could not say. A maternal appeal? Or maybe she just saw in Ruth a middle-aged woman in need of a friend.

"Your eyes are so pretty," Tiana told her that first rendezvous at the diner, a compliment that had Ruth blushing to the roots of her hair. "You don't look like a Ruth," she said.

"Oh?" said Ruth. "What do I look like?"

Tiana studied her face intently until Ruth could feel herself blushing again. "Maybe a Rita. Like Rita Hayworth."

"Really?" said Ruth.

"Or an Ava. Like Ava Gardner."

What a thrill it was to be seen as a Rita or an Ava, to be equated with a star of the silver screen. Not since her college days had Ruth dared to imagine herself as anything more than ordinary. And here, this young woman saw in Ruth something more—more than a middle-aged woman in jeans and a sweatshirt.

Ruth immediately found herself drawn to Tiana's self-assurance and awed by the breadth of the younger woman's experience. Tiana had traveled all over the world, from Central America to Southeast Asia to France and beyond. She'd surfed in New Zealand, worked on a coffee plantation in Costa Rica, cooked for sixty men in a remote fishing village in northern Alaska. She spoke Spanish, Portuguese, and bits of French and Isan. She knew wine, and poetry, and tai chi; she was fluent in food, and coffee, and music. How she'd crammed it all into thirty-two years, Ruth could hardly imagine. How she was still single was even harder to fathom. But she was refreshingly unconcerned by this lack of attachment. Indeed, Tiana spoke very little of men. Maybe that was the secret to her brimming life, remaining unencumbered, an existence Ruth could hardly conceive of after four children and thirty years of marriage.

As for the Streamliner, it made good on its promise that "nothing could be finer than eating at the Diner." The diner was a far cry from the greasy spoon its name seemed to suggest. The coffee was robust, the muffins nothing like the store-bought bran confections Ruth had grown accustomed to, and the omelets so much more than the standard ham and cheese. The Streamliner possessed a style all its own, one that infused rustic European cuisine with a culinary ethos Abe would have characterized as "granola." Ruth told herself halfheartedly that Abe wouldn't appreciate the diner, but the truth was that she wanted the diner to be her place, not theirs. These were not Abe's people; they didn't buy life insurance. These were Ruth's people. They wrote poetry, blew glass, maybe played mandolins. Their sophistication was practically Parisian next to most of the island's denizens. The thought of Abe at the counter opining about interest rates was incongruous. For Ruth, the Streamliner Diner was nothing less than a revelation; more than a restaurant, it was an institution, vibrant and joyfully noisy, humming with that energy Ruth had gravitated toward in her university days, but something more, too, a warmth, and the promise of familiarity.

Over the course of three or four coffee dates, Tiana introduced Ruth to the entire staff of the diner, women every last one of them but for the teenage dishwashers, who were boys with spiky hair and T-shirts emblazoned with band names and slogans that likely would have offended Abe's sensibilities: Dayglo Abortions, Circle Jerks, and the most egregious of all, Rock Against Reagan. The diner women were a dizzyingly diverse cast of characters: Barb, and Kiki, and Jewel; Gabby, and Judith, and Heidi; Toni, Alexandra, Leigh Anne,

Greta, Lindsey, and Mary Beth. While these women shared a common notion of community, they were anything but uniform in their ideologies. Judith was a Buddhist, while Alexandra was a self-described Taoist, and Jewel subscribed to a deity called Ramtha. Heidi was a devout atheist. Mary Beth believed in extraterrestrials. Toni practiced numerology and read palms. Likewise, their lives were self-styled: Greta lived in a converted school bus. Kiki lived in a yurt. Lindsey drove a vintage Mercedes.

Within a matter of weeks, Ruth was welcomed into the diner fold, and overnight, the Streamliner became her second home, the place she lingered half the day while Abe was at the office and Maddie was at school, those hours formerly spent administering to her domestic obligations, folding laundry, Windexing mirrors she was afraid to look into, watering flower beds nobody appreciated. This time was now passed at the diner counter, talking to the girls as they worked, or whoever happened to sit next to her, whether it was Steve, the mural painter and garden sculptor; Misha, the cellist and actor; Rene, the wreath maker and masseuse; or Maya, the voice artist and sometimes belly dancer. They all accepted Ruth as what she wished to be: a poetess and a farmer. And though in most cases she was old enough to be their mother, they treated her as an equal. Not that there weren't older patrons in their midst, resident characters, white-bearded fishermen, and carpenters, men who enjoyed lively conversation and the company of those Streamliner women, whose brand of rugged individualism they heartily subscribed to themselves.

When Ruth wasn't at the diner, she was filling notebooks again, verses and vignettes, whole poems. And for the first time in her life, she was sharing them. Not with Abe, of course, but with Tiana, and Judith, and Heidi, and Alexandra, after hours at the diner, or early mornings at Pegasus Coffee, where they sometimes gathered before work. To Ruth, this community of creative souls represented an antidote to the times. Their built-in support system, their self-reliance, their autonomy, their unique customs, all of it embodied the ideal of the collective that the baby boomers had tried so desperately to achieve. And it seemed that some of them—those she met at the diner, those who weren't peddling plastics or selling insurance, those who were renting, not owning, those who were either childless or whose children wore their hair past their shoulders and ran with the wolves—had finally achieved it in their thirties.

After two months of Ruth loitering at the diner, Judith offered her a job.

"You know your way around a kitchen. If you're gonna be here all day, why not get paid? You'll free up space at the counter."

The thought of working at the diner had not once occurred to Ruth in her endless hours drinking coffee at the counter, discussing everything from goat farming to the novels of Robertson Davies. Ruth didn't need the money, any more than the diner needed another body in the kitchen. The proposition seemed less about employment and more about fully belonging to the Streamliner.

That evening at the dinner table, Ruth announced her intention to enter the workforce for the first time.

"Aren't you kind of old to be getting a job, Mom?" said Maddie.

"Good for you," said Abe. "How'd you come by it? You applied, or . . . ?"

"One of the owners offered it to me," said Ruth.

"Great," said Abe. "Can't beat that. You know, I've been meaning to eat there, but I'm not really a breakfast guy beyond coffee and toast. While you're at it, find out who insures the place."

Ruth and Abe had survived Leonard, and Karen's death, and so far, five years of Ronald Reagan, and while there was no denying that their marriage had grown distant and utilitarian, Abe had once again proven himself a supportive spouse. Whatever distance between them Ruth may have begrudged, she forgave him because of his tolerance.

The diner saved Ruth from what had begun to feel like a life by default. The diner empowered her; it reconnected her to a larger world of ideas and people and experience. To survive the utter chaos of the morning rush at the Streamliner was one thing, but to laugh through it was something else altogether; to feel like you were a part of something vital and thriving embodied a thrill and a sense of accomplishment that the slow, grinding slog of parenthood had never quite achieved with any regularity. Too often, nobody had ever been there beside Ruth to appreciate it when she cooked breakfast for six, cleaned the dishes, packed the lunches, and sent everybody on their way. Lacking anyone with whom she might share the accomplishments, she had stopped acknowledging these pleasures herself.

Nothing beat the solidarity of those late Sunday afternoons closing the Streamliner after a harrowing day, as she and the girls, once the dust had settled, prepared the restaurant for the week ahead, bantering and complaining and laughing as they prepped, and ordered, and restocked, listening to *A Prairie Home Companion* on public radio. Occasionally, Ruth and Tiana and Heidi would steal out back of the restaurant to smoke a joint by the dumpster. Marijuana was something Ruth had partaken of only twice in her life, once with Fred and Mandy in the back of Fred's car at Magnuson Park beach, and once with Anne and Royce Holiday out by the pond, where they had gleefully insisted upon her compliance. Ruth had not particularly enjoyed the experience on either occasion. But smoking with Tiana and Heidi felt like a rite of passage.

Many changes were afoot. Ruth's wardrobe was completely transformed within a matter of months. Gone were the frumpy jeans and the matronly hair, gone the shapeless gardening boots. In their place Ruth wore a sassy bob with a high nape, bold patterned blouses with low necklines paired with flowing, breathing skirts and leather Birkenstocks. Though Ruth worried these wholesale changes might look like a midlife crisis to her husband and the fellow congregants at Seabold Methodist Church, Bess Delory was there to support her as always.

"Nonsense! You look more like you than ever! My goodness, you look twenty years younger with your hair off your face. And that blouse—gorgeous! Are those camellias?"

But not everyone in Ruth's life was so accepting of her remade appearance, especially her fifteen-year-old daughter.

"Ugh, Mom, it's embarrassing. What are you wearing?" Maddie complained. "You're supposed to be a mom. You look like a bag lady."

Abe met this metamorphosis with curiosity and mild amusement, teasing Ruth affectionately about her granola stylings, but Ruth could feel the force of his renewed attention, even when her back was turned, and that, too, was empowering.

For all the fresh influences in her life, none were more far-reaching than Tiana, to whom Ruth owed her new lease on life. Two months into Ruth's tenure at the diner, Tiana had already displaced Bess Delory as Ruth's primary companion. When not convening at the diner, Ruth and Tiana took afternoon walks around Gazzam Lake, or Battle Point Park, or out in the mudflats at Manitou Beach at low tide, barelegged to their knees as they squelched through tidelands. Since they had entire lifetimes to share, these early stages of their friendship might be described as breathless. Their investigations ranged widely, from art to philosophy to politics. In the arenas of politics and religion, Ruth found Tiana refreshingly unencumbered by affiliations, her theological inclinations tending toward those Eastern and new age philosophies that best suited her. Politically, she landed somewhere far to the left of any party platform, her political philosophies, like her religious convictions, a mishmash of ideologies best summed up as agrarian communistic gynocentrism. Abe would've had a field day with Tiana had Ruth ever allowed such a summit to occur, but like her diner life as a whole, Ruth cultivated and maintained her friendship with Tiana outside of Abe's purview.

Abe apparently entertained no misgivings regarding Ruth's extracurricular activities. He seemed genuinely pleased that Ruth was living her best bohemian-granola life, if not relieved to be excluded from the proceedings. While Ruth clung firmly to her Methodist and Democratic roots, she was endlessly fascinated by Tiana's maverick philosophies and outlandish notions, pseudoscientific propositions such as "morphic resonance," "antediluvian civilization," and "the science of magic." It was not the ideas themselves that intoxicated Ruth, rather Tiana's ravenous curiosity and contagious enthusiasm for them.

But more than intellectual, Ruth's attraction to Tiana was compelled by something else, a sort of kinetic energy produced whenever the two of them were in proximity. Tiana's effortless, almost androgynous beauty was like a gravitational force. The graze of Tiana's shoulder aroused a certain flutter in her chest; the touch of Tiana's fingers stood Ruth's arm hairs on end. These were new feelings for Ruth. That they were mutual seemed undeniable, though still difficult for Ruth to account for, no matter how many times Tiana complimented her eyes, or her well-preserved figure, or her mental acuity, or her command of language. Such was Tiana's charm that she might have attached herself to anybody she wanted. Why she'd chosen Ruth in the produce section of T&C remained a mystery.

For all that Tiana and the diner family had done to help Ruth survive the hormonal chaos of menopause, for all the comfort, and encouragement, and occupation they offered, there was no correcting the chemical disequilibrium that visited Ruth daily, those moments of inexplicable agitation, incongruous tears, or incomprehensible grief. Add to this the seismic shifts in Ruth's identity, all the newness, all the adjusting and recalibrating, and her grand climacteric was bound to reach a crescendo.

It occurred on a rare Sunday when Ruth had skipped church, during a particularly harried brunch rush at the diner: checks flying; orders stacking up; sourdough smoldering in the toaster; potatoes smoking on the grill; the overwhelming cacophony of the diner—the scrape of forks on ceramic, the clinking of glass, the discord of thirty simultaneous conversations—beating on Ruth's eardrums, even as the demands came flying at her from every direction (*How's that Mediterranean scramble? Table two is missing a BLTA. Where's my combo? This was supposed to be a deluxe*); the impatience of Lindsey at the waitress station; the impossible wall of heat rising off the grill sopping Ruth's face with perspiration, blurring her vision. On top of it all, that particular Sunday would have been Karen's twenty-eighth birthday.

When Lindsey, arms akimbo at the register, demanded her combo for the third time, something in Ruth snapped. Dropping her spatula on the grill with a clang, she tore off her apron, dropped it in a heap, and fled the cramped kitchen. She hurried past the register, nearly upending Lindsey as she rounded the corner, quickening her pace down the narrow aisle past gawking diners, nearly clipping Kiki, arms full of plates, on her way past. Once Ruth hit the open air and pushed past the horde waiting on the sidewalk to be seated, she rounded the corner, passing the line of diners gaping through the window this time, before she arrived at the dumpster in back, where she broke down.

It was only a matter of seconds before Tiana joined Ruth there.

"Oh, sweetie," Ruth said.

Tiana wrapped Ruth in an embrace and held her firmly but tenderly as Ruth's body slackened in her arms. But as Ruth felt the pressure of Tiana's chest, almost boyish, pressed against her own, her heartbeat palpable, along with the soft stirring of her breath in Ruth's ear, a single sensation overrode the rest, an arousal, not purely sexual, though acutely sensual. Perhaps Tiana felt the quickening of Ruth's heartbeat as she squeezed her harder. When she finally relinquished her grip, she held Ruth at arm's length and smiled sympathetically.

"Hey, you," she said, and that was all.

The next instant, Ruth felt her mouth upon Tiana's, a kiss unlike any Ruth had ever known, a far cry from the gruffness of Abe, whose dry lips arrived at hers like a formality. This exchange with Tiana was ardent to the point of desperation and must have lasted five seconds before they finally separated. When Ruth looked up, her heart galloping in her chest, she nearly swooned from the shock of what she saw next, or rather whom.

There, parked in the rear lot of Town & Country in the station wagon, looking out the driver's-side window directly at them, was Abe.

"What is it?" said Tiana as the blood drained from Ruth's face.

"My husband," said Ruth.

Minutes later, Ruth was in the passenger seat beside him in total silence, both of them staring straight ahead out the windshield at the line of green dumpsters behind T&C.

"I've been meaning to come in for weeks," he said, as if he owed her some explanation for his presence there. "Today was the day."

A deafening silence settled back into the car as they continued to avoid eye contact. It lasted a minute, maybe even two, Ruth all but paralyzed in her befuddlement.

"Well," he said finally. "Are you gonna say something? What was that?"

Ruth did not answer; she couldn't, for she could not account for something she didn't understand herself.

"Don't you think she's a little young for you?" he said.

"It's not like that," said Ruth. "Whatever that might have looked like, it wasn't."

"It looked like my wife kissing another woman."

"It was, but not like that."

"Like what, then? That was no peck on the cheek."

"I don't know what it was," said Ruth. "I was distraught, I was thinking of Karen, I screwed up an order, Lindsey was yelling at me, I ran out. Tiana followed me out. She talked me off the ledge, and then . . . it just . . . happened."

"And that was the first time?"

"It was," said Ruth. "The first and the last."

"Mm," said Abe.

It was clear as he gazed out the window that he was deeply troubled. God, the confusion he must have been feeling, the poor man. Surely, he must have had a million questions that he couldn't bring himself to ask: *Are you a lesbian? Do you love me? Do you hate me? Why is this happening?*

Ruth should have told him it had absolutely nothing to do with him. While that much seemed obvious, it might have been a comfort to tell him so. But Ruth couldn't bring herself to speak. So they continued to sit in silence for a minute until it began spitting rain on the windshield.

"Aren't you supposed to be in there working?" he said at last.

"Yes," she said.

"Well, then . . ."

Is That What You Think?

All things considered, to Abe the job had seemed like a good idea. It would offer Ruth a new sense of purpose with Maddie on her way out of the house. The money she earned would be mostly symbolic, for it was never a matter of need. That the Streamliner had become so much more than a job, that it had become some sort of personal revolution, was more difficult to resolve, undermining Abe's fundamental expectation of a world governed by stability, normalcy, and reason.

While kissing another woman struck Abe as a puzzling manifestation for a midlife crisis, who could blame Ruth for wanting to reinvent herself? She'd devoted her entire adult life to serving her family, sacrificing everything for her husband and her children; didn't she deserve the opportunity to dabble in something new? How could Abe deny her this liberation, wherever it came from, whatever it meant?

Looking at these women with their Birkenstock sandals and their hairy legs, their "goddess" muffins made of morning glory seeds, their chamomile tea, listening to public radio and reading tarot cards, turning their backs on convention in favor of a lifestyle more suited to twenty-year-olds, you'd think it was still 1968. Nearly two decades on, these women, some of them now approaching middle age, having largely rejected the institution of marriage, still hadn't opted back into the mainstream. Abe couldn't see the appeal for Ruth.

Still, he'd managed to hold his tongue, mostly because he was afraid that if he pushed back, it might spell the end of his marriage. He resolved himself to let Ruth work herself through this crisis of identity on her own terms. Thus, the incident with Tiana was never mentioned again, leaving Abe to guess at its meaning. While Ruth's relations with Tiana, whatever exactly they amounted to, somehow did not feel like quite the same threat to Abe as Leonard Haruto had, the infidelity (indeed, if it could be called one?) still vexed him. At least he had not been forced to witness firsthand his wife's indiscretion with Haruto as he had with Tiana. Never before had Abe seen two women kissing the way Ruth had been kissing Tiana. Was Ruth a lesbian? Had she always been a lesbian? Had the Streamliner Diner made her a lesbian? Had Abe made her a lesbian? Any way Abe figured it, the possibilities were troubling. Where were these lesbian inclinations in 1955? Surely, Ruth would not have acted on such impulses back at UW, or would she have? Or had she? Abe tried to picture her kissing Mandy Baterman the way she kissed Tiana, but he couldn't imagine it.

Had Ruth quit her job at the diner that afternoon, or at least taken some time off, stepped back and removed herself from this other life to some degree and reconcentrated her energies on the home front and her marriage, Abe might have been able to forgive all of it. But Ruth maintained her alliances with the Streamliner Diner, where Abe was condemned to remain an outsider, if not as a male of the species and symbol of the status quo, as Ruth's husband, and as an impediment to her continued development. Under these circumstances, how could Abe feel anything but in the way? Even when Ruth began to solicit Abe's participation, he distrusted the invitation as conciliatory rather than genuine.

"You should come in and eat during my shift."

"Food's too frilly for me—all that guacamole, the artichoke hearts, too many grains. I'm a bacon-and-eggs man."

"Well, we have that, too. Or just have coffee."

"Too strong. Puts my nerves on edge."

But when Ruth persisted, Abe felt he had no choice but to accept this olive branch, no matter how much he dreaded the prospect. And so, one Saturday morning, Abe circumnavigated the crowd of waiting parties out front and waded through the cramped foyer, proceeding past the hostess station and the teeming dining room, where he packed his large frame onto the lone empty stool at the counter, unbeknownst to Ruth, whose back was turned as she busied herself at the grill, shoulder to shoulder with Tiana. Here, Abe found himself wedged between a braless woman in green cat-eye glasses and a bearded fellow in a purple beret. Thank God Abe brought a newspaper.

The coffee was radioactive. The eggs were poached. There were onions and peppers in his potatoes. The counter was too mobbed for Abe to unfold his paper, so he was forced instead to gaze across the counter at the back side of his wife and her . . . lover? He might have left his breakfast and made a quick getaway had the check arrived in a timely manner; instead, the guy in the beret insisted on striking up a conversation with Abe over the din of the restaurant.

"So, what do you do?" he said.

"I sell insurance," said Abe.

"Okay, I see, insurance," he said. "But what do you do?"

"I just told you; I sell insurance."

"Oh, wow," said the guy. "A real career man, then. You go to school for that?"

"Thirty years ago," said Abe.

"I'm Thor," he said, offering a toast with his coffee cup.

He was a stoop-shouldered five foot seven in work boots; nothing about Thor conjured the god of thunder.

"I'm an artist," he observed.

"Mm," said Abe.

"Mostly, I work with found objects."

"Ah," said Abe.

"I just installed a piece at Strawberry Hill Park, maybe you've seen it? It's about sixty feet off the road on the west side, near the bathrooms."

"Afraid not," said Abe, scanning the vicinity for a waitress.

Though Abe offered him little encouragement, Thor kept the conversational ball rolling with a veritable catalog of his work. When verbiage no longer sufficed, Thor produced a binder from his ruck-sack and offered Abe a visual tour of his art. Mostly shapes and hu-man figures constructed of hubcaps and rebar.

"I call this one *The Body Electric*," he said.

The Body Electric resembled nothing so much as the bombed-out hull of an old fishing schooner strewn and dangling with metal miscellany. It seemed that one man's found object was another man's scrap metal.

It was a relief when Ruth finally leaned over the counter to ad-dress Abe.

"How was your breakfast?" she said.

"Delicious," he said, checking his watch.

Abe could not escape the diner quickly enough. It was a small comfort knowing that his status as an interloper, whether real or per-ceived, was at least for him a welcome condition. Eggs were meant to be fried, female ankles shaven, scrap metal scrapped.

But when, two weeks later, Ruth insisted that Abe accompany her to the annual diner Christmas party at Fort Worden in Port Townsend, Abe could not wiggle out of it.

"You'll love it," she insisted. "There will be music, and storytell-ing, and games."

The prospect was about as enticing as an evening of iron thumb-screws. What if Thor was invited? All that phony spirituality and self-empowerment. Bulgur salads and beets. Goat cheese. Hand-holding and singalongs. Scrap metal.

But once they got there, even Abe couldn't complain about the setting. Fastidiously arranged atop a wide, grassy plateau dotted with madronas, historic Fort Worden was bordered on the north by a high bluff overlooking Admiralty Inlet and buttressed to the west by a steep, verdant hillside of fir and cedar. The sublime orderliness of the compound had always appealed to Abe, the tidy administrative buildings and barracks aligned strategically and harmoniously. Straddling the bluff and hidden from view were Abe's favorite feature of the fortifications: the batteries and armaments, hulking concrete structures adorned with the rusted remnants of nineteenth-century gun emplacements. Abe had explored their endless tunnels and stairways a half dozen times over the years.

The Christmas festivities took place in an elegantly restored officer's quarters, a U-shaped, white edifice trimmed in green, fronted by a wide porch looking out over the grass sprawl of the parade grounds. The porch was teeming with diner staff and alumni when Abe and Ruth arrived shortly after sunset. Flowing skirts and colorful blouses were out in full force. Jaunty fiddle music spilled out of the open windows, punctuated by laughter. The air was redolent with spiced apple cider and marijuana smoke. It was Abe's nightmare. The party was beyond crowded. The diner family having a liberal sense of personal space, men, women, and feral children pushed in on Abe from every angle as he followed Ruth through the proceedings like a toddler through a supermarket until she finally settled in the kitchen, where she found Judith, and Alexandra, and Mary Beth, and, of course, Tiana, along with a handful of other men and women.

"Ruthie!" someone called out.

And soon they were surrounded. Abe was reintroduced.

"The elusive Abe," said Mary Beth. "He actually exists!"

Though clearly intended as playful, the comment cut Abe for reasons he couldn't quite comprehend.

"We're so glad you came," said Judith.

"Absolutely," Tiana chimed in.

Within moments, the kitchen began to fill up with dinerites, employees and patrons alike, among them Thor, who arrived with a small entourage that included a ruddy-faced folk musician named Carl and a squat woman of indeterminate age whose hair was shorn to a quarter inch of stubble. As each wave of revelers arrived, new conversations broke out, all of them unbearably clever or incomprehensibly obscure. Abe mostly listened in fits and starts, his soul steadily withering under the burden, occasionally sneaking glances at Tiana out the corner of his eye. He found it nearly impossible not to. She was indeed something to behold when you looked past her boyish stylings; her soft features were a fascinating contradiction to her tattooed arms, and her silver eyes were lively, if not a little cold. Abe could definitely understand Ruth's attraction, if that's what it was, and never had he felt paunchier, more middle-aged, or less interesting than beside Tiana.

Amidst all this conversation, Abe found himself caught in the crosshairs occasionally, inevitably by the same query.

"So, what do you do, Abe?"

To which Abe crafted a number of impromptu responses:

I'm a veterinarian psychologist.

I repair antique sewing machines.

I write greeting cards.

I photograph windmills.

"Really?" they would say.

"No," Abe would say. "Actually, I sell insurance."

"Oh, I see," they would say politely.

There was zero chance he was selling any of these people on a home or life policy. Most of them probably didn't even carry auto.

After twenty minutes of these awkward exchanges, while Ruth was engaged in a passionate conversation with somebody named Taffy about the monasteries of Tibet, Abe effected his stealthy egress through the rear entrance and took refuge in the open air. As darkness fell, Abe turned his collar up against the wind and ambled across the grounds to the base of Artillery Hill and started up the trail in the moonlight wistfully, tortured by the possibility that Ruth loved this young woman and that he could never hope to compete for her affections against such a singular creature. For what did Abe know of art, or foreign culture, or gourmet food? He'd never been to Europe or South America, never beyond Canada to the north or Mexico to the south. He couldn't write a greeting card to save his life, he hadn't a creative bone in his body. That Tiana was a woman hardly mattered at that point. As far as rivals went, she was more formidable than Leonard Haruto. Of course, Ruth would choose Tiana over Abe, if ever forced to choose. But Abe would never force such a choice; he was too afraid of losing her.

God, but what an idiot he'd been, taking her for granted all these years, never indulging her free-spirited nature, never adopting her interests, never commenting on her hair. He should have taken her to the Louvre years ago, kids or no kids, or at least the World's Fair back in '62, a mere ferry trip across the sound, a trek he'd refused to make because of the crowds. He'd been a stodgy old man even in his thirties, shaking his fist at rain clouds and taking grocery clerks to task. How tedious he must seem now, on the wrong side of fifty.

At the top of the hill, a little winded from the hike, Abe ascended the narrow steps of the first battery by the light of the moon. It looked like a Mayan ruin with its symmetrical tiers geometrically opposed. Abe stood at the concrete lip looking out across the inlet to Vancouver Island.

Really, he ought to be angry. Tiana was an interloper. Who was she, anyway, beneath that radiant skin and those exotic tattoos? Had she wooed other menopausal women into her lesbian web? Rather than being fascinated by her, Abe should have despised her for horning in on his wife and upending his marriage. But he couldn't summon his ire, because Tiana wasn't the problem, he was the problem.

And the question remained whether he could do anything to solve it, or was it already too late? Ruth had insisted he come to the party, right? She'd clearly left the door open. So, what was he doing up here all alone, when he should have been down at the party fighting for his marriage?

Abe tucked his hands in his coat pockets and walked back down the trail in the fog of his own breath. When he arrived once more at the party, he went from room to room looking for Ruth, but she was nowhere to be found. The thought occurred to Abe in the cramped hallway, enveloped in the smell of patchouli and body odor, fiddles and mandolins assaulting his ears, that Ruth might be out there kissing Tiana somewhere in the darkness, both of them with garlic and pot on their breath.

Abe retreated to the front porch, all but vacant now that the party had moved inside, where he found an unlikely conversation partner and ally in Heidi, the big, bawdy, bottle-redhead waitress from Montana.

"Come to sell me insurance?" she said, exhaling a cloud of cigarette smoke into the night.

"Naw," said Abe. "Just looking for Ruth."

"Sit down," she said, indicating the empty chair next to her.

Clearly out of place at the party, Abe had little choice but to comply. He'd barely met Heidi, a mere five-second introduction across the counter, but he knew her by reputation as a person who spoke her mind without reservation. Nothing wrong with forthrightness. Skip the gymnastics and say what's on your mind. Abe had been saying all along that the world would be much more efficient and less chaotic if everyone would do so. Sure, there were bound to be some hurt feelings, but look at the benefits.

"Not really your crowd, huh?" said Heidi.

"No, I guess not," said Abe.

"They're good people once you get to know them," she said.

"I'm sure," said Abe. "If you say so."

"I do," she said, stubbing out her cigarette on the bottom of her shoe, dropping the butt in a beer bottle at her feet, then immediately fishing a joint out of her purse. "How about it?" she said, lighting up.

"I'm cool," said Abe.

Heidi laughed at this declaration. "If you say so," she said.

"Give me that," said Abe, snatching the joint.

"Careful with that, Poindexter," she said.

Abe took an amateurish pull of the joint and managed not to choke as the smoke billowed out his nostrils, and possibly his ears.

"Nice night," she said. "Finally. God I'm sick of the rain. Only nine months until summer."

"And it lasts a week," said Abe.

"Exactly," Heidi said.

It seemed that in Heidi, Abe had found a dinerite who viewed the world as a reasonable adult rather than an idealist. Somebody who sucked it up and swallowed the jagged pill of reality but still managed to have a laugh.

"So, what's the insurance racket like?" she said.

"You don't really want me to answer that, do you?"

"Why not?"

Abe still wasn't sure whether he was being baited, but he gave Heidi the benefit of the doubt. "It's a good living," he said. "More honest than some jobs I can think of."

"Like politician?" said Heidi.

Abe laughed despite himself. Perhaps it was the pot, or maybe just the company, but Abe was suddenly more at ease than he'd been all night. "Can I ask you something?" he said.

"Shoot," said Heidi.

"So, then, are you all . . . you know, lesbians?"

Heidi's entire manner froze for the briefest of instants as though perhaps she was offended, before she burst into laughter. "Is that what you think? We're all lesbians?"

"Well, I . . . ," said Abe. "Maybe not all of you, but . . ."

Heidi redoubled her laughter as though it was the funniest thing she'd heard in ages. "Wow," she said. "That's funny. I can see it. But speaking for myself, I like men—too much in fact. Hell, I married three of them. I'm not alone there. A few of these ladies have been around the marriage block. So, no, we're not all lesbians. Every one of us is different, Abe."

"I haven't offended you, have I?"

"No," said Heidi. "You're cracking me up because I can see how it might look like that. And you're not entirely wrong. So, let's see: Barb, yes, she likes women exclusively. But Kiki, no way. Greta, yes, Liz, no. Jewel, she's on the fence, probably done a little petting. Gabby, she just hates men—doesn't mean she likes women, though. Alexandra, Leigh Anne, Toni, they're married. Mary Beth and her husband go both ways; same with Tiana. So, you know, it's a mixed bag. Why do you ask, anyway?"

"Just curious," said Abe.

Heidi wasn't buying it. She took another pull from the joint, knowing better than to offer it to Abe again.

"Oh, wow, okay, I see," Heidi said. "You're worried Ruth is gonna be converted into a lesbian. Hahaha, that's funny! I wouldn't sweat it, Abe, nobody's indoctrinating anyone around here. Let me tell you something about the sisterhood: It can be a powerful intoxicant, but it's not permanent."

Abe didn't believe that. He could see how the women shared among themselves, how they listened to each other's laments and supported each other unconditionally. They were bound by experience in a way men and women could never be bound, not fully.

"Ruthie is just trying to discover herself," Heidi assured him. "That's a good thing, right?"

For the first time all night, Abe was glad that he came to the party.

Heidi stubbed the joint out and tucked it in her purse. "You going back in?" she said.

"Nah, I think I'm gonna take in the view," said Abe.

Heidi left him alone on the porch with an encouraging pat on the shoulder and reentered the party, where Christmas carols had erupted. Abe turned his collar up once more and descended the steps and walked a hundred yards out onto the great empty expanse of the parade grounds, and looked out over the bluff, the cold, crisp stars wheeling above, the brisk wind biting his cheeks, behind him the officers' quarters, warm and orderly, lit up like lanterns, the distant sound of the diner Christmas festivities hanging in the air, the loneliness of the darkened bluff as palpable as gravity itself.

While Ruth was trying to find herself, Abe, too, was forced to admit that he was totally lost. Standing there, he couldn't help but reach into the past for some clarity, some beacon in the darkness. He thought about the kids, each one of them in turn, and recalled them as toddlers: Anne, and Karen, and Kyle, and Maddie, their different personalities, their different temperaments. He recollected himself and Ruth as younger people, bound more closely together then, if only by necessity. He could still recall that first whiff of farm air in the spring of 1959, remember the first night he and Ruth slept in the house, baby Karen between them. God, how he yearned for that newness. That had been his adventure. It was perfectly obvious from his current vista that their necessary bond, that imperative by which they were bound inextricably, was in the past now and could never be recovered, for the years and the necessity had flown. It wasn't that Abe wanted the years back. No, the mere thought of reliving them was ponderous enough. Nor was it that Abe wanted to rewrite his past to reach some different conclusion, although the possibility had crossed his mind many times over the years. This was nothing so specific as regret, rather something closer to melancholy, an ineffable sorrow.

As Abe was standing out there on the empty parade grounds in the dark, lost in the vastness, he was startled by a sudden touch. Before he could turn to face her, he knew by her touch that it was Ruth who'd taken hold of his waist and pressed her body into his back for warmth. She didn't say a thing, nor did Abe. They just stood there near the edge of the bluff, looking out over the water glimmering in the moonlight.

"Can we go home now?" said Abe at last.

"Yes," said Ruth.

The Disadvantages

2024

There were disadvantages to having her own room at Twin Pines, loneliness being one of them. Ruth had never thought she'd miss the racket of the ventilator or the extra nurses coming and going, but ever since the night her roomie Tish was hurried out on a gurney, Ruth had found that the silence in the room was at times deafening, especially late at night. Isolation was always there, of course, it was woven into the very fabric of the universe, in the vast spaces between the heavenly bodies, despite their irresistible attraction to one another. So, too, this isolation was a fundamental aspect of the human condition, to be born alone and die alone. Ruth had felt it as a girl in Shelton, where she was an object of curiosity and suspicion to her classmates, and even to her parents. She'd known it in those early days at UW, her first time away from home, before she'd befriended Mandy and the other girls at Leary. She'd known it as a young mother at the little one-bedroom house on Roanoke, marooned at home all day long, even as her young children tugged at her apron for attention. And it had visited her, too, alone on the farm at the ages of thirty, and forty, and fifty.

Like most people with a knack for survival, Ruth had learned long ago that this unsettling sense of aloneness, of separateness, could be held at bay with companionship: a lover, a friend, a familiar face. Even the nearness of strangers could suffice to some extent. And when that connection wasn't possible, Ruth tried to stay busy with her hands, journaling and gardening, cooking and cleaning. And when tasks failed to bring solace, poetry had served Ruth, comforting her in fits and starts, and in moments of clarity and sureness, it allayed her fears, if only temporarily.

However, bedridden in an aftercare facility, there was very little Ruth could do to ward off the loneliness.

God, but what a relief when Abe arrived for his daily visit like clockwork, conveying a dirty canvas shopping bag, no doubt full of magazines and newspapers and crosswords to help Ruth fill the hours.

"Brought fortifications," he said.

"God bless you," she said.

Time, Newsweek, yesterday's *Kitsap Sun,* a half-finished puzzle book, but something else, too, something unexpected. Ruth recognized the leather-bound journal immediately. Where on earth had he dug it up? She held it to her nose and sniffed it, and instantly that April afternoon came rushing back, that second day of their vacation in 2000, the day she'd bought the journal at the little boutique, five blocks from the hotel, along with the beret and the scarf, both of which were long gone. But the journal survived, which in itself was not so surprising. To be sure, there were others ferreted away in the back of closets, in boxes in the garage, notebooks dating back as far as college. Notes, observations, aspirations. Bits of verse, whole poems, enough to fill several chapbooks.

"It was the only one I could find that still had blank pages," Abe explained. "I almost drove to Paper Products to get a new one, then I remembered they closed ten years ago. Is it moldy, is that why you're smelling it?"

"Where was it?"

"In a box in the attic."

"What were you doing in the attic?"

"Good question," he said. "I went up there with a flashlight looking for something, but by the time I fought through the cobwebs, I forgot what I was looking for. I found those glass votives you were looking for ten years ago, though."

"You shouldn't be climbing a ladder like that!"

"Fair enough," he said. "But it was important."

"So important that you forgot it."

"Touché," said Abe.

Ruth smelled the old journal again.

"We can dry that out if it's moldy. I just thought you might want it."

"It was sweet of you to bring it," she said.

She smiled, acutely aware of the slight crookedness of her new smile, along with the attending ache in her jaw. As she clutched the journal, there was a slight welling in Ruth's chest. That people think of us when we're not around, that they go out of their way to do little things simply because they hope to please us, we sometimes take for granted. They may not always be matters of great inconvenience, these small acts of consideration, but they add up to a great deal.

Ruth opened the notebook arbitrarily, landing on two lines of verse, the beginnings of an unfinished poem:

How deep the blue sky
What a gift the sun's golden magnificence

Perhaps the sentiment was a little blundering, the language a little trite, but it had been true when Ruth wrote it nearly twenty-five years ago, and it was still true today.

"The heat gun!" Abe cried out, startling Ruth from her ruminations.

The exclamation was so arbitrary, so devoid of context, Ruth thought Abe was having one of his moments.

"The heat gun! I just got to thinking of your moldy notebook, and it hit me. That's what I was digging around for up in the attic!"

"You really shouldn't have been up there. You could fall and break your neck."

"That corner in the basement, below the broken gutter," he said. "You know, behind the washer, it's waterlogged again, and it's starting to attract the carpenter ants."

"Mason is supposed to take care of the ants. That's what we pay him for—pest control."

"I forgot to tell him about it last Thursday. So, I figured I'd blast it for twenty minutes with the heat gun, problem solved. Well, last time I used the heat gun was up in the attic, under that eave, after that damn atmospheric river, or whatever they called it, back in two-thousand-whenever-it-was. I remember, because I'd plugged it into the extension cord, and it drew too much power and blew the damn breaker. I got so preoccupied with the breaker box, I never finished in the attic. Anyway, it's up there, if you want me to dry out that notebook."

It didn't matter that his stories were uneventful and largely pointless, it was so good to hear his voice, good to feel his presence there.

*

After four hours sitting with Ruth at Twin Pines, then fighting traffic through Poulsbo on the way home, Abe finally arrived back at the farm in the late afternoon, where John Duncan had already called it quits for the day, leaving his tool belt slung over the new handrail, perhaps as a signal that he'd finally complete the ramp in the morning and clean up the mess he'd left from the demoed stairs. Abe navigated the construction cautiously on his way to the front door.

He should have asked John to let the dog out, for he soon discovered that Megs had peed in the kitchen again, poor girl, in the very same place as always, as close as she could possibly get to the back door. No sooner had Abe located her under the kitchen table than he heard the listless thud of her tail three times on the linoleum as she looked up dolefully at him.

"Aw, it's okay, old girl," said Abe. "C'mon, I'll take you out back for a stretch and a pee. Then we can eat an early dinner, how does that sound?"

Eventually, he managed to coax her out from under the table, and she labored across the kitchen and out the back door, into the yard, where she immediately squatted to pee. When she was finished, she turned around again directly without so much as a nose to the ground or a sniff of the afternoon air, and labored up the steps one at a time.

In the kitchen, Abe heaped paper towels on the puddle, then dished out a can of the three-dollar organic grain-free chicken formula, but Megs exhibited little interest in it.

"C'mon, girl, you gotta eat."

Megs approached the bowl dutifully and gave it a sniff.

"Attagirl," said Abe, less than optimistic as he exited the kitchen.

Retiring to the living room, he lowered himself into his La-Z-Boy and reached for the remote, which felt heavier than usual. He almost didn't turn on the TV, and having finally remembered, briefly considered retrieving the heat gun from the attic, but decided against it, heeding his wife's mandate.

After five minutes of KOMO news, Megs ambled into the living room and lowered herself onto the braided rug at the foot of his chair, licking her lips twice and paying out a sigh.

Abe bent over and patted her on the head.

"That's a good girl, Megsy. Your mama will be home soon," he said. "That'll cheer you up."

The Scattering

1988

Ruth had been taught as a child that a church was not a building, that a church was people. Likewise, a household was people, just as the Streamliner Diner had been people. Thus, when Judith and Alexandra sold the restaurant in '87, though the new owners kept the name and largely maintained the same standard of culinary excellence, the people who'd accounted for the Streamliner Diner's singular appeal scattered, seemingly all at once: Judith moved to Kingston and opened a hotel; Heidi moved back to Montana; Gabby and Jewel both moved to the city; Mary Beth and her husband fled south to Ashland, Oregon; Kiki moved to Eugene to finish grad school, Barb north to Canada; and Tiana relocated to Todos Santos to start a gallery with her new boyfriend, and that was the last of her. Gone, nearly every one of those women who had accounted for the diner's distinctive spirit, on to their next adventures, some thrilling new chapter in their lives. Gone with them were those lively conversations upon which Ruth had come to depend, those breathless philosophical interrogations and muddy walks that had sustained her through her midlife bewilderment, those vital connections that had helped to reshape her flagging self-image. Gone, all of it.

Ruth found herself back on the farm with an empty nest and little occupation to fill the hole left by the sudden conclusion of the diner renaissance. Abruptly, she stopped journaling or writing verse, as her appetite for poetry, like all the rest of her appetites, flagged. There was, of course, the Seabold Methodist Church, reliable as the tides, unconditionally supportive, though short on adventure. There was also Ruth's enduring friendship with Bess Delory. God bless Bess, steadfast, dependable, convivial, kind, though hardly the personification of the erudition and curiosity Ruth had enjoyed with the diner women. And then there was Abe, also dependable, also steadfast, intelligent in many ways, though not intellectually companionable in the way of Tiana, or Judith, or Mary Beth.

In the absence of diner culture, the onus rested squarely on Ruth to address these deficits. She might have started a book club, or volunteered at the historical society, or dabbled in adult education at Seattle Central Community College. Instead, she gave in to the familiar condition of stable despair, gradually defaulting to her former self. It was only a matter of months before the flowing skirts had found their way to the back of the closet, replaced by the frumpy jeans befitting a woman who'd recently received her second free AARP tote bag.

Finally sensing Ruth's months-long gloominess, perhaps, or more likely fresh off a lucrative day in the insurance trade, which accounted for the bulk of his good moods, Abe shocked Ruth one Friday evening with a dinner invitation.

"What say we go out tonight, grab a bite? No kids, no finicky teenagers, what's to stop us?"

While Ruth initially greeted the idea with a cautious enthusiasm, grumpiness soon set in as she tried to find something appropriate to wear. She hated her wardrobe, most of which hardly fit anymore or hadn't aged well. She finally settled on one of her old diner blouses, a taupe and turquoise affair with a Southwestern motif, a hand-me-down from Judith that no longer suited Ruth, with its boxy shoulders and its wide neckline. She hated how her body was changing, too, how that pooch around the middle she'd so effectively staved off through four children was now insistent at her waistline, drooping over like a fold of pizza dough.

"Haven't seen that one in a while," Abe observed when she emerged from the bedroom dressed for dinner.

Though the comment was clearly innocuous, it annoyed Ruth nonetheless. For it seemed to Ruth that Abe had not seen her for years, regardless of her wardrobe. She could have dyed her hair purple, and he wouldn't have noticed.

Ruth's irritability continued to ramp up throughout the car ride to town. Between Abe's inane attempts at conversation and her general nerve-worn state of anxiety, itself inexplicable, it was all Ruth could do to stop herself from snapping at Abe's insipid running commentary.

"Look at this rain, wonder if it'll clear up. Lookie there, the Coles finally replaced their garage door, it's a wonder nobody stole their lawn mower all those years. Say, is that Darrel Rapada's old coupe?"

To make matters worse, without a reservation there was a twenty-minute wait in the drafty foyer of the Saltwater Cafe. Abe, not the world's most forbearing personage when it came to waiting, managed to occupy himself with a serendipitously discarded copy of the *Sun*'s regional section, as Ruth impatiently surveyed the dining area, struck by the cheap artifice of the place, a dressed-up fish-and-chips joint with cloth napkins and smoked glass mirrors. Even the clientele was discouraging. Not a familiar face. Everybody so normal, so safe, so devoid of character. Who were these people, Californians? It used to be that islanders had a distinct character, even if you couldn't put your finger on it.

"Finally," she muttered when the host arrived to seat them.

"Relax," said Abe. "It's Friday night."

But Ruth couldn't seem to relax, no matter how hard she tried to talk herself into it. Whatever had gotten under her skin was hot and prickly now and wanting to be scratched like a rash.

As if a night on the town was not novel enough, they ordered cocktails, Ruth a Manhattan and Abe a Sazerac. Neither of them had ever been a drinker, not even at college. Abe, of course, was moderate in all things, while Ruth had never much trusted alcohol beyond a half glass of wine, never liked that the more she drank, the less dominion she exercised over her thoughts and the less control she seemed to have over her actions. Still, there had been the occasional eggnog or wine during the holidays, the cold beer at a summer barbecue, the wedding toast, and other customary occasions that called for alcohol.

The first sip of her Manhattan seemed to take Ruth's edge off immediately, but halfway through her drink the alcohol began to dull her senses, until she was beset once again by moodiness. It didn't help that the salmon was poached to a rubbery beige, the butter separated, fine little bones ribbing the filet. The oversteamed vegetables—carrots and broccoli and crumbling cauliflower—were the stuff of Ruth's unhappy childhood. The "potatoes" were in fact oversalted French fries, limp and oily as wet salamander and raw in the middle.

Abe didn't seem to mind his bowl of chowder, despite the thick film on top.

"Fair," he said. "Too much pepper, but not bad."

And there was Abe in a nutshell, it seemed to Ruth. Fair. Not bad. Bland, and white, and tasteless as a bowl of chowder. Never enough pepper.

"It looks like a bowl of mortar," Ruth said.

She could feel her syllables rounding at the edges as her words began running together. What exactly he had done to arouse her contempt didn't matter. Her anger had been simmering for months. The fact was, tonight he was actually making an effort for once. He'd been sweet to suggest a night out. It was hardly Abe's fault if the Saltwater Cafe wasn't La Tour d'Argent, or even the Martinique. Still, going out to dine at all had been a nice gesture. He even wore a bow tie. So, why did she want to lash out at Abe? Was it because it took him so damn long to make the effort? Was it because he'd been forever stunting her growth with his staid and steady presence? Or was it simply the bow tie, that enduring symbol of his conservatism? The way he sat too upright, the way he chewed, the way he went to his napkin after every bite, even his order, clam chowder and a side of chips, so pedestrian, so obvious, like a tourist wherever he went. There was no end to Abe's irritating qualities.

"Well, sold a homeowner's policy to your church friend Jan Heron this afternoon," he said, wiping the edge of his mouth daintily.

"Of course you did," said Ruth.

"No-brainer," he said. "Farmers upped their premium after that fir fell on their garage last month. They were paying out the nose for detached structure, boilerplate coverage. I was able to get her a lower quote and fifteen hundred dollars in additional coverage."

"How thoughtful of you," said Ruth.

Abe searched her face for an explanation as Ruth glared defiantly back at him.

"What's gotten into you tonight?" said Abe. "Bad day?"

"They're all bad," said Ruth.

"Is this the hormones again?"

Though he'd said it delicately enough that it was not intended as an accusation, Ruth could hear the exasperation in his tone, as though he was thinking: *Oh, boy, here we go again.*

"It's always the hormones, isn't it, Abe?" said Ruth, loud enough to draw the attention of the neighboring table. "If it's female, it must be hormones."

He tried to silence her with a meaningful glare, a look that said to Ruth: *Don't embarrass me. I have a reputation to uphold.*

"Hormones, hormones, always the hormones," Ruth said. "It was hormones with Karen, too, remember? Locked herself in her room, hormones. Ran away, hormones. Killed herself, hormones."

As ever, ready to nip this or any conflict in the bud, Abe shifted directly into damage control mode, setting his napkin on the table and waving for the check, before withdrawing to the restroom to avoid further engagement. Decisively passive in Abe fashion.

Ruth remained at the table, stewing as she followed Abe's lanky progress across the dining room, annoyed with his jerky gait, his narrow shoulders, his mindful posture, disgusted at the fact that he was incapable of confrontation.

"Ech," she muttered under her breath as she watched him disappear into the corridor, before dispensing with the last of her Manhattan in a single gulp.

The alcohol was sitting like a weighted blanket on her shoulders by the time Abe returned from the bathroom, evading her eyes.

"What are you so afraid of?" she said, loud enough to silence the dining room.

But Abe did not take the bait.

"Don't forget your purse," he said gruffly as he left a hundred-dollar bill on the table.

Ruth's thoughts were leaden as she stood to leave, Abe already ten paces in front of her, his good posture beginning to fail him under the weight of the unpleasantness.

The drive home was eerily silent, Ruth glowering out the side window and Abe gripping the wheel until his knuckles were white. When he pulled up in front of the house, Abe got out of the car and walked straight up the steps without opening her door as he had as a matter of custom since 1953. Ruth sat in the passenger seat for a moment, her mouth dry, her thoughts a dull irritant. After considerable groping in the darkness, Ruth located her purse by her feet, pushed the door open, then nearly slipped climbing out of the car.

Abe was already in his chair with the remote in his hand, agitation working on the lines of his forehead, as he watched the late news. He didn't even look at her when she came in and walked straight to the kitchen, where she began immediately to scour the cupboard for alcohol. She found nothing beyond a half bottle of dry vermouth and an open jug of Carlo Rossi sangria from two Thanksgivings ago. She poured out an unreasonably tall glass, splashing the countertop and resisting the impulse to wipe it up. Instead, she left the puddle of wine there like a challenge. Chances were, Abe would walk right by it five times before she cleaned it up in the morning.

Though she had no desire to be around Abe, the living room was as much hers as it was his, so she took her place in the chair opposite Abe with her glass of wine and settled into a sullen silence. After a moment, Abe took a lame stab at diplomacy.

"I'm sorry about the hormones comment," he said, looking straight ahead at the Schick commercial on TV. "You weren't acting like yourself."

But Ruth wasn't having it.

"And who is that, Abe? How exactly do you presume to know me?"

Though Ruth was making a concerted effort to enunciate her words, it wasn't quite working.

"The damn mailman knows me better than you do," she said.

"That's not even remotely true," he said.

"Try living with you," she said.

"You know, it's not like you're a joy to live with," he said, raising his voice for the first time. "It used to be things were good enough around here, or so I thought. We've built a pretty nice life. And when I say 'we,' I mean mostly I have. I'm the one who bought this farm, I'm the one who accounted for all the food on the table. I'm the one that bankrolled all your improvements, your raised beds, and your greenhouses, and your marble countertops."

"Pff," said Ruth. "Hail the great man."

"Well, he's served you well enough, hasn't he?" shouted Abe. "He may not be Julius Caesar, but he's worked his butt off for thirty-five years so you could have all this. So you could grow your flowers and read your poetry."

"Ha! Is that what I was doing?"

"When you weren't kissing gardeners and lesbians!"

"I was raising children and cleaning house!"

Even in her deteriorating state of stupefaction, Ruth wondered once again what had possessed her to air these old grievances now. But still, she couldn't resist the reckless impulse.

"Healthy children," said Abe. "Well-fed children, educated children.

And a pretty nice house, too, I might add. And acreage for all your projects!"

"There you go again," said Ruth, straight out of the Ronald Reagan playbook.

"My God, when was the last time you were happy, Ruthie? When you were kissing that Tiana woman by the dumpster?"

"At least she had a soul," said Ruth.

"Is that what those tattoos on her arms were?" said Abe. "Her soul?"

"You wish you had guts," said Ruth. "You walk around convincing yourself you have guts, but you don't."

Even when she said it, Ruth knew the statement was out of left field and she was only lashing out like a sick cat.

"Well, I guess I don't know what you mean by guts."

"Of course you don't," said Ruth. "You wouldn't know it if it kicked you in the balls!"

Here, Abe shook his head grimly, then ran his hands over his drawn face and drew a deep breath.

"Okay," he said, releasing the breath. "I don't know what any of this is about, but I'm sorry."

"Don't bother," she said.

The minute she heard Abe pulling up the driveway, the euphoria of conflict gave way to a wave of remorse that crashed upon Ruth, even as she took one last slug of Carlo Rossi.

*

Abe checked into the Evergreen Motel in Poulsbo around ten thirty P.M. without so much as his spit kit in his possession. Even in his state of emotional befuddlement, he was peeved to find that his AAA card wasn't in his wallet. Maddie had probably taken it to college without telling him, probably Ruth's idea, though Abe would have insisted she take it himself had he thought of it. The point was, at least he'd have known about it and ordered a duplicate.

"Can you take my word for it?" he asked the clerk, a kid in his twenties.

"Sorry, we need a number."

Abe sighed. The whole country was going to hell. It used to be a man's word was enough. He sure as heck wasn't about to call Ruth for the number, though it would have saved him nearly ten bucks.

Squalid might have been an improvement for Room 213, which was perfectly forlorn in its shabby neatness and a decade outdated with its green shag carpet and burnt orange bedspread. The folded hand towel at the edge of the basin, the fake wool throw blanket at the foot of the bead, the ceramic cup of potpourri on the dresser— these paltry touches of hominess only made the room worse.

Abe's hand was still shaking as he dropped the car keys on the nightstand. How had the night gone so wrong? The evening had begun hopefully. Abe was confident that he'd come home imbued with the requisite energy to lift Ruth's spirits, or at least distract her from the perpetual funk she'd been wallowing in for, what, three months, now? Years, really, if you accounted for all the other funks. This was more than one bad night fueled by alcohol, this was the culmination of years of repression, decades even, of bitterness, resentment, jealousy, outrage, all of it simmering until tonight, when it finally boiled to the surface.

As inflamed as he was by Ruth's assault on his character, Abe was dogged by the suspicion that he'd had it coming somehow. Certainly, he'd lost his cool, and he was not proud of that. The thought occurred to him that maybe he should call Ruth after all and apologize, or at least let her know he'd checked into the Evergreen for the night. But that part of him still incensed by her behavior vetoed any such diplomacy. She'd caused this—let her worry.

Abe slept on top of the covers in his slacks and socks, if you could call it sleep. His general agitation conspired with the bright lights from the parking lot and the traffic on 305 to keep him awake most of the night. By morning, he had talked himself into swallowing his pride and putting the previous night behind him. People said things in anger, it came with the territory of marriage. It behooved Abe to be what he viewed as the bigger person in this instance. He almost stopped at Central Market for flowers, but he wasn't quite ready to go to those lengths. Instead, he returned to the farm empty-handed, a practiced apology on his lips, where he found Ruth on the sofa with an ice pack on her head. He was about to humbly offer his penitence and ask for his wife's forgiveness when she beat him to the punch.

"Don't you have something to say to me?" she said.

Abe's emotional turnabout was absolute and instantaneous. "Me?" he said, incredulous. "My God, you're the one who . . . you can't be serious."

Ruth's grim expression answered that question immediately.

"Oh, this takes the cake," Abe said. "Unbelievable."

Huffing and puffing, he strode past her and down the hallway to the bedroom, where he yanked a clean shirt and pair of slacks out of the closet and changed his clothes angrily, muttering his misgivings. He didn't bother shaving, though he was showing the better part of two days' growth. He briefly considered packing a spit kit and searching the desk drawer for the AAA card on his way out the door, but he was in too much of a hurry to escape.

Abe was halfway out the front door, striding past the kitchen, when he discovered Ruth hunched there at the table, sobbing inconsolably into her hands.

Immediately, his emotional pendulum swung back to repentant as he leaned down to comfort her.

"Oh, Ruthie, I'm sorry," he said.

She choked back a sob and looked up into his face. "No," she said. "It was me. I'm sorry."

Abe motioned for Ruth to stand, and when she got to her feet, he wrapped her in an embrace, his confused heart still drumming three measures ahead of the beat.

Something Else

2024

Ruth awoke suddenly at three A.M. and couldn't get back to sleep. For the better part of an hour, she lay in her bed at Twin Pines, staring at the ceiling as the sounds of the dormant facility washed over her: the custodian trundling his cart down the corridor, the clock on the wall, the metronomic tick of the second hand, the distant drone of muted conversation as an idle female staffer engaged in a personal call at the darkened reception kiosk. Though she was hopelessly awake, Ruth's thoughts were neither excitable nor numerous. More than the dire deliberations or worries she'd come to associate with insomnia, she was plagued by sensations: a heaviness of chest and limb, an aching of the spirit, a yearning, palpable but vague, which Ruth soon recognized as loneliness. Was there a lonelier place on Earth than a hospital bed at night?

The television might have served as a welcome distraction, as it had for much of the past two weeks, particularly in those hours when Abe was not occupying his post at her bedside. But TV was strictly prohibited at this hour. Even a reading light was forbidden. She thought about journaling by the paltry light spilling in from the hallway, and almost reached for the old leather-bound notebook, but she knew it was useless. All the verse in the world could not buffer her from this loneliness. Beyond sleep, there was no occupation left but the life of the mind and body. And so, Ruth had no choice but to dwell in this desolate state.

God, how she wished Abe could have been there beside her in the darkness, to talk in whispers, about the future, or the past, insurance, taxes, anything at all, just so long as she could hear his breathing and know that he was there, that she was not alone. Lying there in the stillness of Twin Pines, Ruth felt like the last person alive. Was this perhaps a taste of the emptiness that awaited Ruth in the beyond?

When Ruth could abide these thoughts no longer, she pushed the call button, if only to intrude on this oppressive mood.

The phone conversation at the kiosk ended abruptly, and the squeak of rubber-soled footfalls followed, approaching down the hallway. Soon the night nurse appeared at the foot of the bed, a young woman whom Ruth did not recognize.

"You're new," observed Ruth.

"Yes. I'm Annabel," she said.

"Hello, Annabel."

Her scrubs were a pale pink and baggy. Ruth strained to discern her features in the dim light but couldn't quite do so.

"Come closer," she said.

"Is everything okay?" said Annabel, stepping nearer.

Annabel was perhaps thirty. Pretty, round faced, and heavy through the middle. Her voice was even but warm, friendly but professional.

"Yes, I'm fine," said Ruth. "Thank you."

"Did you push the call button?"

"Did I?" said Ruth. "I must have pushed it by accident, I'm sorry, dear."

Annabel smiled. "It happens," she said. "Since I'm here, do you want to try to go to the bathroom?"

"No, no," said Ruth.

"Is there anything else I can do for you?"

"No, dear, I don't think so, thank you."

"All right, then," said Annabel. "You get some rest, okay?"

"I will," said Ruth.

"Good night," said Annabel, turning to leave.

But there was something else, though Ruth couldn't say what. With no immediate cause to keep Annabel at hand, Ruth wasn't ready to let the young woman leave.

"Actually," said Ruth, "would you mind terribly staying for a minute?"

"Of course," said Annabel.

"Have a seat, would you?"

Annabel seemed ambivalent on this matter. Perhaps bedside vigil was discouraged by her professional credo, or maybe she had other duties to tend to. It might have been that the possibility simply made her uncomfortable. But after a brief hesitation, Annabel circled the bed and sat in Abe's spot, where she lingered in silence, and no doubt anticipation. But Ruth did not pursue the interaction straightaway.

Finally, Annabel broke the silence.

"Is there anything in particular you wanted?"

"Just company," said Ruth. "Just for a few moments, dear. We don't need to talk. Unless you want to."

They both opted for the tick of the clock, the faint rumble of the wheeled custodial cart, the hushed but steady rasp of Ruth's breathing. The stillness must have been agonizing for poor Annabel. How to explain to someone so young this desolate sensation that threatened to pull Ruth downward like an undertow?

Ruth felt she owed her something in the way of conversation.

"You know," she said at last, "there's a poem called 'Annabel.' I wish I could remember it."

"I'd like to hear it," Annabel said.

"Google it on your phone sometime," said Ruth. "It's by Poe."

"I will," said Annabel.

Before it could settle in once more, the silence was disrupted by the distant buzz of the switchboard at the reception desk.

Annabel rose to her feet. "Well, I'd better . . ."

"Yes, you go now, dear, I'm sorry I kept you."

"You're sure you don't need anything? I can come back after—"

"No, no, I'm sure," said Ruth.

Watching the young woman leave, a crushing isolation beset Ruth once more. Though ostensibly in her best condition since the surgery, her vitals stable, her cancer in remission, she was nonetheless certain she was going die, that her blood pressure was going to plummet without warning at any second, and there would be no saving her this time.

To ward off this anxiety and keep death at bay, Ruth turned to the only place left to turn.

God, please spare me long enough to go home.

Those Human Elements

By the midnineties, the insurance game was changing faster than ever, and as with most changes, Abe was resistant to it. Personal lines commissions were going down as independent agents saw direct sales cutting into their market. Technology was also becoming a factor, and not in a good way. Email, spreadsheets, computer ratings, all of it came as a personal affront to Abe, who'd made his name and established his place in the industry, as well as the community at large, owing to those human elements once imperative to the success of the insurance agent: personability, trust, familiarity.

Abe's plan had long been to pass the torch at Bainbridge Island Insurance, as Todd Hall had passed it to Abe almost thirty years ago, but the reality was that Abe had nobody to pass it on to. With so much turnover in the office over the years, he'd never quite developed a qualified protégé. There had been Ted DeWitt way back when, but Ted had been a bean counter, not the face of an agency. Thus, when Marsh McLennan and Company made a lucrative offer to buy out Bainbridge Island Insurance, Abe accepted the terms with little hesitation.

Not that Abe was ready to retire—the prospect was terrifying. But it was a transition he'd have to make sooner or later, and Marsh Mac's offer had all but made the decision for him.

Abe's retirement party was a collaborative effort between the Bainbridge Island Chamber of Commerce and Kiwanis. The festivities took place on a Friday night at the St. Barnabas social hall, where Abe had attended so many Kiwanis functions over the decades. San Carlos catered the affair. Abe had not only insured Lee and Marianne's restaurant since day one but paid out on two separate claims, a kitchen fire their first year of operation as well as a flooding incident last fall. This was good enough for a 30 percent discount.

The hall itself was nothing remarkable: low ceiling, linoleum floors, overhead fluorescent lighting, the walls adorned with Anglican church literature, and a stack of pamphlets in the lobby emblazoned with the church's blue, red, and gold compass symbol. A hundred and twenty people showed up to bid Abe his farewell from the workforce—recent employees, former employees, longtime customers, fellow Kiwanians, local business leaders, neighbors, and friends, including the Duncans and the Jacobsons. In fact, it was the Duncans' eldest son, John, from the chamber who served as the master of ceremonies.

"Hat tip to Ruth Winter for helping us get this thing organized," he said. "Technically, that's still Mrs. Winter to me."

This comment drew the first of what would be two dozen polite chuckles to punctuate the evening.

"Thanks to San Carlos for the food," said John. "Great chimichangas, Lee!"

Todd Hall, eighty-two years young and under two hundred pounds for the first time since high school, carting an oxygen tank with twin plastic tubes snaking up his nostrils, led off the roast, after a little difficulty getting up the riser to the podium.

"When I first agreed to sell Bainbridge Island Insurance to Abe back in the day, I was drunk," he said. "Abe saw to that, didn't you, Abe?"

Everybody sniggered, even as Abe felt his face color. For, though the story was offered in jest, it was nonetheless true; Todd had imbibed several double MacNaughtons that afternoon.

"But seriously," said Todd. "I always knew Abe would do great in the insurance racket. He had all the tools and none of the ethics."

This prompted another smattering of laughter from the group.

"One time," said Todd, "Abe and I went to the art museum in downtown Seattle and Abe accidentally knocked over a statue. The museum administrator ran up to us, waving his arms, and said, 'Hey, that's a five-hundred-year-old statue!' And Abe said: 'Thank God, I thought it was a new one!'"

Encouraged by the ensuing chortles, Todd went right back to the well of tired insurance agent jokes.

"As you all know, Abe is just a big kid at heart. The only difference between Abe and a whole life policy is that the whole life policy eventually matures."

Though friends and associates all laughed as though in recognition, the truth was that Abe was born middle-aged, something Ruth had gleaned within five minutes of meeting him in 1953. Still, Abe was touched by their amusement, their warmth, their mere attendance at such a pitiable celebration on a Friday evening in June. Here it was, the culmination of his life's work, four decades of ambition and toil, of planning, and plotting, and scheming, and staying one step ahead in an ever-changing landscape, of peptic ulcers and parental absenteeism, nearly a half century of blood, sweat, and tears memorialized in a church social hall, replete with old jokes and warmed-over chimichangas. And yet, Abe could not help but be honored by all the fuss.

Ted DeWitt was next up at the podium. Still at Safeco nearly thirty years after Abe had landed him a job as underwriter, Ted was a bit jowlier, a bit balder, a bit more bag-eyed than Abe remembered, for Abe had only seen Ted a handful of times since he risked his livelihood for Abe, or more precisely risked it for Kelly Mathison and her children.

"Everything I know about the insurance business, I learned from Abe Winter back in the late 1960s," said Ted. "No wonder I'm still broke."

This prompted a chuckle from the crowd.

"Seriously, though. The first thing Abe taught me was that needing insurance was like needing a parachute. If it wasn't there the first time, you probably won't be needing it again."

Though the well of tired insurance jokes was a deep one, Ted pivoted to a more genuine note, sharing the story of how Abe had suffered through Ted's inept performance in sales but had seen his strength as an adjuster and went out of his way to set him up with a great job at Safeco. Standing left of the stage, his plastic cup of club soda getting flatter and warmer by the minute, Abe scanned the crowd until he found Kelly Mathison, knowing she had no idea what she owed to Ted DeWitt. Kelly happened to catch his gaze and blew a friendly kiss to him. She looked great, happy, and fit in her midfifties, her second husband standing beside her in Dockers and a blue dress shirt. More than the jokes or the fond remembrances, it was gratifying for Abe knowing that at least once, he'd done the right thing.

After the roast, Abe had a moment with Ted at the makeshift drink station, where Ted poured himself a plastic cup of white wine and Abe freshened up his club soda.

"Thanks for the speech, Ted," Abe said, clapping him on the back.

"Of course," said Ted.

"Incidentally, she's here, you know?" said Abe.

"Who?" said Ted.

"Kelly Mathison," said Abe, lowering his voice.

The name didn't seem to light any bulbs for Ted at first.

Abe lowered his voice to a conspiratorial hush. "The woman whose husband, you know . . . back in '76."

"No kidding," said Ted. "I haven't thought about that in years."

"You're a good man," said Abe, and he meant it.

"Ditto, buddy," said Ted.

Five minutes later, Abe found himself face-to-face with Kelly and her husband, Kurt.

"So, what's next?" Kelly asked.

"Hang gliding," said Abe.

"Really?" said Kelly.

"Nah," he said. "To be honest, I have no idea."

"Well, that's exciting," she said.

"If you say so," said Abe.

Abe wished it were exciting. But he didn't want to learn karate at sixty-five, he didn't want to fish, or hunt, or drive all over kingdom come in an RV. He didn't even want to go to France, or Egypt, or South America, as much as Ruth aspired to such adventures.

Abe barely saw Ruth throughout the evening, so busy was she with her duties as devoted wife. Abe finally caught up with her as the festivities wound down, the social hall half-empty, plastic cups tipped sideways on fold-out tables, Kiwanians breaking down the riser, chamber volunteers removing the streamers.

"Congratulations, mister," said Ruth, pinching his cheek before planting a kiss upon it. "Well done."

Abe took his wife's cheerfulness to heart. It humbled him that after all they'd been through, Ruth seemed genuinely excited by the prospect of seeing more of him.

Leaning down to her five and a half feet, Abe planted a kiss on her forehead.

"Now the leisure begins," she said.

*

As it turned out, Abe's retirement was not all that Ruth might have hoped for. Now that it was Abe's turn to empty nest, without an office to escape to, she found him insufferable: often touchy, frequently irascible, nearly always edgy. And yet, for all his restlessness, he refused to go anywhere.

"Let's go to France," she'd say. "You know I've always dreamed of Paris."

"Too expensive."

"What about Mexico?"

"And get dysentery?" said Abe. "No thanks."

"Okay, Brazil."

"I'll tell you what, you go. Take Bess Delory down to Mazatlán or something, knock yourselves out. I'll hold up the fort."

But Ruth never called his bluff. Why not? Nothing against Bess Delory, but Ruth was not convinced they'd make the most companionable travel mates, and it was doubtful Abe would permit Ruth to go alone. And even if he would consent to it, as much as she'd longed to explore foreign locales as a younger woman—the bustling markets of Delhi, the waters of Tolantongo, the pyramids of Giza—now, a year shy of social security, the thought of traveling solo was more than a little daunting.

Ruth should have pushed him; he probably would have given in eventually. Instead, she begrudged Abe for his lack of curiosity and adventure. For all his initiative and prescriptive bootstrapperism, now that he was lost on the far side of middle life, he was not at all interested in finding himself. Moreover, the antagonism that had marked their political differences through the Reagan and Bush eras had extended well into the nineties. By 1997, Abe's distaste for Bill Clinton bordered on pathological. The mere sight of the man on the evening news every night invariably aroused Abe's contempt.

"People first, my buttocks!" he'd shout at the television.

"I don't understand you," Ruth said from her side of the living room. "All the man's done is double down on Reagan's economic policy, condemn big government, and play nice with Republicans. And you don't like him why?"

"Because he's slick," Abe complained. "I don't trust him."

"You said the same thing about Kennedy."

"You're damn right."

"Frankly, I'm beginning to think it's personal," Ruth said. "Are you sure it's not his good looks that offend you?"

"Ha! That peanut head, good-looking? Are you kidding? You know what I see when I look at Bill Clinton? I see Royce Holiday with a haircut."

Their squabbling extended well beyond the arena of politics. With both of them at home so much, their opposition had never been so ubiquitous; whether it was the temperature in the house, the volume of the TV, or when to feed the dog, Ruth and Abe could agree on virtually nothing. Even dinner conversation, once a bilateral neutral zone reserved for small talk, had become an uneasy accord.

"What do you mean by 'too bright'?"

"I don't mean anything."

"Well, you said it, didn't you?"

Nothing was too trivial to put them at odds. It got to where Ruth and Abe did their best to avoid one another, no small task in the same household, especially when the upstairs sat all but vacant, as it had in the decade since Maddie moved out. When Ruth was certain she couldn't stand it a minute longer, she took the initiative.

"I think we should talk to someone," said Ruth in the kitchen, while Abe was eating his All-Bran.

"What does that mean?"

"Like a marriage counselor," she said. "Someone to mediate, to help us understand each other better, to help us develop some tools."

Ruth was 99 percent sure that Abe would wave the proposition off, if not mock the idea outright, but to her astonishment, after brief consideration, a spoonful of cereal poised halfway between his mouth and the bowl, he consented.

"Fine," he said. "We'll talk to someone. But nothing churchy."

Just when Ruth had written him off as totally inflexible, Abe had subverted her expectations again. But the smooth pavement of his acquiescence did not last long. Two days later, Ruth produced a pair of referrals.

"Why does it have to be a woman?" he said. "Why not a man?"

"These were the best referrals," she explained. "And why not a woman?"

"Because she'll just take your side."

"This isn't about sides, that's the whole point!"

She had him cornered.

"Fine," he said. "But if she starts taking sides . . ."

Despite Abe's considerable reservations, their first session with Tamara Selvar was a revelation. She wore her hair medium length, and dressed sensibly in slacks and fitted blouses, and wore flats. No jewelry, no makeup. Not traditionally feminine, and yet, not a lesbian so far as Abe could tell. Selvar's manner was the sort of straightforward and assertive that demanded accountability, and Abe liked that, even when she put him on the spot.

"Now, let me ask you a question, Abe. Where do you see your marriage in ten years?"

Abe considered momentarily. "The same, I guess. The way it's always been."

"Is that fair, do you think?" said Dr. Selvar.

"Well, it's worked so far. Sure, we've had our ups and downs, but that's marriage, right? It's not all moonlight and roses."

"How much moonlight would you say there is?" said Dr. Selvar.

"Well, I . . ."

"Ruth?"

"Not much. None, actually."

"Abe, would you agree with that?"

"Well, I . . . I mean, it's not like we're twenty years old, you know?"

"So, you believe romance is synonymous with youthfulness?"

"Well, yeah, mostly."

"And why is that?"

"Because young people are naïve, they're hopeful, they don't live in an adult world."

The more Tamara Selvar drew Abe out with these interrogations, the more Abe was forced to reckon with his own unreasonableness.

"Abe, what would you say you love most about Ruth?"

"I . . . well, I mean, a lot of things."

"Give me an example."

"I love that I can count on her."

"How?"

"She's always there for me."

"That sounds like it's more about you. What does it say about Ruth?"

"She's dependable."

"Okay, but that's still more about you than Ruth, isn't it? Tell me something else you love about her."

"Okay, she's fun."

"Fun how?"

"I don't know, she's game for about anything, I guess."

"Give me an example."

"She likes crosswords. She's good at them. I can ask her for just about any word and she'll get it."

It seemed to Abe that his every explanation was more inadequate than the last. Whose idea of fun and exciting was a crossword? Only with Tamara Selvar to bear witness, week after week, did Abe begin to suspect how stubborn and incompatible he must've seemed to his wife.

After two months of weekly sessions, their relationship was making strides. On Friday evenings they began going to movies together at the Lynwood Theatre, where Abe was learning to hold his tongue about exorbitant ticket prices and oversalted popcorn, to suppress his sighs when the drama skewed too sentimental or strayed too far from realism. And the more he held his tongue, the less he found these things bothered him, as though giving voice to his misgivings had been the problem all along.

"It was charming, wasn't it?" Ruth said about the French film they'd seen at the Lynwood that mild fall evening.

They were walking past Walt's grocery on the way to the car, the last pink vestiges of sunset still visible on the western horizon, the briny scent of low tide heavy in the autumnal air. Abe had already forgotten the name of the film, but it had been slow as molasses, painfully sparse and uneventful, and he was practically cross-eyed from reading subtitles for what amounted to an impossibly long two hours. But the truth was, the movie had not been without its charms. Some of the scenery was nice. The music wasn't too loud, as it often was in the American movies. The theater wasn't all that crowded. And Abe especially liked the ending of the film because it meant he could finally empty his aching bladder in the lobby bathroom.

"Yeah, it was nice," he said.

"I'm glad you thought so," said Ruth.

More and more frequently, their conversations assumed this agreeable and uncomplicated tenor. Abe found that it was actually refreshing not to voice his opposition, particularly to things of such little consequence. He came to realize that it wasn't always necessary to voice an opinion at all. Nobody had to be right or have the last word. Sometimes you just let a subject exist without trying to own it. You listened instead of talking, you considered instead of deflecting, you looked for common ground instead of points of contention. Sometimes playing well with others was as simple as getting out of your own way.

This tack was not limited to cinema. It could be applied to the ideological hornet's nest of partisan politics, a battleground for Abe and Ruth through a dozen administrations. Abe no longer baited Ruth with political differences. He held his tongue about Clinton's campaign financing, even the overnight stays in the Lincoln Bedroom— over five million dollars! He did not hold Ruth accountable, as he once might have, for Al Gore's limp legalistic defense of those fundraising calls from the White House office. Likewise, Abe did not yell at the TV when the news cut to President Jiang Zemin's red-carpet welcome, as though Ruth had been the one to welcome him personally. Sometimes it wasn't worth it to voice an opinion, or even have one. What mattered were the things he and Ruth could agree on: crossword puzzles, sourdough toast, gifts for the great-grandkids, fresh eggs, Sunday drives to the south end of the island, and blackberry cobbler in the fall.

Even their intimate relations saw a turnabout. Though missionary remained the bedroom standard, Abe learned how to tantalize Ruth in new ways, to graze, and pet, and tempt her with his touch, gradually, as Ruth began to let her desires be known, and Abe began to listen, and defer his immediate pleasure to greater effect for everyone involved. It turned out, you could teach an old dog new tricks, so long as it was willing to learn. Maybe he still had a few surprises in him, after all.

V

L'Aventure

2000

A week in advance of Ruth's sixty-fifth birthday, Abe booked a reservation at the newish Four Swallows restaurant, the finest dining experience Winslow had to offer, if Abe was to believe Al and Terri Duncan. As it happened, Ruth's birthday fell on a Saturday, so Abe planned on making an evening of it; an early dinner, followed by a seven P.M. showing of *Snow Falling on Cedars* at the Lynwood Theatre.

They arrived at Four Swallows promptly at five thirty, Ruth attired in the same baby-blue sequined dress she'd worn to Abe's retirement party, and Abe in a baggy gray Kenneth Cole three-piece, now ten years out of commission.

"You look stunning," Abe said over the rim of his water glass.

"Oh, stop," said Ruth.

"At least you don't smell like mothballs," he said.

They were situated in the main dining room, a rectangular area of maybe three hundred square feet, looking out the single-hung window at the four-way stop on Madison.

"It doesn't matter what they call this old place, I always feel like I'm eating in someone's house here," Abe said.

"You are," Ruth observed. "That's part of the charm."

Indeed, they were sitting in what had a century earlier comprised the Grow family living room. The old yellow two-story farmhouse, long an island landmark, had been occupied by a half dozen other restaurants over the decades: the Cherry Tree, the Island House, That's-A-Some Italian. Nothing ever seemed to stick for long. But for the foreseeable future, it was Four Swallows, its most expensive iteration yet.

Ruth ordered the pork medallions with the cherry reduction. Abe ordered the cast-iron skillet steak, medium-well.

Abe had never been good at surprises, and once again, it seemed he'd tipped his hand.

"What is it?" said Ruth. "Why are you grinning?"

Without further ceremony, Abe produced a decorative pink envelope (five bucks at Paper Products!) from his inside coat pocket, casually presenting it to Ruth.

"Joyeux anniversaire, mon amor!" it said on the front in Abe's unsteady hand.

"How sweet," she said, patting his knee beneath the table. "And such a pretty envelope, too. Sweetheart, for the record, there's a 'u' in *amour*—m-o-u-r."

"Noted," said Abe. "Well, c'mon, open it."

"Am I being subpoenaed?" she said.

"Something like that," said Abe.

Ruth pulled back the flap and fished out the contents of the envelope: a colored pamphlet from the travel agency, and a second envelope, letter sized, embossed with the light blue Continental Airlines icon.

"What is this?"

"Take a look."

Donning her 2.5 readers, Ruth removed the itinerary from the second envelope and peered down at it, still visibly confused.

"I don't understand," she said.

"Isn't that what you always wanted?"

Stunned momentarily, Ruth nearly let the envelope slip from her grasp. "Oh, Abe!" she said. "I don't know what to say."

"April in Paris," he said. "Not bad, right?"

"You mean . . . both of us?"

"It'll be romantic," he said.

Abe, in fact, was dreading the prospect of Paris. He'd never particularly cared for the Martinique, all that rich food—goose liver, and hollandaise sauce, all those mousses and pâtés. Then there was all that high culture to consider, walking around museums, and all that climbing steps, and admiring old churches. And the language barrier. Not to mention the twelve-hour flight or the cost of the tickets. Abe would have preferred nine days in Indianapolis or Milwaukee, or, better yet, right there at home in the familiar environs of the farm, with Ruth's cooking and his chair in front of the television. Instead, he'd pulled out all the stops for Ruth's benefit, even booking a table six months in advance at what the travel agent had assured Abe would be the finest of dining experiences at Joël Robuchon's Michelin-starred restaurant, which included something called an eight-course prix fixe with wine pairings. Abe would be sure not to forget his Tums that night.

"Are you sure about this?" said Ruth.

"Of course," he said.

Despite his reservations, Abe gradually managed to generate some enthusiasm for the trip throughout the winter. He was determined to put a happy face on this adventure. It wasn't enough to say that Ruth had earned such a pilgrimage, nor that she deserved it. That Ruth had not been to Paris shamed him, for he had stood in her way. Paris was an ideal Ruth had aspired to since before Abe ever met her, one that dated back to her sophomore year of high school in little backwater Shelton, from which vantage Paris must have seemed like Mars. This romance with Paris had largely accounted for her collegiate love of cafés and museums, along with her lifelong love of cooking, and poetry, and all things elevated above the humdrum reality of life with Abe.

For Ruth, this would be the journey of a lifetime.

*

Indeed, Paris was heaven for Ruth! The cafés—Les Deux Magots, and Chez André, and Café de Flore! The boulangeries and the bistros! The buskers, and the street painters, and the smells too various to catalog!

They stayed in the heart of Paris at the Intercontinental, a charming hotel on a quiet side street three blocks off the Champs-Elysées. The establishment was a welcome departure from the Evergreen Motel in Poulsbo. Rather than impress with its luxury, the Intercontinental wowed with its quaintness and unpretentious elegance, its truffles and handwritten welcome notes upon check-in, its warm, attentive staff, and its old-world charm that managed to feel contemporary. Their second-floor room was small by American standards but airy and filled with natural light, the bed dressed in fine linen, the toiletries of higher quality than the Irish Spring of the Evergreen Motel.

They spent the first afternoon and evening recovering from jet lag in the little room, where Abe fell asleep fully clothed within ten minutes of their arrival. But even in the confines of their tiny quarters, Ruth could feel the pulsing possibilities of Paris pressing in around her as she looked out the window at a small stretch of avenue Marceau.

On the second day, at a small boutique in Hermès, Ruth bought a leather-bound journal, a light scarf, and a beret, which she would wear for the remainder of their stay. They spent the next seven days eating, and drinking, and walking until their feet were blistered, exploring virtually every corner of the City of Light, far beyond the touristy trappings of the Champs. Daily, Ruth put her limited French to the test, the rusty rudiments of which she'd studied freshman year of college, which she'd dutifully amended with a stack of Berlitz self-teacher CDs for months prior to their departure.

The weather was perfect throughout their stay, midsixties and sunny, not a single day of rain, though not even a downpour would have dampened Ruth's enthusiasm. Oh, the cornucopia of culture! Of course, there was the Arc de Triomphe, and the Eiffel Tower, everything from the pamphlets, but more impressive still, there was Manet's *Olympia* at the Musée d'Orsay! The rose windows, gargoyles, and flying buttresses of Notre-Dame! The Père-Lachaise cemetery, the Picasso Museum, Sacré-Coeur! Ruth had been daydreaming of such wonders since high school. And here she was, at last, at large in Paris, free to explore its cultural wonders far and wide.

Ruth and Abe strolled the verdant quays along both banks of the Seine, admiring the bridges and gardens, dodging cyclists and dog walkers, pausing at monuments and statues long enough for Abe to remove his shoes and rub his aching feet. They trudged up Montmartre, circled the basilica and Saint-Pierre, before wending their way down the cobbly streets, through the throng of pushy merchants and winded tourists. At one point they were all but assaulted by an aggressive restaurateur, a portly gentleman with a sweat-stained white shirt, a dirty apron, and three days' growth of stubble.

"Non merci, nous n'avons pas faim," Ruth politely observed, even as he blocked their passage.

The Frenchman was not easily dissuaded.

"Come now, sit, sit, I insist. I serve for you the very best in all of Paris."

When Abe tried to push past him, the younger man went so far as to seize his arm, but Abe wrested it from his clutches immediately.

"Easy, there, Pierre. We already have dinner plans," he said.

They spent an entire afternoon wandering the length of the Canal St.-Martin, past the locks and over the cast-iron bridges, pausing to rest on park benches and watch the students and tourists move past.

On the fourth day, they doggedly ascended the one-thousand-six-hundred-odd steps of the Eiffel Tower, which Abe began referring to as the "Awful Tower" around step five hundred. It was the first time he'd voiced his dissent during the odyssey. But once they finally reached the observation deck on the top level, even Abe could not belie his wonder at the vista, a panorama of the city from Sacré-Coeur to the Grand Palais, across the Seine to the Trocadéro square and gardens, flanked by the Palais de Chaillot and its museums, and far off, the skyline of the city's financial center, the modern buildings huddled together as if to keep the old city out.

"It's really something, isn't it?" he said.

"It's everything," said Ruth.

On the fifth morning, they cabbed to Shakespeare and Company, Ruth's bucket-list bookstore, where they spent hours among the shelves, Abe mostly browsing history and biography as Ruth piled up two hundred dollars' worth of poetry books. But twenty pounds of books could neither deter Ruth's appetite for wandering and wondering or even slow her down. She was a blotter, soaking up Paris, spectacle by spectacle, scent by scent, with every perfumery, boulangerie, florist, or bistro they passed.

"Do you smell it?" she would say. "Isn't it wonderful?"

Though it was clear to Ruth that Abe did not share her obsession with the cultural wonders of Paris, he was an incredibly good sport throughout the trip, walking the soles of his tennis shoes bald at sixty-eight years of age, enduring the crowds, the lines, his indigestion, a multitude of trifling cultural misgivings. Through it all, he remained game for whatever as Ruth pushed them to wring the most out of every minute, trudging up and down virtually every side street, not to mention two whole days crisscrossing the Louvre, where more than anything else, the art seemed to baffle Abe.

"So, did her arms fall off, or was it always that way?" he said of the *Venus de Milo*.

"To be honest, I don't find her particularly attractive," he said of the *Mona Lisa*.

"Why are they naked?" he asked, regarding *The Pastoral Concert*.

"The kid's gonna break that lamb's neck," he said of Leonardo's *The Virgin and Child with Saint Anne*.

Though Abe may have been over his head culturally, he offered little protest. For that alone, Ruth couldn't have loved or appreciated him more. His intrepid enthusiasm, though clearly manufactured, was at its core sincere. The fact was, he simply wasn't wired for all this newness and adventure. The constant adaptation, the abrupt transitions, the incessant spontaneity. Her husband's curiosity was easily sated until it came to problem-solving, to devising solutions for the practical problems that dogged quotidian life—the management and leveraging of finances; the prioritization of tasks; the navigation of a busy schedule, confusing road map, or exhaustive tax form. Searching, for Abe, meant solving.

On their seventh day, they visited Notre-Dame, a spectacle that even Abe could not fail to appreciate.

"My gosh, it's really something," he proclaimed after two hours of exploration.

From Notre-Dame, they followed the street map to Rodin's studio, where they found the house under renovation and the studio closed. But circling round back, they arrived at the garden, where Ruth marveled at the meticulously kept grounds, the hedges, the ivy, the grass, all trimmed and edged to geometric perfection, the yellow forsythia and the deep-blue ceanothus in full bloom. And oh, the sculptures—the size, and scope, and pure drama of them!

Once again, the magnificence and pageantry were largely lost on Abe.

"I always thought he looked constipated," he said of *The Thinker*.

"Look at the size of those hands," he said of *The Kiss*.

"Hmph," he said of *The Gates of Hell*. "Quite an imagination. Suppose there's a bathroom out here somewhere?"

Poor Abe, so out of his element, so morbidly incurious at times, but also so consistent, and calm, and tolerant in his willingness to indulge that which opposed his nature. And for the better part of eight days, he endured admirably. It wasn't until the boat tour of the Seine, late in the morning of their penultimate day in Paris, that Abe's patience finally gave out. It was no small wonder, what with all the waiting in line, and the stultifying crowd on deck pressing in on Abe whose general disposition had already been nosing toward irritability since shortly after he was forced to don his moldering, sweat-soaked sneakers once again, walking eight blocks to eat what he characterized as "dessert for breakfast." Already sweaty and short of breath after the day's hike, and God only knew how existentially exhausted from eight days of unwanted cultural edification, he finally lost his composure when he found himself pinned to the rail by an obese couple intent on snapping pictures over his shoulder.

"My God, what is with the French? Do these people have any sense of personal space?"

"Sweetheart, they're mostly Brits and Americans."

"Whoever they are, they're pushy," he said, loud enough for the obese couple to hear.

"It's just crowded, dear."

"Then they should sell fewer tickets! It's like a cattle car out here!"

Ruth patted him on the cheek, then leaned in to plant a kiss there. "You just need a nap, grumpy bear."

Indeed, after the ninety-minute tour and the cab ride back to the Intercontinental, Abe lay down to nap without even taking his sneakers off. Miraculously still energized, Ruth sat beside him on the bed, thumbing restlessly through a volume of Louise Colet, before she could no longer help herself.

*

When Abe awoke from his nap in the hotel room, the late afternoon sun angling through the window, Ruth was gone. She wasn't in the bathroom. Poking his head out into the hallway, he looked in both directions to no avail. Checking his watch, he saw that it was after five o'clock. Didn't she realize they had a flight in the morning? They'd need a good night's rest if they hoped to make it home in one piece. It would be after ten P.M. by the time they landed at Sea-Tac, and past midnight by the time they got off the ferry. Somebody would have to drive back to the farm in the dark, and Abe was hoping it wasn't him. The sensible thing to do this afternoon—and they had discussed the matter explicitly—was to stick around the hotel, eat an early dinner downstairs at the restaurant, and go to sleep before eight o'clock. So, where had Ruth gone off to?

Slipping into his tennis shoes, still swampy from the week's ceaseless walking, Abe proceeded down the stairs to the front desk, where he made inquiries with the concierge.

"Apologies, monsieur, I did not see your épouse leave the hotel. Perhaps she's just taking the air, no?"

"Apparently so," said Abe. "Thank you."

Abe might have left it at that, but it irked him that Ruth had strayed from protocol. For nine days, he'd done everything she wanted. His only ask was that they scale things back and get some proper rest on the final day. Thus, he was annoyed as he walked down avenue Marceau in search of Ruth. Paris was not helping his mood. Twice he nearly stepped in dog piles. Here was a city celebrated for its sophistication, yet nobody picked up after their dogs. How could a culture claim such erudition when they were dodging dog crap every five steps? And how could they get anything accomplished working four days a week? Maybe they should devote the fifth day to cleaning up after themselves!

God, Abe couldn't wait to get home. He'd have plenty of time to appreciate the French experience later, eight months from now, when he was at home in his slippers, eating leftover turkey and watching the news. He was tired of mentally converting francs into dollars, tired of not knowing what the heck people were saying, tired of armless statues and stained glass, wrought iron and cobblestone and cheese, and the suffocating sense of history that Paris all but forced down his throat. And while Abe was not unaware of the irony of begrudging a culture for its insistence on tradition and its stubborn resistance to change, Abe couldn't help himself. He missed what he knew.

After considerable wandering around the neighborhood, Abe finally located Ruth on a side street, seated alone at a crowded sidewalk café, unintentionally chic in her twenty-year-old diner hand-me-down blouse and baby-blue beret, coffee cup at her elbow, as she scribbled in her leather-bound journal, oblivious to the activity around her.

His annoyance dissipated in an instant. Even at a distance of forty yards, he couldn't suppress a smile watching Ruth in her element. She was still the woman he'd married nearly half a century ago: intelligent and free-spirited, curious, adventurous, and intent on discovery, everything Abe never was, nor ever would be, though it heartened him to know that through Ruth he might one day achieve a respectable balance. But what about Ruth? Had she sacrificed too much in service of their marriage?

She looked so content sitting there by herself, filling up that journal. When she lifted her eyes from the page to gaze into the near distance, Abe spun around abruptly, lest she spot him. The least he could do was leave her to herself on this, her final day in Paris.

Abe was waiting on the bed when she returned to the room, clutching her journal, shortly before sunset, cheeks flushed from excitement.

"You're glowing," he said.

"Am I?" she said. "I guess I just feel so . . . alive."

Abe felt anything but; he was punchy, and achy, and nerve-worn, a persistent irritability festering just beneath the surface of his skin. And yet, to see Ruth thriving buoyed his own spirits to such an extent that he was suddenly willing to do it all over again, even if it killed him. He'd do it for her. He'd do anything for her.

"Here's an idea," he said, swinging his feet off the bed. "I change the tickets, we stay another week. We'll have to eat some kind of surcharge, obviously, and we may have to switch hotels, but we could—"

"No," she said. "This has been perfect. I'm ready to go home."

The Prunes of Wrath

2024

As desperately as Ruth had yearned to escape Twin Pines, as much as she missed her own bed, her own toilet, her side table and lamp, her view of the orchard and the pond out the living room window, she was not without reservations when it came to returning to the farm. What if it was all too much for Abe? Maybe they'd both be better off with Ruth in assisted living. Maybe it was time to give up the fight, to capitulate to the wishes of her children, and let the farm go. They had lives of their own to govern; Ruth could hardly blame them for wanting to run damage control on the affairs of their infirm mother.

Ruth's leg ached as Abe assisted her into the passenger seat. Buckling in, she took what she hoped would be her final look at Twin Pines, God willing.

Avoiding the highway as usual, Abe navigated them home by way of the old route, north down Viking Way to the 305 junction.

"You hungry?" Abe asked.

"No," she said.

"Well, anyway, I've got smoothie fixings at home. No bananas this time. You warm enough, you want me to turn the heat up?"

"I'm fine," she said.

"What about the radio, you want some music?"

"Thank you, hon, I'm fine."

When they reached the farm, Ruth was surprised to find that the front steps were gone completely.

"What's this?" she said, leaning on her walker.

"It's a ramp," said Abe. "Had John Duncan build it. I thought we'd better make a few upgrades."

"You paid him, didn't you?"

"He's retired," said Abe.

"Tell me John didn't do all this for free," she said.

"Yes, I compensated him, of course," said Abe, who in that very moment resolved to send John Duncan a check. "Careful, the walkway is slick."

Abe followed Ruth up the ramp, granting her a short rest in the foyer before he led her to the back of the house and walked her through the other modifications he'd hired John Duncan to make in the bedroom and bathroom. In addition to displacing the dresser to allow for a wider berth on Ruth's side of the bed, chrome handrails had been installed on either side of the toilet, as well as in the shower.

"It's all up to ADA snuff," Abe said proudly.

Lowering herself onto the edge of the bed, Ruth found her reservations were already on the wane. Here was proof that Abe could handle this.

*

The oncologist was a woman named Dr. Megan Wyatt, very professional, and not one to mince words when it came to the rigors of radiation.

"This is going to be some rough traveling, Ruth, I'm not going to sugarcoat it. We're talking about a lot of pain, a lot of discomfort, which we'll manage as best we can. We're talking about fatigue, nausea, intense burning inside and out."

Here, Dr. Wyatt addressed Abe directly:

"Our first order of business is to get Ruth's weight up. I've scheduled treatments to begin in a little over two weeks, and we'd like to see her weight up by at least five pounds. I'll schedule a Zoom with the nutritionist."

"What's a Zoom?" said Abe. "Is that one of those computer meetings?"

"We can schedule an in-person consultation, if you prefer."

"Yes, please," said Ruth and Abe in unison.

Thus began the feeding: Ensure Pluses twice daily, beef broth, smoothies with two different protein additives, whatever Abe could force upon Ruth.

"I'm telling you, I can't eat another bite," she pleaded. "I'm gonna explode."

"Two more bites," said Abe.

How well Ruth could remember issuing that identical directive countless times to her infant children more than a half century ago. Now, on the opposite end of the transaction, Ruth found herself every bit as resistant as Anne, or Karen, or Kyle, or Maddie.

"I'm telling you, I can't hold any more," she said. "I'm going to be sick."

"You have to," said Abe. "Dr. Wyatt's orders."

Ruth complied reluctantly at every meal, if you could call them meals, seven and eight a day.

"Please not again," she entreated.

But much to Dr. Wyatt's approval, Abe had managed to get Ruth's weight up six and a half pounds by the first session.

"When this is over," said Ruth, "I'm fasting for a year."

Abe was almost as nervous as Ruth before the first radiation treatment. He waited in the lobby through the half-hour session, that sterile, overly lit way station that would become his second home over the next six weeks, through a dozen issues of *Modern Health and*

Living and *Entertainment Weekly*. It was a relief each afternoon to see Ruth emerge from her treatment and make her way down the corridor deliberately behind her walker, accompanied by Dr. Wyatt's nurse assistant.

The first week of daily treatments was mostly painless, a little dryness inside Ruth's mouth, a slight sensitivity on the skin of her cheek below the ear. But by day eight, the pain kicked in with a ferocity that even Dr. Wyatt had not prepared her for. The entire right side of Ruth's face began to burn as the radiation ravaged the inside of her mouth. It was a good thing she'd put on the weight, for the pain of her mouth, raw and blistered and impossibly tender, rendered eating nearly impossible. Still, Abe remained steadfast in his charge.

"Dr. Wyatt said we've got to keep your weight up," he insisted, foisting another Ensure Plus and straw upon her.

Not only was the pain debilitating, but the right side of her face had blossomed to a chafed and flaking scarlet red, worse than any sunburn and excruciatingly painful to the touch. They managed the pain as best they could, but the pills could do only so much. Ruth did her best to remain stoic through it all, downplaying it at every opportunity so as not to burden Abe with her discomfort. Dear Abe was tireless in his ministrations, though Ruth could see he was exhausted, his face drawn and colorless.

"Maybe this Sunday, we ought to take you to church," said Abe. "They keep asking about you. Pastor Persun left another message this morning."

"I couldn't," she said. "Not looking like this. I'm not ready to go out in public."

"It's not public, it's church."

"I'll get there eventually," she said. "But not now."

By the third week of radiation, Ruth's concern for Abe had nearly begun to eclipse her own difficulties. It was clear to her that Abe was beginning to slip mentally, likely owing to the stress of caring for her. More frequently of late, she'd observed his momentary confusion, the donning of that thousand-yard stare, sometimes even when he was driving, like on their way to her radiation as he entered the new roundabout at Johnson Way for what must have been the twentieth time. Midway through the rotary, Abe went walleyed and stopped suddenly, nearly causing a pileup.

"Are you okay?" she said.

"What the hell is this doing here? There's not supposed to be a traffic circle here."

"Honey, keep driving," she said.

He pulled through the intersection without further incident, but Ruth could see his hand quaking on the steering wheel.

Even in her tenuous state of health, when Abe was supposed to be caring for her, Ruth was compelled to look after him.

"Get some rest," she told him after they made it home from the clinic. "I'm starting to worry about you."

"Look," he said. "I forgot about the roundabout, okay? Sixty years, no roundabout, and all of a sudden the darn thing is there in the middle of 305. I was just confused for a second, that's all. Next time I'll take Lemolo and we'll drive the back way past the marina."

But Abe, overwhelmed at times by his responsibility as Ruth's caregiver, had recently had occasion to wonder himself whether he might be losing a step mentally. Of late, he'd been given to abstraction at inopportune moments. He was becoming increasingly forgetful and, to hear Ruth tell it, repetitive.

"Sweetie, you must have told me that four times today."

One evening, Abe had been talking to Kyle on the phone, and in midsentence had completely lost his bearings.

"Dad?" said Kyle when the phone line went quiet. "Dad? Hello?"

"Oh, yeah, sorry, son. You were breaking up."

It was the strangest thing, for Abe had no recollection of where his mind had fled in that moment, and it couldn't have been more than three or four seconds in duration, but still, it was troubling. Was he losing his marbles? Was this the beginning of dementia? Would he wind up in six months' time in some nondescript elder-care facility called "Shady Brook" or "Pleasant Acres," smelling of baby powder

330 *   Jonathan Evison

and hand sanitizer, being spoon-fed by a nurse who he was convinced
was Barbara Bush? Or would he simply stop breathing in the middle
of the night as Ruth constantly fretted? These were eventualities Abe
dared not broach with Ruth.

But recently, basic tasks he'd once taken for granted, things he
had done a hundred times before, were becoming more complicated,
it seemed. Such as when Abe went to the Safeway pharmacy to pick
up Ruth's prescription earlier in the week. When he'd finally gotten to
the front of the pickup line after a twenty-minute wait, the clerk
punched in Ruth's name and scrolled up and down the screen momentarily, as Abe watched on.

"Sorry, I'm not finding it," said the clerk. "Nobody called it in. Let
me give the doctor's office a call."

"He's in Hawaii," said Abe. "The office is closed."

"Do you have the prescription?"

"Yes," Abe said. "On my wife's computer."

"Did you bring it?" said the clerk.

"The computer?"

"The prescription."

"Young man, you act like I walk around with internet. My generation is not plugged in like yours. We still deal with people."

"Uh, okaaay," said the clerk.

"Look here, I know what you're thinking. I'm no dummy, I have
five grandchildren—you think I don't know all about twerking and
PG chat? That doesn't mean I have to use it."

"You mean ChatGPT?"

"Sure, whatever, I don't care. Understand something here, young-
ster, I'm not a boomer—believe it or not, the boomers came *after* me!
And my generation, we don't walk around with personal computers in
our pockets, that's not our world. We didn't burn draft cards, either.
What don't you understand about that?"

"Well, you have a phone, right?" said the clerk.

"Yes," said Abe.

"Let's see it."

"It's at home on my wall, where it belongs."

The clerk laughed despite himself. "You're joking, right?" he said.

"I'm not joking," said Abe.

"You actually have a landline?"

"I have a telephone, yes," said Abe. "And not that it's any business of yours, but I also own a cellular device. My wife bought me one three years ago at Christmas and I don't even turn it on anymore. It's in a drawer with the lightbulbs and the extension cords. Are you starting to get the picture, here? Now, I need to get my wife's prazosin, and it's your job to help me, is it not?"

At that point, the young man went after his supervisor, who soon arrived in a white smock and proceeded to repeat almost verbatim what the clerk had tried to explain the first time.

"I don't carry email with me, don't you understand?" said Abe.

"Well, then go home and email it to us."

"You want me to email an email? And then what am I supposed to do, come back here?" said Abe.

"Yes."

"And waste all that gas? Not to mention the time? Look, let me make this real easy: It's p-r-a-z-o-s-i-n, or maybe u, you've got your spell-checker on there, figure it out."

"Sir, we don't have the prescription on file, and we'll need to see it in order to fill it."

"It's prazosin, I just told you that! I even spelled it for you!"

"But the prescription, we'll need to see it."

Abe nearly lost his mind, but somehow he managed to maintain his composure.

"So, you're telling me I'm supposed to go home, then send the email to you here at the store, the one that says prazosin?"

"Yessir."

"And then I am supposed to come right back here in person?"

"Exactly."

"All this to pick up my wife's prazosin, which you've got back there somewhere?"

"Yes, but you need to bring the prescription."

"Ridiculous," said Abe, throwing his arms up. "Let me speak to your manager."

"I am the manager."

"What's your name?"

"Von."

"Von what, Von Trapp?"

"Stevens, sir."

Abe paid out a sigh.

"So, you're telling me I waited in line for twenty minutes, and I'm not leaving here with my wife's prazosin?"

"No, sir, I'm afraid not. Not without a prescription."

The world had truly gone mad. Abe was practically trembling as he stomped away from the pharmacy counter in search of the juice aisle. He walked all the way to produce, then halfway back before he located the aisle, where he scanned the shelves impatiently for a full five minutes trying to locate the prune juice. There, he found every cranberry combination known to man, Cran-Apple, Cran-Cherry, Cran-Raspberry, eight different kinds of lemonade, apple juice, grape juice, guava nectar, pomegranate juice, for heaven's sake, but no prune juice!

Finally, a young employee in a hairnet, with a name tag that said Zach, stocking sodas nearby, interceded on Abe's behalf.

"Can I help you find something?"

"Prune juice!" Abe all but shouted at poor Zach.

"Oh, right there on the bottom shelf," he said.

Indeed, there it was, a single narrow slot reserved for prune juice; one lousy brand, and that was it.

"Why is it way down there?" Abe demanded.

"It's not very popular," said Zach. "The Poulsbo store doesn't even order it anymore."

"Is that right?" said Abe. "Not very popular. Well, who do you suppose buys it mostly?"

"Um . . . old people?"

"Exactly!" said Abe. "And what are old people not very good at?"

"Um . . . going to the bathroom?"

"Bending down, you imbecile! Why the Tom, Dick, and Harry would you put the prune juice way down low where old people can't reach it?"

"Well, I never really thought of it that way," said Zach.

"Of course you didn't! All you grocery peddlers think about is raising prices and cutting a few ounces off the size here and there— as if we won't notice!"

God knows, poor Zach must have endured some kind of sensitivity training, because he was seemingly imperturbable, a portrait of grace despite Abe's unreasonable outburst.

"Here, let me get that for you," he said, hefting the prune juice off the bottom shelf and presenting it to Abe.

"Who said I wanted to pay six bucks for an inferior brand?"

"Well, it looks like it's the only brand."

"Exactly! And it's six bucks, and it's way down there where only a midget could reach it!"

"Uh, I think they're just called little people now," he said. "Just sayin'."

Abe drew a deep breath and held it in. His life had become one indignity after another. Seething with outrage, and more than a little ashamed of himself, he accidentally let the bottle slip from his grasp and watched in disbelief as it exploded in the aisle, attracting the undivided attention of every shopper in aisle nine.

Abe stood frozen a moment, lightheaded as frustration and embarrassment coursed through his veins. He gazed stupidly at his empty hand, then at the gigantic mess on the floor, then back at his empty hand.

"You okay?" said the stocker.

"Of course I'm okay," lied Abe. "What the heck are you waiting for, somebody is gonna slip and break their neck."

Abe stormed out of Safeway, red-faced and slightly confused—no prazosin, no prune juice, and no idea where he'd parked the car. Indeed, in his flustered state, it took him ten minutes walking back and forth across the lot from the UPS Store to the High School Road entrance to locate the Subaru, now squeezed between two F-350s, in the side lot. He could hardly open the door to climb in. From there, it took another three minutes to find the car keys, which he'd inadvertently dropped on the driver's-side floor. Before he started the car, he sat in the driver's seat for a moment, overwhelmed by the immediate future. The kids were right, Abe was not fit to care for anyone, not even himself. What if it got worse, the lapses more frequent, what if he wandered off and forgot who he was, and somebody found him in the middle of an intersection with his pants around his ankles?

Abe finally managed to regather his senses and started the car. On the way home, however, in his state of preoccupation, he drove right through the light at Day Road and had to turn around in the casino parking lot and backtrack.

By the time he finally reached the farm, he'd forgotten why he'd ever left.

"Are you okay, hon?" Ruth asked when he appeared in the bedroom, where she was upright doing the *Times* crossword.

"Yes, fine," he said.

Golden

2004

It was Anne who took charge of planning Abe and Ruth's fiftieth-anniversary celebration.

"Dad, I gotta warn you, this isn't gonna be cheap," she cautioned.

"Whatever it costs," said Abe. "I mean, within reason."

"You want it to be special, right?"

"Of course," he said. "Within reason."

With Abe's blessing, Anne reserved the Seabold Community Hall only a quarter mile south of the church, a lovely old stand-alone hall constructed early in the previous century. The setting was lovely, a broad grassy acre nestled in the thick of old-growth cedar; there was plenty of parking in the gravel lot and only three steps to navigate. As with the Grange Hall on North Madison, or the Island Center Hall on Fletcher Bay, Abe must have driven by the Seabold Community Hall a thousand times without ever having been inside it. With its high ceilings and hardwood floors, its tall windows and broad sills, its antique light fixtures and electrical outlets, the old hall was the perfect venue in which to honor the fortitude of a marriage that had lasted longer than the Bulgarian Empire.

Anne saw that the hall was dressed up in bunting and strung with banners, each corner brimming with colorful balloons. Twelve fold-up tables were spaced evenly about the ballroom, clothed in white, each one adorned with a bouquet of fresh flowers, arrayed with plates and crystal glasses, cloth napkins, and silver all around. At the front of the hall, a small riser had been erected, with a PA and a microphone placed in a telescoping stand.

Out of seventy invites, sixty people attended the party, including the Duncans and the Jacobsons, Bess Delory, Judith and Alexandra from the Streamliner, the grandchildren, even Todd Hall's ninety-two-year-old widow, Jean. At six P.M. sharp, the Golden Oldies took the stage. A Dixieland ensemble, who came as a referral to Anne by none other than the Kiwanis, who had for fourteen years running hired the band for their Fourth of July parade float. Each of the band's five members was as old or older than Abe. To the delight of the white-haired in attendance, the Golden Oldies delivered rousing renditions of "Lazy River," "Tiger Rag," and "Sweet Georgia Brown" during the pre-dinner set.

The dinner was catered by a gay couple named Eric and James, the fare baked Mediterranean chicken kabobs, a pecan-berry salad, and a rosemary sea-salt batard. Though the cost was not what Abe had considered "within reason," the food did not disappoint.

Once the tables were cleared, and the Golden Oldies had wrapped their second set ("Heebie Jeebies" being the consensus highlight), the event proceeded according to Anne's itinerary, as each of the Winter children in descending order took the mic at center stage to offer a short tribute. The children were to be followed in turn by Abe and Ruth themselves.

After everything Abe had managed to screw up since 1954, every insensitive comment, every unreasonable request, every ham-fisted romantic gaffe, he wanted to get the speech right, and so he'd practiced it for two weeks in front of the mirror, Petey the fox terrier as his audience.

"Whaddaya think, Petey, should I lose the joke about the Clintons?"

The cheerful murmur of the hall died down the moment Anne took the stage, thanking in turn Eric and James for the wonderful food, the Golden Oldies for the wonderful music, and finally, all who attended the evening's celebration.

That Anne, their first child, was just a year shy of fifty seemed impossible. Wasn't it just a couple years ago that Abe was picking her up from Girl Scout camp? Why, Abe could've sworn it was just last week he was teaching her how to drive the old Ford station wagon, the aptly named Country Squire, in the empty IGA parking lot. It was a cliché that they grew up in a blink of an eye, but it was true none-theless.

"When I think of Mom and Dad's marriage," began Anne, "I think of Sisyphus."

Right off the bat, she got a laugh.

"Mom is Sisyphus," she said. "And Dad is the rock."

The room was in stitches now.

What a beautiful thing it was to be laughed at lovingly, to be looked back upon fondly, not for your strengths but for your weaknesses. Was there a truer sign of love?

"But you gotta hand it to them," said Anne. "Fifty years, that's quite an accomplishment. I don't know how you did it, Dad. Eighteen years of Mom's cooking was more than enough for me."

Abe laughed along with everybody else, though in truth Ruth was an excellent cook and everyone knew it.

"But really, Mom, Dad, what you've done is impressive. Not only did you get it right the first time, unlike some of us, you made it last, you did the work. So, congratulations on fifty, and here's to fifty more."

Kyle was next to step up to the microphone, wrapping his big sister in a hug as she left the stage. To see them linger in a genuine embrace like that, to know that their affection had survived everything

Abe and Ruth had survived and more, was to know a satisfaction as great as watching them take their first steps. For it meant that despite all the challenges and obstacles of their partnership, the petty pridefulness, the obfuscation, the self-sabotage, the calamity, and sorrow, and tragedy, he and Ruth had still managed to foster something vital and enduring.

"Fifty years," said Kyle. "Yowza. How many eras is that? Seriously, though, I can't say I'm surprised that we're all here today."

Looking at Kyle up there onstage, now a man in his midforties, with salt-and-pepper-flecked hair, a little paunch around the middle, a leather belt, adult shoes, Abe could still see him at sixteen years old in the kitchen in shoulder pads and jersey, drinking milk straight from the carton. He could see him at eight, arms folded, brow furrowed in protest, not eating his green beans.

"The thing about Mom and Dad is that no matter what happened, you knew they would always be together. Nothing could break them apart. Almost like they were, well, stuck with each other."

The room chuckled in recognition, even as Abe's eyes began to burn.

When Maddie took the stage, Abe thought she looked softer than he'd seen her in ages. Her hair for once was its natural light brown, free of green or blue or purple dye. He could count on two hands the number of times he'd seen her in a dress. Despite the years, he could still see his youngest daughter as the little girl she once was, and it seemed like only last week that he was helping her into her rain boots and cutting the crust off her sandwiches.

"By the time I came around," she said, "Mom and Dad had already survived the sixties somehow. Can you even imagine? My dad, Mr. Bow Tie, and my mom, the hippie sympathizer. But they made it work, and they still make it work. God knows, I couldn't have done it. I can hardly keep my houseplants alive."

Another comedian. It was strange, listening to his grown children, at thirty-four, and forty-four, and nearly fifty, talking about him, reflecting on the life he'd helped provide for them. Strange, how he still felt as protective of them as he did when they were two, and twelve, and sixteen years old. God, he was proud of them.

Finally, Abe's moment arrived. Despite his rehearsals, and the fact that everybody there was practically family, his hand was trembling when he took the mic from Maddie, pulling her in for a hug, and planted a kiss upon her forehead as the microphone squalled feedback.

"I love you, kiddo," he said.

Looking out at the gathering, all those familiar faces, Abe wasn't sure he could get through the speech, or even get it started. But he managed to, barely.

"A lot of you have asked me this week, 'Abe, what is the trick to getting to fifty years?'" he said. "Well, let me tell you, if I've learned one thing over the past half century, it's that the key to an enduring marriage, at least my enduring marriage, can be summed up in one word. A single word. One word that epitomizes the long haul, one word that exemplifies patience, and understanding, and loyalty. And that word," said Abe, "is Ruth. Without Ruth, we never would have made it this far."

Abe did not dare look down from the stage at Ruth for fear his composure would wilt in an instant.

"Not only is my wife more beautiful after fifty years than the day I met her, she is kinder, smarter, more empathetic, and more patient than ever before. I cannot say the same for myself, a grumpy old man complaining about gas prices and long lines, but I'm grateful as heck that Ruth stuck with me all these years. I remember the first day I met her."

Over the next ten minutes, Abe delineated in broad strokes their lives together, from their courtship at the University of Washington, to the little green house on Roanoke, to those first days on the farm. From there, he proceeded through four children, an entire career, all the way to retirement, and finally returned to the here and now.

"Looking back on all of it," said Abe, "it's easy to forget the troubled parts, but the fact is they tested us again and again. And I wouldn't trade those challenges for anything. Looking at my life, backward and forward, from the past to the future, I see so many possibilities, so many paths taken and not taken, but along every one of those paths, whatever I imagine, whatever might have happened, whatever will happen, one thing is always the same: You are by my side, Ruthie."

Tearfully, Ruth watched Abe leave the stage and descend the steps, Al Duncan greeting him with a handshake and a pat on the back that morphed into a manly hug.

Only once Abe resumed his seat at the table did Ruth ascend the riser and take the mic from the stand, looking out upon a lifetime of friends and loved ones, all gazing up at her, eager with anticipation. She dared to peer straight at Abe, his bow tie crooked, his face flushed with emotion, his long legs crossed, as he looked courageously back at her.

"You know, Annie was right," Ruth said. "Abe is a rock. My rock. And I've been crashing against that rock like a monsoon for fifty years."

Could it really be fifty? Taking a broader view of the decades, it almost seemed possible once Ruth accounted for politics and hairstyles, births, deaths, graduations, and weddings. But when she zoomed in on any one moment, like her and Abe lying at Magnuson Park beach in July of 1954, or date night at the Martinique in 1969, or standing on the moonlit bluff of Fort Worden in 1985, or being accosted by a French restaurateur on a Paris sidewalk in 2000, fifty years seemed impossible. That Ruth had given all but her childhood and adolescence to this partnership, that she had not chased after her dreams in full measure, was no fault of Abe's. While he might have encouraged her a little more, Abe always accepted her for who she was, or who she was becoming, invariably tolerated her mercurial forays and experimentations into impropriety, and even lesbianism. And never in fifty years, not once, not intentionally, had he asked her to be anyone but herself.

"A few minutes ago," Ruth continued, "you heard Abe give me all the credit for our long-lasting marriage, but it's not true. If Abe's been guilty by way of his reliance on me, I've been equally guilty in my dependence on Abe. When was the last time I lit the gas barbecue, or unclogged a sink, or jump-started the car? It's not news to anybody here that Abe and I haven't always seen eye to eye. The Democrat and the Republican. The flaky liberal and the stodgy conservative. The poet and the pragmatist. The wave and the rock. So, how did we make it work in spite of all these differences? The answer is acceptance. And patience. And yes, sometimes compromise. What we call balance is not always symmetry. Sometimes we need a complement, a contradiction, a counterpoint, to be our best selves."

Here, Ruth hazarded another look around the whole gathering until her eyes landed directly on Abe, where she managed to quell an emotional uprising, but just barely.

"Sweetie," said Ruth, looking into his face, "I just want to thank you for being my counterpoint."

Into the Quiet

2019

By eighty-four years old, the mileposts marking Ruth's passage through life, once a freeway teeming with destinations and diversions, were situated farther apart along a road that was but a single-lane highway leading one place. Ruth was no longer in a hurry, no longer harried or constrained by the ticking clock. These were the days of surrender, the days of relief, the days of idling and routine, early mornings, and afternoons, and evenings that each bled into the next with little if anything to distinguish them beyond a call from Anne, or Kyle, or Maddie, a doctor's appointment, a trip to Rite-Aid, occasional constipation, fits of afternoon exhaustion, sore joints, and inexplicable cravings for shrimp cocktail and tapioca pudding.

That the demands of her schedule were so light, that the fires of ambition had waned to a glowing ember, her entire purview narrowed to the extent that she could barely see beyond next Tuesday—these were largely welcome developments. For only in her ninth decade did Ruth finally come to share her husband's enduring belief that change was the enemy and that progress was usually a misnomer. Like many octogenarians before her, it no longer behooved Ruth to breathlessly navigate an ever-accelerating world that held little regard for her. She'd grown apathetic about the unreasonable demands of modern life. She no longer cared to have Maddie explain what an app was; she had no interest in self-checkout or the alleged convenience of online shopping. Leave automated customer service to the young. They could have their technology and instant gratification. After eighty years, Ruth knew what she knew, and knew what she wanted, and clung to it as a matter of course. There came a certain liberation with lowering the bar, with simply consigning oneself to the task of getting through each day with as little discomfort as possible. It wasn't the stuff of Nobel Prizes, but it was relatively painless and eminently approachable. She yearned only for her reliable pleasures: her crosswords and her game shows, occasionally a poem or a fresh bouquet of flowers from Town & Country (provided they were under ten dollars). She looked forward to occasional updates from the five grandchildren she hardly ever saw and the greats she'd yet to meet. As much as Ruth wished they were all closer, it was enough to know that somebody, somewhere, was thriving, and that Ruth had contributed to this in some small measure with all those birthday checks, and Christmas checks, and graduation and wedding checks.

Though it had taken him years, Abe had finally surrendered to retirement. The quality of his life or its meaningful continuance was no longer predicated on productivity, and his burning desire for success no longer demanded it. He'd earned the right to sit around on his duff, just as he'd earned the right to complain. Everyone was dying. Everything was expensive. Nothing was made in America. Healthcare was broken. The economy was broken. Democracy was broken. Manners had disappeared. Common decency was at an all-time low. And the Republican Party had lost its way. This was but a partial list of Abe's grievances as he looked toward his own and everybody else's impending demise and was strangely content doing so. He'd been telling the world where it was headed all along. He'd done his part to warn them. Now he was going to sit around and watch everybody else scramble to figure it out.

But the world wasn't all bad. They hadn't canceled baseball, yet, or *60 Minutes,* and the farm beneath a fresh blanket of snow was still a beautiful sight to behold, even if it was cause for great inconvenience. Most important, he still had someone he could rely on to accept him as he was and indulge him, to listen to, and comfort, and care for him, and furnish him with a six-letter word for "strips in geography class" that began with an "I." Take away Ruth, and all he had was his chair.

As for Ruth, she worried over Abe's future frequently. Though he was still sharp, and still alert most of the time, still capable of most anything he had been at fifty, there were moments of repose, once every three or four months, when she caught him sitting in his chair looking blank faced, his eyes faraway, mouth slightly agape, like he'd been struck by lightning.

Always, she addressed him in these situations.

"Abe, honey, are you okay?"

"Oh, yeah, what is it, hon?" he'd say, snapping back to attention.

These occasions were isolated, but Ruth could not suppress the fear that as the years wore on they might become the rule rather than the exception. For she'd seen a similar blank look before on the face of Bob Dolinger at church, only three years before his Alzheimer's got so bad that he couldn't recognize his own son. Then there was Abe's breathing at night. Sometimes in bed, when he stopped snoring, Ruth reached out in a panic to feel his chest, just as she had with each of her children as infants, certain that they'd stopped breathing.

"Abe, honey," she'd say, shaking him. "Abe!"

"Hm, what? What is it?"

Ruth worried that one of these nights she would reach out and he wouldn't respond. But he always did. And every morning he awoke when she woke, and together Ruth and he marked another easy, uneventful day, watching the news and doing crosswords, eating their big meal early in the day, napping, and sometimes, on warm afternoons, sitting out on the front porch on the rockers, drinking decaf, Abe admiring the farm as Ruth scrawled in her journal. Nothing about those quiet, painless days intimated the trouble that lay behind them, or the trouble that lay ahead.

The Day Draws Near

2024

By the fifth week of treatment, Ruth had crossed a new pain threshold. The burning, blistering ravages of radiation were like nothing she'd ever experienced. Every breath, every utterance, every sip of smoothie, was excruciating. On top of the physical discomfort, there was the mental anguish of missing her favorite foods—tomato soup, spaghetti, orange juice, anything the least bit acidic. The entire right side of her face was as red and chafed as if she'd just stepped out of an arctic wind for the first time in three weeks.

"My God, look at me," she said into the bathroom mirror, Abe flanking her left shoulder.

"A little red is all. You can't even see the scar."

"You're just humoring me."

It was true, and they both knew it.

"Ruthie, let's face it, we're older than dirt," Abe said. "We can't afford vanity at this point, it's a losing proposition."

"I suppose you're right," she said. "Old habits die hard."

Still, setting aside her pride, it took Ruth a month of haranguing before Abe was able to convince her to return to church. By then, her fellow congregants, their countless entreaties left unheeded, were bordering on mutinous. God knows how much time they'd spent praying on her behalf; they had a vested interest. They wanted their Ruth, now.

"Oh, I've missed them so much," she said. "You'll come with me? You don't mind?"

"Of course not."

It was a Sunday in early February when Ruth clutched his elbow firmly as Abe escorted her across the gravel parking lot of Seabold Methodist Church without her walker. Though spring was rumored to be near, the day was brisk and the sky concrete gray. Even as they inched their way toward the front entrance, joints stiff, feet numb, hands frigid against the chill air, the finest of snowflakes began to flutter down from the heavens like gossamer, dimpling the puddles before them.

"My God, does it ever end?" Abe wondered aloud.

"Don't take the Lord's name in vain," she said.

Finally, they reached the open doors of the reception hall, where a blast of warm air met them. Ruth was greeted vigorously.

"Oh, Ruth! You've been in our prayers."

Abe himself was afforded a celebrity's welcome; this being only his fifth or sixth appearance of the decade, he'd become the stuff of legend.

"We're so glad you could join us, Abe," said Pastor Persun, taking Abe's freezing hands within her own.

Once they'd managed to appease the welcoming committee, Abe and Ruth moved into the sanctuary, where they took a seat in the second pew, the front row being unoccupied. Just to the left of the tiny chancel, still behind the organ despite her arthritic knuckles and failing ears, was ninety-three-year-old Bess Delory, hunched from decrepitude, red hair gone white as ash and thinning, gazing weak-eyed from behind the 3.5 readers perched on the bridge of her nose as she stared down at the sheet music. Though Abe had never been of a musical persuasion, it was clear that Bess hit a few wrong notes along her halting way through "Blessed Be Thy Name Forever," though nobody so much as winced.

Casting a look around, Abe figured Seabold had to be the world's oldest congregation. Aside from a reticent granddaughter (or, more likely, great-granddaughter) of nine or ten years old near the back, there wasn't a soul under seventy years in attendance, excepting the old blond Lab sprawled at the foot of the altar, who had to be at least that in dog years. Abe couldn't help but wonder if the aging demographic was a churchwide Methodist phenomenon or just a Bainbridge Island trend. As denominations went, Methodists being cut from the most liberal of cloths, it seemed to Abe that given the nutty and incomprehensible tenor of the current epoch, Methodist numbers ought to be skewing younger rather than older, that the congregation should be growing, not shrinking. But there they were, a thinning herd of Methuselahs, stooped and wheezing, exhausted daily by lunchtime, but present and accounted for on Sunday morning.

Pastor Persun was a known lesbian, nearing the conclusion of her two-year appointment at Seabold Methodist as she stood at the pulpit smiling out at her venerable flock. Fittingly, she chose for that Sunday's sermon the subject of community, speaking on the central importance of the congregation, of paying witness, and of completing the circle. Abe was no expert on such matters, though he had by virtue of longevity endured Pastor Nordan, Pastor Dearsley, and a dozen other pastors over the course of his infrequent visits to Seabold the past fifty years, and while Pastor Persun may not have been the best orator among them, nor the most earnest or charismatic, she was the most conversational, and, it seemed to Abe, the most genuine. Perhaps it was her very lack of formality, a certain ease about her manner that felt lived-in rather than rehearsed; Abe couldn't say exactly. Maybe it was experience.

Not once during the sermon did Abe surreptitiously sneak a glance at his watch.

He could have sworn that Pastor Persun was talking directly to him and Ruth when she read from Ecclesiastes: "'Two are better than one, because they have a good reward for their toil. For if they fall, one will lift up the other.'"

Abe couldn't argue with that. Reaching over, he clutched Ruth's hand in her lap, and she squeezed it ever so slightly.

Turning his attention to the foot of the altar, Abe watched the old Labrador retriever, his pink, lump-riddled belly exposed, the rise and fall of his chest a steady but labored bellows. Watching the dog, and listening to Pastor Persun, the thought occurred to Abe that only a Methodist would allow a dog in a church. Leaning toward Ruth, he said in what he intended to be a whisper:

"We should bring Megs next time . . ."

Ruth shushed him with a stern look.

Despite the remonstration, the idea heartened Ruth. It meant Abe was coming back.

"Now," said Pastor Persun, "I'd like to turn our attention to the book of Hebrews, chapter ten, verses twenty-four and -five."

To watch Abe trying to navigate the Holy Bible, it might have been the Shenyang phone book. He finally gave up looking for Hebrews and peered over Ruth's shoulder, where she'd already located page, chapter, and verse, following along with squinted eyes as Pastor Persun read.

"'And let us consider how to stir up one another,'" she said. "'To love and do good works, not neglecting to meet together, but encouraging one another, and all the more as you see the Day drawing near.'"

As Ruth sat there beside him, the thought came to her that of all the doubt and isolation we endure, most of it is born of that singular source that by its very nature is opposed to congregation: the self, that flawed and miserable embodiment of the irrefutable loneliness that is being human, the condition that accounts for our desperate yearning toward any connection that might save us.

"So, let us strive to understand and encourage one another, truly," concluded Pastor Persun.

"Amen," said Ruth.

For, setting aside all our differences, acknowledging the forces intent on tearing us apart, all we have to distinguish ourselves from nothingness, to buffer us from inevitable ruin, is each other.

Ruth squeezed Abe's hand a little tighter. To hold his hand was to be felt, to be tethered to something solid amidst the vast confusion of the universe, even as her day drew near, and surely that day was not far removed.

Here Again

2024

E very year, late February arrives like a respite, an occurrence as predictable to Bainbridge Islanders as rain on the Fourth of July, a string of sunny days to rouse the farm from its sodden winter funk: blue skies and the promise of spring, the tall grass shaking off its frost, the mossy ground softening underfoot, the bare fruit trees beginning to bud, the daffodils, and the crocuses, and the cyclamen just pushing up through the soil, the hellebores and early poppies beginning to blossom.

It is upon such a day that Abe coaxes old Megs down the ramp to the Subaru. She lumbers half-blindly across the driveway, where Abe lifts her into the back seat and settles her onto the old beach towel so familiar to her.

Next, Abe helps lower Ruth into the back seat, where she buckles in beside Megs.

"You got enough room back there?"

She nods solemnly in lieu of a reply.

Abe circles around to the driver's seat and climbs in, his heart in his throat as he proceeds slower than usual up the puddled driveway.

"Is she comfortable?" says Abe, eyes in the rearview mirror.

"I think so," says Ruth from the back.

"How about you?"

"Keep your eyes on the road," she says.

It seems almost a crime to say goodbye on such an achingly beautiful day. How deep the blue sky, what a gift the sun's golden magnificence. All around, the world stirs with beginnings, swells with the promise of life, as the mild breeze whispers of burgeoning possibilities. What a glorious world to leave behind.

At the signal on Day Road, Abe reaches back to stroke Megs's head.

"How's she doing back there?" he says, eyes once more in the rearview mirror.

"Resting," says Ruth.

Ruth has begun to sob quietly. And again, the grief wells in Abe's throat as the light turns to green.

Abe checks in at the Day Road Animal Hospital, while Ruth waits in the car with Megs. Five minutes later, he returns, hefting Megs out of the back seat and setting her on her feet in the muddy parking lot, where she stands stoically, head slightly down, tail between her legs.

"You wanna come in?" Abe says to Ruth.

"Of course," she says.

"Let me get the walker out of the trunk," he says.

"I don't need the walker," says Ruth.

Abe assists Ruth out of the back seat, and she steadies herself on his shoulder as they cross the squelchy lot at a tortoise's pace, Megs trailing lethargically at their heels. In the lobby, they proceed straight past the desk into the examination room, where Dr. Garman, to whom Abe and Ruth still refer as "the new vet," though he's been there for seven years, who has treated Megs for everything from fleas to hypothyroidism to benign tumors, is already awaiting them.

The paper crinkles as Abe hefts Megs onto the table, her breathing labored, her brown eyes at once dull and imploring. She seems neither anxious nor frightened but indifferent, and, Abe would like to think, resigned to her fate. But he's not resigned himself. Of all the dogs on the farm across the decades, Petey, and Rowdy, and Daisy, and Duke, Megs was perhaps the most companionable, the most easygoing, the steadiest presence in their lives.

Dr. Garman is a portrait of patience and understanding. It occurs to Abe that the man must do this daily. Indeed, his bearing is practiced, his voice modulated to soothing effect, his manner appropriately subdued. He's a pro. In another life, he might have done well selling insurance.

"I thought I'd give the three of you a moment, if you'd like," he says.

"Yes," says Ruth. "Please."

And as soon as Dr. Garman leaves the room, Ruth is sobbing again, and Abe's eyes, too, begin to burn as he strokes Megs's head. The old Lab sighs deeply in response.

"That's a good girl," says Abe. "That's a sweet, sweet, good girl."

The room is a blur of tears when Dr. Garman returns.

"Are you ready?"

"Yes," says Ruth, choking back a sob.

And without further ceremony they proceed with the awful task.

After what amounts to a long, full life, the fall of darkness seems mercifully, ambiguously brief. Abe and Ruth lavish Megs with their touch as her breathing slows, Ruth stroking her rump, Abe scratching her gently behind the ears, until the light fades altogether. They linger for a moment with Megs's lifeless form, Abe still scratching behind the ears.

"Such a sweet girl," he says.

"Her suffering is over now," says Ruth.

They leave the facility heavy of heart. The walk across the parking lot to the car is endless. The tattered old towel is still in back when Abe helps Ruth into the passenger seat.

"They'll call us about the ashes?" she says.

"Yes," says Abe.

They drive home in silence, the sun's golden magnificence flooding the interior of the Subaru, even as their lives are forever diminished. They pull up in front of the house, where Megs's bed is still on the porch.

When Abe opens the passenger door, he offers Ruth an elbow, leading her deliberately up the ramp without the walker to the front porch, her limp still perceptible. Abe lowers first Ruth, then himself, into the sturdy rockers, their white paint chipped and peeled, their runners worn smooth. Between them, Megs's ragged bed sits empty.

"What about the bed?" Abe says. "I suppose I should—"

"Leave it for a while," she says. "It's not hurting anything."

"I suppose not," he says. And then, after a pause: "Cup of decaf?"

"I'm good, thanks," she says, reaching over to set her hand upon his. "I just want to sit."

"Me too," he says.

And so, Ruth and Abe sit, as they've sat ten thousand times before, side by side in silence, gazing out across the farm, past the flower beds, and the vegetable garden, and the pasture, still wet with dew. Past the greenhouse and the barn, beyond the orchard and the pond. Past the edges of the land they've lived on for so long, through the stands of venerable cedar and fir, and into eternity.

Acknowledgments

Huge thanks to my early readers: Thomas Kohnstamm, Zachary Cole, and my wife, Lauren. For his indispensable input on everything related to the insurance industry, thanks to my old friend Todd Hall, and thanks to the many Bainbridge Islanders who helped me get the times and places and feelings right, including Karen Beierle and the Bainbridge History Museum. Thanks to Gary Lothian for his input on Paris. Thanks to my mom, whose dogged battle with oral cancer, and grit and determination, were the impetus to write this novel. Thanks to everyone at Dutton: Emily Canders, Nicole Jarvis, Ella Kurki, Aja Pollock, Craig Bunn, Juli Meinz, Alice Dalrymple. Thanks to my long-suffering agent, advocate, and friend, Mollie Glick (and her spectacular assistant Via Ramono!), and to my wise, patient editor, John Parsley, for his belief and stewardship.

About the Author

Jonathan Evison is the author of the novels *Again and Again; Small World; All About Lulu; West of Here; The Revised Fundamentals of Caregiving; This Is Your Life, Harriet Chance!; Lawn Boy;* and *Legends of the North Cascades*. He lives with his wife and family in Washington State.